"W.E.B. Griffin is the best chronicler of the U.S. military
ever to put pen to paper—and rates among
the best storytellers in any genre."
—*The Phoenix Gazette*

Praise for the Men at War novels
by W.E.B. Griffin . . .

THE LAST HEROES
THE SECRET WARRIORS
THE SOLDIER SPIES
THE FIGHTING AGENTS
THE SABOTEURS

"WRITTEN WITH A SPECIAL FLAIR for the military
heart and mind." —*The Winfield (KS) Daily Courier*

"SHREWD, SHARP, ROUSING ENTERTAINMENT."
—*Kirkus Reviews*

"CAMEOS BY SUCH HISTORICAL FIGURES as
William 'Wild Bill' Donovan, Joseph P. Kennedy Jr., David
Niven, and Peter Ustinov lend color . . . suspenseful."
—*Publishers Weekly*

W.E.B. GRIFFIN'S CLASSIC SERIES

PRESIDENTIAL AGENT
Griffin's electrifying new series of homeland security . . .

"The prolific, mega-selling Griffin is well on his way to a
credible American James Bond franchise. It's slick as hell."
—*Monsters and Critics*

continued . . .

BROTHERHOOD OF WAR

The series that launched W.E.B. Griffin's phenomenal career . . .

"AN AMERICAN EPIC." —Tom Clancy

"FIRST-RATE. Griffin, a former soldier, skillfully sets the stage, melding credible characters, a good eye for detail, and colorful, gritty dialogue into a readable and entertaining story." —*The Washington Post Book World*

"ABSORBING, salted-peanuts reading filled with detailed and fascinating descriptions of weapons, tactics, Green Beret training, Army life, and battle." —*The New York Times Book Review*

BADGE OF HONOR

Griffin's electrifying epic series of a big-city police force . . .

"DAMN EFFECTIVE . . . He captivates you with characters the way few authors can." —Tom Clancy

"TOUGH, AUTHENTIC . . . POLICE DRAMA AT ITS BEST . . . Readers will feel as if they're part of the investigation, and the true-to-life characters will soon feel like old friends. Excellent reading." —Dale Brown

"COLORFUL . . . GRITTY . . . TENSE." —*The Philadelphia Inquirer*

"A REAL WINNER." —*New York Daily News*

ALSO BY W.E.B. GRIFFIN

THE SAB★TEURS

W.E.B. GRIFFIN

AND WILLIAM E. BUTTERWORTH IV

JOVE BOOKS, NEW YORK

THE BERKLEY PUBLISHING GROUP
Published by the Penguin Group
Penguin Group (USA) Inc.
375 Hudson Street, New York, New York 10014, USA
Penguin Group (Canada), 90 Eglinton Avenue East, Suite 700, Toronto, Ontario M4P 2Y3, Canada
(a division of Pearson Penguin Canada Inc.)
Penguin Books Ltd., 80 Strand, London WC2R 0RL, England
Penguin Group Ireland, 25 St. Stephen's Green, Dublin 2, Ireland (a division of Penguin Books Ltd.)
Penguin Group (Australia), 250 Camberwell Road, Camberwell, Victoria 3124, Australia
(a division of Pearson Australia Group Pty. Ltd.)
Penguin Books India Pvt. Ltd., 11 Community Centre, Panchsheel Park, New Delhi—110 017, India
Penguin Books (NZ), 67 Apollo Drive, Rosedale, North Shore 0745, Auckland, New Zealand
(a division of Pearson New Zealand Ltd.)
Penguin Books (South Africa) (Pty.) Ltd., 24 Sturdee Avenue, Rosebank, Johannesburg 2196,
South Africa

Penguin Books Ltd., Registered Offices: 80 Strand, London WC2R 0RL, England

This is a work of fiction. Names, characters, places, and incidents either are the product of the authors'
imagination or are used fictitiously, and any resemblance to actual persons, living or dead, business es-
tablishments, events, or locales is entirely coincidental. The publisher does not have any control over and
does not assume any responsibility for author or third-party websites or their content.

THE SABOTEURS

A Jove Book / published by arrangement with the authors

PRINTING HISTORY
G. P. Putnam's Sons hardcover edition / June 2006
Jove premium edition / June 2007

Copyright © 2006 by William E. Butterworth IV.
Excerpt from *The Double Agents* copyright © 2007 by W. E. B. Griffin.
Cover design © 2006 by mjcdesign.com.
Cover photograph © Jack Delano/Corbis.
Cover typographic styling by Lawrence Ratzkin.
Text design by Meighan Cavanaugh.

ISBN: 978-0-515-14306-5

JOVE®
Jove Books are published by The Berkley Publishing Group,
a division of Penguin Group (USA) Inc.,
375 Hudson Street, New York, New York 10014.
JOVE is a registered trademark of Penguin Group (USA) Inc.
The "J" design is a trademark belonging to Penguin Group (USA) Inc.

PRINTED IN THE UNITED STATES OF AMERICA

10 9 8 7 6 5 4 3 2 1

**THE MEN AT WAR SERIES
IS RESPECTFULLY DEDICATED
IN HONOR OF:**

*Lieutenant Aaron Bank, Infantry, AUS,
detailed OSS
(Later Colonel, Special Forces)
November 23, 1902–April 1, 2004*

*Lieutenant William E. Colby, Infantry, AUS,
detailed OSS
(Later Ambassador and Director, CIA)
January 4, 1920–April 28, 1996*

It is no use saying,

"We are doing our best."

You have got to succeed in doing

what is necessary.

—*Winston S. Churchill, British Prime Minister*

THE
SABOTEURS

I

[ONE]
Villa del Archimedes
Partanna, Sicily
1215 25 February 1943

I do not want to die that way, Professor Arturo Rossi thought as he looked through the doorway at the far end of the tiled hallway. *It's utterly terrible . . . inhuman.*

His light olive skin paler than usual, the tall, slight fifty-five-year-old felt himself swaying, faint from all he had seen.

The bruised, disfigured bodies of four men lay strapped to battered wooden gurneys inside the room. The ancient villa on the hillside overlooking the Mediterranean Sea had six such rooms off of the common hall, three on either side, each of cold coarse stone with the windows to the outside boarded over. More than thirty men also lay bound to gurneys in the other rooms, lit by harsh light— alive, but barely.

A warm hand gently gripped Rossi's left upper arm, steadying him, and he turned to look at his soft-spoken old friend from the University of Palermo.

Dr. Giuseppe Napoli, his wild mane of white hair flowing, had brought Rossi here to witness with his own eyes the unspeakable acts that were being committed by the German *Schutzstaffel*—the SS.

Rossi had followed the elderly physician's stooped walk down the hallway in shocked silence. He had glanced through the staggered doorways and noticed that the condition of the men worsened room to room, from mildly sedated with no obvious illness to grave with astonishing symptoms.

And then they had come to this last room, with its horrid stench of death.

It was the worst of all.

The torsos were mostly covered by dirty gray sweat- and blood-stained gowns, the arms and legs exposed, and the wrists and ankles secured to the gurneys by worn-leather straps. All the bodies bore some sort of rash. The legs on a couple also showed small open wounds—infected and festering—while the arms and legs of the others were spotted with blisters filled with dark fluid.

Rossi noticed that the smell of rotting flesh was made worse—if that was possible—by the unemptied tin buckets hanging beneath the gurneys. These held what had been the contents of the men's bowels, which with all Teutonic efficiency had passed through a hole fashioned in the gurneys for unattended evacuation.

Rossi quickly turned away from the doorway. His throat contracted, and he felt his eyes moisten, then a tear slip down his right cheek.

It was clear that these men—all Sicilians, as his friend had warned him—suffered greatly in their final weeks and days. Yet the contorted faces of the dead suggested that not even death had brought them any real peace.

Rossi realized that what disturbed him—beyond the obvious outrage at such atrocities against his fellow man—was that foreigners could come in and inflict such terrible things upon Sicilians in their own country in a villa named for Archimedes, perhaps the greatest of all Sicilians.

And that they could do it with what appeared to be absolute impunity.

But how can anything be done about something no one knows—or admits—is happening?

The villa, built by the Normans nine centuries earlier, overlooked the sea a little more than ten kilometers up the coast from Palermo's Quattro Canti quarter—the "four corners" city center—and the Norman-built Royal Palace, as well as the University of Palermo.

Far enough away so that any screams or gunshots or whatever would be lost to the blowing winds. And the secret remains safe. . . .

"So now you know," Napoli whispered.

Rossi looked at his friend, who held a cotton handkerchief over his nose and mouth. Rossi could see in his eyes genuine sadness and more than a little fear.

Rossi nodded softly and risked another glance around the cold, hard room.

"The Germans have brought yellow fever here," the doctor continued. "They use these human hosts to keep the virus alive . . . and, I think, to serve as an example of what they are capable of doing. I fear that this is just the beginning. I hear the Germans are experimenting else-where with other unorthodox methods—worse ones that also could be brought here."

Rossi had heard such stories, too, when he had visited the University of Rome. Quietly told, they described what was happening in the concentration camps run by the SS. Humans treated worse than laboratory rats. Bodies dissected without benefit of anesthesia. Legs and arms and torsos collected and stacked dispassionately, like so many cords of firewood.

The stories recounted conditions and acts so horrific, it was said, that German soldiers had to be bribed with bonuses of cigarettes and salamis and schnapps in order for them to agree to serve there.

And now, here in Sicily, this outrage of using humans—Sicilians—to keep alive a deadly virus strain.

"Where are they getting these poor people?" Rossi asked softly.

"Sturmbannführer Müller of the SD—"

"The *Sicherheitsdienst*?"

Napoli nodded.

Rossi knew the reputation of the SD, the SS's intelligence branch. They were ruthless in the execution of their job: to take out any threat to the Nazis.

"—he has ordered them brought in from the island prisons."

"That's where they took town leaders who opposed Mussolini. Many were mafia."

"And many of these here are mafia. Sturmbannführer Müller says the SD, with Il Duce's blessing, wants to neutralize them. This way, they're not a possible threat—and they're no longer 'useless eaters.'"

Rossi nodded slowly. That was another of the stories he had heard in Rome. As far as the Nazis were concerned, you either actively contributed to the war effort or you were a burden—a useless eater.

"So Müller says at least now they are useful," Napoli said.

Rossi stared him in the eyes.

"For what? I do not understand why they bring this virus."

Napoli checked behind them and down the hallway before responding.

"They're useful in the preparations for the Americans and British," he said softly.

Rossi shook his head.

Napoli went on: "There is much talk that they could invade Sicily and then Italy on their way to Germany. As Hitler has not sent many German soldiers here—perhaps cannot send many, as rumors suggest he is stretched thin on other fronts—he needs other methods to defend against such an invasion. And so the few forces that he has sent—Müller, for example—have very short and very mean tempers. . . ."

The two men glanced at the bodies on the gurneys.

Rossi softly finished the thought: ". . . And they are not at all unwilling to do the unspeakable."

They stood there a long time before Rossi broke the silence.

"What about Carlo? He would never stand for this."

A brilliant mathematician and a kind man, Dr. Carlo Modica was, like Napoli, in his seventies, and had served as the head of the University of Palermo for almost ten years. In his specialty as a metallurgist, Rossi had at times worked closely with him.

Napoli put his hands on Rossi's shoulders.

"Carlo is the reason I felt you had to see this for yourself."

"You're not telling me that he is permitting this?"

Napoli stared him in the eyes.

"What I am telling you, Arturo, is that Sturmbann-führer Müller made it clear to Dr. Modica that his participation would be in his best interest. Müller said that it would send a good message to others if someone in such a prestigious position participated."

Rossi's eyes grew larger.

"With all due respect, I would like to hear Carlo tell me that personally."

Napoli dropped his hands to his sides.

"He cannot," he said softly, and his eyes moistened.

"Why?"

"Because Müller has put me in his place here."

"I don't—"

"Carlo was injecting the virus in a—" he paused, searching for the right word "—in a 'patient' when the 'patient' struggled. Carlo was pricked by the needle or scratched by the 'patient' . . . that part is unclear . . . but the result is that he somehow infected himself. . . ."

"He has yellow fever?"

Napoli shook his head.

"*Had* yellow fever."

He nodded to the men on the gurneys.

Rossi looked, then looked harder, and suddenly was sick to his stomach.

He now recognized the grotesque body on the far right as that of the gentle mathematician.

Dear Holy Mother, Rossi thought, and motioned with his hand in the sign of the cross.

"None of us is safe," Napoli whispered.

[TWO]
Woburn Square
London, England
2010 25 February 1943

Major Richard M. Canidy, United States Army Air Corps, bounded unnoticed up the stone steps to the first-floor flat at 16 Woburn Mansions. Solidly built and good-looking, the twenty-five-year-old displayed such confidence in his quick stride that if any bystanders had seen him approach the massive wooden door of the flat they would have mistakenly believed that not only was he supposed to be there but that he may very well have owned the place.

The flat instead was home to the beautiful Ann Chambers, with whom he had recently shared—and he hoped soon would again share—some very special times.

No matter how much that idea appealed to him, however, right now it was not the reason for his haste to get to the flat—and inside.

If I don't get the door open in the next second, he thought, *I'm going to piss my pants. My back teeth are floating. . . .*

Canidy knew that the door had a solid-brass handle-and-lock set, the type with a thumb latch that, when left unlocked, a simple depressing of the latch caused the bolt to pull back from its place inside the doorjamb and the door could then be swung inward. And he knew that it was old and worn.

If the lock isn't busted, he thought, *odds are good she's left it unlocked again.*

In one fluid move, he found the handle in the dark with his right hand, pushed on the latch with his thumb, and leaned forward in anticipation of the door's swinging inward.

A split second after the electrical pulses traveled from his thumb to his brain, and the brain interpreted these pulses to mean that the latch did not depress and that the door was in fact locked, his brain received priority electrical pulses of information from his right shoulder—in the form of a sharp pain—that the brain then interpreted to mean the door had not swung inward . . . that it had not moved at all.

Dammit!

He winced and yanked at the door handle, pushing at the latch again and again, causing the lock set to rattle.

The door remained locked, but the rattle told him that there was more than a little slop in the old mechanism.

Hitting the solid door did his bladder absolutely no

good, and he found himself doing a little anxious dance
to try to hold back the inevitable.

He quickly pulled out his pocketknife, opened the
blade, and carefully slipped it in the crack between the
door edge and the doorframe, just above where the bolt
engaged the strike plate. As fast as he could, he worked the
knife blade downward and then methodically back and
forth, the blade little by little depressing the bolt against
its spring until the bolt was clear of the doorjamb.

And the door swung inward.

He entered the flat and slammed the door shut behind
him, the bolt clicking back in place.

It was even darker inside the flat, but the absence of
light only served to heighten Canidy's sense of smell.
And he could very much detect the sweet, delicate scent
of a woman.

He stumbled around in the dark till he found—
actually, ran into—the lamp where he remembered it
being and clicked it on.

The flat, nicely furnished with ornate old furniture
covered in well-worn fabrics and soft leather, opened
onto a large main room, off of which were two smallish
bedrooms, a single bath with a toilet and a shower, and a
kitchen. There were dark hardwood floors throughout, as
well as thick woolen rugs. A marble fireplace topped with
a four-by-five-foot mirror graced the main living area.

He made a beeline for the head.

The leak surprised even him with its duration; he considered timing it with his wristwatch chronometer. He
pledged never to pass another crapper without at least

considering how full his bladder might be *and* the distance to the next crapper should he choose not to stop.

When he had finally finished and went to wash his hands, he caught himself making a massive yawn. Now he did check his watch.

Only eight-fifteen? Jesus, this has been a long day—didn't think we'd ever get wheels-up out of Casablanca this morning—and she may not be here for some time. Wouldn't want to miss what could be a long, passionate night....

He walked to the couch, turning out the light as he passed the lamp.

He yawned again, and shortly after he lay down and his head hit the tasseled pillow he was snoring.

As Ann Chambers rounded the darkened street corner, she caught her right heel in a crack in the sidewalk that had been left uneven by the bombs of the Luftwaffe.

"Shit," she whispered in her soft Southern drawl.

When the heel caught, it had stuck fast, and her foot had come completely out of the shoe, causing her to place her stocking-covered foot on the cold ground. She reached down and grasped the heel to pull it free of the sidewalk and found that it had almost completely separated from where it attached to the sole.

The twenty-year-old blonde sighed. This was her second-to-last pair of really nice—and really comfortable—shoes, and she wasn't sure how soon the replacements she had written home for would arrive. She did a lot of walking—everyone in London did a lot of walking—and for her, comfortable shoes rated high on the list of absolute necessities.

So that she would not tear the small leather tag that barely connected the heel at the back, she put down her heavy, black leather briefcase and used both hands to carefully tug at the heel until it pulled free.

Ann held up the shoe, trying to get a decent look at the damage in the dim light. She thought that there might be a small chance she could repair the shoe herself because she knew there was next to no chance of getting a cobbler, even if she could find one that hadn't been blown out of business, to do so in a timely fashion.

A nicely dressed middle-aged man approached and stopped.

Great, she thought. *Just what I need now. . . .*

"Can I be of any help, lass?"

Ann, still kneeling, looked up at him.

"Thank you, but no."

"You're sure?"

The only thing I need is protection from strangers who can't take no for an answer.

"Yes," she snapped.

She saw him make a face and immediately felt bad. Being frustrated about the broken shoe—not to mention going home to an empty flat—was not his fault.

In a softened tone, she added, "I'm almost home. Thank you."

He turned smartly on his heel. "Very well."

As the man walked away, she stood up and looked again at the shoe and still couldn't tell how badly it was damaged.

She frowned, then—despite the fact that her right foot was close to numb from the cold—removed her other shoe, collected her briefcase, and padded all but barefoot in her now-torn hosiery the final block to her flat at 16 Woburn Mansions.

As she went, she could not help but be saddened again by the ugly gaps in the buildings. German bombs had destroyed large sections of the city—the damage had been utterly indiscriminate—and there was more and more of the destruction almost every day.

It was no different here at Woburn Square, where bombs had taken out ten of the twenty-four entrances and reduced what not very long ago had been a lush and meticulously kept park to nothing more than a burned fence and bare trees.

Adding another insult, the once-manicured park was now pocked from where crews had dug dirt to fill sandbags and dug out small shelters, for those who could not reach a basement or subway shelter quickly enough when bombs began to fall.

Sixteen Woburn Mansions had survived, but its windows now were boarded with plywood and its limestone façade scorched black from the fires that had raged up and down the street.

Ann walked up the short flight of stone steps, dug into her briefcase, and came out with a key ring, then put one of the keys in the heavy brass lock of the massive wooden door and, when she heard the loud metallic *clunk* of the tumbler turning, depressed the lever above the handle with her thumb, leaned her shoulder into the door, and walked inside.

She went to the lamp, clicked it on, and sighed. It was good to be home. Ann appreciated the fact that while her flat was not what one would describe as opulent, it was certainly comfortable—and superior to most flats in London, particularly the ones on Woburn Square that now were nothing but rubble.

And most important, for now, it was hers alone.

Sixteen Woburn Mansions had been assigned to the Chambers News Service, through its London bureau chief, by the Central London Housing Authority acting on a memorandum from CNS's main office in Atlanta, duly relayed through the SHAEF (Supreme Headquarters, Allied Expeditionary Force) billeting officer, that had stated that the flat was intended to house all five CNS female employees in London, names to be provided as soon as they were available and could be forwarded from Atlanta.

And while the flat technically did indeed currently house all of the female employees of the Chambers News Service London bureau—in the person of one Miss Ann Chambers—what the bureau chief did not know was that it had been Miss Chambers who initiated the memorandum from the Atlanta office just after having obtained an assignment to the London office and just prior to her arrival in England, and that while it was theoretically possible there would be more female employees sent to serve in the London bureau, for the near term at the very least it was not at all likely.

This caused Ann some genuine mixed feelings. She knew that she was bending the rules. She knew that people in London were packed in flats, and ones smaller than hers. But she also knew that she would give up the flat in a heartbeat when she was sure that it had finally served its purpose—helping her have a private place to land the love of her life—and she was determined that that was going to be soon . . . very soon.

After that, she promised herself, she would make amends for this bit of selfishness.

The bureau chief suspected, of course, that Ann had used the system to her advantage, but it made no sense to fight it.

For one thing, Ann Chambers was the daughter of the owner of Chambers Publishing Company and the Chambers News Service—and, accordingly, was the London bureau chief's boss's boss.

For another, she was a fully accredited correspondent, and a damned good one. She had real talent, wasn't afraid of hard work, and consequently turned in solid feature articles that the news service sent out on the wires around the world. Her Profiles of Courage series about ordinary everyday citizens serving in extraordinary roles during wartime had become wildly successful.

Why, then, would the bureau chief want to upset the apple cart over what, at least for the time being, was a technicality? As far as he knew, more female employees might be on the way; he certainly could use them.

There was no question that Ann was more than earning her keep. Which was a good thing because there was no doubt in anyone's mind that the last thing that Brandon Chambers, chairman of the board of the Chambers Publishing Company, would have stood for was blind nepotism. He was a tough, no-nonsense businessman—some said a real sonofabitch, a reputation that Chambers wasted no effort to dispel or even dispute—who had built a world-class news service from the ground up and would not make a token hire of a family member unable to pull his or her own weight.

Early on, Ann had shown that she had a way with words—much like her father—and so while it came as no real surprise to Brandon Chambers, he was nonetheless not happy when out of the blue she showed up at his Atlanta office and announced that she had dropped out of Bryn Mawr and said that if her father did not give back the part-time correspondent job that she had held off and on since high school, she was reasonably sure Gardner Cowles—who owned *Look* magazine and a lot else—could find something for her to do. And very likely make it a full-time position.

Cowles was Brandon Chambers's bitter competitor and just cutthroat enough to find great glee in providing Ann Chambers with a job at *Look* magazine, which was regularly beating the life out of *Life*.

Thus, there was no changing his daughter's mind. "I wonder where she got *that* lovely stubborn personality trait?" Mrs. Brandon Chambers had said with more than a little sarcasm when her husband phoned with the news of their daughter's plan—and Ann went to work that day in the Atlanta home office as a full-time Chambers News Service correspondent.

Now, some months later, she had had herself transferred to the London bureau.

That, too, had triggered howls of protest from the corporate office of the chairman of the board—he never believed any woman should be a war correspondent, and certainly not someone of his own flesh and blood—but it quickly became another father-daughter battle lost by Brandon Chambers.

Dick Canidy had been asleep twenty minutes when he snored so loudly that he woke himself up. It took him a moment to get his bearings, and as his brain told him where he was he heard a key being put in the front door, the lock turning, and the door opening.

He started to jump up but stopped to admire the silhouette of the well-built young woman in the doorway. Ann closed and locked the door and carefully found her way across the flat in the dark.

He laid his head back on the pillow. Her presence excited him. He could feel the beating of his heart beginning to build and a slight sweat forming on his hands. After a moment, he ever so slightly caught her scent . . . and smiled.

He watched as she padded to the fireplace—*Is she barefoot?* he wondered—and dropped her shoes and leather bag to the floor—*She is barefoot! Or at least in stockings.*

Ann groped around until she found the matches, then lit the candles at either end of the marble mantel. They started to glow brightly, the light filling more and more of the flat, and he lay in the shadows on the couch.

Jesus Christ, if I say anything now it's liable to scare her out of her skin!

Then she started to take off her outer clothes.

Now, this could get interesting. . . .

Ann put down the matches on the mantel, then pulled off her overcoat and without turning tossed it over the back of the couch. She slipped her V-neck sweater over her head—uncovering a white blouse that fitted her form tightly—and was about to throw it on the couch, too, when she had a second thought.

She put the armpit of the sweater to her nose, sniffed with more than a little apprehension, grunted *Ugh*—then threw it to the couch.

When she next adjusted her skirt, pulling it up at the waistband and twisting it slightly, the wool caused her buttocks to itch and she found herself vigorously scratching her fanny with the fingernails of both hands.

Those unfortunate events now handled, Ann arranged the candles to her satisfaction, then examined herself in the mirror and fixed her hair mussed by the sweater.

Looking at herself, she could not help but think of Sara Spenser and the profile of her that she had spent the day writing.

For most of the last week, Ann had followed the

nineteen-year-old, spunky, petite brunette as she'd served
with the Light Rescue Section of London's Civil Defence.

Under a 1914 tin hat, draped in baggy woolen men's
pants and heavy overcoat and clunking around in
"Wellies"—men's rubber Wellington boots—three sizes
too big, Sara worked twenty-four-hour shifts, carefully
but quickly digging through rubble to uncover victims
whose homes or businesses had been bombed and then
carrying them by canvas stretcher to the buses converted
into ambulances that waited nearby.

It had taken a couple of days—and one long, teary
night over pints of stout at the Prince's Bangers & Mash
Pub—to get Sara to open up, really open up, but Ann
had, and she learned that Sara was all that was left of her
immediate Spenser family.

Her brothers had died in battle, and her parents and
grandparents were killed during a blitz when a series of
bombs leveled their neighborhood. There were somewhere some second cousins twice or thrice removed, but
for all the contact between the families, she said, "They
may as well be bloody Aborigines. Could be dead, too.
Who knows? That's how close we are."

Ann was not sure if it was Sara's matter-of-fact delivery, or the realization that Sara was about Ann's age and
given some tragic turn Sara's story could be Ann's story,
or all the beer they had consumed—or a combination
thereof—but Ann was terribly saddened for Sara.

Sara, however, would have none of it. She would not
accept pity, she said. "Others have lost everything, yet

here I am alive and well and with my life ahead of me. I can—I *must*—carry on."

Ann had found strength in Sara Spenser. She was impressed with her brave front, and perhaps even more so with her ability to find humor in some of the most difficult of times.

Sara had turned heads with her laughter that night in the noisy pub as she told Ann about the time her Light Rescue Section had been removing rubble of another bombed-out building, first evacuating victim after victim still alive to the ambulances, then dealing with the dead, then uncovering an older gentlemen, looking a bit bewildered but clearly alive, pants around his ankles and surrounded by debris one would expect to find in a water closet.

Sara had taken a deep swallow of her stout, then recalled, "As I helped him pull up his trousers, I asked if he was all right. He nodded and said, 'It's just that it's rather odd that one moment, here I am sitting on the loo, and the next, when I pull the chain, down comes the bloody house!'"

Ann had spent exhausting days running around London's bomb-debris-filled streets to track down stories and interview people, then often-sleepless nights awaiting the haunting sounds of the air-raid sirens.

More than once she had wondered why she didn't just go home to Atlanta . . . or even back to Bryn Mawr. Return to the safety and sanity of the States. But then she realized that she might not meet a person such as Sara otherwise, and she knew there was no way she could *not* be here. Writing about the war had become her duty.

In the glow of the candles in the mirror, Ann smiled at herself.

And I didn't really come here for the work. I came here for Dick.

And then her throat caught.

Where the hell is he? It's been almost two weeks since he left and not a word. For all I know he could be lost or captured or . . . She tried to force herself not to think it . . . *dead.*

Although Major Richard M. Canidy wore the uniform of the United States Army Air Forces, Ann Chambers knew that the dark-haired aviator worked for an outfit called the Office of Strategic Services. More than worked for it—was pretty high up in it.

It was more or less known that the OSS was a military intelligence operation, a secretive collection of spies, analysts, and such from various branches of the military and the government and corporate America, some very highly connected, reflecting in part the fact that its head, Colonel William J. "Wild Bill" Donovan, enjoyed the confidence and close friendship of President Franklin D. Roosevelt going back to their days in law school at Columbia.

But that was all she knew—despite her sniffing around on the side—and it was more than Canidy was willing to tell her. Even this current mission of his was one he had said not one word about.

Except to say good-bye here at the flat in a very special, very personal way.

Which was why, she thought, and made a mischievous grin in the mirror, *the flat would always be kept only for her. Her and Dick.*

If he ever comes back.

Dick, with the warmth and smell of Ann on her coat and sweater, thought that he had nearly died and gone to heaven. He moved under their weight and caused a spring in the couch seat to creak.

He looked toward Ann and saw her eyes dart in the mirror, searching.

After a moment, she turned toward the couch.

What the hell. Now or never.

As he started to sit up, he said, "Hey . . ."

Ann had heard a noise. *Was it the floor creaking?*

She held her breath and looked in the mirror, searching to see if there was someone in the room behind her. She saw nothing, then quickly turned to look more carefully.

Then she thought she had heard a man's voice—*Dick's?*—but knew that that had to be impossible.

Just imagined it, she thought, *just wished it.*

She shook her head, telling herself it had been too long a day.

Then suddenly she saw the clothes she had tossed on the couch were . . . *moving?*

She started to scream—but then there was Dick Canidy coming out from under her coat, the sweater still on his head.

He was dressed in uniform, his eyes smiling, his arms open wide.

"Hey, baby!" he said. "Surprised?"

Ann caught her breath, then felt slightly unsteady on her legs.

"Dick!" she cried softly.

She padded across the room into his arms, pulled the sweater off his head, buried her head in his neck. She felt his arms wrap around and hold her tightly. It was an incredible feeling.

She turned to look up at him, smiled, and they kissed deeply.

When finally they had separated, Dick lovingly cupped her face with both of his hands. He thought he noticed something on her cheek, gently angled it toward the candlelight, then saw on her fair skin a line of tears that glistened with the reflection of the flame.

He felt his body quiver, slightly and involuntarily, as he realized just how incredibly beautiful he found Ann and how deeply she affected him.

"Miss me?" he said softly and kissed the tears.

Ann was already unbuttoning Dick's shirt.

———

"So how did you get in the flat?" Ann said as she poured port into the wineglass that Dick Canidy held, filling it about halfway.

They were lying side by side on the floor before the fireplace—which now crackled as it burned brightly—on top of giant pillows covered in a fine silk fabric and under a goose-down-stuffed, cotton-fabric-covered duvet.

Ann put the cork back in the squat fat bottle, placed the bottle near the fire to keep it warm, then snuggled up to Canidy.

He offered the glass to her, raised an eyebrow, and she leaned forward and took a big sip, then leaned forward and kissed him. She wondered if it was possible to feel any more warmth in any more places of her body at once.

Canidy smiled and finally said, "Getting in places—mostly where I'm not supposed to be—is what I do for a living."

He shrugged.

"This place is no challenge—boarded windows, half the building missing—"

"Is that where you were?" she pursued. "Where you weren't supposed to be?"

"Annie," he said, sighing. "You know I can't—"

"I know, I know. But you can't blame me for trying."

She looked into his eyes.

"I worry about you. I worry about you and me."

"Shhhh," he said, looking back into her eyes and gently touching his index finger to her lips. "Stop. Don't. We're fine. And now that I'm back and certain problems have been solved, I plan to be around for as long as I can."

Beaming, Ann quickly sat up, and as she did the duvet slipped, exposing her bosom.

Dick smiled and kissed her left breast.

"Promise?" she said softly, modestly pulling up the duvet.

"I go where I'm ordered, Annie. I can't—"

"Promise?" she repeated, this time more forcefully. "Please?"

Dick took the glass of port and put it beside the bottle, then wiggled under the duvet and wrapped himself around her.

"Promise," he said softly, knowing sometime— probably soon—he would have to break it.

[THREE]
Brooklyn Army Base and Terminal
Brooklyn, New York
0545 26 February 1943

"Tony the Gut" Lucchese, the five-foot-seven, 220-pound gang boss of local 213, International Longshoreman's Association, stood near the edge of the industrial dock as icy gusts came across the East River.

Son of a bitch! the thirty-five-year-old thought, turning his back to the wind. *I'm gonna freeze my fuckin' nuts off out here.*

He took a final puff of what was left of his stub of a cigar, threw the butt into the dark water, then thrust his hands into the pockets of his heavy woolen overcoat, his fat fingers hitting the grip of the .357 caliber revolver he'd put in the right pocket.

Lucchese looked up as an olive drab jeep floated past, hanging from a cable of a loading boom on the dock, then shivered violently and wondered if the shiver had been caused by the bitter cold—or his outright fear.

Seventy percent of the war goods and soldiers shipped to Europe passed through New York area terminals—much of that going through the Brooklyn terminal.

The ILA controlled it all.

The union saw to it that the loading went on smoothly round the clock—and on time, like that bastard Mussolini ran his trains—because not only was the shipping critical to winning the war, keeping the pace steady was important to the ILA boys doing the skimming.

The more they moved, the less anyone noticed a container here and pallet there had been "misplaced" in transit.

This was not lost on Lucchese.

It don't take no Road Scholar to figure out I can get whacked for doing this thing, he thought.

And Lucchese knew that if they didn't whack him for causing the loading of the ships to slow—or stop—then they'd likely do it for him going behind the ILA's back and working for Harry Bridges in the first place. The head of the stevedore unions on the West Coast, from Seattle to San Diego, was trying to muscle his way in on East Coast business—and the ILA locals weren't happy about that shit at all.

Lucchese mindlessly kicked at the snow with the toe of his boot. He still had time to back out of this thing, time to save his ass. Just pick up the phone and call it off.

But . . . Bridges's boys would be really pissed, and he would blow this, his big chance to move up when Bridges came in, to be at the front of the line—to be the real player they kept saying he should be.

Lucchese pushed back his round, pressed-steel safety hat. He scanned the lines of railroad flatcars and semi-truck flatbed trailers that waited to off-load tanks and trucks and munitions and medicine and food and more—everything desperately needed to fight and win a war. The lines went back as far as he could see in the dimly lit dockyard.

At the head of the lines, booms on the dock and ships moved like giant fingers lifting the pallets and containers and vehicles into EC2 (Emergency, Cargo, Large Capacity) ships. Each 441-foot-long vessel could transport the same amount as three hundred railroad cars, and a dozen EC2s were moored here, taking on cargo, while a couple dozen more were staged in the bay, waiting for their turn at the dock.

It was no secret that these so-called Liberty ships were being built in record time at U.S. shipyards on the East, West, and Gulf Coasts—and being sunk by enemy torpedoes damned near as fast.

Convoys, each with scores of Liberty ships, rushed eastward across the Atlantic, only to be hunted down by packs of German U-boats. Hundreds upon hundreds of the ships and their crews were blasted into the icy-cold depths—seven and a half million tons of critical cargo lost in 1942 alone.

The Nazi submarines were so deadly effective that the Allies considered a Liberty ship to have earned back its cost if it made just one trip across the Atlantic Ocean.

Which made, the nervous Lucchese knew, today's act all the more volatile, if not reprehensible.

A ship horn suddenly blew and Tony thought he'd shit his pants.

Aw, fuck it. I gotta do this thing.

Tony the Gut walked up to the door of the tin box of a dock office that he shared with International Longshoreman's Association gang bosses Michael Francis "Iron Mike" Mahoney and Franco Giuseppi "Little Joe" Biaggio. He grabbed the knob, then stopped short of turning and pulling it.

He was still anxious, not to mention breathing a little heavily from the walk, and the feeling in his ample belly still was not a good one. Maybe not so much dread. Maybe more like a mix of emotions—fear for sure, anxiety . . . hell, even a little excitement muddled in there.

Yeah, Lucchese thought, *that's all. C'mon, you can do this!*

He took a deep breath, exhaled, turned the knob, and pulled the door open.

The twelve-by-twelve paneled office held—barely— the wooden desks of the three gang bosses. Space was tight; if two of the men leaned back in their chairs at the same time, they hit. Each desk was pushed up against a wall of its own. The top of Lucchese's desk butted the bottom of the grimy plate-glass window—with the dusty, three-month-old MERRY CHRISTMAS! & HAPPY NEW YEAR! banner draped across the top—that overlooked the waterfront. Mahoney's was opposite it, at the foot of a large chalkboard that was a grid of white boxes in which the gang bosses kept track of who worked loading what ship and at what job—winch drivers, boom men, jitney drivers, and so on. The third desk, Biaggio's, was against the wall directly across from the door.

They shared the office's one battered telephone, coal black with a long, frayed cord. It was on Biaggio's desk, next to a filthy ashtray and a beat-up RCA radio softly playing music.

Biaggio, a compact five-foot-three, 120-pound thirty-year-old with piercing gray eyes and a mostly bald head that he kept trimmed to the scalp, was talking on the phone when Lucchese entered the office. The bitter cold wind blasted in from behind him, carrying some snowflakes.

"Close the goddamned door already," Mahoney snapped, grabbing at papers being blown about his desk.

Mahoney, who was thirty-two and had thick black hair that he kept slicked back, stood as tall as Lucchese but weighed 160, every ounce of muscle toned from long hours at Nicky's Gym.

Biaggio looked up from his desk, said, "I gotta go," into the phone receiver and put it in its cradle.

He caught Lucchese's attention.

"We need to talk, Tony. Have a seat."

Lucchese looked at him. Biaggio was the brightest of the three, on top of everything. He'd been brought in by the ILA not quite six months ago, when the union hall boss said Lucchese "could use a little help, what with the push to load ships faster and all."

Biaggio showed that he could handle his own work and at the same time know what was going on with Lucchese's and Mahoney's gangs.

Since just after Biaggio first arrived, Lucchese had tried—but usually failed—to be one step ahead of Little Joe. The second-guessing tended to annoy Biaggio, but Lucchese never stopped.

Must be that boom thing he's worried about, Lucchese thought now.

He said, "Engineering's fixed that winch on that ten-ton—"

"Sit," Mahoney said pointedly as he stood up.

Lucchese stared at him.

"What the hell's up with you?"

"Tony, don't make this harder than it has to be," Biaggio said quietly. "Sit. Please."

Lucchese moved toward his chair, making an agreeable gesture with his hands up, palms out. He shrugged out of his heavy coat and dropped his huge frame into the wooden chair. He nodded toward the phone.

"I'm expecting a call, just so's you know."

"We know," Mahoney said.

Lucchese raised an eyebrow, his face questioning.

"Everything," Biaggio added, staring at Lucchese. "We know everything."

Lucchese looked blankly at Biaggio.

What the hell? Everything?

Biaggio stared straight back, said nothing, just let that information take root. He then, with some element of theater, pulled a pack of Lucky Strike cigarettes from his shirt pocket, slid one from the pack and put it to his lips. He produced a scratched and dinged stainless-steel Zippo lighter from his pants pocket and, with a flourish, lit the cigarette, clicked the top closed with a flick of the wrist, and put the Zippo on the desk.

He held the pack out to Lucchese.

"No, thanks," Lucchese said and cleared his throat, hoping that no one noticed the nervous slight stammer.

He felt himself starting to sweat, despite the cold office, and hoped that that was not evident, either. A cigarette could calm him.

"Wait. Yeah, Little Joe, I'll have a smoke."

After he'd lit Lucchese's cigarette and put the Zippo in his pants pocket, Biaggio continued: "Look, we know who you've been talking to, who you're waiting to talk to"—he glanced at the phone—"and, most important, we know why. So don't try bullshitting us."

Lucchese felt his stomach twist into a knot. He took a pull on the cigarette and looked out the window.

Biaggio said, "You want to tell us why?"

Why what? You don't know shit, Lucchese thought.

He said, "Tell you why what?"

"Why you're doing this thing?" Biaggio said, his tone suggesting that he was beyond annoyed.

Lucchese inhaled deeply, then let it out.

"What thing?"

Mahoney slammed his fist on the desk. "Don't bull-shit us!"

Lucchese slid his chair back and away, toward the door.

"What the fuck is your problem?"

"You!" Mahoney said, clearly upset. "You—"

"Easy, Mike," Biaggio said.

Biaggio glanced out the window. No one was paying any particular attention to the gang bosses' office. Men and machines worked at a steady pace. A jeep on a cable swung past the window.

Biaggio locked eyes with Lucchese.

"Harry Bridges," Biaggio said slowly.

Oh shit! Lucchese thought.

He automatically glanced at the phone, then hated himself for it when he saw that Biaggio's eyes had followed his eyes to it.

Lucchese did not trust himself to speak at first. He took a puff, exhaled. Then: "Yeah? Okay, so what about Bridges? It's no secret a bunch of us from the ILA listened to him speak."

"But after that," Biaggio said, " 'most everybody took the hint and forgot about him."

"And what if I didn't?" Lucchese said.

Biaggio sighed. He stubbed out his cigarette in the half-full ashtray on his desk, lit another. He picked up the whole phone and slammed it on Lucchese's desk.

"What you're gonna do when it rings is this," Biaggio said, his eyes cold gray. "You're gonna tell Bridges that you've done this thing, that it's happening, then you're gonna say you gotta go and you hang up. That's it."

"It's not Bridges who's calling," Lucchese said defiantly.

This, he knew, was of course true—if not entirely transparent—because he also knew it was one of Bridges's men who was supposed to call.

Biaggio shook his head, then exploded: "Then you fucking well tell whoever calls that you've done the fucking thing and it's fucking happening! You got that?"

He paused, caught his breath.

Then he more quietly added, disgusted, "Jesusfuckingchrist, Tony. How stupid do you think I am?"

Slowly shaking his head, Lucchese looked down at his boots, then up and out the window, avoiding eye contact. This had all seemed so much easier when it was being planned.

How'd it go bad? Who talked?

As he watched a cable swing two U.S. Army one-ton Ben Hur trailers past the window en route to a ship hold, Lucchese thought that he might cry.

The phone rang.

Tony turned to the sound, looked at the phone, looked at the clock on the wall showing 8:01, looked at Biaggio.

It rang a second time.

"Go on and get it," Biaggio said after a moment.

But it had stopped ringing.

"I'm supposed to answer on the third ring next time they call, at two after."

Lucchese looked up at the clock and watched the second hand tick around the face.

When the phone had rung three times, Lucchese put the receiver to his ear and said, "Yeah?"

Biaggio sensed Mahoney moving, and when he looked at him he saw that he was leaning down and pulling his Colt .38 caliber revolver out from where he stashed it in the bottom drawer of his desk. Mahoney swung out the cylinder of the snub-nose, checked to see that it was loaded, then softly clicked the cylinder back in. He pulled up his left pants cuff, tucked the pistol in his sock, snugging it inside the top of his leather boot, then pulled the cuff back down. He looked at Lucchese.

"Uh-huh," Lucchese was saying into the phone, his eyes glued on Biaggio. "That's right. It's done. I've passed the word."

Lucchese listened for a moment, said, "Right," then hung up the receiver.

He looked at Biaggio. "Now what?"

Biaggio stubbed out his cigarette.

"You wait," Biaggio said. "Right there, by the phone."

"Another call?"

"Let's go, Mike," Biaggio said, standing up. "We got work to do."

"A call from who?" Lucchese pursued.

Little Joe and Iron Mike ignored the question.

Lucchese watched them pull on their heavy coats and thick knit caps and steel safety helmets, then go through the door without saying another word.

The icy wind blew in, and for a moment there was the loud drone of the heavy equipment outside before the door slammed shut with the wind.

The gang boss office was now quiet except for the sound of the radio playing. Softly, International Longshoreman's Association gang boss Anthony Christopher "Tony the Gut" Lucchese started crying.

"Oh, God . . ." he sobbed.

As Biaggio and Mahoney walked away from the office, they were aware of a U.S. Army six-by-six—a Truck, General Purpose, two-and-one-half-ton 6×6, meaning all wheels were powered—hanging from the cable of a ten-ton boom.

The GMC "deuce and a half," an Army workhorse, had an open cab with a canvas-covered cargo area and was painted olive drab with white markings, including that of a three-foot-diameter star-in-a-ring that about covered the whole door. It was not uncommon for a Ben Hur trailer to be hooked behind a six-by-six.

"Okay," Biaggio said to Maloney.

They gave the signal—each pulled a knit scarf from an overcoat pocket and simultaneously wrapped their necks—then turned to walk toward the farthest Liberty ship.

Immediately, they heard the pitch of the ten-ton boom winch become deeper, straining under a heavy load. The six-by-six hanging on the ten-ton boom cable was now beginning to swing toward its ship hold.

Then there came a great screaming of winch gears and the cable started to unspool rapidly as the giant GMC truck fell from the sky.

As he stared intently at the phone, waiting for it to ring and wondering who it would be, Tony heard a terrible noise on the dock outside the office.

He looked up at the plate-glass window in time to see a blur of olive drab with a white star fill it.

In his last conscious moment, Tony the Gut saw the window explode—its shards flying into the office and spearing his flesh—and felt the office ceiling collapse on his head.

A huge truck tire came to a rest on his back, crushing out his last breath.

[FOUR]
OSS London Station
Berkeley Square
London, England
0745 28 February 1943

Colonel David Kirkpatrick Este Bruce, the distinguished-looking chief of London Station, heard the rapping of knuckles on the wooden doorframe and looked up from the stack of documents that he had been reading since he had arrived at six o'clock.

Bruce had the calm and detached manner of a high-level career diplomat, which is what he had set out to be when he'd joined the diplomatic corps after graduating from Princeton University. His face was stonelike, chiseled, and his eyes burned with an intensity that caused him to appear older than his years, though he had turned forty-five just two weeks earlier.

His number two, Lieutenant Colonel Ed Stevens, a beginning-to-gray forty-four-year-old whose strong face always seemed to be in deep thought, stood in the doorway to the empty outer office of Bruce's administrative assistant.

"Good morning, sir," Lieutenant Colonel Stevens said, and held up an envelope stamped TOP SECRET. "This just came in from Colonel Donovan."

Bruce glanced at a side table. It held photographs in silver and wooden frames of Bruce with politicians and military leaders—one showed him with British prime minister Winston Churchill at the polo grounds, another with General Dwight Eisenhower in Algiers—and there was a silver-framed image taken of Bruce in an Adirondack chair with his wife, Alisa, sitting on his lap.

It had been snapped in Nantucket some years earlier—a decade, if not longer—and it had captured the young, vibrant couple in a relaxed, carefree moment. A visibly half-in-the-bag Bruce, in a tailored dark suit, had the top button of his crisp white shirt undone and his orange-and-black rep necktie loosened, while his wife, in pearls and a dark silk cocktail dress, held her high-heel shoes in one hand, a drink in the other.

It was one of Bruce's favorites because it froze in time a very rare moment when their vast wealth did not matter—Bruce had a great deal of his own money when he married Alisa, née Mellon, the richest woman in America.

At that moment, they had been simply happy, a loving couple—which wasn't necessarily the case now, and one reason Bruce found himself more and more on edge.

"'Morning, Ed," Bruce said almost absently, waving him in the office.

Next to the papers on the deeply polished desk was a silver service for coffee—a large carafe, three clean cups and saucers in addition to the cup and saucer Bruce had used, and sugar and milk in their bowl and pitcher—and Bruce motioned toward it.

"You'll forgive my manners when I ask you to please pour yourself a cup," Bruce said, taking the envelope.

"Thanks. I believe I can manage," Stevens said agreeably, as Bruce broke the seal on the envelope, flipped past the two TOP SECRET cover pages, and began to read.

Bruce grunted.

"Interesting," he said. "Not exactly surprising." He put the sheets back in the envelope and looked at Stevens. "Damned good news, as far as I'm concerned."

Ed Stevens, settling into one of the two chairs in front of the desk, did not reply immediately, but when Bruce continued to look at him, seemingly expecting some comment, Stevens said cautiously, between sips of coffee, "Canidy is due here this morning."

"Good. I've said it before, and I'll say it again. I've always thought that Canidy is out of his depth here, and he is helping prove my point with his reckless acts."

He poked a finger at the stack of documents.

"There's a message in here from Howell confirming that Howell arrived in Washington with Fulmar and the Dyers. Just that. Nothing more."

Stevens felt unease at what he recognized as Bruce's obvious anger. The slight that had triggered it clearly had not been forgotten nor forgiven.

David Bruce had learned on February 14—two days after celebrating his birthday—in an EYES ONLY personal message from Colonel Donovan that a mission was taking place in Bruce's backyard, one of such extreme importance—"Presidential," Donovan had written—that Bruce was deemed not to have the "Need to Know."

That was difficult enough for the chief of OSS London to swallow, but what made matters worse was the fact that Stevens—*My deputy, for Christ's sake!* Bruce had thought disgustedly—did have the Need to Know, though Donovan had said that Stevens was privy only to limited details in order for him to act should he suspect that any actions by OSS London Station—or by Bruce personally—might undermine the mission.

It was not a perfect situation, the OSS director apologized, but it was a necessity, one made by direct order of FDR. Donovan promised to bring Bruce into the loop as soon as possible.

It turned out that Donovan didn't have to; of all people, Canidy had done it for him, in a TOP SECRET—EYES ONLY message that he had sent from German-occupied Hungary.

Dick Canidy was Eric Fulmar's OSS control officer. He had sent Fulmar, his prep-school classmate and the American-born son of a German industrialist, to Germany to smuggle out Professor Frederick Dyer, whom Canidy understood to be an expert in metallurgy and in the manufacture of jet and rocket engines. The fifty-nine-year-old professor was disgusted with Nazis in general and Hitler in particular, and it was hoped that he would assist the Allies not only in the pinpointing of the factories that were producing these engines, which would then be bombed and thus preserve Allied air superiority, but also in the advancement of the Allies' own development of jets and rockets.

What Canidy—and Stevens and Bruce and everyone except a select few on the secret list controlled by the President—did not know was that Dyer was more importantly also a scientist with expertise in nuclear fission, and his escape would (a) deny the Germans his work in the race to develop an atomic bomb and (b) help the Americans in theirs—code-named the Manhattan Project—at which they had already had considerable success, including the first uranium chain reaction on December 2, 1942, in a lab secretly built in a squash court under the football stands of the University of Chicago.

An escape route had been carefully planned, with a series of OSS and British Special Operations Executive agents and resistance members set to smuggle Fulmar and the professor and his daughter from Marburg an der Lahn in Germany (where Fulmar was leaving a long trail of German SS bodies) to Vienna, then Budapest, and ultimately to the coast of the Adriatic Sea, where a fishing boat would ferry them out to the island of Vis, on which Canidy waited with his hidden B-25 aircraft.

That had been the plan. But, as plans can, it went bad—placing the President's extreme mission, as well as the lives of Fulmar and the professor, in jeopardy.

Canidy had sent a message from Vis saying that only Gisella Dyer, the professor's attractive twenty-nine-year-old daughter, had made it out via the Hungarian pipeline. Fulmar and the professor were serving ninety days' hard labor in Pécs, in southwest Hungary, their punishment for being black marketers, ones who failed to pay off local officials.

When word got back to OSS Washington, Donovan made a cold-blooded decision: If in ten days Canidy failed to rescue Fulmar and Professor Dyer, Canidy was ordered to terminate them to keep them from falling into the hands of the Germans on their trail.

When Donovan then learned that Canidy, risking everything, had gone after them himself, and then that the OSS team and the C-47 sent to support him was declared late and presumed lost, Donovan had had to cut his losses: He ordered a squadron of B-17s, ostensibly en route for a raid on Budapest, to take out the Hungarian prison as a target of opportunity.

But the C-47 hadn't been lost—it'd been forced to land.

And then, as the B-17s leveled the prison at Pécs, it'd taken off with Canidy and Fulmar and Professor Dyer . . . mission accomplished.

Bruce reached out for the carafe and poured himself more coffee as he thought how that damned loose cannon Dick Canidy had again gotten away with not following the standard operating procedures.

But maybe not, he thought, judging by this morning's message. *Maybe Donovan is about to call Canidy on the carpet.*

Bruce caught the look in Stevens's eyes and realized that he had put him in an awkward position.

"Sorry, Ed. Forget I said anything."

Bruce thumbed through the pile of messages until he found what he was looking for and passed it to Stevens. "You've seen this?"

"Yeah," Stevens said after he scanned it. "Another request from Sandman for Corsica."

"I know getting the weapons is no problem. But do we have the cash on hand that they request?"

"Can you give me a minute?" Stevens asked and nodded toward his office, signifying that he wanted to check something.

"Of course," Bruce said, then picked up his coffee cup and turned his attention to the decrypted message from the OSS agent on the Axis-held French island of Corsica.

Two months earlier, in mid-December, the Office of Strategic Services had made history with the landing of the first OSS secret agent team inside enemy-occupied Europe. To the great relief of OSS stations from North Africa to London to Washington, the team, with minimal difficulties, had had textbook success from the time its clandestine radio station, code-named PEARL HARBOR, had, on December 25, 1942, sent to OSS Algiers Station the first of what would become almost daily messages that detailed German and Italian strengths and strategic locations and more.

It was remarkable for the OSS on a number of levels, not the least of which was that it garnered the young agency genuine credibility—albeit grudgingly in some quarters, such as the British SIS, which had been formed in the sixteenth century and had absolutely no patience for the stumbles of the infant American intelligence organization.

General Dwight David Eisenhower, the supreme Allied commander, while not exactly a cheerleader for the unorthodox methods of Colonel Donovan and his merry band of spies, became a cautious convert when, at Allied Forces Headquarters in North Africa, he was provided with the OSS intel relayed from Corsica.

The covert team, using its growing web of local connections, had reported that only twenty-five thousand Italians had taken the island; that they'd done it with relative ease because the Vichy government had ordered the French army's two battalions there not to resist; that these battalions were demobilized and their general put under house arrest; and that the Italians had limited their strength on the island only to the west and east coasts and to major highways inland.

Building on that team's success, the OSS was continually assembling and training more teams. Two were on standby to go in as soon as possible, one of these an emergency backup to the first—as relief, when the team was exfiltrated, or as replacement, in the event that its cover was blown. The rest were being trained for SO— Special Operations—OSS agents sent in to support the local resistance, the Corsican Maquis, with tools for sabotage and harassment of the enemy.

As Bruce read the most recent report from the agent on Corsica—this report including a list of the local gendarmes that the team had recruited and their needs— there was a light tap at the door.

"Good morning, sir," the pleasant voice of a woman said.

David Bruce looked up and saw Captain Helene Dancy, Women's Army Corps.

Captain Dancy was Bruce's administrative assistant, an attractive brunette in her thirties who had left a position at the Prudential Insurance Company as executive secretary to the senior vice president for real estate. She was professional and thorough, with the golden ability to get things done when others would have long ago given up.

"Good morning, Captain. Everything well with you this morning?"

"Just fine, thank you, sir."

She nodded at the stack of reports.

"And you? I see you've managed your usual early start. Anything for me?"

"Never early enough, it would seem," he said with a tone of resignation. "Colonel Stevens just left to find something. I have nothing for you right now, but should Stevens require help that could change."

"Certainly, sir."

"Were you able to locate Captain Fine?"

"Yes, sir. Late yesterday. And I just passed by him in the hall. He said he would be by momentarily."

Bruce glanced at the file on his desk that held the TOP SECRET message from Donovan.

"So should Major Canidy. While I'd like to keep Canidy at bay, I don't think that that's going to happen." He paused. "But I might be able to use that to my advantage."

"Sir?" Captain Dancy said. "I don't follow."

"Never mind it, please. Just thinking aloud. Show them in when they get here."

Captain Dancy had finally sat down at her desk after having replaced the coffee service in David Bruce's office with a carafe of fresh coffee and clean cups when a tall scholarly looking man in the uniform of a United States Army Air Forces captain entered her office.

"Sorry I took so long," Captain Stanley S. Fine said.

"Not a problem," Captain Dancy replied with a smile. "Colonel Bruce said you were to go right in when you got here."

She had long been impressed with the thirty-three-year-old Fine and not just because she knew that before joining the OSS and before being a commander of a B-17 squadron (this despite his great desire to be a fighter pilot) he had been a Hollywood lawyer. That, of course, *did* impress her—the movie business had that effect—but what Captain Dancy really understood about Captain Fine was that he was a very wise man and she knew this judgment of his character was widely shared, including by both Colonel Donovan and Colonel Bruce.

"His nose out of joint that I'm late?" Captain Fine said.

"You're not late. And I don't think that it's you he's—"

"Stan!" a familiar voice called from the hallway just outside the door. "I need a moment with you."

Captain Dancy recognized the voice, and was not surprised when a moment later Major Richard Canidy appeared in the doorway.

"—It's him," she said, finishing her sentence with a smile in her voice.

"'It's him' who?" Dick Canidy said, mock-innocently. "I could not possibly be guilty of that for which I have been unjustly accused." He paused. "Could I?"

Captain Dancy liked Major Canidy as much as—if not more than—she did Captain Fine. And for some of the same reasons—Dick was a bright guy, one who was genuine and caring—as well as for some other reasons—Dick was damned dashing, with a real magnetism that on occasion caused her to lament the differences in their ages.

"You tell me, Major Canidy," Captain Dancy said in a

conspiratorial tone, then added warmly, "It's nice to have you home safe."

"Thank you, Captain."

"Can whatever it is you need to discuss wait till lunch?" Fine asked.

Canidy thought about it for a second. "Fine, Captain Fine."

Captain Dancy stood, shaking her head.

"If you two will follow me, please," she said, and started for the office of the chief of OSS London Station.

David Bruce, holding a coffee cup saucer in one hand and sipping from the cup in his other, was in deep thought looking out one of the tall windows when his office door opened and Captain Dancy announced, "Sir, Captain Fine and Major Canidy are here."

Bruce, still looking down at the street and sidewalk, said, "Thank you. Send them in, please."

A moment later, Fine and Canidy said, almost in unison, "Good morning, sir."

Bruce turned away from the window in time to see Captain Dancy leaving the office and pulling the door closed behind her.

"Good morning," Bruce replied. He looked them in the eyes for a moment, then said, "Please allow me to say that I am deeply relieved that you both made it back."

He looked at Canidy and added, "That didn't always seem to be the case."

"Thank you, sir," they replied.

"You certainly deserve some time off after that mission," Bruce said. "But I'm afraid it's going to have to wait. The sooner we get going on this, the better."

Fine and Canidy exchanged glances.

"Get going on what?" Canidy said to Bruce. "We haven't—"

There was a knock at the door and it swung open.

"Colonel Stevens, sir," Captain Dancy announced.

Lieutenant Colonel Ed Stevens was standing there behind her, a worn-leather briefcase in each hand.

"Come," Bruce said almost impatiently.

When Ed Stevens entered, Fine and Canidy came into his view.

"Stan! Dick!" Stevens said.

He put down the briefcases, went to them, and embraced them one at a time, giving each a loud double pat on the back. When he was confident of his voice, he added, "Damn, it's good to see you guys!"

Lieutenant Colonel Stevens took a step back and composed himself.

"Thanks, Ed," Canidy said.

"It's good to be back," Fine added. "Thank you, Ed."

Stevens nodded and smiled, then collected the briefcases and turned to Bruce.

"I knew we had these funds in the safe. I'm having them see how much more we can get, and how soon."

"Funds?" Canidy repeated.

When Stevens nodded, Canidy turned to Bruce.

"This have to do with what you're talking about, David?"

Bruce ignored the question. He pointed to the couch.

"Put them there, Ed," he said.

He looked at Canidy and Fine.

"Can I offer you some coffee?" he asked. "Helene just made it."

As Bruce poured everyone a cup from the new carafe brought in by Captain Dancy, Stevens placed the briefcase from his left hand on the couch first, then the one from his right hand beside it.

He worked the combination lock on the left briefcase, pushed the buttons to unlock its clasps, and after the clasps sprung open with a dull *click-click* he slowly opened the case. Then he repeated the process with the right case.

Stevens looked at Bruce.

"Nice," Bruce said, stepping over to admire the worn currency that was in fat bundles secured with paper bands. "I don't care how much one might be around money, you just can't help but be impressed with cold, hard cash—seeing it, feeling it, smelling it."

There were appreciative chuckles.

Canidy offered, "I've always thought that bank tellers were not being completely truthful when they said that they were unaffected by all the money they handled day in and day out."

"They were just saying something they felt obligated to say?" Fine said.

"That's my guess," Canidy said. "That, or they're just damned liars looking for a chance to skim it."

"There's always that temptation," Bruce said matter-of-factly. "Or out-and-out steal it all."

"Anyway," Stevens said, pointing to the left briefcase, "in here is a half-million francs, and—" he pointed to the right one "—this is a hundred thousand in lire. It's a start, and more is on the way. We had another two hundred thousand francs, but our contact at Banque Oran became suspicious of a series of deposits by the owner of a restaurant that had suddenly become quote very successful unquote and when the bills were inspected, about one in ten were found to have had sequential serial numbers."

Bruce grunted.

"The Fascists really can't think we are that stupid," he said. "That's insulting."

"More likely a stupid mistake on the restaurateur's part. Careless. Or lazy. Just stuck the new bills in with old ones in a single batch, not bothering to spread out the ones with sequential numbers over time. After we discovered that the money was marked, but before we could turn him, I'm told somebody shot him."

Bruce shook his head. There was no room for mistakes in this business. Especially sloppy ones. Yet, there seemed to be no end of them, either. And it was too bad he'd been killed; you could never have too many double agents.

"That amount should satisfy Sandman's immediate request," Bruce said, glancing at the pile of documents on his desk that included the message from Corsica as he sat down.

He motioned for Canidy and Fine to take their seats in the armchairs in front of his desk and they did.

"Yes, sir," Stevens agreed and closed the cases, then moved one to take his seat on the couch.

"Sandman?" Canidy said, eyebrows raised in question.

Bruce bristled at the temerity.

As a rule of thumb, the asking of questions in the OSS was discouraged; in fact, the act could, depending on the magnitude of the subject, carry significant penalties including but not limited to, say, confinement in an obscure stockade at the far end of the world for the duration of the war plus ninety days—if not longer. One either had the Need to Know or one didn't. Lives—indeed, the war—could be lost if too many knew too much.

Looking at Canidy, Bruce knew that he knew this. But Bruce also knew that he was still pissed that Canidy and Fine and Stevens, his goddamned deputy, had had the Need to Know about the smuggling of Professor Dyer and his daughter out of Hungary—while he didn't.

Intellectually, he could understand the logic. Emotionally, however, was something else.

Yet here was Canidy once again questioning at will.

Bruce was honest enough with himself to recognize that he had more than a little resentment toward Major Richard M. Canidy, USAAF.

What bothered Bruce wasn't the fact that despite the gold leaves of a major pinned to his A-2 jacket epaulets, Canidy was not an officer of the Army Air Forces. Assimilated ranks were issued all the time—particularly in the OSS. Because civilians in a military environment attract

•

attention and because little attention is paid to majors, especially at the upper levels of the military hierarchy, it had made good sense to arrange for the Army Air Forces to issue an AGO card from the Adjutant General's Office to "Technical Consultant Canidy" that identified him as a major. That way, should someone inquire of Eighth Air Force or SHAEF (Supreme Headquarters, Allied Expeditionary Force), a record would exist of a Canidy, Major Richard M., USAAF.

And what bothered Bruce was not the fact that Canidy, with a bachelor of science degree in aeronautical engineering from the Massachusetts Institute of Technology, 1938, had, as a lieutenant junior grade, United States Navy Reserve, been recruited from his duty of instructor pilot at Naval Air Station Pensacola to be a Flying Tiger with Claire Chennault's American Volunteer Group, then from there been tapped to be a "technical consultant" to the Office of the Coordinator of Information, the first incarnation of the OSS.

Canidy had proven himself a warrior—particularly in China with the Flying Tigers—as well as a natural leader, and Bruce respected that.

No, what bothered the strictly ordered sensibilities of David Bruce was the fact that Canidy was simply too young and too reckless—particularly in light of the fact that being the officer in charge of Whitbey House Station, OSS-England, made him the third-highest-ranking OSS officer in England.

And, getting to the meat of it, what really bothered Bruce the most was not only the fact that Canidy pulled damned dangerous stunts—invariably leaving a mess for the diplomatic-minded such as Bruce to clean up—but that he damned well got away with them.

Which, of course, left Canidy with no problem asking questions that he should not be asking.

"Ed," London Station chief David Bruce finally said, "why don't you fill in the details?"

"Yes, sir," Lieutenant Colonel Ed Stevens said, then looked at Major Canidy and Captain Fine. "You're familiar with 'Pearl Harbor'?"

"You're referring to the OSS team," Canidy said, "not to the Territory of Hawaii."

Stevens nodded.

Stan Fine said, "We are."

Stevens stood and went to the desk and picked up the carafe. He raised the pot to ask everyone, *More?*, and poured after Bruce slid his cup closer, then warmed up Fine's and Canidy's cups, then finally his own.

"Sandman is in Algiers," Stevens continued, "training additional teams for insertion into Corsica. The next team will take in this cash, sharing it with the team already in place. You're familiar with the makeup of the teams?"

"The recruits are Corsicans," Canidy began, "from the French Deuxième Bureau at Algiers."

The French Deuxième Bureau was the intelligence arm of the French army's general staff.

"Right," Stevens said. "An officer and three men. The officer is the intel leader, and the liaison and the two radio operators report to him. So Sandman took the four-man team in by *Casabianca*—"

"The French sub?" Canidy said.

"Exactly. They infiltrated at night onto the beach by rubber boat. First wave ashore, they took wireless radio sets, money, weapons—"

"Lots of Composition C-2," Bruce interrupted.

"Lots of C-2," Stevens confirmed with a smile. "Then the sub backed just offshore, where it laid on the bottom for twenty hours. Meanwhile, the team went inland, established its base, then the next night returned to the beach—a different spot that'd been prearranged—and signaled the sub, which had been waiting subsurface, watching with its periscope. It surfaced, and full supply—more pistols, Sten nine-millimeter submachine guns, ammo, et cetera, et cetera—was completed."

Stevens took a sip of coffee, then continued: "In days we were getting reports from Pearl Harbor, making it successful on a number of levels—"

"So much so," Bruce interrupted again, "that our plan now is to send in teams to France."

There was silence as Canidy and Fine drank from their cups and considered that.

Stevens went on: "There's more, but for now understand that we're going to use the Corsica model of inserting teams in France to supply and build the resistance. That said, it's going to be more difficult. We got lucky in Corsica; the Germans and Italians took the island with next to no troops, and continue to hold it in a very sloppy manner. The French there hate the Fascist Italians, of course, and so far don't seem afraid to take our help to rise up against them."

"Conversely, France is crawling with Krauts," Canidy said. "And with a lot of Frogs who want to get along with the Krauts."

"Right," Stevens said. "We're confident that enough of the French will fight; it's just going to be harder getting to them."

"And that's where we come in?" Canidy asked. "C-2 and suitcases of cash—I'm in."

Canidy thought that he noticed a just-perceptible smirk from David Bruce.

"That," the chief of London Station replied evenly and with a straight face, "is where Captain Fine comes in. Captain Fine will be flying this money to OSS Algiers, where he will give it to Sandman and then begin the setting up of teams for France. Right now, Major, since you've just successfully come from German-occupied territory, I'm simply interested in your observations."

"Well," Canidy shot back, "my first observation—"

"Dick!" Fine said, cautioning him.

"Before you go off half-cocked, Major," Bruce said, "you should know that I have my reasons."

"Reasons?" Canidy parroted.

David Bruce knew that he shouldn't, but he felt some small pleasure picking up the envelope and handing it to Canidy. "For you."

Canidy reached out, practically snatched the envelope, and opened it. He flipped past the outer cover sheet

stamped TOP SECRET, then past the inner one stamped
TOP SECRET—EYES ONLY BRUCE STEVENS CANIDY and
read the message without expression.

```
TOP SECRET
OPERATIONAL IMMEDIATE
FROM OSS WASHINGTON FOR OSS LONDON EYES
ONLY BRUCE STEVENS CANIDY
QUOTE USING MOST EXPEDITIOUS MEANS CANIDY
IS TO REPORT TO THIS OFFICE AND TO ME RE-
PEAT ME DIRECTLY STOP CANIDY IS NOT REPEAT
NOT TO ATTACH HIMSELF TO OR ASSUME AUTHOR-
ITY OF ANY OP OR MISSION STOP DONOVAN END
QUOTE
```

Canidy put it back in the envelope.

"Any idea what this is about?" he said.

Bruce locked eyes with him, waited for a moment, then
said, "Officially? No. Unofficially?" He paused, seemingly
deciding if it was wise to go on. "Unofficially, I think it's
rather clear."

Canidy waved *Go on* with his hand.

Bruce said, "You are damned lucky to be alive and free
as opposed to alive and in the hands of the *Sicherheitsdienst.* You knew too much to go behind the lines. What
if you had in fact been captured?"

"But I wasn't," Canidy shot back. "And I accomplished the mission."

"At an incredibly great risk," Bruce replied icily. "And
not without significant loss. The Hungarian pipeline is

blown, and last word we got from the OSS radio station was code that they had been discovered and were about to be captured."

Canidy's face tightened. He looked past Bruce and stared out the window.

"Judging by the wording of Colonel Donovan's message," Bruce went on calculatingly, "I presume he feels the same way."

After a moment, Canidy locked eyes with Bruce.

"Maybe you're right," he said, putting his cup and saucer on the desk. "I greatly regret the loss of any agents, but I did what I thought was the best under the circumstances. . . ."

"And you did do the best considering the circumstances," Fine offered.

"Thank you, Stan," Canidy said.

Then he stood, and took the envelope that held his top secret order from Donovan.

"If you'll excuse me, I think I should pack."

II

[ONE]
Unterseeboot 134
30 degrees 35 minutes 5 seconds North Latitude
81 degrees 39 minutes 10 seconds West Longitude
Off Manhattan Beach, Florida
2305 27 February 1943

Kapitänleutnant Hans-Günther Brosin—who was twenty-six years old, had a clean-shaven, soft-featured face, a head of loosely cropped black hair, and a compact five-six, 130-pound build that one might expect of a seaman who had volunteered to go to war in the confines of a tube only thirty feet tall and two hundred long—not only was not happy with his present assignment, he was highly pissed.

In his mind, it was one thing to have to follow orders that you knew went contrary to everything you understood your training to be—and, without question, the training of a *Kriegsmarine* U-boat commander and his crew was to hunt down and kill enemy vessels—but it was entirely another thing to follow orders that not only essentially repeated those of a mission that had been risky beyond reason but that very much repeated orders of a risky mission that had in fact proven to be a complete and utter failure.

The vessel's two-week-plus passage across the Atlantic Ocean—during which the U-134, running under strict radio silence, had come across a convoy of Liberty ships carrying war matériel eastward and the crew had not been able to fire a single one of its fourteen torpedoes because Kapitänleutnant Brosin's orders specifically forbade any enemy contact unless it was in an act of defense *and* "necessary to ensure the success of mission"—had in no way tempered his anger.

I am the commander of a fully armed man-of-war, he thought, *not of a passenger ferry.*

Brosin looked up from the chart that plotted their course to the shores of America, and studied the cause of his contempt.

Richard Koch and Rudolf Cremer were the leaders of the two two-man teams he was to put ashore. Koch's partner was Kurt Bayer, and Cremer's was Rolf Grossman. They were all in their late twenties and of average size and looks (none of the four appeared distinctly German), each dressed in all-black woolen clothing, complete with knit cap, and wearing a black leather holster that secured a Walther P38 9mm semiautomatic pistol and an extra eight-round magazine.

Brosin was unaware—his orders strictly spelled out that he was to transport the teams and see that they made it to shore; he knew not who they were nor what they were doing, and they did not offer the information nor did he ask it—that all four men had spent years in the

United States before the war and that if they had not already returned to the fatherland by December 1941 they had in the months immediately afterward. Koch and Cremer had served in the military; Bayer and Grossman, civilians, were selected in large part for their knowledge of America, then were trained for their mission by the Abwehr, the military's secret service.

The teams were moving four black stainless steel containers, each roughly the size and shape of a large stuffed duffel, complete with black-webbed shoulder straps. One by one, they staged the heavy containers near the base of the ladder that led up to the hatch in the conning tower.

Feeling Brosin's eyes on him, Koch glanced over at him, and nodded. Brosin did not respond.

Koch, a good six inches taller and forty pounds heavier than Brosin, had come to respect the commander—at the very least for his obvious professional care for his men and his ship, and surely for his temper. In view of the latter, Koch had—as difficult as such a thing was to accomplish on an undersea boat—managed to keep his distance from the captain the whole two weeks. And, as overall leader, he had made sure that Cremer and Bayer and Grossman had done the same. At one point, when they had confined themselves to their bunks to memorize the details of their mission orders for after landing—every phase had to be accomplished by memory only—two days passed without the captain seeing his unwanted human cargo.

Crouching, Koch helped Cremer position the last container, gave him a pat on the back, then, being careful as he stood upright so as not to strike his head on any of the ship structure, walked over to Brosin.

"Not long now, Commander," Koch said.

"Not soon enough," Brosin replied evenly, looking right through him.

That, Koch remembered all too well, was exactly what the captain of U-134 had told him when they had had their first meeting—a private one—in the captain's quarters shortly after they had sailed from the bunker at Brest, France.

"Just so we are clear about this," Kapitänleutnant Hans-Günther Brosin had said, waving his copy of the mission's secret orders. "Landing agents from a U-boat on the shore of America was an idea that bordered on suicide when it was attempted only months ago and it is an idea that is more than suicide now."

"Commander, not attempted but successfully—"

"I count Kapitänleutnant Linder," Brosin interrupted, holding up his hand in a gesture that stopped Koch, "as a personal friend. He, as one professional to another, personally told me the complete details of how U-202, under his command, put ashore the four Abwehr-trained agents on the Long Island of New York. Including the fact that, as the agents and their containers of explosives moved to shore by raft, the U-boat became grounded on a shoal of sand."

"Perhaps if the captain had—"

"*Ach du lieber Gott!*" Brosin snapped. "There is no *per-*

haps! This boat is the same type as U-202, and I can tell you, Herr Koch, as I know every detail of this ship, stem to stern, that for it to float requires a minimum water depth of five meters. And what is *more*—"

He heard his voice echo down the ship. He had quickly been losing his temper and realized it.

He paused, took a deep breath, then with a lower voice had continued: "And what is more, Herr Koch, a U-boat's only measure of safety is the silence of the depths. If she is in less than thirty meters—and certainly if she is in five, ten meters of water, or, worse, is aground—she is a sitting duck. As was the U-202."

He shook his head.

Brosin went on, his disgust clearly evident: "Are you aware that when the emergency measures of dumping fuel to lighten the boat, then using her diesel engines full power astern, did not seem to be helping free her from the shoal—an act that not only resulted in the loss of more precious fuel but also served to ruin any stealth the boat might have enjoyed—Kapitänleutnant Linder had ordered the crew to begin to *scuttle* her?"

"Commander, I am more than—"

"Of course you are. And so, too, you are of course aware that the agents—those four in New York and an-other four the next day put ashore just south of here—were almost immediately captured? And those not put to death by the Americans were sentenced to spend their lives in prison?"

When Koch wordlessly stared back at Brosin, the cap-tain threw up his hands.

"It was insanity to embark on such a mission," Brosin said with disgust, "and it is insanity to repeat such a failure."

"And, Commander," Koch had said matter-of-factly, "as it was the U-202's and Kapitänleutnant Linder's, so is it our duty to serve as ordered."

"That does not mean I will repeat mistakes made."

"Nor will I, Commander," Koch had replied coldly. "With respect, that is why this time we land during winter. And in deeper water. You will recall that Kapitänleutnant Deecke had no such problem with U-584 landing its agents on the Florida shore. And U-584 is a Type VIIC"—he paused for effect—"the same as this boat."

"I have made my position clear," Brosin said and stood up. "There is no margin for error."

"Understood, Commander," Koch said, rising. He started to leave, then added in a light and hopeful tone: "Remember, it is the new year. Victory for the Führer and the fatherland is soon, my friend."

"Not soon enough," Brosin had said.

Now, more than two weeks later, U-134 was within ten miles of the uppermost east coast of Florida.

Brosin turned to his executive officer, who stood with his forehead against the periscope, eyes pressed to its rubber eyecups.

"Good, Willi?"

"Nasty weather up top, sir," Wachoffizier Wilhelm Detrick, a squat, dark-haired twenty-one-year-old, said.

"Rain, light wind from the northwest. Visibility is not great. But nothing in sight, sir."

"Take us up, then, Willi. Keep her running on batteries, prepared to go immediately to full diesel power, if necessary."

Brosin paused and looked at Koch and his teams, then added: "The sooner we get this over with, the sooner we can get back to our real work."

"Yes, sir," Detrick said.

[TWO]
Manhattan Beach, Florida
0201 28 February 1943

United States Coast Guard Yeoman Third Class Peter Pappas, who was five-foot-five, 130 pounds, and blessed with the chiseled look of a Greek god bronzed by sun and salt, tugged the hood of his poncho tighter around his head, trying to seal out the cold rain that was dripping in around the brim of his hat.

The rain had been coming in what seemed like almost regular intervals the whole time—two hours so far, with two to go—that he had been patrolling the beach. The wind had been light but steady out of the northwest. A very, very quiet Saturday night, and now early Sunday morning.

Pappas stopped at another one of the somewhat regular indentations between the sand dunes, paths cut by the feet of countless beachgoers during warmer and happier times. He looked inland and saw nothing suspicious.

Then, with his handkerchief, he wiped rain from the lens of the U.S. Navy binoculars hanging from his neck, raised them to his eyes, carefully fitted the eyepieces to his eye sockets, then made a 180-degree sweep of the beach and ocean, slowly scanning from north to south.

And seeing absolutely nothing but black-gray sand, black-gray sea, and black-gray sky.

Again.

He snickered. He had just remembered the line he'd joked with the girls to get them to meet him at night on the beach: "Want to go watch the submarine races?"

Damned submarines, he thought, the smile long gone. *Joke's on me now.*

It had been about a year ago when, as a seventeen-year-old senior at Tarpon Springs High School, Peter Pappas first began to seriously consider joining the United States Coast Guard.

Being around boats and water was more than natural for him. His grandparents had come from Greece and settled into what then had been a village of fishermen and sponge divers. In time, Pappas's father and uncles had followed their father into the business that had fairly rewarded their families for their hard labors. And so, too, had Pappas begun working the boats as a young boy, learning the business from the bottom—literally, cutting sea sponges from the floor of the Gulf of Mexico.

By age seventeen, though, after five-plus years of pulling

sponges and filleting fish, Pappas had more than convinced himself that he needed to do something with his life other than work the family boats.

Actually, it had been Ana who had convinced him. Not that Anastasia Costas had told him that specifically, but Pappas could figure out that a sponge diver had little chance at a long-term relationship with the only daughter of Alexander Costas, Esquire, mayor of the town of Tarpon Springs.

Pappas had the Greek-god-like looks and a seemingly endless, easy charm that went a long way to masking the fact that he had not necessarily been blessed with smarts. He was a nice guy, even honest (something that could not be said of many of the boat guys), and that coupled with the looks and charm had caught the attention of fifteen-year-old Ana. And he intended to keep it.

When Pappas had looked around Tarpon Springs and considered his options, he found few. He had not excelled academically—it had taken some tutoring for him to actually graduate high school—and he certainly had not performed well in any sport. Working long hours on the boats had not allowed for any athletics.

Then, last summer, as the *Sophia*, one of his father's two wooden work boats, headed for port loaded with sea sponges and grouper and snapper, he had seen a Coast Guard cutter rumble past. The ship was at least one hundred feet long—more than three times the length of the *Sophia*—and fast. More impressive, though, was a crew member at the stern: He stood at what Pappas was pretty sure had to be a machine gun. Maybe a .50 caliber. And he seemed to be making a slow salute or wave in Pappas's direction as the cutter continued past.

Pappas, hosing fish guts off his boots and the deck, had made his decision then and there. Joining the Coast Guard would give him the opportunity to be paid to travel far, if he wanted. Or he could stay close to home, as this cutter proved was possible. And with the United States having just been bombed into the war, women loved a man in uniform. Including Ana.

When Pappas went to enlist, the United States Coast Guard recruiter down there in Tampa could not have agreed with him more.

"And I can request where I'd want to be assigned?" Pappas had asked him.

"Hell, son," the recruiter said, handing him a pen and the enlistment papers, "you can *request* anything you want!" He pointed. "Your autograph goes right there."

Pappas had not requested Jacksonville Beach, Florida.

The last place on God's green earth that Pappas expected to be in the middle of winter was on a deserted beach in a cold rain. With the world at war and being two-thirds water—that was one thing he had actually absorbed when he hadn't been daydreaming at Tarpon Springs High—Pappas figured the odds should have been in his favor that, rain or shine, he would instead be manning, say, a USCG cutter .50 caliber machine gun in the act of protecting U.S. merchant marine ships shut-tling war supplies.

Or something, for Christ's sake.

Certainly not a yeoman third class on coast watch, standing on a dune in wet sand up to his ankles and look-ing out through binoculars at the black-gray seas of the Atlantic under an even blacker-grayer layer of clouds.

Sure, there had been more than a little hysteria about the security of America's shores after they caught those Kraut spies last summer, but that had long ago died down. And what idiots would again try doing something with subs that had already failed them? Even the Krauts couldn't be that stupid.

So far, Pappas had heard only what sounded like some drunken celebrating—at one point that naughty, deep-throated laugh of a female having too much fun—but that had been inland, toward the bungalows and bars of the town of Jacksonville Beach, the voices carried out on the wind.

Here on the beach, he had not seen anything all night, and he had no reason to think he would see anything all morning. Especially in this impossible soup.

And, he thought, *for Christ's sake, what if I did? They didn't even issue me a weapon. Just a damned whistle, these binocs, and as a special treat—whoopee!—a hoagie sandwich.*

Peter thought about Ana.

At least that part of his plan had not soured. Yet. They still wrote to one another, though the span between her letters seemed to be getting longer each time, and the length of her letters shorter and less, well, personally detailed.

He reached inside his poncho and felt in his breast pocket for the letter that he'd received from her just a few days ago. She had written after Valentine's Day, all excited about the chocolates he had arranged to have sent to her, but the letter otherwise was filled with generalities, and certainly no specifics about their plans together.

Peter was more than aware that if he had not volunteered to join the Coast Guard, he very likely would have been with Ana on Saturday night—and maybe into this Sunday morning—and there would have been absolutely no chance that she was with some other guy who also had found her many fine qualities desirable.

He suddenly felt very sad and lonely.

And while he was a little hungry—*Hell, I always seem hungry*—the hoagie sandwich, a thick, soft roll slathered with butter and packed with turkey, was really not going to be much of a consolation.

Pappas walked toward one of the footpaths between the dunes until he found a weather-beaten log that looked as if it had been beached there for decades. He sat on it.

He considered rereading Ana's letter—it was upbeat and would probably cheer him—but realized it simply was too dark to see much of anything, let alone read a piece of paper. Besides, the rain would make the ink on the letter run and likely dilute the delicate fragrance of the perfume that she had misted it with and he didn't want to risk ruining a letter that he had read only three times so far. And who knew when she'd write next?

Instead, he put the binoculars beside him on the log, then dug down in his wool coat till he found the inside pocket that held the wrapped-in-waxed-paper hoagie. He pulled it out, pulled back the paper, and was surprised to discover that it was somewhat warm, at least in relation to the conditions outside his poncho.

Pappas again thought of the letter and the perfume and suddenly had a mental image of Ana. The vision caused a stir in his groin. He could see Ana, deeply tan and in her black swimsuit, the one with the low-cut front and the back open impossibly far down. She was lying on her side, on a towel just above where the gulf surf rolled to its highest point on the bright white sand.

He looked at the sandwich, looked into the dark distance, shrugged.

Pushing back the pangs of hunger, he ducked his head completely inside the poncho, brought the sandwich in under the same cover, then unbuttoned his fly, made himself accessible, ran his fingers through the bun in order to coat them with the butter, and, his hand thus lubricated, reached down and found himself again as he pictured Ana peeling off her black swimsuit.

[THREE]
Unterseeboot 134
30 degrees 36 minutes 5 seconds North Latitude
81 degrees 39 minutes 1 second West Longitude
Manhattan Beach, Florida
0130 28 February 1943

The German submarine was motionless on the slick surface of the Atlantic Ocean three hundred yards off the
shore of the United States of America and barely afloat in
a water depth of thirty-one feet.

Its conning tower was crowded. Kapitänleutnant Hans-
Günther Brosin stood there, as did his executive officer,
while a line of sailors worked to move the four stainless
steel containers from down below out through the conn
hatch and onto the deck, where the two teams of
commando-trained agents were quickly and efficiently
inflating the last of the six-foot-long rubber rafts and
preparing the three coils of three-quarter-inch-diameter
line that would be tied end to end to eventually tether all
of the rafts to the U-boat.

Brosin glanced up nervously at the thick clouds.
Though there was a steady, cold drizzle, he was content
to suffer it in return for the air cover that it and the
clouds provided.

It was eerily still and calm and quiet . . . too damned
quiet. What little wind that there was came out of the
northwest, causing the only surf—if the absence of such
could be called that—to be a soft lapping of waves on the

shore. No surf and no wind meant no natural sounds to mask any loud noise that they might make.

As Brosin fitted the soft rubber eyepieces of his Carl Zeiss binoculars to his eyes and made a slow sweep of the coastline, he said, "What is our time, Willi?"

Detrick trained a penlight on the chronometer strapped to his wrist.

"Nine and a quarter minutes so far, sir, twenty and three-quarter to go."

"An eternity," Brosin muttered. Then he asked, "Engines?"

"On standby, crew awaiting your orders."

When Brosin took the binoculars from his eyes, he saw that Richard Koch was coming up from the deck to the conning tower.

As the agent approached, Brosin said, not kindly, "What is it? Troubles?"

Koch held out his hand. "As this will be our last communication, Commander, I wanted to say thank you. We go now."

Brosin nodded. "Go with God," he said more warmly, shaking Koch's hand. He then added, in a serious tone: "But go quickly. This exposure becomes more dangerous by the moment. In precisely twenty minutes, we will be under way, with or without the rafts."

Brosin knew that while it was not absolutely critical that the U-boat take the four rubber boats with it when it left, everyone would be better off if it did—the agent teams especially.

They could hit the beach, strap the stainless steel containers on their backs, and move inland without having to take time to deflate and then bury the boats. Only their footprints would be evidence of their having been there, and in an hour's time, with the rain, those would be gone, too.

And if no rubber rafts were found, then there would be no reason for anyone to look for whatever vessel had launched them.

Koch lightly clicked his heels, nodded once in deference, and left the tower for the deck.

Brosin turned to Wachoffizier Detrick.

"If there is no signal within fifteen minutes to retrieve the boats, Willi, personally see that the line is cut."

"Yes, sir."

Richard Koch dipped the wooden oar blades into the sea, pressed for leverage the toes of his boots into the crease formed where the floor of the rubber boat met the transom, and slowly leaned back, pulling on the oars as he did.

The whole boat seemed to contort and simply move in place at first. It felt as if the rubber ring that formed the sides of the raft just flexed around the weight of the cargo—Koch and the stainless steel container—and that the boat made no forward motion across the water.

Koch raised the blades out of the water, leaned forward, dipped the blades, and again leaned back and pulled. More flexing of the raft, but not as much as the first time. And when he made another cycle, he could sense that he was making progress, that the rubber boat was moving forward.

Between his raft and the U-boat, Koch could hear the dipping of the others' oar blades and similar sounds of progress.

Getting the men and the containers from the U-boat into the rafts had gone almost as they had practiced it at the sub pens in France. They first had tied off each boat—as an act of safety in the event one went in the drink before anyone wanted it there—to a short line that was secured to the ironwork that protected that deck gun mounted just fore of the conning tower. Then, after the boats were inflated with a foot-operated bellows, they were slipped over the side. One had gone in upside down and had to be recovered, drained of seawater, and re-launched.

Next, a rope ladder was produced and deployed, and the first agent, Bayer, made his way down it, along the port side of the sub, and into a raft being steadied by a sailor holding as best he could to the short length of line tied to the bow. Once the agent was in the boat, seated on the center bladder of inflated rubber that served as his rowing position, one of the stainless steel containers, tied to another line and with its web shoulder straps placed against the hull to muffle any metal-on-metal clanking, was slowly slid down the port side. The container was secured on the deck of the raft by a strap affixed to the floorboard, and the sailor then cast off the short bowline and the next raft was pulled forward and positioned at the foot of the rope ladder.

With each agent, the process had been repeated almost flawlessly. The exception was Rolf Grossman.

When Grossman's container was lowered over the side, the sailor, his fingers tired and cramping, accidentally let the rope slip and in the quiet of the night the container hit the water with a remarkable sound. The resulting splash nearly soaked Grossman with cold seawater, and it took some effort for the quick-tempered agent not to spring from the raft and up the ladder to let loose a string of expletives—if not a fistful of knuckles—at the sailor.

In addition to the short length of line on his boat, Koch had another. It was tied to a hard point on his bow and, at the other end of the line, to another coil of line on the U-boat deck that in turn was tied to yet another coil of line that was secured to the ironwork that protected the U-boat's deck gun. A sailor played out the coiled lines as Koch rowed away.

Koch now led the tiny flotilla to just shy of shore. He kept a steady rhythm as he cycled the oars. And after some time, he felt the raft suddenly rise higher on a swell than it had on any swell since he had left the sub and he knew that meant the water was getting shallower, that he was almost ashore.

He dipped the blades and pulled hard on the oars, once, twice, then, on the third pull, he at once felt the blades strike the sand bottom and the raft slide to a stop to the sound of rubber scraping on the beach.

Koch quickly shipped his oars and practically leaped out of the boat and onto the shore. He scanned the area, saw nothing in the darkness, then reached in the boat and, with a good deal of effort, pulled out the stainless container and set it on the sand. He turned and tugged hard at the raft to pull it up and out of the water.

Next, he carried the container higher on the beach, up past some driftwood and old logs, then ran back to meet the other rafts.

One by one, as they repeated the pulling ashore of the boats, Koch used hand signals to indicate that the agents should move the containers to the collection point on higher ground.

As Cremer and Bayer and Grossman did so, Koch took the loose end of the short line of the nearest raft and tied it to his boat, then tied the next raft to that one, creating a train of rubber rafts ultimately tethered to the U-boat.

He was tying the last raft when Cremer returned.

"Herr Hauptmann, shall I make the retrieval signal?" Cremer whispered in German.

"Not 'Herr Hauptmann,'" Koch hissed in English. "From now on, we use our American names."

"Yes, sir—" Cremer began in English, then corrected himself. "Okay, Richard."

Cremer stepped to the water's edge, removed a black tin flashlight from his pocket, held it to the highest point he could reach over his head, then pushed its switch six times to make the agreed-upon signal of two series of three flashes each. When there was no immediate response from the U-boat, he quickly repeated the two series of three flashes.

He heard a sound of something rushing through the water just offshore and realized it was getting closer. It sounded like a small school of fish rushing across the surface. Then he noticed a line tied to the first raft was drawing taut—fast. The line stiffened and the raft practically shot off of the shore. It took him a moment to understand that someone on the U-boat had seen his first signal and the sailors had begun to pull on the line. The delay, he guessed, had to have been due to the length of the line and the taking up of its slack.

Cremer put the flashlight in his pocket, then hurried over to the next raft in line. He positioned it in the water, toward the U-boat. Koch was about to do the same with the third raft when he heard footfalls squeaking in the sand as someone was fast approaching.

"Sir!" Bayer whispered excitedly.

"It's Rich—" Koch began to correct Bayer as he turned away from the raft to face him.

Koch stopped when he saw Bayer standing there with Grossman. He couldn't believe his eyes, but when Cremer ran up with his flashlight and turned it on there was no disputing it.

Between Bayer and Grossman stood a young man— really, only a kid; his huge eyes showed stark terror— wearing the uniform of an American coastguardsman.

Bayer had the young man's hands bound together with rope cut from one of the containers, and Grossman had his Walther 9mm pistol pointed at the kid's head. They had used a length of material cut from the poncho to gag his mouth.

"Turn off the goddamned light!" Koch whispered, in German, and when it went dark he leaned closer to Bayer's ear and snapped, "What is this?"

Bayer replied in German: "I was having no luck finding the placement of the containers. I went up to the dunes, by some logs, and heard moaning."

"Moaning?" Koch repeated.

"*Ja,*" Bayer said, a hint of laughter in his voice. "And when I finally saw where it was coming from—a poncho—I saw it was shaking. A happy shaking, if you get my meaning, Herr Hauptmann."

Koch looked at him incredulously. *"Scheist!"* he said.

"He has no weapons," Grossman said. "What do you want to do? I can kill him, but then we have a body."

Koch considered that quickly. Grossman would have no trouble strangling him—cutting his throat or shooting him was out of the question; too messy and noisy—but they couldn't leave the body on the beach or toss it in the sea.

The kid clearly constituted some sort of beach patrol. And if he didn't check in with someone, that someone would come looking for him, and if they found his body there would be problems that the Germans did not need. Same if they tried to bury him. Someone would eventually find the grave site. Worse, it would require the teams to burn valuable time digging a grave, burying the body, then covering their tracks.

There was the sound of laughter coming from a short distance inland, and a woman's cackle caused Koch to be distracted for a moment. Then, behind him, there came the sound of the third raft beginning to crunch across the sand as it headed for the sea.

Koch turned and looked at it a long moment as it slid away.

"This way!" he said, running for the last raft in the line. *"Schnell!"*

With more than a little effort, Bayer and Grossman lifted and dragged the young American in the soft sand behind Koch.

"In here!" Koch said, pointing to the raft.

The American squirmed and made angry grunts as they placed him on the floor of the raft. Grossman smacked him hard on the top of his head with the Walther and the protests stopped for a moment. When the kid stirred, Grossman hit him again with the pistol, this time behind the right ear, and he went limp.

"Take those oars and put them in the other boat!" Koch ordered as he rushed to wrap the kid's ankle with the strap that had secured the container to the raft. He then took the end of the line that bound his hands and ran it down to the ankles, trussing him to keep him from jumping overboard in the event there came such an opportunity.

The line that tied the fourth boat to the third boat now began to tighten, then became quite taut. Koch suddenly realized that with the added weight of the kid, the fourth boat was stuck high and dry. He signaled for each man to move to a corner of the boat and they lifted and carried the raft into the water.

Slowly, the train began moving smoothly out to sea again.

"That should make a nice surprise for the commander," Koch said as the last raft and its cargo floated from view.

The men chuckled.

"Enough of this," Koch said. "Let us go before he is discovered off his post—and then we are."

U-134 had been moving slowly in reverse under the quiet power of batteries for about five minutes—Kapitän-leutnant Hans-Günther Brosin having given the order to be under way immediately after seeing through his binoculars the first blink of light from the agent's six-pulse signal.

After the first two sets of three flashes, there quickly had followed another two sets, and Brosin wondered if there was any particular reason for that—were the agents simply more anxious than necessary or did they need to get the rafts off the beach right away because they were in immediate danger of being discovered?

There was a flash code for that contingency, of course, as well as for others, but Brosin knew that invariably there were gray areas when something happened that was not addressed by some specific signal. So instead of having the U-boat sit in the shallow sea while the deck crew of five hand over hand pulled in the line in order to retrieve the rafts, he ordered another five sailors to go

down and help them pull against the extra strain of the
U-boat backing away from shore.

The sooner they were in deeper water, the sooner he
would feel better.

Moments after he had given the order to get under
way, as the sailors were hauling in the line, there came another odd occurrence.

The line tethering the rafts suddenly became very
taut. It pulled forward the seamen who were retrieving it
due to the fact that the ship was of course motoring in
the opposite direction. This created the real danger of
pulling them overboard, and Brosin was just about to
bark the order that they let loose of the line and that the
engine power be cut when whatever obstruction there
had been was overcome, and the sailors were again re-
covering line hand over hand.

Now, with his binoculars, Brosin could see the first of
the four rafts coming into view through the drizzle.

"What is our depth, Willi?" Brosin asked.

The executive officer relayed the question down below and a moment later replied, "Thirty meters, sir."

Brosin watched the first raft reach the submarine. The
sailors cleated the line, ran to the raft, and manhandled it
aboard. Two seamen began deflating the recovered raft
while the others returned to pulling in the line that tethered it to the following rafts.

Satisfied that the recovery process was progressing
well and nearly completed, the captain let the binoculars
hang from the strap around his neck and turned to his
executive officer.

"Bring her around, Willi," he ordered, "and set a course of one-two-five degrees. Go to diesel power, five knots to start, then double that once all boats are aboard and stowed."

"Yes, sir," Wachoffizier Detrick said, and called the orders down below.

Brosin looked again at the men on deck, saw that they had the third boat out of the water, then he removed the strap from around his neck, handed the binocs to the XO, and went to the hatch to go below.

Brosin had just stepped from the foot of the conning tower ladder when he heard from above Willi Detrick's excited voice call down through the hatch, "Sir! I think you should see this!"

[FOUR]
Gander Airport
Gander, Newfoundland
0840 4 March 1943

Dick Canidy had sensed in his gut the very early sign that the Douglas C-54, one so new that it seemed right off the assembly line, was going to have problems with one of its four Twin Wasp radial engines.

The Air Transport Command flight had been eight hours, ten minutes, and fifteen seconds out of Prestwick, Scotland—Canidy had immediately checked his chronometer, which he had reset to zero and activated as the bird had gone wheels up—when he detected an odd faint vibration that his aeronautic training had immediately told him was more than a mere aberration.

Not a minute later, it manifested itself again, louder this time, and one of the engines on the left wing of the Douglas C-54 began to shake the plane violently. Then a great cloud of black smoke erupted out of the outboard Twin Wasp, and the pilot rushed to shut it down, feather its props, and adjust throttles and trim to rebalance the aircraft.

This took a few minutes, what to many passengers seemed like hours, but soon afterward they were informed that everything was fine, that the cause of the engine failure was a common oil pressure problem, that the pilots had absolutely no doubt that the aircraft could make this leg's intended destination—the refueling stop of Gander—and that the only inconvenience was that they would just be a bit delayed.

Canidy knew that "a bit delayed" was a huge understatement. Down one engine, they were going to be flying slower than the 250 miles per hour or so that the aircraft had been making.

But he of course knew the rest to be true. The excuse of an oil pressure problem was plausible. And the aircraft was more than capable of cruising along at an altitude of seven thousand feet on the power of the remaining three 1,450-horsepower Pratt & Whitney engines.

That had been the view of Canidy the Professional Aviator.

Canidy the Bus Passenger, however, became miserable after hours of looking at the dead engine with the Atlantic Ocean in the background and was grateful to finally see the coastline of Newfoundland on the horizon, and then the snow-covered airfield itself, a welcome waypoint carved out of the wilderness on what not five years earlier had been an uninhabited plateau of Gander Lake's north shore.

As the Air Transport Command C-54 pilot turned on final, the only sounds in the cabin were the hum of the Twin Wasps and the rush of air over the flaps extended from the wings. The next sounds heard—the *chirp-chirp* of the aircraft wheels gently touching down on the runway—were followed by the raucous applause of the nervous passengers now greatly relieved to have cheated death again.

Canidy looked out the window, trying to avoid getting drawn into the mindless jabbering of the other passengers.

Just before touching down, his field of view allowed him to see hundreds of warbirds parked in neat lines—Douglas Boston light bombers with Canadian Air Force markings, U.S. Army Air Forces B-25 Mitchells and B-24 Liberators, and more—all apparently waiting to be ferried eastward to battle.

They came through here, Canidy knew, because the shortest route between North America and Europe was Gander to Prestwick. He remembered being told that the population of this godforsaken frozen outpost had swollen to some fifteen thousand—a mix of Royal Air Force, Canadian Army, and U.S. Army Air Forces, heavy on the Canucks.

Canidy could not see the warbirds now. All that was visible was a wall of snow that had been plowed off of the runway. He looked across the airplane and saw that there was a wall on either side of them and it appeared as if the plane was traveling along in some kind of winter canyon.

The aircraft came to a gap in the canyon wall—a ramp to the taxiway—and as the C-54 turned into it, Canidy could see that a yellow truck with a FOLLOW ME sign had been waiting there, and now was leading the way.

A moment later, Canidy began to see a row, then two and three rows, of bombers. The C-54 rolled past them, then past two hangars that looked full of aircraft in for repair, then up to the Base Operations building.

Ramp personnel wearing remarkably heavy winter outfits and carrying wands waved the C-54 to a parking pad next to two other C-54s, and the pilot shut down the three good engines.

After a long visit to the gentlemen's facilities, Canidy attempted to get a status report on the aircraft and—though appreciative of having made it alive and well to Beautiful Downtown Gander—an idea of when the hell he could expect to be airborne out of this icebox of an outpost, en route to Elizabeth City, New Jersey, and connections from there to anywhere else but here.

He tried at first to go through channels.

Start with the little guy, he thought. *Be nice. Don't make waves.*

That had been a disaster.

At every step, they gave him a variation on the same bullshit line: "It's going to take more than a little time to pinpoint the problem—a day, maybe longer—then fix it—did you see the full maintenance hangars as you came in?—or arrange for an available backup aircraft and get it in the air, or failing all that, find everyone an empty seat here and there on various other aircraft. We're sorry, Major. It's the best we can do. We didn't break the aircraft on purpose."

And the more Canidy pushed, the more resistance he encountered.

To hell with this, Canidy thought.

He made a direct path to the airfield's Flight Operations.

There he learned from a clerk that another C-54—this one freshly refueled and headed for Washington—had just about finished embarking its passengers.

"As the major might expect," the clerk added, in what he thought was a helpful manner, "the aircraft is completely full. The passenger manifest is closed."

With some effort, Canidy tracked down the Air Officer of the Day and explained his situation. This of course could not have fallen on less sympathetic ears.

"*Everybody's* in a hurry to get home, Major," Canadian Air Force Group Captain Pierre Tugnutt said.

Tugnutt was an officious prissy type, tall and slight, with a meticulously trimmed pencil mustache and thin strands of hair combed over an enormous bald spot, who practically sniffed with contempt as he handed back Canidy's USAAF travel orders.

"I'm not every—" Canidy said to Group Captain Tugnutt before he realized others in the room were watching their interaction and he stopped.

"Captain," he began again, calmly, "could we have a private moment?"

"I believe our business here is complete, *Major*."

"Captain," Canidy replied evenly and with a forced smile, "it would really be in the best interests of both of us." He paused, then nodded toward the small adjoining office. "Please."

Captain Tugnutt's bony face contorted to show his obvious annoyance. He finally said, "Very well."

"Thank you, sir," Canidy said loudly, more for the benefit of those in the room than for Tugnutt.

In the office, Captain Tugnutt said, "Now, Major—"

"Captain," Canidy interrupted, his voice low as he spoke with an edge to his words, "know that I share this with great reluctance."

Canidy produced a small leather wallet containing his OSS anywhere-anytime-anyfuckingthing credentials.

"You get me on that plane, *sir*," Canidy added, "or we get the air vice marshall on the horn."

The AOD raised an eyebrow as he reviewed the credentials—twice, since it was clear he had never seen any like them before—before he handed them back.

"If you'd made these available from the start, Major," Captain Tugnutt said snottily, "there'd been no problem, and certainly no call for threats."

It was all Canidy could do not to suggest that the captain make himself genuinely useful to at least one person by going off and performing on himself what his surname implied.

But Canidy wanted on that damned airplane—and out of Gander—and impressed himself by keeping his automatic mouth shut for once.

As Canidy climbed aboard the about-to-depart flight, he realized that his problems would likely not end with the fastening of his lap belt. He saw his open seat—the only open seat on the whole aircraft—and it was right next to a lieutenant colonel who had a very sour look.

He clearly was not at all happy that his traveling buddy, also a light bird, had been bumped—and, worse than bumped, made to get off of the plane—to make room for a lowly major.

Canidy, not in any mood to deal with another by-the-book type, dealt with the situation in what he felt was the best manner: He ignored it.

Then he thought, *Why the hell not? I'm ordered home to take my medicine, so what's the worst that can happen? They send me back to fight the Krauts?*

Canidy pulled a silver flask from his tunic, lifted it toward the prickly lieutenant colonel as if in a toast, said with a smile, "For medicinal purposes," then, in three healthy swigs, drained half of the scotch contained therein, put the flask back in his tunic pocket, pulled his cap down so the brim covered his eyes, and with vivid memories of the bittersweet hours in the arms of Ann Chambers at her flat the previous night—*Or was it the night before? Jesus, I hate this travel*—he slid into a deep sleep.

[FIVE]
Anacostia Naval Air Station
Washington, D.C.
1520 5 March 1943

The change in pitch of the four Twin Wasp radial engines on the Air Transport Command C-54 when the pilot throttled back for a slow descent from its cruising altitude of nine thousand feet caused Major Richard Canidy, USAAF, to stir from his sleep. He had awakened briefly once before when he thought he may have felt another odd vibration, but all engines continued to turn and he had dozed off again.

He cracked open one eye now, then the other, and after his pupils adjusted to the painfully bright afternoon sunlight that was flooding into his window he glanced out over the right wing. He could see a beautiful blanket of snow covering everything on the ground of what he guessed was Delaware. *No, Maryland,* he corrected himself when he recognized the geography of the eastern shore of Chesapeake Bay.

The pilot banked a bit to the right, and when the brilliant sun reflected off the wing, Canidy winced, then turned away from the window.

The lieutenant colonel was still strapped in next to Canidy, and though he did not seem to be as much out of sorts as he had been at takeoff, he was not exactly about to offer, say, his services as a D.C. tour guide—or even share transportation into the district.

Sharing transportation, Canidy saw as he carried his duffel on his shoulder down the aircraft steps behind the lieutenant colonel, was not going to be a problem.

There, parked among a line of olive drab Chevrolet staff cars, was a 1941 Packard 280 convertible coupe. Leaning on its fender, reading a copy of the *Washington Star,* was a stocky chief boatswain's mate wearing an expensively tailored United States Navy uniform. On the chief's sleeve were stitched twenty-four years' worth of hash marks.

Canidy realized that the scene fascinated the lieutenant colonel, and he intentionally picked up his pace across the tarmac enough to move ahead of the lieutenant colonel.

The lieutenant colonel watched as the goddamned major who had bumped his buddy off of the C-54 approached the chief.

When the major barked, "Ellis!" the chief quickly looked up from his paper, scanned the line of arriving passengers, then even more quickly folded the *Star* and tossed it in the Packard, and saluted the major crisply.

"Major Canidy, *sir*!"

The major tossed his duffel to the chief, who caught it, then moved ahead of the major and opened the passenger door of the coupe. Once the major was in the car, the chief closed the door, put the duffel in the trunk, slid in behind the wheel, and began to drive away.

The lieutenant colonel stood stiffly as the car passed,

the major saluting smartly and smiling from its passenger's seat. It took a moment or so for the stunned lieutenant colonel to answer with barely a wave of a salute.

"How the hell are you, Chief?" Canidy said as the Packard turned left onto South Capitol Street, SE, then started to cross the bridge into the city.

"Doing pretty good, Dick," Ellis replied with a warm smile. "That light bird with you have a bug up his ass or what?"

Canidy picked up the copy of the *Star* and scanned the headlines. "I had to bump his buddy off the flight at Gander, and, if that wasn't enough, the AOD refused to tell him why. And then I wouldn't, either."

Ellis grinned, shaking his head. "Damned good to see you. Didn't think that I would."

Ellis worked for Colonel Donovan as special assistant to the director. He understood that to mean that he was to do "everything and anything" to make the life of the head of the OSS easier and that kept him going round the clock. He was privy to ninety-nine-point-nine-nine percent of everything the director read, wrote, uttered, or otherwise transmitted, and knew all about Canidy having been in German-occupied Hungary.

He was also quite aware that Donovan had called Canidy back from London in a SECRET—EYES ONLY message—Ellis was the one who had hand-carried it to the commo room for encryption and transmittal. That duty of course naturally fell under the heading of doing everything and anything for the director. But, as far as Ellis was concerned, so did an errand to fetch Dick Canidy at the airfield.

Truth be known, Ellis had the greatest respect for Canidy, and would have done anything for him.

"Should I ask about the wheels?" Canidy said.

"I've got orders to drive it once a week so it don't just sit and rot behind the house on Q Street."

The house on Q Street, NW, a turn-of-the-century mansion that had long belonged to the wealthy Whittaker family, was being leased for one dollar a year to the Office of Strategic Services as a place to safely and discreetly house whomever—agents, politicians—was deemed necessary in the course of duty.

Whittaker Construction Company, which had begun by building and operating railroads before the Civil War, now included various areas of heavy construction (ports for ships and planes, hotels, office buildings), and continued to be quite prosperous.

With enormous wealth came very high connections and the majority shareholder of the firm—James M. B. Whittaker (Harvard '39), presently a U.S. Army captain on an OSS mission behind enemy lines in the Philippines—had been known to address the President of the United States as "Uncle Frank," and not always pleasantly.

"Sounds like something Jimmy Whittaker would say," Canidy said.

"Yeah, and so I was doing just that, just about to go on my usual thirty-minute spin, when the boss, who didn't want you looking for him in his office, said to go find you at Anacostia. 'Why don't you take the convertible out to the prodigal son?' is what he said."

"I'm not the prodigal son. Jimmy is. That's why it's his car. Hell, his house. Any word from Jimmy?"

Ellis looked at him blankly. He didn't respond.

"I'll take the absence of bad news to mean good news," Canidy said with a smile.

Ellis, eyes on the road ahead, shook his head.

Canidy went on: "The boss have much to say about me otherwise?"

"Only that he'd meet us after he stopped by his town house in Georgetown."

"That works," Canidy said. "I definitely need a change of clothes."

"A shower wouldn't hurt, either," Chief Ellis said, and smirked as he turned left onto M Street, headed for Rock Creek Parkway.

The house on Q Street, NW—a mansion on an estate— was surrounded by an eight-foot-high brick wall. Ellis brought the Packard to a stop with its bumper against the heavy, solid gate in the wall.

He was about to tap out "Shave and a Haircut, Two Bits" on the horn—mostly because it drove the ex–Secret Service guys nuts, and Ellis didn't much care for them or their holier-than-thou attitudes—when a muscular man in civilian clothing and a woolen overcoat stepped out from a break in a hedgerow and approached Ellis's window, his shoes crunching the snow as he walked.

Canidy thought the overcoat more than adequately concealed what he probably held underneath—a Thompson .45 caliber submachine gun. The man looked inside the vehicle, nodded at Ellis, then disappeared back in the hedgerow.

A moment later, the double gate swung inward, Ellis pulled forward, and just as soon as the car was inside, the gate doors swung closed again.

Ellis followed the cobblestone driveway back to the five-car garage, which was called the "stable" because that was what it had been before being converted to hold automobiles. He parked the car, then went to the trunk and retrieved Canidy's duffel.

"I'll get that, Chief," Canidy said, holding out his hand.

"I can use the exercise," Ellis said, waving him off. "Besides, I know how it feels when you get off that plane from London."

"Nothing a good belt won't fix," Canidy said.

They walked up to the mansion, and Ellis opened the door that led into the kitchen, then followed Canidy inside.

It was a very large space—filled now with the delightful smell of onion and garlic sautéing in olive oil—and had the industrial-sized stoves and cookware and the stocked pantries and huge refrigerators that one would expect to find in a restaurant. And it was noisy.

A short, rotund, olive-skinned man in his fifties, wearing a white chef's hat and coat, was loudly directing a staff of four, waving a large knife as his pointer. Before him on the marble counter were two large uncut tenderloins of beef on a cutting board.

"Chief Ellis!" the chef, now waving the knife at him, said in a deep, thick accent that Canidy guessed was Italian or maybe Sicilian. "You don't interfere!"

"Just passing through, Antonio, just passing through," Ellis replied. "Say hello to Major Canidy."

Chef Antonio approached Canidy, stopped within five feet, put his hands stiffly to either side—the knife still held in the right one—and in an exaggerated fashion looked down at his feet for a long moment, then up and at Canidy.

"It is my great honor, Major," he said formally.

Then he glanced at Chief Ellis and said to Canidy, "Chief Ellis is banned from my kitchen. He interferes, and food disappears." He motioned back and forth over his round belly to illustrate.

Canidy laughed.

"It is my pleasure—Antonio, is it?" Canidy noticed that the chef beamed appreciatively that he had addressed him correctly, then went on: "And you're right, Antonio. I've yet to meet a Navy man you can trust around food or booze. Speaking of which"—he looked at Ellis and nodded toward the heavy wooden door on the other side of the kitchen—"I'm going to get a taste of the latter and take it to my room."

"Your bag will be waiting when you get there. And I

took the liberty of having the staff clean and press the suit you left here. Might be a good idea to dress for dinner. The boss said to expect him about six o'clock."

Canidy nodded. "Thank you, Chief," he said sincerely. As he went though the door, he added, "It's always wise to dress for what might be one's last meal."

III

Dick Canidy left his room on the third and uppermost
floor of the north wing of the mansion and walked down
the long hallway. He had had difficulty getting the top
button of his heavily starched dress shirt buttoned, and,
when he finally did, he could not believe how tight the
goddamned shirt collar felt. He wondered if the cleaning
staff had done something terrible to his shirt—at one
point questioning if it was even his shirt—then decided it
was simply a very heavy starching that likely caused some
shrinkage. Whatever the reason, the collar was extremely
stiff and extremely uncomfortable and so he worked his
necktie back and forth to loosen it, then squeezed fingertips inside the collar on either side of his neck and
gently pulled, stretching the material.

That seemed to provide some comfort, and so he
carefully snugged up his Windsor knot just enough to
hold it in place but not so tightly as to cancel out what
he'd just accomplished. He then closed one button on
his dark gray, single-breasted Brooks Brothers suit jacket,

surveyed himself in the enormous, etched-glass oval mirror hanging at the end of the hallway, then went down the wide stairway.

One of the heavy wooden double doors to the library was partially open and Canidy entered through it, closing it behind him with a squeak from its heavy brass hinges.

It was a huge room paneled with deeply polished hardwoods that held large oil paintings of family portraits of generations of Whittakers. Floor-to-ceiling bookshelves were filled. The dark wooden floor area was segmented by four large Oriental area rugs of equal size, on each of which were the same heavy leather couches and armchairs with overstuffed ottomans arranged facing inward, the design creating a quad of individual areas.

On the farthest wall, above and on either side of the ornate brick fireplace, which crackled with a just-beginning-to-burn fire, there were mounted trophies of great animals—among them a lion, a wildebeest, a zebra, and a pair of spectacular horned heads that Canidy seemed to recall were commonly known as Greater Kudus, which he thought was an antelope or such—in a gallery, near which a rollaway bar service had been positioned.

The bar was Canidy's immediate destination and the soles of his leather shoes made a resounding *thump-thump-thump* in the quiet room as he crossed the wooden floor to reach it.

The service contained a wide selection of spirits, light and dark and very expensive, as well as aperitifs and two brands of VSOP cognacs he had never heard of. Canidy found what he was looking for—a delightful twenty-year-old single malt made by the Famous Grouse folks—and he poured himself a double, neat, in a crystal tumbler.

He took his drink and stepped closer to the fire, and, deep in thought, stood and stared silently at the flames.

So this is how it ends? Canidy thought somewhat morosely. *In a glorious mansion with exquisite scotch? The unwashed amid the trappings of great wealth and comfort and success? How rich!*

He took a healthy drink of the single malt and waited a moment before swallowing, enjoying its deep flavor and warmth on his tongue.

He looked up at the exotic animals. He raised his glass to them.

"Make room for me up there, boys. I'm soon to join your lot. . . ."

As he took another drink, he heard the door hinges squeak across the room and he turned.

Canidy recognized the distinguished-looking gentleman of sixty standing in the doorway. He was stocky yet fit, with a full head of silver hair neatly trimmed and strong eyes set in the ruddy face of an Irishman. He wore a well-cut, double-breasted dark gray suit, a crisp white shirt, and a marine-and-white rep necktie. He had a strong presence; his confidence filled the room.

There was a reason for this, Canidy well knew. Here was a man whose accomplishments were legion—successful Wall Street lawyer and Medal of Honor recipient led the long list—a warrior, a genuine leader, someone whom men would follow anywhere, anytime, for anything, without question.

And here, Canidy knew, was the man he had let down.

"Good evening, sir," Major Richard Canidy said, mustering a voice stronger than he felt. He started walking toward him.

"Dick," Colonel William J. Donovan, director of the Office of Strategic Services, said warmly. "How are you?"

"Getting better by the sip, sir." He raised his glass. "I hope you'll forgive me for starting."

Canidy and Donovan met in the middle of the room and they shook hands with some intensity.

"It's really nice to see you, Dick," Donovan said, his eyes locked on Canidy's.

"Thank you, sir. And you."

After a long moment, Donovan released Canidy's hand, took a step back, and looked at Canidy's glass.

"Do I suspect you're into the good single malt?"

"Guilty, sir."

"Well, then, what the hell." He smiled. "As we say in the business, 'When with evil companions, try to blend in.'"

Canidy grinned, nodded once, said, "Single malt it is, sir," then turned for the bar, and thought, *Helluva way to get my head handed to me. But*—he glanced at the animal trophies—*I can think of worse.*

As Canidy poured another crystal tumbler with two shots of twenty-year-old Famous Grouse single malt scotch, the director of the OSS said behind him, "I read your after-action report."

That was all he said. There was a silence, interrupted

only by the sounds of Canidy putting the bottle back on the tray with a *clunk* and of the fire crackling.

Canidy wondered if he was supposed to say something in reply.

But what? Is this where I throw myself on the mercy of the court—court, my ass; more like the court, judge, jury, and firing squad—and confess to having fucked up, apologize to Donovan for having caused him to bring me home to deal with my actions, and then beg him that I not be sent to some hellhole of a stockade or mental ward where I'll spend the duration of the war cutting sheets of paper into paper dolls and confetti?

"Yes, sir," Canidy said—it was more of a question than a statement—as he handed the drink to Donovan.

"Thank you." Donovan took the glass and raised it to Canidy in a toast. "To successful missions—"

"Sir?"

"—To successful missions that contribute to winning the war."

Canidy touched his glass to Donovan's, but as they both took sips it was clear that Canidy was not completely following the OSS director's meaning.

"Nice," Donovan said, holding the glass in his palm and admiring the booze. "Very nice."

He walked over to the nearest leather couch, sat down, then motioned for Canidy to do the same on the facing couch. Canidy did, and now realized that the arrangement of furniture created an environment where a discussion could be at once open and confidential.

After a long moment, Donovan looked at Canidy. "Anything you want to add that you may have purposefully left out of your after-action report?" he said, his tone pointed yet at the same time assuring.

What the hell is he hinting at? Canidy wondered. *I put everything in there.*

"There were some minor things," Canidy offered. "Operational logistics, communications snafus, that kind of thing."

Donovan nodded.

Am I missing something here? Canidy thought. *Of course I am. And, Christ, it's crystal clear—that sonofabitch David Bruce even spelled it out for me—so why the hell not just get it over with?*

Canidy inhaled deeply, let it out, and said, "There is one thing that I felt best not put in writing."

Donovan raised an eyebrow.

Canidy stood. "I fucked up, sir. And I apologize."

The director of the Office of Strategic Services did not respond.

"It's just that," Canidy went on, "someone had to do something to complete the mission. And so, completely aware of the fact that I was the control—and knew too much to go behind the lines—I ignored that and . . . and I went in."

He took the last sip of scotch, put the empty tumbler on the coffee table, and after a long moment of considering if he should say his next thought, he dismissed it, then mustered the courage to say it.

"Colonel, while I do apologize to you personally, I feel you should also know that I would do it again. I couldn't leave Eric and the professor in there; they knew too much. I couldn't do it—wouldn't do it—and so I would suggest that I am more than a little in over my head. That now said, I'm prepared to—what? I'm not exactly sure of my options. Quit? Resign? Drive a desk and push papers here in Washington?"

Donovan was quiet as he considered that. He looked Canidy in the eyes, looked at his glass, sipped the last of his single malt.

"None of the above," Donovan finally said. "You know that, Dick. In fact, you know too much." He paused. "Your offer—however misplaced—is declined—"

"Sir? I—"

"Let me finish, please. While I appreciate what you've said, more than I think you realize, I did not come here—I did not bring you back from London—to shut you down."

Canidy, not believing what he was hearing, simply stared at the director of the Office of Strategic Services.

"Would you mind, while you're up?" Donovan said, holding out his tumbler to Canidy. "But just half this time. And a water alongside, please."

Canidy nodded, and as he walked to the bar Donovan said, "Tell me your understanding of what we're doing in England."

"As far as the OSS specifically?" Canidy said, uncorking the single malt bottle and pouring.

"Yeah."

"Well, starting with the topic at hand, we're pulling scientists such as Dyer out through our pipelines, as well as running harassment campaigns, such as Eric Fulmar's blowing up of the ball-bearing plant that was in my report. Then there's the Aphrodite Project, B-17 drones packed with Torpex to blow U-boat pens and targets of opportunity."

Canidy delivered to Donovan his drinks, placing the glass of water and the glass of single malt on the coffee table in front of him.

"That, plus some counterintel and psych ops, are all being run out of Whitbey House Station," Canidy said, returning to the bar for his drink and bringing it back to his place on the couch. "And just now, David Bruce told me I'm losing Stan Fine, who Bruce is sending—maybe has already sent—to Algiers to begin setting up teams to go into France to support the resistance the way we've got agents in Corsica."

Canidy watched as Donovan picked up the glass with the water, poured some into the scotch, diluting it by about fifty percent, then picked up the single malt, took a test sip, and, apparently satisfied, put the glass back on the table.

"That's mostly correct about Fine in Algiers," Donovan finally said. "It's all about building a *réseau*—a net—of resistance."

He paused in thought.

"Let me paint you a couple of pictures," Donovan

went on. "First the big one. The Allies are mustering for a large push and Hitler knows it. And it's pretty obvious to anyone paying even half attention that France is key; we take it back, take all of it back, and the march is on to Berlin. What isn't so obvious is how we would take France—simply by going in across the narrow top of the English Channel or by coming up from the south, through what Churchill has intimated as 'the soft underbelly of Europe,' or by doing both—and what must be even less obvious to Hitler is how to successfully defend against any—indeed, all—of that while at the same time battling the Russians.

"Our having done so well with Torch," he continued, "and now with having so many Allied forces in North Africa would tend to suggest preparations for the latter, taking Italy, then in through southern France. Yet no matter which of those options is in play—indeed, if all of them are in play; the President made it clear in his Casablanca Conference speech two weeks ago that the Allies will settle for nothing short of unconditional surrender—Hitler knows that his chances are made far better by Germany's success in the Atlantic."

Canidy nodded. "The starving of England," he said.

"Exactly. Continue to dramatically reduce the flow of supplies—food, fuel, weapons, ammunition—and the Germans' defense of France becomes easier and gives way to the Germans' offense of London. And the U-boats have been wildly successful in taking out our supply ships in the Atlantic and Mediterranean."

The director of the Office of Strategic Services leaned forward and picked up his glass, took a sip of single malt, considered his next thoughts.

He continued: "That's the big picture, dangerously simply put, for Europe. As for a smaller picture—at least as far as the OSS is concerned—it involves what David Bruce has Fine doing. OSS London's Special Operations is working with Britain's Special Operations Executive and the Free French to support the Maquis—young guys pretty much your age—who fled for France's woods instead of being forced into slave labor for the German occupation."

"Small wonder they don't trust the Vichy government, either," Canidy said.

"And for damned good reason. So they've formed groups. There's the Francs Tireurs et Partisans, which is controlled by the Communists. The Organization de la Résistance dans l'Armée, full of followers of Giraud. De Gaulle's faithful are Forces Française de l'Intérieur, which is the strongest, and in large part controlled from London by the Bureau de Renseignement et d'Action. And a smattering of others."

"And we're supposed to support all these various factions?"

"That and pull them together," Donovan said, nodding. "For now, and for after the war. They're *already* fighting among themselves for postwar control. But they need training. They need weapons. Food. Money."

"They need us . . ." Canidy said.

"Exactly. We're having great success in Corsica. And we can do it in France. The vast majority of the French was anti-Axis before being occupied by them, and they can only be more so now. And those who may be on the fence, for whatever reason, can be persuaded to work with the *réseau* by appealing to their patriotism—or to their basic sense of survival."

"When you say 'basic sense of survival' . . . ?"

"I mean life or death," Donovan replied, his tone cool and calculated.

He let Canidy consider that, then said, "Our mission will be to supply and lead the Maquis in guerrilla warfare, sabotaging fuel-storage facilities, rail lines, factories, power plants—anything to rob the Germans of their use. SHAEF will designate targets, which SO and SOE agents will then tell the Maquis to take out. For example, using Fulmar's recent work, it's a ball-bearing plant. If those who run it are receptive to working with the Maquis, then we blow the machinery—forges, lathes, electrical transformers, whatever—to disrupt production for the short term; if, however, they choose to be uncooperative, we lay on an aerial bombing run and blow the whole building. The whole damned neighborhood."

"Making it a French decision if they want their infrastructure to survive the war," Canidy said, nodding. "Effective."

"Quite. And I don't think we will have to resort to the bombing more than necessary. The French, as we're finding on Corsica, will readily accept our arms and support. Perhaps too readily."

"What do you mean by that?"

Donovan considered not answering. After a moment, he replied, "Part of dancing with the devil is that we have to recognize they're the devil for a reason, and that the devil has his own motives."

"For postwar?"

"I'm getting more than a little heat here in Washington when it's suggested that we're supplying the Communists—the devil incarnate—with arms."

"But there is, even if only a little, Allied support for that," Canidy said, making it more of a question than a statement. "'If Hitler invaded hell, I would make at least a favorable reference to the devil in the House of Commons.'"

Donovan smiled. "So sayeth Winston. Yes, there is a reluctant Allied support. Because the success of the Maquis is critical to the success of the American and British and other Allied combat forces to come. And that, Major Canidy, is why I brought you back here."

Canidy looked off in the distance and tried to make sense of it all. Something was not right. A piece of the puzzle was missing. He looked at the director of the Office of Strategic Services, who he saw was watching him, studying him.

Canidy said, "At the risk of losing what little credibility I'm afraid that I might have with you, I must admit that I do not follow you completely. I understand going in and supporting the French resistance—I'm fully prepared to act on that right now, set up SO teams, et cetera, et cetera—but what does not make sense to me, if you'll forgive me for saying, is why you could not have made these orders in a Secret—Eyes Only message. I could be on the ground in Algiers with Stan Fine right now."

"Because you're not going into France."

The surprise was evident on Canidy's face. "But I thought that you just said—"

Donovan held up his hand. "Did you stop to wonder why it's just you and me here, Dick?"

"Yes, sir. I thought my ass was in a crack—"

"And after I made it clear to you that it wasn't, did you not wonder?"

Canidy said nothing. There was nothing to say.

Donovan continued: "The reason that I pulled you back in the manner that I did was so that everyone would think that your ass *was* in a crack. So if you disappear, it won't be unexpected."

"Disappear, sir? To where?"

Donovan did not reply directly. He studied the crystal tumbler as he rolled it in his fingers, making the single malt rise and fall as it slowly circled. "There are, as you know, people who do not like the OSS. People on our side of the war, some very high up. For good or other-wise, one of our chief supporters is the President of the United States."

"One could do worse," Canidy offered.

"Perhaps," Donovan said, agreeably. "But some-times—maybe most times—such connections can cause serious friction, particularly when you take your orders directly from the President. That's why no one under-stood why it was so important that you flew a mission to bring back bags of what was thought to be dirt. And no one understood why it was so important to bring out Professor Dyer. And now no one will understand why it's important you set up and run a resistance net in Sicily."

"Sicily?"

"General Eisenhower, there at AFHQ in Algiers, has made it clear that he does not want us—OSS in general and OSS SO in particular—in Sicily before the invasion. He thinks it will tip our hand to Mussolini and Hitler. Especially if our Special Operations begins blowing up things."

"So we're going into France from the south?"

Donovan ignored that. "The OSS Italian SI desk here in Washington, under a very capable and very young Army fellow by the name of Corvo, has been pulling to-gether men to compile intel on Sicily and Italy. Their work has been limited to interviewing anyone in the States with an interest in the place, from tourists who vis-ited there to Mussolini-hating natives who fled to the States. They're making relief maps of the islands, compil-ing lists of assets, targets of opportunity, et cetera. Natu-rally, this is leading to some internal jockeying as some of the SI guys try to set themselves up as SO, but we've been stalling, using Eisenhower as our excuse. Which is why you're going to set up a resistance net in Sicily, just as is being done in France, one that will not be discov-ered by the Italians, the Germans, the OSS Italian SI—and particularly by Ike."

"Yes, sir."

"It won't be easy. While the Sicilians hate the Fascists,

they're not exactly fond of anyone else, either. You're going to have to develop some leverage with them, because we need intel and we need it right now, something to feed Eisenhower in the event he gets wind of what we're up to—and particularly if we uncover something he doesn't know but should."

He paused to let that soak in, and as Canidy nodded, went on: "Your cover is the extraction of another scientist, this one a Sicilian named Arturo Rossi. He also has expertise in metallurgy. More important, he is a key contact with scientists whose disciplines are of extremely high value to the United States."

"For example?"

Donovan took a sip of single malt before replying. It was obvious that he did not want to answer the question directly and that he was not going to.

"These disciplines," he finally said, "and their importance will become clearer to you in time. For now, know that Professor Dyer said that he and Rossi worked together when they both were visiting professors at the University of Rome. So our immediate fear is that once the Germans figure that out, and find the connection with the missing Dyer and these other scientists, Rossi's life will be at risk, if it's not already."

"I understand."

"It's going to be especially difficult because we don't have any established pipelines, and establishing one means getting through to the tight-lipped Sicilians—"

There came a knock, and Donovan stopped speaking as one of the heavy wooden doors squeaked open.

Chief Ellis stood in the doorway with a natty man who carried in his left hand a tan leather satchel and who wore a dark two-piece business suit, white shirt, and navy blue patterned tie with a matching pocket square. He looked to be about thirty years old and was of average height, with pale skin, dark eyes, shiny black wavy hair that was neatly combed, and a finely trimmed black mustache.

"Major Gurfein, sir," Ellis announced. "And Antonio says he's prepared to serve in fifteen minutes."

"Thank you, Chief," Donovan said as he stood up. "Murray, please come join us," he added, waving him in.

Canidy stood and followed Donovan as Ellis left the room and closed the door.

Donovan shook hands with Gurfein, then motioned toward Canidy. "Murray Gurfein, Dick Canidy. Dick, Murray."

They shook hands.

Donovan put a hand on Gurfein's shoulder, squeezed it, and said, "Something to drink, Murray? Dick pours a deadly single malt."

Gurfein smiled. "That would be a lifesaver."

Canidy brought the drink to where Donovan and Gurfein were seated.

The director of the Office of Strategic Services raised his glass in a toast and Canidy and Gurfein followed.

"Our swords," Donovan said.

"Our swords," Canidy and Gurfein repeated in unison.

After they sipped, Donovan looked at Gurfein. "Nice booze, no?"

"Very."

Donovan turned to Canidy. "For your edification, Dick, the most recent time that Murray and I had the opportunity to share a single malt was last summer at the bar of a very nice hotel in midtown Manhattan, a den of ill repute frequented by the usual bigwigs, including Mayor Fiorello La Guardia himself. Our host was a lawyer by the name of Moses Polakoff."

Canidy drew a blank on the name, and shook his head slightly to indicate that.

"Charles Luciano?" Donovan said.

Canidy shook his head again.

Gurfein offered, "Charlie 'Lucky'?"

Canidy's eyebrows rose. "The head of the mob? Isn't he doing time?"

Gurfein nodded. "Thirty to fifty, courtesy of my former employer."

"Before Murray joined the OSS," Donovan explained, "he was head of the Rackets Bureau of the New York County District Attorney's Office. Tom Dewey, as D.A. for New York County and as the U.S. Attorney for the Southern District of New York, did an incredible job of cleaning out the underworld—Dutch Schultz, Waxey Gordon, Legs Diamond."

"Luciano went down in '36," Gurfein added, "for compulsory prostitution of women. Moses Polakoff is his lawyer. Luciano was in Dannemora Prison till last May, when we had him transferred to Great Meadow."

"Why the move?" Canidy said.

"That's why Murray is here," Donovan said. "When he was running the Rackets Bureau, an unusual situation arose with ONI. One that might help you."

Canidy looked incredulous. "I'm going to ask a Guinea gangster for help?"

Donovan looked at him a long moment. "Time to dance with a new devil, Dick." He glanced at his watch, then at Gurfein. "Why don't you start from the beginning, Murray? But first, shall we eat?"

[TWO]
Manhattan Beach, Florida
0330 28 February 1943

Richard Koch and Rudolf Cremer helped Kurt Bayer and Rolf Grossman dig two shallow holes beyond a line of sand dunes fifty yards inland from the beach in order to bury the black stainless steel containers—now each just top and bottom shells that were nested together after being emptied of the soft bags that contained explosives, detonators, pistols and ammunition, United States currency, and clothing.

Koch thought, but couldn't be sure, that he heard the angry shouting of Kapitänleutnant Hans-Günther Brosin from just offshore. He told himself that he had to be imagining it because of at least two things: Enough time had passed since they had sent the young coastguardsman, bound and gagged, out to the U-boat in the train of rafts being retrieved, which should have put the vessel—and its captain—far out of earshot. And the U-boat commander would not be so careless as to draw undue attention to himself while in the process of trying to get his ship to deeper water before being discovered.

Still, Koch smiled in the darkness at what he imagined as the U-boat captain's furious reaction to his little surprise.

The men filled in the greater part of the holes using their short-handled shovels, then tossed the shovels in on top, too, and filled in the last foot or so of sand by hand. They smoothed out the top of the disturbed sand as best they could, then left it, relying on the rain and wind to blend it all back together.

They stood, and each slung one of the heavy soft bags over their shoulder, adjusted its strap, then started moving southward along the sand-dune line, the team of Richard Koch and Kurt Bayer in the lead and, some ten paces or so back, Rudolf Cremer and Rolf Grossman bringing up the rear.

The plan now called for the two teams to separate as soon as possible. That meant after they had secured transportation—a 1935 Ford sedan, big enough to fit them all for the short time necessary—which Koch told them he had arranged for through an old contact.

On the surface, the car seemed only a convenience, not a necessity—each team member had been thoroughly briefed on the terrain and alternate transportation options by Koch and could find their way alone if necessary—but beyond that, it held other value to Koch.

Richard Koch had lived for three years—between stints as a part-time engineering student at the University of Florida at Gainesville—in Jacksonville, where he worked for the local company that distributed Budweiser beer. He had driven a truck and delivered cases and kegs of Auggie Busch's best brewed hops and barley to Duval County bars in the seaside towns that lined its shore—Manhattan Beach, Jacksonville Beach, and on down U.S. Highway 1 to the St. Johns County line.

Over the course of his regular three-times-a-week route, he had become friendly with many of the bartenders and restaurant managers with whom he had come in contact, but none so well as J. Whit Stevens. "Jay," as he was called, was a stocky, middle-aged blue blood from Philadelphia who had inherited from his eccentric grandmother a popular hole-in-the-wall at Neptune Beach called Pete's Bar.

It was because of his grandmother that generations of the Stevens family had spent their winter breaks at Jacksonville Beach. She was a free spirit in the world of the upper crust, and believed that the Palm Beach–type crowds wintering to the south of Jax were snooty and terribly overrated. She had spent nearly a lifetime trying to take some of the stiffness out of her own husband—Stevens's grandfather—and her son—Stevens's father—but with little success.

And so it surprised no one when, after old man Stevens died of a heart attack at his senior vice president desk in the trust department of Mellon Bank, Grandma

Stevens up and moved permanently to Jacksonville Beach, where, in another free-spirited act, she opened Pete's to help her pass the time.

Stevens's father was also at Mellon, as president of the corporate banking department there, and it had made sense to everyone that Stevens would follow his father and grandfather into banking.

And he did. He graduated from the business school at the University of Pennsylvania and soon became a Mellon junior executive on the fast track. But it was not to last.

Stevens never was comfortable as a button-down type. And all the business of being a blue blood bored him; he'd just as soon push away from a gourmet meal at a gala at the Union League of Philadelphia, loosen his tie as he walked across Broad Street, and go eat a Philly cheesesteak in the 12th Street Market.

The undisputable fact was that genes had indeed jumped a generation—and the genes he had gotten were those of his grandmother.

Clearly, she had recognized that and, accordingly, willed to him the bar—her last defiant act in trying to loosen up the Stevens clan.

This time, she had been successful beyond her greatest hope.

It had been years since her funeral, and that had been the last time that Stevens had put on a suit and tie. He now was prone to well-worn khakis, a faded captain's shirt with epaulets, and a crushed navy blue Greek sailor's cap that was always askew on his unruly sandy hair.

As his grandmother had been, Stevens was also well

liked. This was in part because of his engaging habit of greeting everyone with a pat on the back—a hug for certain regulars—but he knew it also was due to the fact that he had a habit of letting the bartenders at Pete's pour penny draft beer when the happy mood struck him.

From most appearances, Stevens did not take the bar business too seriously. It seemed that the steady customers provided him an easy and reasonable cash flow most of the year and a very good income during the height of seasons, June through August and mid-November to early January. And he had that rent-free two-bedroom apartment above the bar, a bit ratty-looking from the outside but with what had to be an incredible view of the beach and Atlantic Ocean. Why work hard?

But the exact opposite was true.

The proprietor, with his master's of business administration from Wharton, quietly tracked every nickel, knew what a keg cost him wholesale, knew what he lost in retail income when he just about gave away each keg during a "happy mood," and knew by what percentage customer traffic—and revenue—then increased after word got around that Pete's had been giving away beer again.

Most important, he knew that not all of the income found its way onto the cash receipts reported to the Bureau of Internal Revenue. Consequently, Stevens had a hefty fund tucked away for a rainy day—a very rainy day—or for whatever else he decided was the best use of his money.

In addition to the income from the bar, Stevens also dabbled in a number of other cash-generating ventures.

He owned a couple of rental cottages—shacks, really, just bare bone and basic but with great beach access—and these he let in spring and summer (no one ever wanted to rent them in winter, when a cold wet wind blew in steadily off the ocean, and the only heat source in the cottages was the rarely used wood-burning stoves). And he traded cars, some by choice, some by necessity.

It was common—maybe too common—in a beach town environment for jobs to come and go almost as easy as the wind, leaving carpenters and painters and other such tradesmen to wait out the dry spells.

And it only made sense, at least to them, to spend time between jobs where they spent time after work when they had jobs: at Pete's. But drinking when there's no income, and no hope of income anytime soon, made for a bad formula.

Thus, quietly, because he did not want to become known as the Bank of Booze, Stevens allowed a select group to run bar tabs. While those who found themselves in that group thought it was a damned decent service for Stevens to offer to Pete's regulars who were temporarily down on their luck, it was far from a magnanimous act on Stevens's part.

He knew his customers, and which ones were loan worthy and which were ne'er-do-wells. And for the worthy, he charged a somewhat healthy interest rate, and secured it by holding the legal title to the car or truck of the borrower.

When the owner got work, he bought back his title by paying off—in cash—his tab and the interest incurred. If the owner did not get work and the tab reached a point short of the value of the vehicle, it was pay up or default time.

Consequently, Stevens had one, two—on occasion, as many as four—vehicles to his name.

When he could, he kept a couple of them parked outside the bar—it was always good for the place to look as though someone were there, to draw in patrons during business hours and, after hours, to deter others who might not have the best of intentions—and any extras he kept parked out at the rental cottages.

Richard Koch did not have the benefit of being educated at a school of finance—he had been strictly reared in a home of modest means, his father a hardworking diesel-engine mechanic who had brought the family to America but then decided to return home to Germany when Richard was nineteen and old enough to fend for himself—but Koch was frugal-minded, too.

He had managed his personal affairs well by keeping steady employment and spending within his means. He even socked away cash on a regular basis—a little sometimes, more others, till he had just over three thousand dollars.

Koch never needed to use Stevens's loan system, but he was aware of it, and aware that Stevens seemed to be always doing something with cars, and so when, in November 1941, Koch made plans to visit his family in Germany, he spoke with Stevens about leaving his car with him. Stevens was of course agreeable—for a small fee.

That left only one thing to take care of: what to do

with the brick of cash that Koch had saved. He did not want to leave it in a bank—not being a U.S. citizen made him concerned that the money could be confiscated for whatever reason—and he thought long and hard about what to do with it, from burying it to having someone hold it for him.

He finally realized that he already was having Stevens hold his car; why not just have him hold it, too—but not know that he was doing so? He could hide it in the car.

After first taking brown butcher paper and wrapping the cash in two small bundles, then covering the paper with heavy black tape, he went through the Ford looking for a spot that was both safe and not at all obvious. He looked and looked and finally decided on the backseat. He unbolted the seat from the floorboard, taped the bundles to the wire frame underneath, and then bolted the seat back in place.

Then he drove the car to Pete's Bar, parked it out front, locked it, and went inside and handed the keys to Stevens—never for a moment realizing that in a month's time Germany would be declaring war on the United States and in two months' time he would be enlisted in the German army.

In December 1942, Richard Koch had a letter-sized envelope added to a pouch containing other correspondence from the Abwehr. This pouch was then hand-carried to Spain, where it found its way to a Spanish diplomatic courier en route to Spain's consulate office in New York

City. There the envelope was sent by messenger to Eva Carr, one of Fritz Kuhn's faithful in the German-American Bund living on the Lower East Side.

When Eva Carr, a rugged-looking brunette of thirty-five, opened the plain envelope, she found another, note-card-sized envelope.

It carried the return address:

```
Richard Koch
Gen Delivery
NYC NY
```

And it was addressed to:

```
Mr. J. W. Stevens
c/o Pete's Bar
117 1st St
Neptune Beach Florida
```

Attached to the inner envelope was a handwritten note that instructed the recipient to affix the proper three-cent postage to the inner envelope and mail it from a box in New York.

Had Eva Carr opened the smaller envelope, she would have seen the letter therein, written by hand by Koch, that began "My Dear Jay," then opened with a line inquiring as to Stevens's health and well-being, and abruptly segued to announce that Koch would be coming back to collect his car, within the next thirty to forty-five days, and if Koch could so impose on Stevens he enclosed a twenty-dollar bill (in U.S. currency, of course, which had come from German counterintelligence) in order to have someone check out the car to ensure that it was in sound operating order, that it didn't need a new battery or tire or other, that it had a full tank of fresh gasoline, et cetera, et cetera.

The letter closed by wishing Stevens—and Pete's—a successful new year.

[THREE]

Wordlessly, the teams made their way southward in the rain at a half trot, following along the dune line. They came to an occasional footpath—beach access points that connected parking lots to the shore—and stopped, carefully looking for the lone, love-struck couple out for a middle-of-the-night stroll or the drunk who may not have quite made it home, before crossing the path and continuing south.

At one point, they came to a halt at a four-foot-high fence that blocked their way—Kurt Bayer actually ran right into the wall of vertical wooden slats wired together and was grateful that it had flexed at impact—and, breathing heavily, the four had to take time to debate whether it was faster to scale the fence or to run toward the ocean in order to circumvent it.

They chose, after a brief and animated discussion, to scale it and soon were running at a measured pace back toward the south, the path clear of everything but sand and more sand for the next forty-five minutes.

Then they came to another beach access path, and

there in the dark the faded signage announced, unnecessarily:

NO LIFEGUARD
ON DUTY!
SWIM AT YOUR OWN RISK!
TOWN OF ATLANTIC BEACH

It was the last part that Richard Koch had found the most interesting, for it confirmed for him what he thought he both remembered and recognized in the dark and rain of the landmarks through this area.

Kurt Bayer stood there beside him, catching his breath, and they waited for Rudolf Cremer and Rolf Grossman to catch up to them. After a moment, they could hear them—feet squeaking in the sand as they ran—and shortly thereafter their vague shapes came into view through the mist.

Koch could hear their labored breaths. Then he heard Cremer manage to say, "Is—is this—this it?"

Koch whispered, "This should be the path leading to Sixteenth Street, and, if so, just over there about five hundred meters"—he pointed south and slightly inland, past some scrub pine trees and palmettos—"are the cottages."

"Let's go, then," Grossman said, already moving and trying not to sound as if he were breathing as hard as he was.

They passed the pines and palmettos and came to a pair
of darkened cottages, two hexagonal designs built side by
side on pilings six feet above the sand and overlooking
the ocean. Koch knew that these belonged to J. Whit
Stevens because he had twice rented one of them himself.

They were identical, with weather-beaten wooden sid-
ing, wooden decks and railings—some sections warped—
and rusty tin roofs. The windows were shuttered for the
season. Even in the dark it was clear that these were summer rentals, absently looked after with the kind of neglect
where one fixes things only when they break—and maybe
then not even right away—as opposed to performing some
semblance of preventative maintenance.

Koch, after pulling his Walther P38 9mm semiautomatic pistol from the leather holster on his hip, then
hearing the others doing the same, led the men toward
the nearest cottage.

He could feel the sand under his feet becoming more
packed, and then becoming almost solid, as he reached
the point where grass grew at the foot of the wooden
steps leading up to the deck.

Looking around, Koch had hoped—and even half-
expected—that he would get lucky and find his 1935 Ford
sedan, probably coated white with salt spray and sand par-
ticles, parked on one of the crushed oyster shell pads under
the cottages, where Stevens often left cars for long-term
storage out of direct sunlight.

He was more than a little disappointed, if not somewhat pissed, that it wasn't there—in fact, that there were

no cars around—because it meant that he would have to walk to Pete's Bar and deal with Stevens at his apartment.

They went up the flight of steps, and, at the top, Koch found the key that he remembered was kept hidden behind a light fixture beside the main door.

He put it in the rusted padlock, opened the stiff lock with some effort, and threw back the clasp. He grabbed the knob, turned it, and pushed.

Nothing happened. The door was stuck.

Damned thing is either swollen or warped, Koch thought, *or the whole worthless house is leaning, causing the door to bind in its frame. If I open it, the whole damned place is liable to collapse. Oh, what the hell . . .*

Koch turned the knob and hit the door hard with his shoulder once, then twice, and the door finally swung inward on very noisy hinges.

It was even darker inside the cottage.

Koch flipped the light switch by the door but nothing happened. He realized that it was like Stevens to have had the electrical service turned off to save even a cent; probably the water, too.

He felt someone suddenly standing beside him, and when he looked Grossman switched on his flashlight and swept the room with its beam. The light initially hurt Koch's eyes, but he adjusted quickly and could see, with all the dust and spiderwebs, that it had been some time since anyone had lived in or even visited the cottage.

They had entered next to the kitchen, which opened onto a main living area that—when the shutters were removed—looked out over the Atlantic. There was a short hallway connecting to two bedrooms and a single bath.

They fanned out, checking that the rest of the cottage was clear, then went into the main living area and put their bags down on the wooden floor.

Koch took his flashlight and went to the kitchen and started going through the cabinets.

They were mostly empty, save for containers of salt and such, but he finally found the candles he remembered being there. He put one on the table and lit it. Then he took from his pocket a pack of Derby cigarettes. Now that they were inside, it was safe to light one up without being seen, and he did.

"First thing after daylight, I'll go get the car," Koch said, walking over to the couch. "For now, take your pick of the beds in back. I'll stand watch first—"

"Sir," Kurt Bayer said, sitting at the table lit by the candle, "you rest and I'll take watch."

He sat down on the couch, positioning his bag right next to him. "No—"

"With respect, sir," Bayer pursued, "I can rest when you go for the car. Right now, you're tired, and we all need to be rested."

Everyone heard Grossman grunt. It sounded derisive, as if Grossman thought the other junior agent was kissing up to his superior.

That attitude bothered Koch, but he found himself smiling in the dark. He was actually grateful he was teamed with someone like Bayer, not Grossman, because the *Oberschutz,* or chief rifleman, was the coldly ruthless one, a little too quick to cut a throat, or, as he'd done to the young coastguardsman, pistol-whip someone.

"You're right, Kurt," Koch said. "Thank you."

Richard Koch finished his cigarette, stubbed it out, then repositioned a couple of the pillows on the couch, swung his feet up, and shortly, with his pistol in hand and resting on his belly, was snoring.

[FOUR]
Neptune Beach, Florida
0810 28 February 1943

Richard Koch, walking at a fast clip down Ocean Drive, pushed the hood of his sweatshirt off his head. He had pulled it up against the morning chill when he had started out from the cottage about an hour ago, but now that he had worked up a light sweat it wasn't needed. He wore the hooded sweatshirt—a heavy, gray cotton one with the faded orange UF logo—tennis shoes, and black shorts.

Just another local out for his morning walk, he thought, his hands in the sweatshirt pouch below the UF. *One packing a Walther P38.*

At the next corner, Koch cut across the intersection and started walking south on First Street. He could see the sign for Pete's Bar and looked at the parking spaces in front of the saloon—and began to worry.

Of the two vehicles parked there, neither was the 1935

Ford touring sedan. One was a pickup—a 1930 Chevy—with garish yellow doors lettered STAN'S PLUMBING and black fenders (the left front one dented) and a rusted metal framework mounted above the cargo area for the carrying of oversized lengths of pipes.

For whatever reason—probably the need for a plumber—it reminded Koch of a drunk he'd once seen in the men's room at Pete's, throwing up in a toilet overflowing with a nasty mix of vomitus and other solids.

Koch had grown fond of the Ford. He liked the design, especially its nose—the tall, sleek chrome grille that was raked backward with bullet headlamps mounted on either side, just above the twin horns, and then crowned with the stylized V-8 emblem that was repeated inside on the dash.

It wasn't Cadillac fancy, but in Koch's mind it was very nice just the same.

And it has a backseat full of fucking cash.

Koch went around to the back of 117 First Street, to the flight of rusted steel steps that led to the roof and the apartment there. He started up the steps, his shoes making an enormous racket on the steel as he ascended.

If J. Whit Stevens wasn't awake before, he is now.

The sun-faded black, stamped-tin address numbers nailed to the left of the doorframe read 117-A, although nails at the top and bottom of the A had rusted off and the letter was now nearly upside down, hanging by the remaining nail in its left foot.

No surprise. Looks like he takes the same care of his apartment as he does his rentals.

Koch knocked, and the A rocked on its nail.

He heard movement inside the apartment, then foot-steps approaching the door.

"Yes?" an unseen Stevens said from behind the closed door.

"Jay, it's me, Richard Koch. Look, I apologize for bothering you at this hour on a Sunday. Can we talk?"

After a long moment, there was the sound of the deadbolt lock turning, then the doorknob. The door opened about halfway, and there stood J. Whit Stevens in pajamas and holding a steaming cup of coffee.

"Richard Koch?" he repeated, as he studied him.

"I worked for the Bud distributor," Koch said. "Re-member? And I left my Ford with you."

Stevens did not seem to register that for a moment, but then his eyes suddenly went wide.

"Oh, *that* Richard Koch," he said.

"I'm actually here about the car," Koch said. He smiled, glad to be remembered finally.

"Come in, come in," Stevens said in a now-friendly tone while opening the door wide.

As Koch stepped inside, Stevens patted him on the back. "Nice to see you, Richard."

Koch had never been in Stevens's apartment. He was surprised.

It was the exact opposite of the bar and the cottages. Clean—spotless, even—and nicely furnished with a big couch, two reclining armchairs, and assorted tables and lamps and nicely framed art. There was an expensive-looking India rug, easily ten by twelve, woven with an intricate patterned design in red, gold, and black. Against the near wall, a cabinet with beveled, cut-glass doors held expensive china and glassware. Next to it, by the kitchen area, was a beautifully finished wooden table. And on the table were a radio softly playing classical music—Vivaldi's *Four Seasons,* Koch recognized—and a coffeepot next to the morning *Florida Times-Union* paper, which Stevens obviously had been reading when Koch had knocked. He noticed that one headline read: U-BOAT ATTACKS DROP BUT STILL HIGH — 300,000 TONS SUNK IN LAST 30 DAYS.

Stevens walked over to the curtain that covered the eastern wall and pulled on the cord system that opened it, revealing a breathtaking view of the ocean and beach, the sun rising low on the horizon, its golden rays fingering through the gaps of the clouds beginning to break up.

Stevens took in the view a moment, then turned and asked, "Can I get you some coffee?"

"I don't want to impose. This shouldn't take long."

"Very well," Stevens said, nodding. "Have a seat, please."

"Did you get my letter?" Koch said. He remained standing.

Stevens looked as if he were trying to pick his words with care.

"The one with that interesting twenty-dollar bill?" he said conversationally. "Yes, I did." He paused. "But—"

"But?"

"But after the fact."

"What *fact*? Is it wrecked? Stolen? What?"

Stevens looked at Koch a moment, then said, "If you'll excuse me a moment, I've got something for you."

He put down his coffee cup on a table next to one of the armchairs, then went across the apartment, back to a door that was on the far side of the kitchen, opened it, and went through it. The door was left ajar, and Koch could see the foot of a bed inside.

What the hell did he mean by "after the fact"?

He shook his head as he walked over to the window. He looked out over the ocean, idly wondering where out there his U-boat was. Koch heard Stevens's footsteps again, then his voice, now chipper, saying, "Here it is."

He turned and saw that Stevens held a brown accordion folder and was pulling out an eight-by-ten envelope with R KOCH handwritten on it in black ink.

Stevens extended the envelope to Koch. He took it, squeezed upright the brass clasp holding the flap, opened the envelope, then peered inside. He saw papers—the letter he had sent (it still had the twenty-dollar bill in it), some sort of accounting sheet, and a stack of bills, mostly fifties, bound by rubber band—and pulled them out.

"Eight hundred forty-five dollars, less my commission," Stevens said proudly as Koch fanned through the money. "More than the blue book's retail value, even after deducting my fees."

Koch was now reading the accounting sheet that accompanied the cash.

"You *sold* my car?" he said, incredulous.

"For a mint!" Stevens replied.

"Who said you could sell my goddamned car?" Koch said. "And what am I going to do now?"

"I didn't need *your* permission," Stevens said somewhat piously. "The law allows for the placing of a lien after failure to make payment on the storage and maintenance of a vehicle—"

"But I paid you in advance!" Koch said, his temper building. He was about to pull out his Walther but stopped himself.

"Not for the full period," Stevens replied. "Regardless, that's a mere technicality. I got you a very good deal. You should thank me."

"I should fucking *shoot* you," Koch snapped, then was immediately sorry that he did.

Stevens, his face showing fear, took a step back.

Don't be stupid, Koch told himself. *Think!*

Stevens watched with real interest as Koch, nervous as well as agitated, pulled a wrinkled pack of cigarettes from a pocket of his shorts and lit one. The pack had a drawing of a black horse head and the brand name Derby.

Koch ignored the interest, and, after taking a long drag and exhaling, looked again at the accounting form.

Stevens said, "It's all accounted for there on the sheet. There's no need to be this way. You were gone quite a long time, longer than you said—"

Koch looked up at him. "Where's my car?" he said forcefully. "I mean, who bought it?"

Stevens opened his mouth to speak but then closed it without uttering a sound. He thought something over, then shrugged and finally said, "I can get that information—I'm not required to share it—but I'll have to check my files for it."

"How long will that take?"

"An hour, maybe less. It's been sold for at least six months. Getting to the paper could take some digging. Do you have to have it now?"

He's right. I don't. Even if I had the information on who bought it, I'd still need to find the guy. Right now, I need wheels.

"I need wheels," Koch said. "Where can I get another car—and I mean *now*!"

"I understand," Stevens said, thinking about it, "but I'm afraid that I don't have any cars right now."

"Shit!"

"I'm sorry, Richard—"

Koch then remembered the car that he had seen when he walked up to Pete's looking for his Ford. "What about what's parked in front of the bar?"

Stevens thought for a moment. "No car that I own. Must belong to someone who got too drunk last night and left it." He paused. "How desperate are you?"

Koch didn't respond. He thought, *I could just steal the goddamned car.*

"How about a truck?" Stevens said and smiled. "I do have a truck."

Koch considered that a short moment. "Get me the keys to it."

"Now, I have to warn you—"

"Just get me the goddamned keys!"

Stevens looked at him a moment.

"Okay. And so there's no bad feelings about this situation with your car, I'll give you a deal on the truck."

"You sure as hell will," Koch said, and thought, *You don't know how good of one.*

"It's in the safe," Stevens said, turning for the bedroom. "I'll be just a moment."

A moment later when he returned, Stevens held a chrome-plated Smith & Wesson .38 caliber revolver and had it aimed at Koch.

When Koch entered the cottage—passing Rudolf Cremer, who had gone to the door with pistol in hand when he heard the footsteps coming up the stairs—he found that one of the shutters over a window facing east had been pulled back and morning light flooded the main living area.

Rolf Grossman sat at the kitchen table, finishing the field cleaning of his Walther; he had lubricated and reassembled it after getting out the sand that seemed to have collected in its every crack and crevice.

The agents had changed out of their black clothing and now wore the light-colored, casual American-style clothing that they had brought.

Spread out on the floor were the contents of the soft bags: electric blasting caps, two-by-three-inch mechanical time-delay devices (their mechanisms built like a wristwatch's, with gears and springs), other slow-fuse devices disguised as pen-and-pencil sets, ampoules of sulfuric acid, boxes of 9mm ammo, bundles of currency, and more.

The men had taken it all out to ensure that it was divided up evenly between teams, then repacked the gear into olive drab canvas duffels that they had packed.

Kurt Bayer was repacking his green duffel when he glanced over at Koch and saw the bloody cloth tied around his left thigh.

"Ach!" Bayer exclaimed. "What the hell happened?"

Koch walked with scarcely a limp toward the couch and sat heavily on it.

"It's nothing," he said. He looked at the gear spread out. "How soon before everyone is ready to go?"

Cremer and Grossman were now moving quickly toward Koch.

"Do we need to go immediately?" Cremer said excitedly. He looked toward the cottage door. "Is anyone chasing you?"

Koch shook his head. "Relax. Everything is okay. But we should get going as soon as possible."

Grossman pointed at the leg and, in an accusatory tone, said, "What the hell did you do?"

Koch looked at him a moment. "Fuck you. I said everything is okay."

He untied the cloth—what Bayer now recognized had been a white T-shirt—and inspected the wound; a small, oozing red pulp hole on the outside of the thigh that reminded Bayer of a very wet, chewed-up pencil eraser.

"It went in," Koch said matter-of-factly, "and it went out. No serious tissue damage. Bleeding is done. Just need to clean it up."

Grossman took a close look and repeated, "What the hell did you do?"

When Koch didn't reply again, Grossman said coldly, "We need to know how this affects what we do after the teams separate."

"He's right," Cremer added. "Who's going to be looking for us?"

Koch nodded. "All right. Fine. I went to the man who had my car . . ."

J. Whit Stevens had held the Banker's Special five-shot revolver in his right hand.

"I had no reservations about selling your car after your letter came with that twenty-dollar bill," he had said. "I knew then that you were up to something shifty, not just somewhere having fun, overstaying the length of time you said you'd be gone."

Koch, hands in his sweatshirt pouch, the right one holding the 9mm Walther, looked at Stevens and waited for an opportunity.

Stevens misinterpreted the silence. "You don't know what I'm talking about, do you?"

Koch shook his head. "No, I don't. Look, can you put down the gun?"

"I had my suspicions before I saw the twenty you sent. It's a Series 1928 Gold Certificate. They've been out of circulation for years. The size of it—about a third bigger than today's paper money—is a dead giveaway."

Koch thought, *The fucking Abwehr gave us the wrong money? Christ!*

He said, "I don't know what you're taking about."

"Of course not," Stevens said, coming closer. "But I do."

He pointed the pistol at Koch's pants pocket. "Mind if I have a smoke?"

Koch shrugged, then reached into his pants pocket with his left hand and brought out the pack of Derby cigarettes.

Stevens nervously waved the pistol at the pack.

"Nice Kraut brand, *Herr* Koch."

Richard Koch stared back but did not respond as he held out the pack.

"I traveled extensively in Europe before the war," Stevens went on, smugly. "England, France, Austria, Germany. I know a few things about your country, including its brands."

Koch said nothing, just jerked the pack upward so that a single cigarette appeared in the small hole torn in the top of the pack. Stevens reached for it with his left hand—and Koch tossed the pack hard into his face.

There was a sharp *crack* as Stevens's .38 fired. Koch felt a burning sensation in his left thigh but ignored it as he grabbed the revolver while thrusting his right knee into Stevens's groin. Stevens groaned and doubled over, and Koch forced the muzzle of the revolver behind Stevens's left ear—and squeezed the trigger.

Instantly, a small geyser of blood and gray matter erupted from the exit wound atop Stevens's skull and he collapsed to the floor, blood from the wound pooling on the India rug.

". . . And I grabbed the keys to the truck, and came right here," Koch said to Cremer, Grossman, and Bayer at the cottage.

He chose not to mention the three bricks of cash collected from the bedroom safe when he went for the truck key—twelve thousand dollars of J. Whit Stevens's rainy-day fund kept separate from the rest that was kept in the safe embedded in the concrete floor of the bar.

"*Scheist!*" Cremer said. "We have not been ashore a full day and already we have a trail of a missing coast-guardsman and a dead pub owner!"

"We have to move!" Grossman said excitedly, and got down on his knees and started repacking one of the soft black bags.

Koch shrugged.

"No argument," he said. "Give me a minute to clean this scratch and we go."

Ten minutes later, after carefully packing all the bags and making sure that they had left no sign of their presence in the cottage, the four men went down the wooden steps and headed toward the parking pad of crushed oyster shells beneath the cottage.

"What the hell?" Cremer said when he saw the horrid yellow-and-black plumber's pickup. "When you said 'truck' . . ." His voice trailed off.

Koch shrugged, then wordlessly put his bag in the back and got behind the wheel.

Cremer exchanged glances of disgust with Grossman, then they put their bags in the back and climbed in with them, trying to arrange themselves so that they would be inconspicuous to passersby.

As the truck starter ground and the engine caught with a cough, Bayer came running up, tossed his bag in the back—hitting Grossman in the head in the process— then got in the passenger's seat and slammed the yellow door shut.

The truck's tires began to crunch on the shells.

IV

"Luciano is a curious study in contrasts," Gurfein said right before slicing more beef tenderloin and putting it in his mouth.

Canidy, Gurfein, and Donovan, well into their meal, were seated in the small private breakfast area that was off of the mansion's main kitchen.

The huge table in the main dining room was for some reason being used as a conference table—with papers and maps spread all over it—and therefore unavailable.

The private breakfast area's outer wall was a large bay window that overlooked a moonlit open area of the estate that went back an acre or so to where a row of tall evergreen trees heavy with snow masked a section of the stone wall that ringed the property and was patrolled at irregular times by armed guards.

Covered with a cloth of white linen, the rectangular table was somewhat small, about three by four, and intended to comfortably seat two. It was now set for three, using what was considered to be the "everyday" china, leaving little empty space between the nice but simple heavy white plates and the water and wine glasses.

Donovan sat at one end of the table, Canidy at the other, and Gurfein was seated between them, opposite the bay window.

Behind Gurfein—very close behind him—was a narrow ten-foot-long shelf running the length of the wall. It now held half-empty platters of sliced beef tenderloin, garlic-roasted red potatoes, steamed asparagus with a lemon-cream sauce, as well as a glass pitcher of ice water and a half-dozen bottles of Cabernet Sauvignon, one of them empty and another open and "breathing."

At the start, Donovan had excused the staff, saying that he felt sure that he and his guests could serve themselves without risk of starving or other calamity, but if anything should arise to prove him wrong—"And I have been wrong before," he said. "I believe it was a summer day in 1888 . . . when I was five"—he would immediately summon them by pressing the floor-mounted service call button beneath him.

"Contrasts?" Canidy repeated, carefully cutting his last stalk of asparagus. "How so?"

Gurfein hurried the chewing of his beef, and swallowed quickly with some effort.

He said, "Although he's rough and squat and dumpy—looks like a dumb Guinea thug, especially with that droopy eyelid and the neck scar he got from knife cuts—he is actually a cool operator who could run a corporation, if he wanted. A legal one, I mean, because he's clearly running an illicit one. Another example is that there is absolutely no doubt that he is a ruthless killer, more than comfortable with getting his hands dirty, yet he has been a model prisoner. Not one problem since he went in the slam this time. And he's not eligible for parole for another thirteen or so years—1956."

"Will he get it?" Canidy asked.

"Not even likely," Gurfein said. "Not with his history. When he first went up—he was sent to Sing Sing—the prison psychiatrist there diagnosed him as dangerous, and added that, due to his drug addiction, Luciano should be transferred to Dannemora. And he was. He was confined to his cell for sixteen hours a day, the remainder of the time spent working in the laundry, with an hour every other day allowed for some type of exercise."

The state prison Sing Sing was at Ossining, near New York City. Dannemora, the state's third-oldest prison and maximum-security facility—and, accordingly, a cold, miserable place to spend a night, let alone to languish a lifetime—was in upstate New York, about sixty miles from Albany.

Canidy reached for the open bottle of Cabernet. When he held it up, Donovan said, "Please," and Gurfein nodded enthusiastically. Canidy poured a little more wine into their glasses, then into his.

"If I may," Gurfein said to Donovan, "let me begin with a quick history of Luciano, then we can get into recent events. Because of the latter, I had to deeply invest myself in the former, and that in and of itself was a formidable task."

"Of course," Donovan said.

Gurfein looked to Canidy.

"Please," Canidy added.

Gurfein cut a piece of meat and put it in his mouth, clearly gathering his thoughts as he chewed and looked out the window. After he swallowed, he took two healthy sips of wine, then dabbed at his lips with his linen napkin.

"First off," the former assistant district attorney for New York County began, "he is not a citizen of the United States, which is what most assume he is. He was born Salvatore Lucania on November 24, 1897, in Sicily, the third son of five children. When Salvatore was seven, his father, a steam-boiler mechanic by the name of Anthony Lucania, immigrated to the United States and found work in Brooklyn at a brass-bed factory. The following year, Luciano came to the U.S. with his mother and siblings. The family worked hard, stayed out of trouble—everyone except Luciano. He was a tough guy from the start. Before he dropped out of school, in fifth grade, he was already roughing up the little Jewish kids, saying he would protect them from being beaten up in the neighborhood, at school—wherever—if they paid him—"

"And if they didn't," Canidy put in, "then he beat them up until they did?"

Gurfein nodded.

"Classic thuggery," Canidy said.

"Interestingly," Gurfein said between sips of wine, "one skinny Polish Jew fought back. His name was Maier Suchowljansky—"

"Later, one Meyer Lansky?" Canidy said.

"One and the same," Donovan acknowledged.

Gurfein stared at his wineglass a moment, collecting his next thoughts as he methodically worked his thumb and forefinger on the stem, slowly spinning the wine. He continued:

"Even though Meyer 'Little Man' Lansky was five years younger than Luciano, Luciano liked him, respected him, learned to listen to him. They were running rackets in no time. Luciano got busted dealing drugs in his late teens, and spent months in the slam at Blackwell's Island. Despite all that—or, rather, perhaps because of it—Luciano rose quickly in the underworld. He joined gangs, then ran them, running with some important Italian mob guys. Quote Italian unquote is key, because when Luciano wound up working with Joe 'The Boss' Masseria, it wasn't long before it got bloody."

Gurfein noticed that Canidy and Donovan had pushed back from their empty plates and so he turned his attention to what little remained of his meal. After a long moment, his plate clean, he picked up his wineglass and went on:

"As *capo di tutti capi*—boss of all bosses—Masseria made a lot of money, and Luciano, now his number two, made him even more. At one point, thinking he was doing what his boss expected him to do, Luciano suggested that they diversify—get bigger and more powerful beyond their already formidable wealth and influence—by doing business with gangs that weren't Italian."

"Why not?" Canidy said. "Lansky, Luciano's most trusted friend, was a Polish Jew."

"True. No doubt that's what Luciano was thinking. But Luciano's idea was to expand not only with gangs that weren't just Italian—but with gangs that weren't just in New York. He was already envisioning a nation-wide syndicate. Whether he shared all of this with Masseria is unclear. But Masseria would have nothing of the idea of working with non-Italians. Luciano was persistent but ultimately frustrated. He got nowhere."

Gurfein drained his glass, then slid it toward Canidy's wine bottle. "If you would, please?"

As Canidy poured, Gurfein said, "Masseria, however, was beginning to fear Luciano—as any wise boss would with nowhere to go but down. So one night in October of '29 a car pulled up to the curb where Luciano stood on the sidewalk on Broadway and Fifth Avenue, right there in front of the Flatiron Building, which he'd just come out of, and some guys jumped out and forced him into the backseat. They bound and gagged him and drove him out to Staten Island. They beat the living shit out of him, pistol-whipping and stabbing him, then strung him up in a warehouse by his wrists. Before they left him to hang there till dead, they also cut his throat."

"Apparently, not good enough," Canidy said with a grin. He knew how easy it was for someone not properly trained to try to slit a throat—and fail. It was harder, and a helluva lot messier, than the movies made it look.

Gurfein nodded. "That's what makes him one tough Guinea sonofabitch. Beaten and bloody, he still some-how managed to work free of the rope that tied his hands, then he crawled out of the warehouse and wound up getting picked up by NYPD's 123rd Precinct. The cops grilled him, but Luciano, true to *omertà*, said nothing, and they ran him to the hospital, where the cops had no choice but to let him go."

"It's easy not to snitch if you don't know who tried to kill you. Did he?"

"Keep quiet? Yeah, he was faithful to the code—wiseguys don't speak out, especially to cops, about the mob. Did he know who did it? No. Not at first. But over time, his counsel—Lansky—figured it out for him."

"Masseria."

Gurfein nodded. "And Lansky helped his pal plot revenge. So one day Luciano secretly approached Salvatore 'Little Caesar' Maranzano—"

"This is where it turned really bloody," Donovan interrupted. "Masseria and Maranzano were bitter competitors and even more bitter enemies. And so began what became called the Castellammarese War. Many of the immigrants fighting this mob war, including Maranzano, had come from the western Sicilian town of Castellammare del Golf, hence the name." He looked at Gurfein. "Sorry. Please continue."

"Over the next couple of years," Gurfein went on, "it was a real underworld bloodbath. Countless gangsters got gunned down. Masseria had been right to be fearful, because everyone was fearful. And it was in this crazed environment that Luciano set him up. He arranged to meet him at a restaurant in Coney Island, and the hit men were waiting."

He sipped from his wine, then grinned. "So Luciano

got revenge on Masseria for his attempted whacking. And Maranzano, who now called himself *capo di tutti capi*, rewarded Luciano by making him his number two."

"Jesus Christ!" Canidy said. "Same song, different verse."

"Yes and no. As with Masseria, you had Luciano playing second fiddle to the ruthless big boss. But with one difference: Maranzano embraced Luciano's idea of a nationwide syndicate. He wanted to be *capo di tutti capi* of the United States. And in order to accomplish this, he felt he had to take out two obstacles: a gangster in Chicago named Al Capone—"

Canidy finished it: "—and a gangster in New York named Charlie Lucky."

"As you say, 'same song.' And Luciano had played this tune before. So, with Meyer 'Little Man' Lansky's help, he got Maranzano before Maranzano got him."

Canidy sighed. "Is there any end to all this?"

Donovan said, "Oh, it just gets better." He looked at Gurfein. "Pick up with Dewey."

Gurfein nodded, then raised an eyebrow. "Colonel, you know it—and him—better than I do, sir. I suggest you pick up that part."

It was no secret that Donovan had close connections in New York—he had been a United States Attorney in New York, a very successful one in seeing to the enforcement of Prohibition laws, before settling into a highly lucrative private practice on Wall Street.

"There's an interesting twist here," Donovan said to Canidy, rising to the story, but then had second thoughts and turned to Gurfein. "If you don't mind, I'd like to hear your take on it again, Murray."

Gurfein nodded.

"Very well, sir." He looked at Canidy. "You're familiar with Tom Dewey?"

"Just what I read in the papers," Canidy said. "Good-looking, bright guy, fearless. Ran for governor of New York—and lost—in '38 at age thirty-five, thirty-six, prosecuted big-time mobsters and other high-profile bad guys, like the leader of the American Nazis, whatshisname—"

"Fritz Kuhn," Gurfein supplied.

"—Fritz Kuhn," Canidy repeated. "Dewey is running for governor again, and will probably go from there to run for President."

"Simply put, in a short time he's cut a very wide path that's shut down a lot of people," Gurfein said. "You'd think the mob would want to rub him out—"

"Sure," Canidy said.

"—and you'd be right."

"And therein lies the twist," Donovan said.

Gurfein nodded slowly. "With Joe 'The Boss' Masseria and Salvatore 'Little Caesar' Maranzano dead and gone, Luciano and Lansky knew this was their chance to pull together the various factions of the underworld. If they didn't, well, what goes around comes around, right? So with some great dealing and convincing they managed to set up what was called 'the Commission.'"

The director of the Office of Strategic Services said: "Dutch Schultz, Lansky, Frank Costello, Joe Adonis, and of course Luciano as its chairman." He looked at Gurfein. "You tell it."

"It was, I think, 1935—"

"Right," Donovan said. "'Thirty-five."

"—and Dewey was investigating Dutch Schultz. When Dutch went into hiding, Mayor La Guardia started to really put the screws to Schultz's slot-machine racket. Needless to say, Dutch didn't like it, and proposed to the Commission that Dewey be taken out. Jonnie Torrio told him, 'You don't go whacking guys that high,' or words to that effect—"

"That's right," Donovan said. "I'd forgotten Torrio was also on the Commission. And no wonder. It was his gang that a young Luciano first joined."

Gurfein waited to see if Donovan was finished, and when the head of the OSS waved his hand in a *Go ahead* gesture, Gurfein continued:

"See, the Commission was really afraid of their own rackets taking heat—even getting shut down—after the public reacted badly to the news of the immensely popular D.A. being killed by the same scum he was trying to clean up. So when Dutch was told no, he was, shall we say, less than thrilled about not getting his way, and became so pissed that he decided that he was going to do the job himself. That is, have his goons kill Dewey. Word spread among the gangs, and when Luciano and his buddy Lansky got wind of it they knew that they had to stop Dutch Schultz."

"And the only way to do that," Candy said,

remembering the news stories, "was for Schultz to get whacked."

Gurfein took a sip of water and nodded at the same time, spilling water on the table and in his lap.

"Shit!" he said softly, then "Excuse me," and quickly patted at the wet spots with his napkin.

"So, Schultz," he went on, "real name Arthur Simon Flegenheimer, aka the notorious Beer Baron, age thirty-three, got shot in the Palace Chop House in Newark and days later died of wounds suffered."

"And Dewey lived to see another day," Donovan said, "saved, oddly enough, by the mob."

"Fascinating," Canidy said. "But what—"

"Not that that made any difference to Dewey," Gurfein interrupted, adding, "because while Luciano may have directly or indirectly kept Dewey from being killed, Luciano was far from being home free. In fact, quite the opposite. The relentless prosecutor got him good: His team of racket busters raided scores of brothels and brought in some one hundred hookers and madams. After a couple weeks in the city's Women's House of Detention, enough of them talked so that Dewey could bring charges that would stick. And, in the end, Luciano was found guilty of running prostitution rings and sentenced to a record term of thirty to fifty."

"Sounds like Dewey essentially had him tossed in the slam for life and thrown away the key," Canidy said.

"That's what everyone thought," Donovan said. "But then the ONI came calling. They were desperate—*are* desperate—for information on spies, saboteurs."

"Navy intelligence in New York," Gurfein said, picking up the next part of the story, "was having trouble—"

Canidy held up his hand to stop him. "Excuse me, Murray. Hold that thought, please, and pardon me for a moment. I'm going to make a quick visit to the gentlemen's facilities."

"Good idea," Donovan said.

He surveyed the table, now little more than a collection of dirty dishes and glasses, and there followed the sound of his foot tapping the floor. After a moment, Canidy realized that Donovan was pressing the service call button.

"We can have our coffee in the library," Donovan said. "Say, ten minutes?"

[TWO]

A silver coffee service tray was on the coffee table between the couches nearest the fireplace. Three china cups, each emptied of coffee at a different level, were on the table, as was a heavy wooden humidor.

Colonel William "Wild Bill" Donovan was seated on one couch and had leaned forward to open the lid of the humidor and dig out a cigar. His fingers found one, and, after he pulled it out, the heavy wooden lid fell shut with a resounding *bang* that carried well through the large room.

As Donovan went through the ritual of unwrapping the cigar, sniffing its length, then snipping the closed end and putting flame to the other end with an engraved, gold-plated lighter, Major Richard Canidy and Major Murray Gurfein stood at the rollaway cart of liquor.

Gurfein held fat snifters in each hand while Canidy poured into them from one of the VSOP cognac bottles, the brand of which he earlier had not recognized.

A third snifter was on the cart, and Canidy poured into it as Gurfein went to the couches, where he handed one glass of cognac to Colonel Donovan.

"You're saying that Navy intel in New York was getting reports of U-boats in the Upper Bay?" Canidy asked, incredulously.

"Yeah," Gurfein said, opening the lid of the humidor and digging out a cigar for himself. "But only reports. No sightings. Considering all the ships getting sunk not far offshore, and those saboteurs we caught last June who had come in at Long Island by U-boat, it's understandable that people would make that leap of logic. Especially after the *Normandie* went down in the Hudson, moored there at Pier 88."

"The Normandy?" Canidy said.

Gurfein, puffing deeply on his cigar as he held a match to it, nodded.

"The French luxury ocean liner SS *Normandie*," he explained, "was the world's largest ship when launched at St. Nazaire in 1932. She had crossed the Atlantic a hundred or so times when, after arriving in New York, the Coast Guard took her into custody."

"How could they do that?"

"Rather easily. France had been occupied, and they were not about to let the Krauts have her back. So, instead, the U.S. War Department then seized the ship, renamed it the USS *Lafayette*, and began converting it into a troop carrier. That process was nearly completed when, on February 9, 1942, she began to burn. The fire quickly spread, there were explosions and more flames, and the great ship turned on her side and without ceremony sank."

"Jesus Christ," Canidy said. "Incredible."

"Yeah," Gurfein said, sipping cognac. "After that, you would not believe what kinds of reports came in from the public. Everyone who looked even mildly suspicious suddenly was considered a spy or saboteur. One guy was convinced he'd seen der Führer's personal Mercedes—but the FBI, ever quick on their toes, discounted that one when two of their agents arrived to question him at the bar, on East Seventh."

Canidy chuckled. "McSorley's?"

"McSorley's Ale House indeed. They couldn't do anything with him, though. He was dusty as everything else in that hole, half in the bag, and adamant that he'd seen what he'd said he'd seen. He'd slurred, 'Why the hell can't you guys just do your jobs. The goddamned Krauts are right under your noses!'"

Now all three men chuckled.

"Have you seen her?" Gurfein said, his tone now serious. "The *Lafayette*, I mean. She's still there. It's an incredible sight. Bigger than the *Queen Mary*, but now just a burned abandoned hulk. That's a real signal for someone to send."

Canidy shook his head.

Donovan said, "I have, and you're right. It's sad. A magnificent ship burned right before it was ready to sail. You can see why rumors circulated about how it happened."

"Rumors?" Canidy repeated.

"ONI's Third Naval District," Gurfein said, "is responsible for securing the waterfront in New York, Connecticut, and part of New Jersey—"

"And," Canidy interrupted, "it reports to . . . ?"

"The Office of Naval Intelligence here in Washington," Donovan offered, "which means just about directly to Frank Knox."

Colonel Frank Knox was secretary of the Navy.

Gurfein went on: "—their key job being to see that nothing interferes with troop shipments and with shipments of supplies and ammunition. In that capacity, and in the capacity of ensuring the general safety of the waterfront, they're looking for subversive activities both in the harbor and on the coast."

"Okay," Canidy said.

"And because of that, they received all sorts of suggestions as to what happened to the *Lafayette*."

"Such as?"

"Such as the ship was sabotaged by the mob as a very clear way of saying they controlled the waterfront and could do the same to any other ship—or ships—if Luciano wasn't looked upon favorably for early release."

"Any truth to that?"

"None whatsoever," Gurfein said, somewhat defensively.

Canidy wondered what that was about.

Gurfein went on: "There have been suggestions that those with sympathy toward the Axis, particularly Fritz Kuhn's followers in the German-American Bund, set it afire to keep it—and the troops and matériel it would carry—out of the war."

"That's plausible," Canidy said.

"Yeah, it is. But so far, no one has turned up any proof. Just a lot of tips that go nowhere. Since she sank, it seems that every time someone sees a bluefish break the surface of the Hudson or East River he's convinced it's a U-boat periscope and the phones ring off the hook."

Canidy said, "And when the guys from ONI check it all out—"

"They come up with next to nothing," Gurfein said matter-of-factly, then chuckled. "Except maybe the occasional FBI agent lurking in the shadows quote undercover unquote."

"Part of why no one was getting any information," Donovan put in, "was because the mob does control the waterfront. You could put Navy guys everywhere—and they pretty much did—but then nobody talks, nobody answers questions, never mind provides leads, good or bad."

Gurfein took a puff of his cigar and let out a big blue cloud.

"It's like this," he said. "You could be standing in the middle of Fulton Fish Market and pointing to a table stacked high with tuna and asking one of the union boys,

'What kind of fish is that?' Now, if he suspected you were a Navy guy, or working for one, he'd look you square in the eye and say, 'Fish? What fish? I don't see no fuckin' fish,' then grin like he knew he had you."

"Meanwhile," Donovan said, "ships were going down in record numbers. In March '42, fifty were sunk, another fifty in April, more than a hundred in May, and on and on."

Gurfein was nodding knowingly.

"Which suggested," Donovan continued, "at least two grave situations: One, somehow information about when and where ships sailed was apparently reaching U-boats waiting, like sharks before a feeding frenzy, just offshore. Two, these U-boats seemed to have unlimited fuel; that is, they somehow were being refueled to stay on station. There simply were too many being too successful."

"So," Gurfein said, putting his cigar in an ashtray and picking up his cognac, "ONI, being in charge of the waterfront, was under great pressure to get information. And because they were in charge of the waterfront, they knew that the mob ran it and that the mob controlled the fishing boats—if not directly, then had considerable influence indirectly, because the mob controlled the Fulton Fish Market, where catches from Maine to Florida—the entire eastern seaboard—were sold. And the fellow who controlled the fish market was—*is*—Joe 'Socks' Lanza."

Canidy sat back in his seat. "So ONI approached this guy Lanza?"

Gurfein shook his head.

"Not directly. No way he'd talk," he said, then took

a sip from the glass before going on: "Joseph 'Socks' Lanza, age forty-one, a real brawler, an in-your-face kind of guy from the Lower East Side—oldest of nine kids— fought his way to be what's called the business agent of local 124, United Seafood Workers union. A long history of charges—theft, homicide, coercion—that never stuck. No witnesses, no worries. Go figger, right?"

Canidy chuckled.

"It would be funny if it weren't so true," the former assistant district attorney said. "But it's also funny— funny coincidental, not funny ha-ha—that when the D.A.'s phone rang with ONI at the other end of the line asking about a dock boss named Joe Socks, we had the guy under indictment for alleged extortion on the water- front—your basic kickbacks from workers, and beatings if they didn't pay."

"Back to your basic thuggery," Canidy said. "Wise- guy 101."

"So we set up a meeting with a couple of the Navy boys and Lanza's lawyer. We explained that we needed access, we needed answers, we needed tips, we needed anything, and would Lanza be willing to help?"

"What did you offer them?" Canidy said. "Some pos- sibility of a deal on the extortion?"

Gurfein shook his head vigorously. "Not one damned thing."

"Nothing?"

"Absolutely nothing," Gurfein repeated. "We simply appealed to their sense of patriotism."

He puffed on his cigar two times, heavily, exhaled

audibly, then took the cigar into his hand and gestured toward Candy with it as he made his point.

"You have to keep in mind that these Italians and Sicilians came to the United States for a better life and that many have family back in the old country, where Mussolini and the Fascists are making life a living hell. And keep in mind that *Il Duce* went after the mafioso in a vicious manner, appointing a special prefect with extraordinary powers to wipe them out; many wound up in penal colonies on those volcanic islands north of Sicily—the Liparis, in the Tyrrhenian Sea—while some of their bosses had to find refuge in Canada and elsewhere. So patriotism, on the surface—it's not that hard a sell."

He put the cigar back in his mouth and puffed.

Donovan said, "That's not to say that they did not *think* there might be some consideration paid at a later time, especially if their help made a real difference—"

"But," Gurfein, sitting up stiffly, shot back, "we offered *nothing*."

Donovan smiled.

"Yes, Murray, I'm not disputing that. I'm putting myself in their shoes, considering how they might have perceived the situation."

Gurfein looked at the director of the OSS a moment and realized he'd been overly defensive.

"Of course," he finally said softly. "My apologies, sir."

He slumped back in the couch.

"Not necessary but accepted," Donovan said very agreeably. "There is also the very real possibility," the director of the OSS went on, looking at Candy, "that they were open to the idea because the more information collected meant the more they knew about the waterfront. It really was to their benefit."

"And then there's that patriotism thing," Canidy said and beamed at Gurfein.

Gurfein looked at Canidy intensely, then realized he was having his chain pulled. He smiled.

"Okay, okay, I'm not that naïve. So there were *possible* plusses for both sides. Bottom line is, it worked. Slowly at first. Not every guy on the waterfront opened up immediately . . . or at all. Then someone—Lanza, I think—got the idea that with the right words said by the right people—the bosses—word would get out for everyone to cooperate. It'd grease the skids. And what better way to get the bosses to agree than to have the boss of bosses agree?"

"And it was off to see Luciano," Canidy said.

"Polakoff first," Donovan said, correcting him. "In the hotel bar, remember?"

Canidy's eyebrows went up. "Right."

"We got Luciano, without him knowing how or why, moved from Dannemora to Great Meadow," Gurfein said, "after selling it to Louis Lyons, New York's commissioner of corrections. His line was, 'If it saves the life of one American sailor, I'm all for it.'" He looked at Canidy. "That patriotism thing."

Canidy smiled. "Sure, but he's *supposed* to be on our side."

"A lot of people are *supposed* to be on our side but don't always seem to be," Gurfein replied.

"Some of my biggest enemies," Donovan added solemnly, "are here in Washington, not in Europe."

Canidy and Gurfein exchanged glances.

While exceedingly rare, it wasn't the first time that Canidy had heard the OSS chief complain about having to fight more bureaucratic battles than real ones with bullets. But from the look on Gurfein's face, it apparently was a first for him to hear such blasphemy.

"So," Gurfein went on, "they swapped eight prisoners from each prison—"

"Wonder what the seven who moved with Luciano thought they'd done right to deserve better conditions," Canidy thought aloud. "Or what the eight moved to Dannemora thought they'd done wrong."

Gurfein looked at him a moment, then corrected him. "Eight—because Luciano didn't know, either. Polakoff and Lansky had made the move as a condition of their getting Luciano to agree. Their reasoning was to have him closer so their commute to and from New York would be short, but ultimately it was, I think, a test to see how serious we were, to see if we could and would affect the transfer."

"And did he?" Canidy said.

"Agree? Not at first. Ever careful, Luciano said he was not sure who was going to win the war, and he did not want anyone knowing he cooperated. He was also afraid of being deported back to Sicily and having to suffer the wrath of Mussolini or Hitler or—maybe worse—the mafia there. It was only after Luciano considered that he'd been moved to a better place, and there he would be allowed to meet with Lansky and his lawyer whenever he wanted—"

"In the interest of providing information for the war effort," Canidy said, "and not running any rackets."

"Certainly the former," Gurfein said. "As to the latter?" He shrugged. "Regardless, in no time word worked its way down through the ranks that Luciano said to cooperate and they did. They even went so far as to issue union cards to ONI guys to work everywhere from on the fishing boats themselves to behind the counter of the hatcheck rooms in nightclubs."

Donovan said, "And, Dick, that's the kind of access you're going to need in Sicily."

"From Luciano?" Canidy said. "Do you think patriotism is going to cut it again? It's a different dynamic."

"Not necessarily," Donovan said. "What makes you think Luciano would not want to expand into his home country?"

Canidy considered that. Before he could reply, Gurfein spoke up.

"You can ask him for yourself, Dick," Gurfein said. "About the patriotism part, that is. I've got it set up for you to meet Lanza, then maybe Luciano."

[THREE]
Jacksonville, Florida
1130 28 February 1943

As Richard Koch turned the yellow-and-black 1930 Chevrolet pickup truck onto U.S. 1 and drove toward the St. Johns River, he studied the instruments on the dashboard.

He saw that the speedometer did not register—its needle rested below the zero on the dial face—and that the mileage shown on the odometer, which was not turning, was 40,348. With the odometer displaying only five digits, he knew that the numbers had to have rolled all zeros, and that meant that the truck really had, at the very least—who knew when the odometer had last worked—140,348 miles, if not 240,348.

He noticed, too, that the oil pressure and ammeter gauges seemed to be registering properly and in a good range. The needle on the gauge labeled OIL/P.S.I. pointed to 50 and the AMMETER needle bounced between 8 and 10.

He glanced at the gauge labeled FUEL. Its needle was flat against the E.

Does that mean it's broken, too, or we're out of gas? he wondered. *Either way, I have no idea how much gas is in the tank.*

He tapped the gauge glass with his right index finger. The needle didn't respond.

"Damn!" he said.

"What?" Kurt Bayer said.

"We need gas," Koch replied.

After a moment's thought, Bayer said, "They didn't issue us any ration coupons."

Even if the Abwehr had, Koch thought, *they'd probably be the wrong ones. Like that damned twenty they gave me.*

Bayer glanced around the truck, then through the back window to the cargo area where Rolf Grossman and Rudolf Cremer were riding, leaning against built-in boxes used for carrying tools and plumbing parts.

"There's probably a rubber hose back there," Bayer said. "We could siphon some from another vehicle."

Koch nodded. "Yeah, good idea." He looked at the glove box. "Just for the hell of it, check in there."

Bayer opened the glove box door and wads of discolored papers that had been crammed inside came pouring out.

"What the . . . ?" Bayer said as they fell in his lap and down to the filthy floorboard.

He began picking through the mess. There were handwritten receipts on standard forms from plumbing supply shops and blank invoices imprinted in black ink with STAN'S PLUMBING, MANHATTAN BCH, FLA.

After a moment, Bayer's voice sounded excited.

"Well, would you look at this . . ."

Koch downshifted the transmission to slow for a traffic light that was turning red—the wound in his left leg hurting when he depressed the clutch—and then looked over.

A grinning Bayer held up a small form.

On it, next to a tiny shield design that encouraged the buying of war bonds and stamps, it had UNITED STATES OF AMERICA OFFICE OF PRICE ADMINISTRATION GASOLINE RATION CARD at the top, a seven-digit serial number, and, twice the point size of the number, a big letter T. Under that was the handwritten information of the holder—Stanley Smith, who, the form stated, had agreed to "observe the rules and regulations governing rationing as issued by the Office of Price Administration"—his address, and the truck's make and model and license plate number.

Koch grinned at the rules and regulations part—*What a joke*—then his eye went to the T.

"That's good for five gallons," he said. "All we need."

He looked at Bayer.

"But when we stop," he added, "check for that rubber hose. We may need it later."

Koch, after they had finally found a gas station open and pumped fuel in what had been a dry tank, took the U.S. 1 bridge across the St. Johns River into downtown Jacksonville. He drove up Main Street, looking intently in each direction as he went through the intersections at Monroe, Duval, then Church Streets.

"Something wrong?" Bayer asked.

There now was a short coil of half-inch-diameter water hose at his feet, on top of the scattered receipts from the glove box.

Koch didn't answer right away.

A minute later, when they came to State Street, he said, "Damn, went too far. I knew this didn't look right," and turned left, drove six blocks to Broad Street, made another left, and then a right onto Water Street.

There, Bayer pointed out the train tracks.

Koch smiled and nodded, then pointed to a lamppost on the corner with a street sign that had the representation of a train track on it—*Looks like a stepladder,* Koch thought—an arrow, and JACKSONVILLE TERMINAL.

Down the street, a row of two dozen palm trees, each easily thirty feet tall, separated Water Street from the parking lot of the terminal building.

The building itself was quite grand.

"Impressive," Bayer said, marveling at its massive stone façade.

The wide entrance featured a row of fourteen Doric columns towering four stories high. The main building itself rose even higher, topped by a peaked roof.

"Typical American overkill," Koch said, unimpressed. "They say the design is a smaller version of New York's Penn Station, which, of course, was designed to copy the Roman baths." He looked at it a moment before pulling into a parking spot. "Disgusting, if you ask me."

As he pressed down on the clutch with his left leg, the wound in his leg triggered a spasm of pain and he involuntarily jerked the leg. That caused him to dump the clutch—killing the engine and banging Grossman's head on the back window.

Koch turned at the *thump,* saw the big *oberschutz*

vigorously rubbing his skull like a little boy with a boo-boo, and called back, "Sorry!"

Grossman glared back through the window.

Bayer and Koch got out of the truck.

"We'll be back shortly," Koch told the pair in the back of the truck.

"Be quick," Grossman called out as they started to walk across the parking lot toward the giant columns. "I have to piss."

Inside, Bayer thought that the terminal was even more elaborate and massive—if that was possible.

The main waiting room, light and bright, held grand arched windows that towered upward six stories to an ornate vaulted ceiling. The floor itself—the first thing he had noticed—was marble polished to an incredible gleam, which seemed to hold its shine well despite the heavy foot traffic.

And there was a mass moving through. The place was packed with hundreds of civilians and soldiers, some traveling, others there to see off or greet those traveling. They milled about the room or waited on the long wooden benches, talking, reading, couples holding hands. Many lingered in the huge restaurant and in the snack bars and newsstands. A few were even getting trims at the barbershop.

Bayer looked around the great room and saw signage indicating MAIN CONCOURSE and, just before the ornamental iron gates that led to the trains themselves, TICK-ETING.

He lost sight of Koch in the crowd, then saw him walking toward the semicircle of ticketing windows in the marble wall at the right side of the main room.

The idea was for each agent to buy two round-trip tickets to different destinations. They would give these—one for each destination—to Grossman and Cremer, who would travel on one and keep the other as an alternate route, a backup.

The reason Koch and Bayer and not Grossman and Cremer were buying the tickets was so that if someone should later try to retrace their path, there would be no one able to recall either agent having ever purchased a ticket or the destination of those tickets.

And there was enough speculation between them that they had already left a very clear trail.

Bayer navigated through the crowd. He noticed that Koch had gone to a line for a ticket window at one end of the semicircle. Bayer, accordingly, headed to a line at the opposite end.

Bayer's line was shorter. He had only three people in front of him, including a young mother holding on her hip a toddler who didn't want to be held.

Surprisingly, the line moved quickly, though, and after only ten or so minutes of Bayer being annoyed by the toddler at his feet he was at the window.

"Destination, sugar?" the young blonde woman behind the window asked pleasantly.

Bayer was caught off guard for a moment, surprised at how attractive she was. And that Southern accent seemed to drip with sweetness.

He smiled, but didn't reply.

"Where you going?" she said.

"Birmingham," he said, then remembered to add, "Round-trip."

"Atlanta or Mobile?"

He looked blankly at her. "No," he said after a moment. "Birmingham, please."

"Atlanta or Mobile?" she repeated.

Bayer, staring, wondered if he couldn't be heard over the din of the room.

The blonde rolled her eyes.

She said, "You have to connect to get to Birmingham, sugar. You can go to Mobile, then go north. Or you can go to Atlanta, then go west."

Shit! Bayer thought. *We went over this!*

"Atlanta, please," he said, trying not to appear nervous.

"That one departs in fifteen minutes or four hours. Is fifteen minutes a problem?"

He thought for a moment, then shook his head.

"Six dollars."

"Six!" he said.

She gave him a big smile, a flash of bright white teeth.

"It's the Orange Blossom Special, sugar. Real luxury. Air-conditioning and diesel power. You want cheaper, take the coal-fired train to Mobile." She paused. "It departs in two hours."

"No, no," he said, "that's fine."

He pulled out his wallet and removed a ten and two singles.

"Two, please," he said, putting the cash on the marble. "I'm with, uh, a friend."

Her eyebrows went up for a second, then she reached into a drawer, came out with eight tickets—two for each of the round-trip's four legs—then put four tickets each into two sleeves decorated with oranges and slid the sleeves toward him.

"Track 20. Y'all have a nice trip."

Bayer nodded *Thank you*, left the window, and walked toward the front door, making what he hoped was an inconspicuous glance over at Koch. He saw that Koch was still in line, with two people between him and the window.

"It's *that* way!" Bayer heard his ticket woman say.

He turned to look at her.

"The passenger boarding ramp is that way," she called, helpfully, pointing toward the ornamental iron gates. "Track 20."

Bayer waved and nodded, mouthing *Thank you*.

He went out the front door.

When he got to the truck, Cremer and Grossman were standing on either side of the cargo area, looking anxious. Grossman was closing up his duffel.

"Where's Koch?" Cremer said.

"Still in line getting the backup tickets." He discreetly set the two orange sleeves with their tickets in the cargo area. "These are the ones to Atlanta and on to Birmingham. It leaves in fifteen minutes."

"*Fifteen* minutes?" Grossman repeated.

He snatched up a sleeve, stuffed it into his coat pocket, then pulled his duffel out of the truck and swung it onto his shoulder.

"Forget the backup tickets," Grossman said, adjusting his fedora and walking toward the building.

Bayer said, "Where are you going?"

"To take a leak and catch a train."

Cremer looked at Grossman, then at Bayer, and shrugged. He grabbed his tickets and a duffel.

"Tell Koch thanks." He offered his hand, and as they shook he said, "Take care of yourself, Kurt."

"And you, Rudolf." He looked toward Grossman. "Watch yourself with him."

Cremer smiled. He waited a moment until Grossman blended in with the crowd that was entering the building, then followed.

Grossman entered the main waiting area of the terminal building. As he scanned the room, looking for a restroom sign, he saw Richard Koch walking away from the ticket windows. They locked eyes a moment, and Grossman shook his head, then immediately turned and walked in a direction away from Koch.

Just before the iron gates leading to the trains, Grossman saw a sign reading MEN. He entered and found a stall at the far end empty, then squeezed into it with his duffel and closed the door, sliding the latch to lock it.

Two minutes later, his bladder and his duffel both somewhat lighter, he exited the stall.

An anxious young man started for it, but Grossman, wrinkling his face, waved the young man off as he spiked a piece of paper on the coat hook attached to the outside of the door.

The paper, scrawled in heavy pencil, read: "Out of Order."

Koch went out the front entrance of the terminal about the time Cremer entered it, but neither saw the other in the crowd.

Bayer was at the truck, waiting in the passenger's seat, when Koch got there. Koch got in behind the wheel.

When Bayer had explained what had happened to the other two agents, Koch did not seem surprised or upset.

"Good riddance," Koch said.

Koch shifted the truck's gearbox into neutral, then depressed the starter pedal on the floorboard. Nothing happened. He pressed it again and again nothing.

"Dead battery?" Bayer said.

"Hell if I know," Koch replied, opening the door.

They got out and went to the front of the truck. Koch raised the hood. The engine had oil seeping at nearly every seam, and the oil itself had mixed with dirt to create a thin coat of oily, black cake.

Koch located the battery. It appeared to have the same oily dirt coating—how oil got on it, he had no idea—and there was a plume of gray-white corrosive growth on the battery's positive lead post.

"Nice," Bayer said. "More than enough corrosion to make it lose contact. I thought I saw a wrench in the toolbox. I'll get it."

Cremer had made his way with the flow of the crowd along the passenger boarding ramp. He saw that the end of each track had its own white stone train bumper—a big block about four by four by four—with the bold, black track number painted on it. In keeping with the landscape design scheme of rows of palm trees outside the station, each bumper was topped with a potted, four-foot-tall palm, creating a similar row inside.

Cremer came to the palm-topped, white stone train bumper with its black-painted 20. The passenger train there—its cars had ORANGE BLOSSOM SPECIAL lettered on them—appeared to be a very nice one.

He got in line to board behind a well-dressed older man in a dark two-piece suit and hat.

The man looked back at him, smiled, then stepped to the side.

"After you, soldier," the man said to Cremer, appearing pleased to offer Cremer the courtesy of going ahead of him.

Cremer thought he must have looked confused to the man because the man attempted to clarify by nodding at the olive drab duffel on Cremer's shoulder.

Now Cremer understood.

"Thank you, sir," he replied. "But I insist, you first."

That seemed to please the older man even more. He nodded and went ahead.

As Cremer boarded behind the man, he saw Grossman farther down the ramp, looking like another soldier boarding at another doorway.

It took Kurt Bayer longer than he expected to find the right-sized wrench in the toolbox, then more than a little effort to loosen the nut on the clamp that attached the electrical cable to the battery. He took his time, knowing that the corrosion had weakened metal and that if he broke the clamp they were really screwed.

A train whistle blew and Bayer checked his watch. Seventeen minutes had passed since he bought the tickets to Birmingham.

"Must be their train leaving," Koch said.

Bayer nodded and went back to working on the clamp. After a few minutes of painstakingly unscrewing the clamp nut, he finally had it loose of the lead post.

Richard Koch reached in and grabbed the cable. As he began tapping the clamp against the truck's framework, dislodging some corrosion in the process, there came a horrific explosion from behind the terminal building.

The sound from the concussion was such that it caused Bayer and Koch to jump. Richard hit his head on the underside of the truck hood.

They exchanged wide-eyed glances, then looked toward the building.

A black cloud of smoke was rising above the terminal, where the passenger-boarding-ramp area met the main building.

People came running and screaming out of the building. Some were bleeding. A few—all of them men—had their clothes on fire.

"Whatever that is," Koch said, "it's not good for us."

Bayer quickly put the clamp back on the battery post, then tightened it as best he could with the wrench.

The parking lot was becoming chaotic as people raced to their cars to get away from the explosion while others ran from their cars to try to find loved ones inside the terminal.

Bayer wasn't sure but he thought he'd just seen one woman, hysterical, bolt from her car and run to the terminal, leaving the car there with its door wide open and its engine still running.

Koch got behind the wheel of the pickup and tried to start it.

Nothing.

"Dammit!" he said, slamming his fist on the dash.

He mashed the starter pedal again.

Still nothing.

He stuck his head out of the window, looking around the open hood, but he couldn't see Bayer.

"Now, what the hell?" Koch muttered.

As he got out of the truck, he heard Bayer call, "Richard!"

He turned and saw Bayer putting their two duffel

bags into the backseat of a 1940 Ford sedan, then getting behind the wheel.

Koch went to the passenger's door, got in, and Bayer calmly eased away as police cars and fire trucks, sirens wailing, began arriving.

Koch gave Bayer directions on how to take Bay Street east, back to Main, where he could make a left turn to drive north on U.S. 1.

[FOUR]
Penn Station
New York City, New York
1130 6 March 1943

As the Washington–Baltimore–New York commuter train rolled into Pennsylvania Station in midtown Manhattan, its brakes making a long, high-pitched squeal, Major Richard Canidy, United States Army Air Forces, prepared to put the sheet of paper that he had been reading back in its brown accordion folder. Murray Gurfein had given the folder to him when Gurfein had dropped him off earlier that morning at Union Station in Washington, D.C.

The folder was fat, packed with a three-inch-thick stack of research that represented the highlights of Gurfein's background check of Charles "Lucky" Luciano. As Canidy glanced at the last sheet of paper, he found its contents curious though not necessarily surprising:

New York Department of Corrections
Great Meadow Prison
Comstock (Washington County), New York

Medical Evaluation of:

LUCIANO, CHARLES

Inmate #92168

The inmate noted above, a White Male, Age
44, has been examined by this physician
and the following conditions have been
found:

HEAD: Normal. Scalp clean.
EYES: Normal, corrected. Vision, right, 90
percent. Vision, left, 90 percent.
NOSE: Clear.
MOUTH: Teeth good, tonsils not visible.
NECK: Normal, with notable scar. Thyroid
normal.
EARS: Hearing 36/36 both ears.
CHEST: Normal. Lungs clear.
HEART: Strong, with occasional murmurs.
GENITALIA: Negative for penile scars, dis-
charge.
RECTUM: Negative for hemorrhoids.
PULSE: 75 resting, 95 after mild exercise,
77 after 2 minutes rest.
BLOOD PRESSURE: 125/85.

HEIGHT: 5-8.

WEIGHT: 158.

WASSERMANN: Negative.

NOTE: Due to the existence of heart murmurs, it is this physician's opinion that
the inmate NOT be assigned duties that are
arduous (i.e., laundry work).

Signed this 12th Day of May 1942

L A Thume MD

Leo A. Thume, M.D.

Canidy's eye paused on the line noting the results of the Wassermann test—the German bacteriologist August von Wassermann in 1906 designed it as the definitive diagnosis for the sexually transmitted disease of syphilis—and it brought to mind the other wild information on the mobster that Murray Gurfein had supplied in detail at dinner the previous night, including that in the course of running prostitution rackets Luciano had sampled his own product—just as he'd sampled the heroin he ran—enough to contract syphilis once and gonorrhea eight times.

The train came to a complete stop, and Canidy slipped the page back into the folder and then the folder into his leather attaché case—being careful to keep it clear of the Colt Model 1911 .45 ACP semiautomatic—as he and the other passengers on the packed train gathered their belongings to disembark.

The door at the end of the car opened and two New York City transit cops came through. Canidy noted that the policemen were making a fairly thorough visual inspection of the passengers as they passed.

He didn't think anything more of it until he was walking through Penn Station, en route to the cabstand, when he noticed what appeared to be a heavier-than-normal presence of cops. Then he seemed to remember that there had been quite a few D.C. cops in Union Station.

It struck him as odd that he was just now noticing it— *I'm supposed to be more situationally aware than most people*—but then he recalled that that famous sociologist, Dr. Whatshisface, found that everyone allowed people in uniform to be invisible to them.

It was a fact not lost on criminals, who commonly put on, say, a postman's uniform to get an edge when committing a crime. When it came time for witnesses to be interviewed by police investigators, the witnesses would not remember seeing a face—"Just a mailman."

Still, I need to pay better attention, Canidy thought.

The cabstand had a long line of people waiting.

Canidy walked past it, headed east on Thirty-second Street. Two blocks later, he was able to hail a cab from the corner of Broadway.

He got in the backseat, gave the driver the address— 117 South Street—and the car shot south down Broadway.

Someone had left a copy of the *New York World-Telegram* on the seat and he picked it up and scanned the headlines. One was about FDR—what had become the

World's usual daily headline taking the President to task on what he had said—or not said—the previous day about the war, or the economy . . . or the price of blue cheese.

Another headline announced a story on Lieutenant General George Kenney's Fifth Air Force attack on a Japanese convoy in the Bismarck Sea that sank four of its destroyers and all eight of its transports—with half of the seven thousand Japanese troops lost.

And yet another led into an article that carried newly released details on the Allied convoy ON-166, which had fourteen ships sunk by U-boats in the Atlantic in late February.

Then there was one, and the short piece beneath it, that caught his attention:

DEATH TOLLS RISE
IN GEORGIA & FLORIDA

```
10 Dead After Explosions in Train Stations
  Official: "No Connection Between Blasts"


          By Jeffrey Csatari/
          New York World-Telegram


ATLANTA, Mar. 5th — Two more people died to-
day from injuries suffered in an explosion
Sunday night at the Atlanta Terminal Sta-
tion here and in another explosion earlier
at Florida's Jacksonville Terminal.
```

Today's deaths bring the total dead from both blasts to 10. Another 32 people were injured; 4 remain hospitalized.

While some witnesses have called the two explosions at the train stations "highly suspicious," local and federal officials investigating the incidents say that there is nothing to link them except simple coincidence.

"There is no connection between the blasts," said Christopher Gilman, Special Agent in Charge of the Atlanta office of the F.B.I. "End of story."

An official close to the investigation in Jacksonville, who asked not to be identified, said: "It's looking like a faulty gas line to a heater in the men's room was responsible, but we're unable to confirm that at this time."

When asked about the report of a German pistol being found at the scene of the Atlanta Terminal Station explosion, Gilman said, "We have no other comment."

The cabbie accelerated heavily down Broadway, honking the horn steadily, and Canidy looked up from the paper to find that the driver was trying to make it through the light at Seventeenth Street before it turned red.

After another ten minutes of such mindless driving—
and countless near collisions along the meandering route—
the driver turned off of Fulton onto South Street, passed
the fish market, and came to a sudden stop with a squeal
of brakes and screech of tires.

A New York City traffic cop had South Street blocked
off, his patrol car parked at an angle, the fender-mounted
emergency lights flashing red.

"What is it?" Canidy asked the cabbie.

"Dunno," he said, his head out the window, straining
to see past the cop.

Canidy could see only traffic backed up and some cops
getting out wooden barricades with orange and black
stripes and starting to assemble them.

He looked at the street addresses just out of his window and realized he was only a half block shy of the address Gurfein had given him for Meyer's Hotel, where
Joe "Socks" Lanza kept a regular room to conduct business away from the fish market nearby.

He reached into his pocket, pulled out a bill to pay the
fare, said, "Here you go," and grabbed his attaché case,
then slid out of the backseat.

He made his way along the sidewalk, past the line of
cars stopped by the police car and around one of the cops
who was just now erecting a barricade on the sidewalk.

"Hey, buddy!" the cop called. "You can't—"

Pretending he didn't hear him, Canidy kept walking
toward 117 South Street.

A moment later, he heard the cop mutter, "Awfuckit."

Ahead, at Meyer's Hotel—a shabby establishment four stories high with maybe thirty rooms, half of which were at any one time being used by the mob—Canidy saw a small half circle of cops gathered at the entrance of the building. They were looking at something slumped against the building.

Canidy looked closer.

Not some*thing*. Some*one*.

He knew what the body of a dead man looked like.

As Canidy approached the building, he saw that a burly guy in a leather cap and wearing the outfit of a fish-monger—flannel shirt, greasy overalls, knee-high rubber boots—was leaning against the wall.

The fishmonger stepped forward and blocked his path.

"Nobody goes in," the huge guy said.

He was six-two, two-fifty—at least—and Canidy found himself having to look up at him.

"I've got a meeting," Canidy replied, undeterred. "You a cop or what?"

The guy eyed him. "Your name Kennedy?"

When Canidy studied his eyes, he saw a no-nonsense look. "Canidy," he said.

"Yeah. He told me to take you to meet him." The guy looked over his shoulder at the crime scene. "Something came up."

"Apparently," Canidy said.

V

Major Richard Canidy, in the uniform of the United States Army Air Forces, carried his leather attaché as he followed the monster of a fishmonger two blocks south, then, turning onto Fletcher Street, another two blocks west.

We must make a curious-looking pair, Canidy mused.

"In here," the guy said when they got to a twenty-four-hour restaurant on the corner where Fletcher met Pearl. It was all he had said the entire four-block walk from Meyer's Hotel.

They entered, and Canidy saw that the restaurant—a diner, really, small and not brightly lit—was mostly full, with a working-class lunch crowd of truck drivers, heavy-construction workers, postmen, even a couple of street-beat cops.

There was the murmur of conversation mixed with the clanking of forks and knives on plates and, just now, the breaking of a water glass accidentally dropped on the black-and-white mosaic tile floor by the lone busboy hustling to clear a table. The smell of garlic and onion was heavy in the air.

The layout of the rectangular room was long and narrow. On the left, at the front by the plate-glass window looking out onto Pearl Street, was a wooden counter with a dozen vinyl-cushion-topped swivel stools on three-foot-high chrome pedestals. Along the right wall, a series of wooden booths and tables ran from the front window to the back wall, each table set for four customers, and each with a black-framed photograph of a Greek island scene nailed to the wall beside it. At the very back, through a single swinging metal door with a window, was the busy kitchen.

A waiter, having kicked open the swinging door, came out of the kitchen balancing on his shoulder a huge, round serving tray piled high with plates of sandwiches and potato chips and bowls of soups. The light from the kitchen briefly illuminated the darkened booths near the back wall. Then the door swung shut, making a *flap-flap-flap* sound before finally becoming still.

For a moment, Canidy could better see, sitting in the farthest booth and facing the front door, a rough-looking Guinea about the age of fifty, with a cup of coffee in his hand and talking to someone seated across the table and out of Canidy's view.

"Back here," the fishmonger said.

As the guy made his way toward the rear of the restaurant, some of the workers looked up from their meals and nodded and he wordlessly acknowledged the greetings.

They reached the booth, and Canidy saw that the man was dressed like the fishmonger he had followed—long-sleeved flannel shirt, dirty overalls, rubber boots.

And Canidy saw that the man seated across from him, in a cheap black suit, was about five-eight and one-fifty, midthirties, with slight features and pale skin. He also was drinking coffee—but an espresso—and next to his tiny cup there was a copy of *Il Nuovo Mondo*, the anti-Fascist newspaper published in New York, with a photograph of Benito Mussolini on the front page.

"This is the guy," the fishmonger said to the two at the table by way of greeting.

The man in the cheap suit looked up.

"I'm Joe Guerin," he said, moving so that he was half standing with his hand out.

The lawyer, Canidy thought, remembering Murray Gurfein's description.

He shook the offered hand and replied, "Dick Canidy. Nice to meet you."

"This is Mr. Lanza," Guerin added, "my client."

Joe Socks—short and pudgy, with a pockmarked face and a bad haircut—looked at Canidy with cold, hard eyes. Canidy knew from Gurfein's background information that Lanza was forty-one years old, but he sure didn't look it. The hard living showed.

Canidy offered his hand and Lanza shook it with a very firm grip.

"Pleased to meet you," Canidy said, impressed by the mobster's heavily callused hand.

Lanza, stone-faced, replied only with a nod.

"Have a seat," Guerin said, motioning to a place beside himself and opposite Lanza.

As Canidy sat down, putting his attaché case at his feet, the monster fishmonger stepped away from the table and positioned himself in the back corner of the restaurant, out of the kitchen traffic, with a clear view of both the front door and the booth with Canidy, Lanza, and Guerin.

"Our friend contacted me," Guerin began, "and I in turned asked Mr. Lanza if he would be open to this meeting."

"Thank you," Canidy said to Guerin, then looked at Lanza and said, "Thank you."

Lanza made a slow blink of acknowledgment.

Guerin took a sip of coffee, then said, "Oh, excuse me. Would you care for something to eat? The food is very good here."

"Thank you, but nothing right now," Canidy replied. He looked at the cup. "Coffee would be nice."

Guerin got the fishmonger's attention, held up his cup and pointed to it, then to Canidy. The guy walked over to where a waiter was putting cups of coffee and espressos onto a tray, took from it one of the espressos—earning him a sharp look from the waiter—and a moment later slid the steaming cup in front of Canidy.

"Thanks," Canidy said.

The fishmonger wordlessly returned to his post.

Guerin said, "Now, what is it that you need, Mr. Canidy?"

Canidy looked at him a moment, and thought, *What*

the hell am I supposed to do? Come out right here in public and tell a Guinea gangster that I want the Boss to set me up with the mafia in Sicily? This is unbelievably surreal, even for me.

"Did Mur—" Canidy began, then caught himself. "Did our friend give you any indication as to the subject?"

Guerin shook his head. "Only that it is of the utmost importance," he said.

Well, that's just great.

Canidy glanced at the fishmonger, who was staring at the front door. He wanted to look that way, too, to at least see if anyone would be able to overhear what he was about to say. But that did not seem the proper thing to do at this point.

"I'm not sure here is the best place to discuss this," Canidy said finally.

Guerin looked around casually. "Here is fine. Nothing happens without my client's say. Nick, the owner, is protected."

Canidy wanted to reply, *Like nothing happens at your hotel?*

He instead said, "With respect, this is not the place. Things—"

"Things what?" Guerin said impatiently.

Canidy picked up on that.

Oh, to hell with it.

"—Things happen, like the surprise at the hotel."

"That," Lanza said, suddenly and coldly, "was a misunderstanding and it is being dealt with."

"It is not what I want to happen here," Canidy said evenly. "A misunderstanding." Now he looked around the room, then back at Lanza. "A misunderstanding after someone overhears something that they shouldn't."

They stared at each other a moment, then Lanza said quietly, "After some guys at Brooklyn Terminal thought they could slow down the ship loading, we had them kicked in the ass. That led to this other thing just now. All a misunderstanding." He shrugged. "These things, they happen. Then they're dealt with."

"Dealt with"? Canidy thought, looking at the emotionless eyes. *As in, made to go away?*

Lanza went on, his manner conversational: "Let's get back to why we're here. You came to us because of our mutual friend. We have an understanding—an honorable one—with our friend, as you clearly do. That makes you *gli amici*, friend of friend. *Capiche?*"

He paused, glanced at his coffee, looking bored.

"So," he went on, "tell us what it is that you need."

Canidy raised his eyebrows.

"Yessir, Colonel Donovan, mission accomplished. I secured an 'honorable understanding' with the murderous mob!"

Jesus, this is incredibly surreal.

But, okay . . .

"Okay," he said. "I need to speak with Charlie about getting some help like our friend got."

Lanza looked at him with renewed interest. "'Charlie'?"

Canidy nodded.

"And what more could you want?" Lanza said. "We

are already giving every kind of help possible. Here, and all up and down the coast."

Canidy leaned forward and quietly said, "Charlie's home."

"We got Brooklyn covered," Lanza said.

Canidy shook his head. "His real home."

"Yeah, and we got it—" he said, then stopped, and his right eyebrow went up. "You mean . . . ?"

"Yeah," Canidy said.

Lanza's eyes darted to Guerin, who looked back and shrugged.

"What would you be needing in his . . . home?" Lanza said to Canidy.

"Contacts," Canidy said. "Locals with connections, with information, who would be willing to build an underground resistance against"—he put his right index finger on Mussolini's photograph on the front page of *Il Nuovo Mondo*—"certain individuals."

Lanza, showing no emotion, considered that. He said, "Why didn't you go straight to him with your request? Why me?"

Canidy nodded; he had expected Lanza might ask that.

"Respect," Canidy said.

When he said it, he saw Lanza's eyes light up a little.

Murray Gurfein, the onetime New York assistant district attorney, had explained to Canidy that, despite the general perception of the underworld as ruthless and cold-blooded, the mafia prided itself on respect—or at least the appearance of respect. They considered it a vital component in keeping their social order intact. Without respect for the bosses, respect for the organizations, their society would devolve into nothing more than bitter bloody turf battles—conflicts no one would ultimately win.

"When I discussed it with our friend," Canidy went on, "I said I wanted first to develop a relationship with those who I'd be working with, then with their blessing take it higher."

Lanza studied Canidy without saying anything.

"We could have just as easily called Mr. Polakoff as Mr. Guerin here," Canidy said, mentioning Luciano's attorney as a matter of fact. "But it would not have been respectful to the people I also would be asking for help."

Lanza did not respond to that. He said, "And what would Charlie be getting in return?"

Canidy thought of Murray Gurfein being defensive at dinner, and grinned.

"Something funny?" Lanza said.

Canidy heard a Lower East Side tough-guy tone of voice that he figured had to be close to what Lanza used when he was about to put the screws to someone who had not paid his protection money or his kickback.

"No, not at all," Canidy said, earnest but unnerved. He took a sip of his espresso, then looked Lanza in the eye. "To answer your question, he would be getting what he is getting now, a deep sense of patriotism for his part in helping to win the war."

Lanza held the eye contact for a long moment, then looked away deep in thought. He drained his coffee cup, set it down in its saucer with a *clank*, and nodded.

"E cosa mia," he said finally.

Canidy's face showed that he did not comprehend.

"It is my thing," Lanza said with some semblance of a faint smile. "Leave it to me."

[TWO]

When Dick Canidy stepped out of Nick's Café onto the busy sidewalk, after Joe "Socks" Lanza had told him that he was sure he could pull together something for that night and to call Meyer's Hotel in two hours for an update, he decided that he needed to clear his head and think all this through.

And one of the best ways Canidy knew to do that was to take a walk.

First, though, he realized that his original plan for the day—to take the late train back to Washington, which was why he had not brought a suitcase—was now changed and that he needed a place to spend the night.

And he also needed a destination to walk.

May as well be one and the same, he thought.

He went to the street corner, to the bank of three pay-telephones there, picked up the handset of the only phone not being used, dropped in a coin, and asked for the Gramercy Park Hotel.

When he was connected by the operator with the front desk clerk, she said that they had a few rooms available, but since it was getting to be afternoon he would do well to come directly to the hotel in order to secure one.

He said that he'd be there in about an hour—maybe sooner—and hung up the phone.

He started walking north on Pearl and noticed that while the air still was crisp and cold, the sky had cleared and the sun, now shining brightly on his side of the street, felt warm and refreshing.

And after that encounter with a cold-blooded mobster, Canidy thought as he crossed to go west on Fulton, *I could use something—anything—to break the chill.*

Canidy walked along, trying to put his finger on what bothered him—and something did indeed deeply disturb him—about Lanza.

Is it the corruption? His background of coercion, beatings, killings—the basic thuggery? Sure, some of that.

Hell, it was all *of that.*

But don't be naïve, Dick, because the fact is that in all of history there has been corruption, and with corruption comes the violence of coercion, beatings, killings, and more.

After a few blocks, he made a right at the corner of Broadway. City Hall came into view.

And here's proof that there always will be corruption—politicians.

What makes a coat-and-tie pol getting a kickback for awarding a city public works contract any better than a Guinea goon in rubber boots getting one for "protecting" a café owner or the hookers in his hotel?

It's not the absence of violence. Don't kid yourself. Many a politician has met an ugly end for failing to do as agreed—particularly when in bed with the mob.

Canidy walked past the grand City Hall grounds, admiring the building and marveling at the memory of just how much—and how blatantly—Boss Tweed, as New York City's commissioner of public works, and the political machine known as Tammany Hall had stolen in the 1860s and '70s.

What was it, some two hundred million dollars? Corruption of unbelievable proportions.

And who the hell knew how much the Honorable La Guardia had to pay—or still was paying—Tammany Hall for his election as mayor?

And with that kind of money involved, only a fool would believe that no one got hurt—that a kneecap or two didn't get popped, that someone wasn't forced to take a long walk on a short pier—in the process.

So Canidy told himself that it wasn't the ugly underbelly of the mob that really disturbed him.

It was more the fact that he innately, and perhaps too easily, understood how and why the mafia worked.

And he understood that he now had to work with it—"to dance with the devil," as Colonel Donovan had said.

What the mob does is not a good thing. But it is better than anything that Hitler and Mussolini have in mind.

Just shy of crossing Canal Street, Canidy passed a series of storefronts and noticed the window of one in particular that advertised a sale on religious books.

It caused him to wonder, as he continued north, how much of an impact the news of his association with the underworld would make on his father. That is, *if* he told him—and he had absolutely no intention of even suggesting it to him.

The Reverend George Crater Canidy, Ph.D., D.D., was the headmaster of St. Paul's School in Cedar Rapids, Iowa. He was a kind and good man—a true gentle man—whose faith in the Lord Jesus Christ was surpassed—if that was at all possible—by his dedication to the education and well-being of the students put under his care.

The Reverend Dr. Canidy lived in the Episcopal school's dormitory, in a small, separate apartment there, and had his office nearby, which allowed him to spend every possible minute on the mission that he devoutly believed to be one of the highest and most noble callings a man could have.

Dick Canidy loved his father. He respected him—genuinely, in the truest definition of the word, not the bastardized version that he had used with that Guinea sonofabitch just now.

The Reverend Dr. Canidy had had his share of disappointments in life, yet he always had stayed strong while he suffered them silently.

He had long been a widower; Dick had no real memory of his mother—other than a vague recollection of visits to a hospital room with a bad odor in her final months—but knew that her illness had not been a short one and that his father had shouldered the responsibility of her care with remarkable strength and quiet courage.

Afterward, he also had delicately handled the new role of single parent and teacher.

That might have been his toughest challenge, Canidy

thought now, and grinned mischievously as he approached Houston Street.

Young Dick had been somewhat difficult, and the troubles really reached a head when a young man name Eric Fulmar was enrolled a grade behind him in the lower school.

Eric had arrived at St. Paul's with a bad attitude—he knew that he was being stuck somewhere safe for the convenience of his mother, Monica Carlisle, the vivacious and—if you believed the studio publicity people—young actress prone to playing coed roles.

It absolutely was not good PR for Miss Carlisle to have a son—and one so old!—and, even worse, if the truth got out, a child who was unwanted, whose father was a German industrialist close to Hitler.

So off Eric was shipped to Iowa.

There, he and Canidy made fast friends, and in no time they were boys being boys—the pinnacle of which was misbehavior that resulted in piles of fall leaves being set afire . . . and their flames accidentally following a path to the fuel tank of a Studebaker President.

The explosion was spectacular, as was the reaction of everyone to it.

To smooth things over, Miss Carlisle's studio sent a sharp young lawyer—one by the name of Stanley Fine—and with the miracle of a calm demeanor and a checkbook, all was made right.

Everything except the disappointment young Dick saw in his father's eyes.

It was much the same look that, not much later, when Dick was determined to learn to fly at the local airfield, he had seen in his father's eyes when it became clear that the son had no desire to follow the path that the father had hoped—into either the church or academia.

Canidy, dodging a cab as he crossed Tenth Street, knew that it would be quite the same look if the Reverend Dr. Canidy were to learn of his most recent dealings with the murderous and the corrupt.

Dad would not care for it one bit. He's like most people. He wants to believe in the good, and only the good—and that's okay.

It just leaves dealing with the bad to guys like me, and that's okay, too.

Except . . . except maybe that's what's so troubling to me.

How can a father and son be so different?

Then again, maybe we're not.

It's not as though I'm dealing with these goddamned Guinea gangsters because I want to; in fact, I don't want to.

I'm doing it because it's necessary.

A block south of Union Square, Canidy came to the storefront of an expensive lingerie shop and Ann Chambers came immediately to mind.

But Dad would like Ann.

He looked in the window, at the display, and had graphic thoughts about the lingerie and Ann.

And what about Ann?

That is one incredible woman—and a long way, in many ways, from the young coed I first met two years ago at her family's Alabama plantation.

Beautiful, smart . . . and determined. Her capacity for affection and care is off the chart.

And it's not as if I have none of those feelings for her.

I'm just not accustomed to having feelings for only one woman for any length of time. Fifteen, twenty minutes max, making me one sorry sonofabitch.

So then . . . where is this going, this "relationship"?

The war is not going to end tomorrow, or next week, and I can't keep promising her that I won't go away—then immediately break that promise.

This is what I do.

And now I'm off to Sicily?

I'm going to need some help with that, help handling these mob guys.

Maybe I can get Fulmar. Or Stan Fine. Screw David Bruce.

Sicily! Jesus!

Ann won't like that . . . me gone again to parts unknown.

Canidy noticed a display of silk hosiery.

I'd be smart to bring back some of those for her. And some soaps and fragrances. Yeah, after I hit the hotel I'll head back here, then over to Kiehl's, over on Third Avenue and—what?

He looked at the street sign—it read 13TH.

That's it. Third and Thirteenth. Come to think of it, without my Dopp kit I need deodorant and stuff, too. But first, the room.

[**THREE**]
Gramercy Park Hotel
2 Lexington Avenue
New York City, New York
1415 6 March 1943

Dick Canidy pushed hard on the gleaming brass bar of the heavy revolving door of what he considered to be one of the city's best-kept secrets.

The Gramercy, built in the 1920s of brick in a renaissance revival style, had a simple elegance that was in keeping with its quiet but very nice neighborhood. It even had a private park across the street.

It was, Canidy believed, every bit as elegant as, say, the Roosevelt up on Madison at Forty-fifth—only some twenty or so blocks north—but a world away from the feel of a crazed city outside your door.

So without really trying, the hotel drew a wide spectrum of guests, including high-level politicians and a slew of celebrities on the way up—or down. There were all kinds of stories about the stars, including, Canidy recalled hearing, that Humphrey Bogart had been married to his first or second wife—or maybe it was both of them—in the rooftop garden.

Some of the well-heeled kept apartments here, and it was not unheard of for one of the elevators to open on the ground floor and have, say, a couple of Old English sheepdogs come bounding out, pulling a resident off of the elevator—clearing a path between the regular guests—on their way to the private neighborhood park.

All of this served to give the place the comfortable feeling of home—a very nice home—and Canidy tried to stay here every opportunity he could.

As he entered the hotel lobby, he could see people seated in the oversized armchairs beneath the understated chandelier. There were others moving to catch one of the elevators to the left of the room. And directly ahead of him was the front desk with, to his great disappointment, a line of three people.

He joined them—two young men and a woman a bit older—and began to worry that he had taken too long to get to the hotel. The woman he had spoken to on the telephone had said that there had been only a few rooms left. Now, clearly, there were a few people in front of him, and there was no telling how many had come and gone in the time since he called about an hour ago.

The front desk was actually a massive slab of dark polished stone, some eight feet long, set atop finely milled oak paneling. Filling the wall behind the two clerks working the desk was an impressive honeycomb of at least a hundred cubbyholes, also fashioned of oak, each box about six by six inches, with a brass number affixed to the bottom lip. Visible inside them were room keys, messages, an occasional envelope.

At the head of the line was a young man in a business suit. Canidy heard him give his name and room number and ask if there had been any messages. The clerk turned to the wall of cubbyholes, reached into one, and retrieved a small stack of note-sized messages. The young man took them, thanked the clerk, and turned away as he thumbed through the stack, now leaving two people ahead of Canidy.

Next in line was a woman of about fifty, well-dressed, and when she approached the desk the clerk smiled and warmly greeted her by name.

Canidy overheard her ask the clerk for another key to her room.

"Because," she said, making a face and turning to gesture at the young man behind her, "my son seems to have locked both my key and his in his room."

The clerk turned to the cubbyholes, reached in one and then in another, taking a duplicate key from each, and then gave one to the mother and one to the son.

As they left, Canidy sighed with relief.

He stepped up to the desk.

The clerk—his name tag read VICTOR—smiled.

"How may I help you, sir?" Victor said.

"I called a short time ago about a room."

"Welcome to the Gramercy. One moment, please. I'll see what we have available."

Victor went to a wooden, open-topped box filled with five-by-seven-inch index cards. He flipped through the cards, wrinkled his face once, then twice. He pulled out one card, looked at it, then shook his head as he put it back in the box. He flipped farther back. His eyebrows went up suddenly and he smiled.

He turned to Canidy with the card.

"We do have something," Victor said and smiled again. "A very nice one-bedroom suite."

"Suite?"

"Yessir," Victor replied, producing a blank registration card and fountain pen. "It overlooks the park. Very nice."

Canidy knew that the Gramercy's rooms were huge, and that the smallest of the huge were on the twelfth floor.

"Nothing smaller? Maybe something on twelve, overlooking Twenty-first?"

The clerk's eyes brightened a moment, indicating that he caught that this was not Canidy's first visit. Then he frowned and shook his head. "No, sir. I'm afraid not."

Canidy did not respond.

What's a suite going to cost?

What do I care? It's not my money.

And the OSS has nearly limitless funds.

Still, I don't like just throwing it away.

"Is there a problem?" Victor said.

Canidy looked at him.

Well, hell, it's just for one night. Who knows what miserable place I'll be sleeping in tomorrow night, or the next.

Canidy was about to open his mouth when Victor leaned forward.

Quietly he said, "I do believe that for a regular guest such as yourself I can offer one of the singles on twelve *if* you'll allow me to upgrade you to a suite for the same rate."

Canidy's eyebrows went up. "That would be very nice. Thank you."

"My pleasure."

Victor watched as Canidy began writing his name on the registration card. The clerk turned his head, almost touching his left ear to his left shoulder, as he tried to read the card so that it was not upside down.

" 'Canidy'?" Victor said, looking thoughtful.

"Richard," he confirmed, looking at him.

The clerk turned to the cubbyholes and from one with a brass tag stamped MISC he pulled out an assortment of odd-sized pieces of paper. Canidy recognized some of them as being message notes like the first man in line received when Canidy joined the line.

The clerk pulled one of the message sheets from the stack, put the bulk of the papers back in the cubbyhole, then turned to Canidy.

"This came for you"—he glanced at the line on the form where the time had been handwritten—"twenty minutes ago."

What the hell? Canidy thought, the hairs on the back of his neck standing on end. *No one knew I was coming here.*

Hell, I didn't know until an hour ago.

He looked around him, checking the lobby. He saw nothing but the same mix of harmless-looking guests going about their business.

He quickly took the form from Victor, somewhat offending the clerk with his brusqueness, and scanned it.

All that was written on it, on the appropriate lines, was: "3/6, 2:05, Mr. Canidy, WOrth 2-7625."

Canidy looked at Victor. "There's no name on the 'from' line. Any idea who called?"

Victor reached out for the form, looked at it, then looked at Canidy.

"No, sir," he said. "I'm sorry. I didn't take this. The operator did."

"Where's WOrth?"

Victor looked again at the message. "That would be a number for the Lower East Side, down around the fish market."

Canidy nodded. "Thank you. Can I get that room key now?"

[**FOUR**]
Suite 601
Gramercy Park Hotel
2 Lexington Avenue
New York City, New York
1445 6 March 1943

Dick Canidy got on an empty elevator, pushed the 6 button, and when the doors had closed removed the Colt .45 ACP semiautomatic from his attaché case and slipped it in the small of his back.

Who knew I was here? And how?

Does the mob have insiders working here, too?

The elevator stopped and opened on the sixth floor. He stuck his head out, looking down the hall to the left and then to the right.

Nothing.

He glanced at the small signage on the wall opposite the elevator. It listed a series of room numbers that included 601, with an arrow pointing left.

He went left down the hall, found the door, put in his key and turned it.

He reached inside the door to the suite and flipped on the light switch, then entered and closed the door behind him. He went quickly through the suite, throwing light switches and checking the bedroom, the closet, the bathroom, under the bed.

There was nothing unusual—and certainly no one—in any of the rooms.

It had to be one of the guys using the pay phones outside the diner. One of them worked for Lanza and had been waiting there to follow me, then got lucky when he overheard my phone conversation. He may have even seen the number that I dialed.

But then they called ahead, left the message at the hotel before I had a chance to call them.

Did they do that to send a bigger message—"We can find you"—or was it them just not thinking.

Either way, it's not good.

Dammit, Dick! Watch your back!

He looked around the suite and now noticed that it was very nice.

It had an outer room with two large couches and two oversized armchairs with ottomans, all upholstered in the same fine, light-colored fabric. There was a large oval coffee table, with copies of *Time* and *Look* and the *Saturday Evening Post* magazines on top and a big bowl of potpourri, which gave the room a pleasant, floral scent. A side table between the oversized armchairs held a thin brass lamp and a black telephone.

Canidy put his attaché case on the coffee table—
almost dumping the bowl of potpourri—went to the
door, locked the deadbolt, then stuck the .45 in his front
right pants pocket. The pistol butt stuck out, but that
didn't bother him.

He walked over to the closed curtain that covered one
wall. The curtain went from the floor to the ceiling, and
when he pulled back one side he saw that Victor, the
front desk clerk, had not exaggerated about the view.

The suite did have a very nice perspective on the
whole neighborhood, and especially on the private park
across the street. The room was up just high enough to
see everything, yet not so high for details—the park's
nicely manicured topiaries, dense bushes planted in intricate checkerboard and circular patterns, and such—to be
lost in the distance. There was a woman sitting on one of
the wrought-iron benches, and he could almost distinguish what she was reading, while a wirehaired terrier
pawed at a ball at her feet.

He let the curtain fall closed, then went through the
door into the bedroom.

It had elegant wallpaper with vertical pinstripes in
navy and silver. The light pine headboard and footboard
of the king-sized bed matched the bedside tables on either side and the enormous dresser with its large mirror.

What a waste for one person! Ann would love this!

Canidy went into the bathroom, took a leak, then
washed his hands and face at the white porcelain sink.

He removed one of the thick, soft white-cotton hand
towels—each one, including the fat bath towels, had

GRAMERCY PARK HOTEL stitched in neat green half-inch-high lettering—from the chrome ring affixed to the white-tiled wall and, almost like he was praying, buried his face in it.

What the hell am I getting myself into?

Then he looked up and at himself in the mirror above the sink.

Make the call.

In the outer room of the suite, he went to the armchairs, pulled the pistol from his right pocket, and put it on the side table next to the telephone. He then reached into his pocket for the message with the Lower East Side phone number and sat in the armchair to the left of the phone.

He picked up the receiver, double-checked the number on the message, and asked for 962-7625.

The call was answered on the third ring.

"Dunn," a deep male voice said.

"Is this WOrth-two-seven-six-two-five?"

"Yeah."

"My name is Canidy. I have a message to call but no name."

"Yeah?"

"You didn't leave this number?"

"What'd you say your name was?"

"Canidy. C-A-N—"

"Hang on."

Canidy heard the *clunk* sound of the receiver being put down on a hard surface, then the sound of footsteps, then, faintly in the distance, the sound of the man's voice relating their conversation. After a moment, the footsteps grew louder and the receiver was picked up from the hard surface.

"Hello?" a different voice said in Canidy's ear.

"This is Richard—"

"Yeah, I remember," the voice said sarcastically. "We just met."

Lanza?

"Listen," Lanza continued, "that thing we talked about? I got someone you want to meet. Eight o'clock tonight, you go out of your hotel, walk to the northeast corner of the park across the street, and a car will be there to pick you up. Got it?"

I didn't tell him what hotel. Clearly, he knows. And he's not making anything of it, just letting me twist knowing that he knows.

"Eight," Canidy said, "northeast corner. Got it. What—"

"And get out of that uniform. You won't need it. Get in something you won't care if it gets dirty. Or wet."

Wet?

Canidy heard the connection break.

He checked his chronometer. It was three o'clock.

Five hours. Not a lot of time.

Canidy, the .45 tucked again into the small of his back, took the elevator back down to the first floor. At the front desk, Victor was still there, and Canidy asked him where the nearest shop was that he could buy some casual, rugged clothing.

"For any special purpose?" Victor asked.

Yeah, Canidy thought, *something that can get dirty and wet.* "You know, Victor, mob kind of stuff."

Hell, I don't know.

"Khakis, flannel shirt," Canidy said, thinking about what Lanza and the monster fishmonger had been wearing. He didn't mention the rubber boots.

"Leonwood's," Victor said immediately.

"What's that?"

"The outfitter L.L. Bean?"

"Yeah, Leon Leonwood. But he's in Maine."

"Uh-huh. That's the main story—with and without the *e*—but there's a small basement store on the other side of Union Square that sells last year's clothes and returns at a deep discount."

Canidy's face lit up. "Perfect! Good stuff at a cheap price."

Victor took a slip of paper and wrote "Leonwood's, 867 Broadway @ 17th" on it and slid it across the polished stone.

"Thank you," Canidy said and turned to go through the revolving door.

An hour and a half later, a grinning Canidy walked up the basement steps of Leonwood's and out onto Broadway.

He carried a big, nondescript brown paper bag packed with three pairs of khakis, two in navy and one in brown; a pair of tobacco-colored, waxed-canvas pants; three flannel shirts in dark, solid colors; a pair of black leather boots; a dark brown field coat; three pairs of black woolen socks; two packages of white cotton boxers and T-shirts; a woolen knit cap; and one wooden duck call, something that he had always wanted and Leonwood's was just about giving them away.

Jesus, I spent a bundle. But for what I got, I saved a bundle, too.

And for what I saved, I can now go to that nice lingerie store and then over to Kiehl's.

Candy had more trouble in the lingerie store than he had in Leonwood's. A lot more trouble. He had been shopping for a half hour and had yet to pick out one nice thing to buy for Ann.

Operative word: *nice.*

He kept looking at items, picking them up, then feeling guilty and putting them back on the shelf.

This was a helluva lot easier at Leonwood's. There, I knew what I needed.

Now I don't know if I'm shopping for Ann—or for me.

He was finally rescued by a pleasant young woman salesclerk.

She walked and talked him through the merchandise, starting out with the silk hosiery.

Damn! I could have picked those out on my own, but no, I had to go straight to the lacy stuff.

One very small but very expensive box later, he was on

his way to Third and Thirteenth, his brown bag only slightly heavier and his wallet significantly lighter.

Filling a shopping basket at KIEHL'S SINCE 1851 was accomplished with much more ease. Canidy pretty much went through the women's section of the store, putting one or two of everything in it.

How can I go wrong? This stuff's been winning women's hearts for almost a hundred years.

He had various bottles of skin moisturizers, face cleansers, bath oils, some kind of cream that softened and removed calluses from feet—and more.

And he splurged on himself, buying a small bar of moisturizing soap to use when he shaved and a stick of antiperspirant.

Now, as he headed back to the hotel, he had a second bag, one nearly the size of—and at least the weight of—the one containing the clothing.

This day is getting more surreal by the moment.

Who would believe I'd be shopping at the same time that I have a date with the mob?

Canidy went through the revolving door of the Gramercy Park Hotel. He looked toward the front desk; if Victor was there, he wanted to thank him for sending him to Leonwood's. But Victor wasn't, so Canidy went to the elevators and caught the next one up.

In his room, he put down the bags on the big bed and went through the one containing his clothes, laying out what he would wear that night.

He checked his watch. Six o'clock.

He realized that he had not eaten since breakfast that morning. In Washington.

Have I really covered this much ground in just one day?

I need to catch a nap.

His stomach growled.

And . . . I need something to eat.

The Gramercy's lounge was off of the lobby, and Canidy, passing the polished-stone front desk, could already hear the lively crowd before he entered.

The lounge featured a terrific massive wooden bar, small round tables with plush, intimate seating, and a gleaming grand piano at which a fellow was playing what Canidy thought was a Duke Ellington piece.

He took one of the empty seats at the bar and asked the bartender for a menu. While he scanned it, the bartender put a glass of ice water and small bowl of orange fish-shaped crackers in front of him. Canidy popped a couple of the crackers into his mouth.

Mmmm. Cheddar-flavored. Nice.

The crackers almost immediately made him thirsty and he looked at the small forest of spigot handles on the draft beers, saw a good Hessian family name that he recognized as a brewery in Bucks County, Pennsylvania, got the bartender's attention and pointed to it. When the lager was delivered, he ordered something that he thought would be quick: a steak sandwich with chips.

He sipped his beer and munched on the cheddar crackers, looking in the mirror to watch the crowd in the room.

So who here has mob connections? He grunted. *Besides me, that is.*

The piano player? One of the waitresses?

The bartender?

Murray Gurfein said that through the unions the mob touched just about everything.

He also said the mob was good about getting union cards issued to the Navy guys for undercover work at the docks, on boats and trucks, in hotels and restaurants.

Not quite five minutes later, the bartender produced a plate with his sandwich.

Canidy looked at him with new interest.

Bet he's a spook with—what did Gurfein call it?— "Local 16 of the Hotel and Restaurant Workers International Alliance and Bartenders Union."

"Thank you," Canidy said, then grinned as he picked up the sandwich.

Nah, he thought, taking a bite. *On second thought, even the mob wouldn't let a Navy guy near the booze.*

The sliced steak on a fresh, hard-crusted baguette turned out to be not only quick but first-class. The beef was a sirloin strip that had been lightly marinated and perfectly grilled to medium-rare, the chips were actually more like steak fries, and the fat pickle was crisp, ice-cold, and almost oozed garlic.

Candidy finished his meal in no time—*I didn't realize how hungry I was*—and he waved for the check as he finished the last of his beer. He signed it to the room and left.

Back in the suite, he took a hot shower, then pulled on his new clothes.

He folded his uniform and put it in the cleaning bag from the closet, then called downstairs for it to be picked up.

"I'll need it cleaned and pressed," he said into the phone, "and returned by first thing—"

He yawned, long and hard, and looked at the clock on the bedside table. It showed seven-thirty.

Fifteen minutes. That's all I need.

"—in the morning," he finished, then added: "And I'd like a wake-up call for seven-fifty, please."

"Yessir, a wake-up call for seven-fifty a.m."

"No, p.m."

There was a pause, then, "Yessir, seven-fifty *p.m.*"

Candidy set the alarm on the windup clock beside the bed as a backup, then pushed aside the rest of the clothes that he had bought and lay down on the bed.

The next sounds he heard—the nonstop *ring-ring ring-ring* of the phone and the clanging of the alarm clock—shook him from a deep sleep.

He looked quickly at the clock. Eight o'clock.

"Damn!"

He jumped up, collected his thoughts.

He went to the curtain, pulled it back, and looked out at the northeast corner of the park. No car appeared to be waiting.

Okay. Maybe he's late, too. Let's go.

He took his .45 off of the bed, stuck it in the small of his back, pulled on the new field coat, stuffed the woolen knit cap in his pocket, then rushed out to the elevators.

He pushed the DOWN button, but neither elevator responded. The indicators over the doors—a half circle of numbers with an arrow, the one over the left elevator pointing to 10 and the one over the right to 1—did not move.

Hell, I'm only on the sixth floor.

He ran down the hallway, pushed open the heavy metal door, and took the bare concrete stairs of the fire escape down two at a time.

He opened the door marked FLOOR 1 and saw that he was down the hall from the main lobby. He went to it, then out through the revolving door.

When he got to the northeast corner of the park, he looked around in the dim light. He still could see no car that seemed to be there for him.

There was, however, a sudden movement behind him, against the fence that circled the park. His hair stood up on the back of his neck, and the pistol in his back seemed a very long way away from his right hand.

Just as he started to turn toward it while reaching for the .45, the movement surged toward him, causing him to jump back.

A well-fed cat then flew down the sidewalk.

Jesus. Get it together or it's going to be one long night.

He saw a cab circling the park. It made the turn onto the street where he stood, began to slow, then pulled to the curb in front of him. The back door opened.

"Get in," a vaguely familiar voice said.

Candidy did, but there was no one else in the car, only the driver, who was huge.

The monster fishmonger.

Candidy slid in and pulled the door closed. "Where are we going?"

"Not far."

He drove off with a heavy foot on the accelerator.

Candidy kept track of their route. The cabbie fishmonger—*What the hell else does he do?*—made a number of turns and soon was flying south down Second Avenue, headed for the Lower East Side.

No surprise there, I guess.

After a bit of jogging down different streets, Candidy saw a sign reading SOUTH STREET and he decided that they were headed for Meyer's Hotel.

Maybe all the dead bodies have been cleaned up by now.

Without slowing, they drove right past Meyer's Hotel.

What the hell?

Two blocks later, the fishmonger turned east and, now driving slowly, wended his way down to dockage on the East River.

Beyond a tall wooden piling with a sign reading PIER 10 there was moored a rusty steel-hulled vessel about seventy feet long. A cargo truck was alongside it, on the

wooden finger of the dock, and what looked like steve-
dores were moving something off the boat.

"This is it," the fishmonger said.

"*It* what?"

"The *Annie*," the fishmonger said, then looked over
his shoulder. "Get out."

[FIVE]
Room 305
The Adolphus Hotel
1321 Commerce Street
Dallas, Texas
1540 5 March 1943

Rolf Grossman was anxious.

The German agent paced the spacious room of the
downtown luxury hotel where he and Rudolf Cremer
had been staying since Wednesday, when they had arrived
by train from Birmingham.

All week they had been trying to keep a low profile—
especially after Grossman's screwup Sunday night when
he dropped his Walther PPK somewhere in the Atlanta
train station—and now that something was finally about
to happen, he was unbearable.

"How much longer?" he said.

Cremer, sitting at one end of the long couch by the
open window, looked casually over the top of the afternoon edition of the Dallas *Daily Times-Herald*.

He did not like this behavior just before they carried
out an operation. Grossman always became too agitated

and his heightened attitude tended to make him careless. Losing the damned pistol was an obvious example.

Both men were dressed in simple black suits, white shirts, and black leather shoes that could stand a shine.

Cremer glanced at his Hamilton wristwatch.

"Soon," he said. "The commuter rush begins in about twenty minutes. Be patient."

Grossman walked around the suitcases that they had bought in the second-hand store in Birmingham and that they now had placed by the door and went to the Westinghouse radio that was on a table beside one of the two beds. He turned the ON-OFF/VOLUME dial and the speaker crackled. He tried to tune in a station by turning the other dial, but all he got was static. He hit the side of the radio with the open palm of his left hand.

"I've hated this hotel since we got here," Grossman said disgustedly. He almost spat out the words.

"I like it," Cremer said in an even tone. "That beer baron—"

"A traitor to our country, if you ask me."

Cremer shrugged. "So you keep saying. Busch began making beer in America in the middle 1800s. I don't think it is fair to judge him now, almost a hundred years later, using your standards for this war."

Grossman grunted. "You are either German or you're not."

"Remind me of your family background again?" Cremer said.

Grossman had confided during the long train trip from Birmingham to Dallas that his mother was French.

He glowered at Cremer.

"All I know for sure," Cremer went on, "is that he built a very nice hotel in a place that is not very nice. It has none of that cowboy nonsense we've seen everywhere else."

Adolphus Busch, as might be expected of one so named, saw to it that the hotel bearing his name was heavily influenced by European design. He built a bit of Bavaria on the north Texas prairie, creating an oasis of elegance in a town that was otherwise rather rough around the edges.

The guests Grossman and Cremer had seen clearly were wealthy, though the two noticed that their dress was not necessarily always up to the standards of what might be expected of, say, the German upper class attending functions at the Hotel Berlin.

Granted, almost without exception the women of the Adolphus dressed quite fashionably, and many practically dripped in diamonds.

The clothing of the men, though, covered a wide range.

Some of them wore well-fitted suits with pointed-toe, Western-style boots, their black leather skins buffed to a deep shine. Instead of a necktie, a few had on a bolo, a finely braided leather cord that was clasped at the shirt-collar button by an elaborate slide fashioned by craftsmen of silver and gems.

Most of the other men at the Adolphus, however, were not concerned with such niceties. They had the weathered look of ranchers—hardworking and honest men—and it reflected in their clothes. If they happened to have on suit coats, the garments were not freshly pressed—one had even showed dirt—and their boots, whether the toes were pointed or rounded, went unpolished.

As it happened, this worked in the favor of Cremer and Grossman.

Cremer said, "No one has looked twice at us here, proving no one would expect to find a couple of German nationals suspected of blowing up things hiding in an expensive hotel."

Cremer flipped the pages of the Dallas *Daily Times-Herald,* found what he was looking for, then folded the paper.

"Especially," he added, "when those agents appear to be blowing up things on the East Coast."

He held out the folded paper to Grossman.

"Here. Read this."

Grossman walked over, took the paper, and found the article.

POWER OUTAGES SPREAD

Baltimore Latest to Lose Power;
3 Cities in 3 Days Go Dark
Governor Calls for Calm

By Michael B. Goldman
Daily Times-Herald Washington Bureau Chief

WASHINGTON, D.C., Mar. 5 — The mayor of Baltimore, MD, last night called his entire police department on duty after more than half of that port city's downtown area lost electrical power.

The outage began at 6 o'clock and lasted for more than five hours.

Confusion struck commuters the hardest, with busy train stations coming to a halt and city streets gridlocked until well after midnight.

Hospital emergency rooms were reported to be operating at peak capacity with record numbers of injured being admitted. A hospital representative who would not speak officially put the figure at "hundreds."

"It is important to have a strong police presence at such times," Mayor Sean Mac-Donald said, explaining his emergency action. "The public expects it."

By this morning, power and calm had returned to downtown Baltimore.

But, according to some, there was anything but calm among the general population.

"People are scared," said Maryland state representative Silas Rippy, a Demo-

crat whose district includes downtown Baltimore. "This is exactly what happened on Tuesday in Carolina and on Thursday in Virginia. They're calling it a 'coincidence.' This is no coincidence. We want — and we deserve — real answers."

Downtown areas of Charlotte, NC, and Richmond, Va., lost electrical power this week, causing injury and panic.

According to Baltimore Power & Light, the cause of the Maryland power failure also was faulty equipment.

"It is an unfortunate coincidence," said Carl Hemple, BP&L Director of Public Relations. "This particular power grid happened to have the same equipment — indeed the same series of manufacture — as the others that went down. It appears that all of the grids were weakened by what we all know has been a worse than usual winter season. It's just that simple."

Agents from the Federal Bureau of Investigation, who had been looking into the event in North Carolina and Virginia, and now are reviewing this one in Maryland, agreed.

"The fact is that it is similar equipment failing under similar conditions,"

said Special Agent Mark Davis of F.B.I.
headquarters here in Washington. "All
grids are being inspected, and any weaknesses found are being corrected."

That explanation, Representative Rippy
said, was not good enough.

"Hundreds upon hundreds have been
hurt," he said. "First it was the train
stations. Now this. Who and what is next?"

Maryland Governor Harold Clarke called
on citizens to remain calm.

"Let's all exercise good judgment," he
said from his office in the capitol. "And
please join me and pray for those injured
in this unfortunate event."

Grossman handed the newspaper back to Cremer and
said, "The cover story of the government is good. But it
does not seem to be believed."

Cremer nodded. "Possibly. But the good news is that
the public is reacting just as we had hoped. Bayer and
Koch are doing a good job. Steady, small attacks. Let the
people cause their own problems." He looked directly at
Grossman. "That's what we need to do, too. No more
big blasts."

Grossman glared back.

"Okay," he said. "Enough. I told you that it was a
mistake to use so much explosive in the Atlanta train station lockers."

He looked at the coffee table, where there were two identical sets of explosives and primers laid out.

"These should be just enough to cause the necessary confusion," he said.

Cremer nodded, then looked at his watch. He put aside the newspaper.

"Okay. It's close enough to time. Let's go."

Grossman went to the table, picked up one set of the explosives, and put it in a small black leather case.

They took one of the five massive elevators down to the first floor, then crossed the richly carpeted lobby and went down the steps to the entrance.

A doorman opened one of the large beveled-glass-and-bronze doors, tipped his hat, and said, "Good day, gentlemen," as they passed onto the busy sidewalk.

They walked up Commerce Street, keeping pace with the crowd of businessmen and secretaries who appeared to have just left their offices.

Ahead of them, a couple of men in suits and ties went through the revolving door of the fancy bar and grill that was a part of the Adolphus. The bar had large, inviting windows overlooking the sidewalk. Cremer looked inside as they passed and watched the two men who had just entered join an animated crowd of businessmen and -women standing at the long, classy brass bar for Friday happy hour.

At the street corner, after waiting for the light to change, Cremer and Grossman crossed Akard Street—

dodging an automobile running the red light—and continued along Commerce.

About halfway up the block, a series of department store windows began. The goods in the large displays looked very much like what they had seen all week on guests at the hotel—very fine and expensive clothing and jewelry.

Almost at the end of the block, they came to a large elaborate entrance into the department store itself.

Grossman glanced at Cremer, who nodded, and they followed four attractive young women through the doors under shiny metalwork that read: NEIMAN MARCUS.

Inside, Cremer followed one of the women—a blonde—to the right while Grossman continued straight, behind two brunettes.

The store was full of customers, mostly women, but more than a few men. An off-duty Dallas policeman, in uniform and armed, working as store security, was riding the escalator to the second floor, scanning the first-floor crowd as he ascended, and then was gone.

The blonde walked slowly past one of the brightly lit glass display cases, admired the earrings there, then continued walking. Cremer stopped and feigned interest in the jewelry while keeping an eye on Grossman.

As planned, Grossman was approaching the counter in the corner that displayed leather goods—wallets, purses, belts, and more.

After he casually looked at the contents of one case, a nicely dressed, dark-haired salesgirl behind the counter walked up and began speaking to him.

Grossman nodded, pointed to something in the display, and the salesclerk took out a key, unlocked the back of the display, and pulled out a wallet.

Grossman casually put the small leather case with the explosives on the counter beside an open black box containing leather key rings and took the wallet.

"Can I help you?" a young woman's voice asked, startling Cremer.

He turned and now saw a pretty redheaded salesclerk standing behind the display with the earrings.

"Oh, no," he said and smiled. "Thank you, but no. I just got distracted."

"These can do that," the redhead said, looking at the earrings.

"Yes, yes they can," Cremer said and started walking toward the leather goods section.

When he reached it, Grossman was at the end of the counter, shaking his head and frowning as he handed back the wallet to the salesclerk.

Cremer heard him say, "Not quite what I need. I'll just keep looking."

"Very well," the salesclerk said, then saw Cremer and turned to help him. When she had reached him, she asked, "Can I help you with something?"

"Yes, please," he said and pointed to a purse at the end of the counter farthest from Grossman. "I'm thinking of something for my girlfriend."

As the salesclerk showed Cremer a large brown purse, he saw Grossman in his peripheral vision walking away from the display—without the small black leather case.

Fifteen minutes later, Cremer held a small brown paper bag with vertical stripes and the store logotype on it.
In it was a half pound of warm salted cashews.

He put a handful in his mouth, then, chewing, went
out the doors on the opposite side of the store that he
and Grossman had entered, turned left on the sidewalk,
went down Main Street for two blocks, made another
left, onto Field, then came back to Commerce, turned,
and went through the glass-and-bronze doors of the
Adolphus.

Grossman had his suitcase in hand when Cremer
reached the room.

Cremer looked to the coffee table; the second set of
explosive and primer was no longer there.

"Okay," Cremer said, nodding, "you go on. I'll see
you at the station."

Cremer guessed that it was maybe six hundred meters
from the hotel to Union Station and so far every step of
the way he had half-expected the explosive to go off in
that fancy department store with the Jewish name.

Grossman had set the fuses too short in the train stations in both Jacksonville and Atlanta. He had almost
blown himself up in Atlanta.

Cremer had told him to set up the trigger—an ampoule of acid that caused a slow burn until it activated the
fuse—so that it would not fire for at least an hour.

But with Grossman having again been so anxious,
Cremer knew that there was a good chance he had

screwed that up and so half-expected the bomb would go off at any moment.

He came to South Houston Street and made a left turn.

And when it does blow, it will certainly cause a curious new twist for the Americans to consider.

First it had been train stations and power plants on the East Coast.

And now Neiman's—a Jude Speicher—in Texas?

How will officials explain this as a "coincidence"?

He joined the crowd making its way to and through the front doors of Union Station.

Especially when the train station down the street from the store gets hit, too.

Inside the terminal, half a dozen Dallas policemen watched the people walk through.

He saw a freestanding sign that read TO TRAINS and had an arrow with U.S.O. above it. He snugged his hat down on his head, and as he headed for the sign he heard the keening of fire-engine sirens down the street. Three of the cops went running out the door.

He looked at his Hamilton and shook his head in disgust.

Only thirty minutes.

VI

Dick Canidy stood on the dock on the East River and watched the taillights of the taxicab with the fishmonger at the wheel disappear into the distance.

He sniffed, then groaned.

Jesus, that's raw.

The massive timbers of the dock reeked of dead fish, despite the cold temperatures, and this was on top of the heavy odor of diesel fuel that over the years had been spilled and then soaked into the wood. He idly wondered how bad the assault on the senses must be in the summer heat.

Canidy saw that the dock had piers about fifty yards long jutting into the river, most with boats moored to them, and longshoremen on and around the boats.

He looked at the activity out at the end of the wooden finger with the PIER 10 sign. He could make out the shapes of the cargo truck and the big boat there but not much detail.

There was light shining from across the river—from the Brooklyn Terminal, where a line of Liberty ships was being loaded—but there were almost no lights here on the dock and those few that were burning had been masked or otherwise dimmed. Even the Brooklyn Bridge looming in the distance was mostly darkened.

There was of course a reason for this. It had been almost a year since the order had come—in April 1942, as the vicious U-boat attacks off the East Coast continued to escalate—for all unnecessary lighting on the New York waterfront to be turned out.

The wind gusted, and Canidy buttoned up his jacket, then pulled the woolen knit cap from his pocket and pulled it on his head, grateful that he now was dressed for the winter woods of Maine, or at least the New York City equivalent.

As he moved toward the boat, he began to pick out details. What from the distance had been a great bulk of rusty black-painted steel hull rising from the river now had rigging and winches and cables and crew—and a name.

ANNIE was painted in tall, white block lettering high on the black bow.

She was an ocean fishing vessel. Three-quarters of her seventy-foot length, from the stern to just shy of the white pilothouse on the bow, formed a large, flat, open working area with heavy-duty fishing equipment for long-lining (running out miles of baited hooks for hours at a time) and a series of hatches above deep cargo holds. A steel mast towered behind the pilothouse, and its boom, controlled by a series of steel cables, reached from the foot of the tower almost to the back of the boat.

Canidy stopped beside the cargo truck and watched as a guy in a thick, dark woolen sweater and black rubber overalls operated levers that were connected to the winches that moved the boom.

The boom was in the process of lifting a crate—Canidy could now see that it held the iced-down carcasses of large billfish and sharks—from one of the ship holds. Two other men were standing on the back of the cargo truck, waiting to guide the crate onto a stack of other crates already there.

"Watch it, there!" the taller of the two guys on the truck called out to Canidy.

Canidy turned and looked at him.

"That crate's gonna swing right over your head," the guy went on, "and you really don't want to be there when it does."

Canidy looked at the crate hanging from the boom cable and saw that a steady stream of what looked like water flowed from its lowest corner. He then took a closer look at the crates on the truck; they were dripping wet, and a slimy liquid ran in rivulets from them, down the truck bed, then drained onto the dock and through the cracks between timber, making, he thought, as it hit the river, a sound similar to the taking of a massive leak.

He stepped back some twenty feet, what he thought was a sufficient distance, and now stood next to the gangplank that led aboard the *Annie*. From there, he watched the crate swing right over where he had been standing—leaving a very wet trail as it went—and then with a different whine from the winch, be lowered to the truck, where the two men manhandled it into place on a stack of other crates before the cable went slack.

The cable was unhooked and the winch operator manipulated the levers. The winches made a high-pitched whine as the cable was recovered and the boom swung back aboard.

The taller man jumped down from the truck and walked toward the gangplank.

"You Canidy?" he said as he approached.

The thick accent clearly was Italian—probably Sicilian, Canidy guessed.

The man, a head taller than Canidy, looked to be about thirty-five and solidly built. He had an olive complexion, thick black hair that was cut close to the scalp, a rather large nose, and a black mustache.

"Yeah, I'm Canidy."

"C'mon aboard," he said, brushing past.

As Canidy followed him to the rusty pilothouse, the truck on the dock started its engine and with a grinding of gears began to pull away with the crates of fish.

Canidy saw that the deckhand who had been working the boom was now securing it and the cable, and the guy who had been on the truck had moved down the finger of the dock and was beginning to untie the starboard bowline from a cleat.

The tall man went to the steel door of the pilothouse, opened it, and went through it.

Canidy began to follow, but the man turned and pointed to the bow of the boat.

"You mind tending to lines?"

Canidy looked forward. "Sure," he said.

"Come back when we're under way."

Under way? Where the hell are we going?

Is this godforsaken rust bucket really seaworthy?

Canidy shrugged and went back out the door, then to the bow.

He heard the sound of a motor struggling to start, then a rumble of exhaust, and he felt a vibration in his feet as a big diesel engine came to life. A moment later, there was another slow rumble, and the vibration from the deck was more pronounced.

The guy on the dock holding the bowline coiled it, shouted, "Line!" then tossed it aboard.

Canidy caught it, then recoiled it and secured it to a cleat.

The guy, after having pushed the gangplank aboard, was now at a cleat midway on the dock, untying the line there.

Canidy went toward him, stepping over the gangplank. As he got closer, the guy shouted, "Line!" and threw it.

This time, Canidy missed the rope.

It landed on the wet deck. He picked it up, and as he began to coil it he realized that this rope was markedly different from the first.

It had a cold slime on it, and it smelled of fish.

Shit! It's the same slop that leaked from the crates!

His hands began to ache from the cold and wet.

He saw that the guy on the deck was now at the dock cleat at the back of the boat and very shortly would be throwing the line aboard. If Canidy didn't get there first, that line was going to get slimed, too.

He quickly coiled the line in his hand, in the process slinging slop onto his pants.

Well, that's what Lanza meant by dirty and wet. . . .

He secured the line, then rushed toward the stern. He hit a slippery spot, started to slide, and, for one terrifying moment, thought that he would skid off of the deck and into the damned river.

He regained his traction, and, in a somewhat comic fashion, fast-walked the rest of the way.

"Line!"

Canidy got to the stern just as the rope came sailing aboard.

He secured it, then looked back and watched as the guy on the dock jumped aboard at the stern, miraculously landing solidly on the fish-slimed deck.

If I'd done that, I'd have slid all the way to New Jersey.

The guy tipped his hat to say thanks for the help, and Canidy turned for the front of the boat.

As he walked to the pilothouse, he could see the tall man inside, lit by small spots of light from the instrument panel, motioning for him to come in.

He went to the steel door and entered.

It was bare-bones inside the pilothouse—a ragged captain's chair on a pedestal, two old wooden folding chairs against the far wall, two wooden bunks bolted one above the other on the back wall, and nothing more. A pair of Ithaca Model 37 12-gauge pump shotguns with battered stocks stood on their butts in a makeshift rack to the left of the helm.

Canidy noticed that it felt slightly warmer inside but figured that was mostly because there was no wind. The smell of fish still was strong.

The tall man was alone, standing at the helm, facing forward and scanning the river beyond the bank of windows.

"Thanks for the hand with the lines," he said, looking at Canidy in the reflection of the window.

"No problem," Canidy said, rubbing his hands.

"There's a wipe rag by the door, if you want."

Canidy looked and found a crusty, brown-stained towel hanging on a small peg.

Better than nothing, I suppose.

He got the slime off his cold hands as best he could, put the towel back, then walked toward the helm.

The tall man kept his eyes on the river, navigating the *Annie* past a Liberty ship that was moving toward the Brooklyn Terminal docks.

He extended his right hand to Canidy.

"Francesco Nola," he said.

Canidy took it. The grip was firm, the hand rough. "Richard Canidy, Captain."

"Call me Frank."

"I'm Dick." He looked out the window. "Mind if I ask where we're headed?"

Canidy saw Nola grin slightly.

The captain said, "I was told you're looking for information." He paused. "I thought you might want to go along as we refuel a U-boat."

Canidy stared at Nola's face in the reflection, trying to determine if he was serious.

After a moment, Canidy said evenly, "If that's a joke, it's not funny."

They were out of the East River now, entering Upper New York Bay.

Nola used the open palm of his right hand to gently bump the twin throttle controls forward. There was a slight hesitation, as if the engines had become flooded with fuel, then the rumble grew a little louder and the bow came up as the boat gained speed.

"No, it's not funny at all," Nola finally responded.

Canidy saw in the reflection that the captain's face had tensed.

Nola added, "It certainly wasn't when I was accused of it."

He was refueling U-boats? Jesus H. Christ! I should shoot him myself!

"Do I understand you to say—"

"Your government boys impounded my boat out at Montauk last year, about six months after I bought it."

"'My boys'? What boys?"

"Your government bureau of investigating."

"The FBI?"

"Yes. They said that I was using the *Annie* to run fuel to the German submarines."

"You're here now, so I assume you weren't?"

"No," he said coldly. "I was not."

Canidy smelled something different in the air, then realized that it was a warm draft coming from a floor vent. The engines had warmed and were producing heat for the pilothouse. A fishy-smelling heat.

"But they still impounded your boat?"

"Yes. I found out—much later—it was because I had had the boat in the docks at Massapequa, being worked on. When my *Annie* had been the *Irish Lass,* belonging to someone else during Prohibition, she was a rum-runner. And when these workers, the ship—what is the word?"

"Shipwrights?"

"—these shipwrights went deep into the holds, they discovered bulkheads that were not right. They removed them and found the large compartments. One had fourteen cases of vodka still in it. I was shocked. But, so what? It is legal to have liquor now. Yes?"

"Yeah."

"But word got back to Montauk that the *Annie* had been a rumrunner, and that it had these special bulkheads. Then the story became that the owner of the *Annie*—who looked Italian and spoke the language like a native—had sympathies to Mussolini and the Germans and instead of running rum behind those bulkheads he was running diesel fuel in bladders to the U-boats. And as everything about the story was true except the part about Fascist sympathies and fuel running, it all became the truth. People believe what they want to believe, yes? And the government took my boat."

Candidy looked off to starboard and could see in the distance the lights of the military terminal on the western shore of the bay, at Bayonne, New Jersey. Liberty ships were being loaded there, with more in the bay waiting their turn, just as at the Brooklyn Terminal.

"I do not blame them; it's their job," Nola went on and gestured toward the ships at Bayonne. "These U-boats are causing great damage to our efforts to win the war."

He stopped and chuckled to himself.

"Listen to me. 'Our' efforts. I am doing nothing. I am not a U.S. citizen. I am only a Sicilian fisherman. And not even that now."

He turned and looked at Canidy.

"If I could," he added, his voice rising, "I would blow those bastards and their U-boats out of the water myself!"

Canidy saw that there was a burning intensity in Nola's eyes.

Is he trying to convince me of something with this little speech?

"I will tell you something," the captain continued, his face softening somewhat. "I did not want to leave Sicily. I *had* to, because of that bastard Mussolini." He paused. "It is not safe for me there. Mussolini's men do unspeakable things. And they accused some of my uncles and cousins of being mafia and took them to the prisons on the small islands. It was only time before they accused me of the same."

Canidy saw that Nola had tensed, his hands gripping the helm tighter.

"And I had to leave for my Annie."

The boat . . . ?

"You see, my wife is Jewish. I would not stay. We could not."

Is he going to cry?

He is crying.

Nola cleared his throat. "Please excuse me. This all means so much to me. I'm not a U.S. citizen. But I want to fight those bastards. For my wife, for my uncles and cousins, for my country."

Canidy didn't say anything. When it was clear that the captain had finished, at least for the moment, he said, "You were talking about the *Annie*. How did you get your boat back?"

The captain was looking forward again, hands a little relaxed on the wheel.

"The Navy," he said.

"The *Navy* got it back?"

Nola nodded. "Without my boat, I was out of work. Mr. Lanza asked me why I had stopped selling my catch at the fish market. I told him my story. He said he'd look into it. A week later, I got a call—'Come get your boat.' Mr. Lanza said he had the Navy get it back."

He had Murray Gurfein get it back for you. But no need to split hairs.

Nola added, "Now, Mr. Lanza tells me that you need information for the war." He looked in the reflection at Canidy. "I am at your service. My family of fishermen is at your service."

What the hell am I going to do with fishermen?

Unless . . . they have a boat.

Candidy said, "Does your family have a boat?"

"Nothing like the *Annie,* of course."

Great! Maybe it's actually seaworthy.

"I understand. But a boat that could get men around the islands unnoticed?"

"Yes. Two."

"Two boats?"

Nola nodded. "Two—what is the word?—*fleets.*"

[**TWO**]
Office of the President's Physician
The White House
1600 Pennsylvania Avenue, NW
Washington, D.C.
1815 6 March 1943

"That will be all for now, Charles," the President of the United States of America said, wheeling himself through the side door into the nicely appointed office.

The valet—Charles Maples, a distinguished-looking older black man with gray hair, wearing a stiff white shirt and jacket, black slacks, and impeccably shined black leather shoes—had just put a large wooden tray holding a pitcher of ice, a selection of liquors in crystal decanters, three crystal glasses, a carafe of coffee, and three china mugs on the doctor's spotless oak desk.

Seated in deep comfortable armchairs across the room were William J. Donovan, director of the Office of Strategic Services; and J. Edgar Hoover, director of the

Federal Bureau of Investigation. Both wore dark suits and ties. They stood up.

"Good evening, gentlemen," the President said.

"Good evening, sir," they replied almost in unison.

The valet said, "Please, let me know if I can be of further service."

"See that we're not disturbed," Roosevelt replied.

"Yes, Mr. President."

The valet went out the main door and it quietly clicked closed behind him.

Roosevelt—without a suit coat but in pants, white dress shirt, and a striped bow tie, and with a cigarette holder clenched in his teeth—rolled his wheelchair over to where Donovan and Hoover stood.

"Please, sit," he said.

The FBI and OSS heads shared a New Year's Day birthday, a fervent sense of patriotism, and, to varying degrees, the ear of the President—but that was it.

There was not any sort of animosity between them—in fact, they thought well of one another—but there was certainly a difference in both how they perceived their missions and how they carried them out.

The FBI head saw things in black and white, while the OSS chief acknowledged the many shades of gray.

Hoover, forty-eight years old, had been head of the bureau for just shy of nineteen years. He devoutly believed that the law was the law—period—and ran the FBI with an iron fist.

There was no questioning his competence and his success. The FBI under his leadership had become an extremely efficient law enforcement agency.

The most efficient one, the brash Hoover would be first to say. And he unapologetically corrected anyone who thought otherwise.

The FBI director had the habit of seeking out the limelight in the interest of making himself—which was to say the bureau, since Hoover *was* the FBI—look better.

In the 1930s, he had made a name for himself and the bureau by going after the mob—"the despicable thugs who threaten our law and order and, in turn, our very civilization," he declared.

He assigned special agents to spend whatever was necessary—months, years, and who knew how much money—to hunt down such vicious gangsters as "Pretty Boy" Floyd and "Machine Gun" Kelly.

When the agents found a mobster, Hoover swooped in on the night of the bust, and was there, front and center, when the press's camera bulbs popped.

It actually was brilliant PR—at which Hoover proved to be a very clever player—because the better his FBI looked in the eyes of the public, the more it helped to get money and other considerations from his connections on Capitol Hill and Roosevelt's inner circle at the White House.

And Hoover had his ways to get what he wanted.

Among other things, he kept secret dossiers on anyone he thought to be (a) suspicious and possibly dangerous—subversive or worse—to the United States, and (b) possibly dangerous—now or in the future—to Hoover and the FBI.

The head of the FBI enjoyed his high profile and power and let nothing threaten it. If he had to go public with information—for the good of the country of course—he did so.

And if just the threat of going public served the same purpose, so much the better.

Conversely, as fast as Hoover ran to the klieg lights—in the process making grandstanding an indelible hallmark of the FBI—Donovan went to the safety of the shadows.

Donovan, twelve years Hoover's senior, had long worked quietly—and extremely effectively—behind the scenes for Roosevelt.

After Donovan had returned from the First World War a hero and then run a successful Wall Street law firm, Roosevelt, who was serving as assistant secretary of the Navy, secretly attached him to the Office of Naval Intelligence. Thus began Donovan's long and secret service of quietly gathering intel at Roosevelt's request.

As this was happening, it came time to clean up what had become a corrupt Bureau of Information—what in 1935 would become the Federal Bureau of Investigation—and heading the list of candidates was one William Joseph Donovan.

But Donovan, still the soldier spy in the shadows and wanting to stay there, quietly campaigned for a young Justice Department lawyer named John Edgar Hoover to get the job.

Donovan's behind-the-scenes hand in Hoover landing the position was not lost on Hoover. He was grateful, and came to consider him a friend and mentor.

Which only served to make matters worse when Hoover got word that the President was considering a new secret organization. This agency would be above all others, collecting intelligence worldwide, as well as conducting counterintelligence operations and more. And Wild Bill Donovan—whom Roosevelt had asked to draft its plans—was to head it up.

Hoover knew he had to put out this potential inferno—a real threat to the power of his FBI—fast.

Using every bit of his finely honed political skills, he tried to impress upon the President that what this new organization did was indeed exactly what the FBI already did, simply on a larger scale, and that any such organization should be—must be, to optimize its efficiency—under the purview of Hoover.

Roosevelt, graciously and with masterful maneuvering, let the FBI director know that he valued his counsel and insight, but said that he had made up his mind. As a bone, he threw Hoover the oversight of all of North, South, and Central America.

Thus, in 1941, William J. Donovan, a civilian, was made Roosevelt's coordinator of information, at a pay rate of one dollar per annum. And in 1942, when COI evolved into the Office of Strategic Services, he was recalled to active duty as Colonel Donovan and made its director.

———

Donovan noticed that Roosevelt looked more tired than usual.

Behind the frameless round spectacles clipped to the bridge of the President's nose, there were dark sacs under his eyes. His thinning hair showed more gray working its way up from his temples. And he seemed somewhat slumped in his chair.

Not surprising, Donovan thought, *not with war being waged on damned near every continent. And he'd never admit a weakness, but that polio is sapping his strength.*

It was then that Donovan answered two unasked questions in his mind—where Roosevelt had just come from, and why they were meeting in the physician's office.

The President clearly had been in his secret War Room, which was here on the ground floor of the White House, between the Diplomatic Reception Room and his physician's office. He spent more time in there than he would ever acknowledge, though records of who came and went—and when—were, of course, meticulously kept.

That answered question one.

Donovan was one of very few who knew of the War Room's existence. Aside from the three shifts of officers from the Army and Navy who staffed it round the clock, the only ones who knew about it were presidential advisor Harry Hopkins, Admiral William Leahy, General George Marshall, and British prime minister Winston Churchill.

It had been Churchill's visit in December 1941 that caused it to be built. The prime minister had brought a portable version of his own War Room that he had in underground London. The traveling model was complete with reduced maps that pinpointed key information on the war.

Roosevelt liked the idea of his own full-sized War Room and quietly had one drawn up.

Now fiberboard covered the walls of a onetime ladies' cloakroom, and maps of the world, in large scale, were affixed thereon. As intel came in, the officers continually updated the maps, marking with pins, coded by color and design, everything from the locations of ships (destroyers had round red heads) to the locations of political leaders (Stalin was a pipe, Churchill a cigar).

Donovan knew that early every morning, Roosevelt would come to the physician's office for his daily checkup and massage, then slip undetected into the War Room next door to be briefed on the overnights.

And Donovan was a member of a group that was even smaller than the one that knew about the War Room: those who had actually been in it.

Not even Eleanor Roosevelt was allowed inside.

Clearly, FBI Director J. Edgar Hoover—who, as they awaited FDR's arrival, had idly wondered aloud why they were meeting in the physician's office—not only had not been in the War Room but also did not know about it.

And, at least as far as tonight was concerned, would continue to be kept in the dark.

And that answered question two.

"I appreciate you gentlemen coming on such short notice," Roosevelt said, sounding more energized than he appeared.

"Yes, Mr. President," they said, almost in unison.

"Can I get anyone a drink or coffee?" the President asked, motioning toward the service on the desk. "Or perhaps one and the same?"

"Not for me, sir," Donovan said.

"I would love a taste, sir," Hoover said. "But, no, thank you. I have to get back to the office tonight. And I've had more than enough coffee for one day."

"Can I get you something, Mr. President?" Donovan said.

Roosevelt shook his head, rubbing his eyes and massaging the bridge of his nose. "I can wait, Bill. Thank you." He then lit the cigarette in his holder, exhaled a blue cloud, and said, "Then let's get on with it—Edgar, any news?"

FBI director J. Edgar Hoover nodded as he reached into his suit coat pocket and brought out a folded sheet of paper. He unfolded it and scanned it.

"According to our labs," Hoover began in an officious tone, "the residue taken from the crime scenes at the train terminals in Florida and Georgia and from the electrical transformer stations in North Carolina, Virginia, and Maryland tested to be from the same family of explosive: *cyclotrimethylenetrinitramine*."

"In layman's terms?" the President said, puffing deeply on his cigarette.

"The Germans call it hexogen—" Donovan offered, earning him a glare from Hoover.

He now had Roosevelt's attention, and finished, "—the Brits call their version Royal Demolition Explosive, or RDX. Here it's just cyclonite. Very common. Very effective."

Roosevelt looked back at Hoover.

"So," the President went on, "then all of the East Coast attacks can be linked?"

"Well, as Bill says, it is a very common compound—"

"You're telling me that you don't know, Edgar?" the President interrupted.

"No, sir, not that I don't know. I'm telling you that it's possible—if not likely—that some of these attacks could be sympathetic ones."

"Sympathetic?"

"Copycats," Hoover explained. "People who either have some ax to grind with America—or your politics, sir—or who simply like seeing things go *boom* and the public's reaction."

Roosevelt considered that a moment.

"What about the German pistol that was found in Atlanta?"

Hoover nodded. "We do have that. And we have had it tested for ballistics and we pulled the fingerprints. Right now, the prints are being run, but so far there has been no conclusive match."

The President looked off across the room as he thought that over.

Hoover added, "Mr. President, if you're wondering if the pistol is the key clue that these are German agents responsible, know that there could be thousands of Walther PPKs in the United States, ones imported before the war. It is not an uncommon firearm, despite being of German manufacture. We simply do not have enough evidence to determine beyond any doubt that this is all the work of German agents."

The President looked at Hoover. "What about Dallas? What have we found out from there?"

"We do not have those details yet, sir," Hoover began. "As you know, the explosions at the department store and train station took place just last night—"

"Of course I know!" the President interrupted, his voice rising. He pointed at a copy of the *Washington Star* that was on a side table. "The whole damned country knows."

"Yessir," Hoover replied softly but evenly. "Mr. President, please understand that I have every man available on this. We will have answers. And we will get those responsible."

Roosevelt suddenly made a toothy grin behind his cigarette holder.

"Just as you did the first ones?" he asked.

"Yes, sir," Hoover began strongly, but then his voice faded as he finished, "Mr. President."

Roosevelt knew that the capture of the German agents had absolutely nothing to do with the FBI's ability to root out foreign agents on U.S. soil and bring them to justice.

What had happened in June 1942 was that German U-boats in OPERATION PASTORIUS deposited eight agents trained in sabotage onto the shores of the United States, four on New York's Long Island and four near Jacksonville, Florida.

The ones in Florida infiltrated with no problem.

The four in New York, however, were almost immediately discovered by a coastguardsman walking the seashore. They told him that they were fishermen, gave him a cash bribe, and he left—to alert his superiors.

A manhunt for the agents began on Long Island, but too late, and the agents were able to board the Long Island Railroad and make it into the city.

That they had managed to get that far was not good enough for one of the agents. George Dasch was having serious doubts about his role in the mission, as well as its overall success, and in the hotel room that he shared with another agent, Ernest Burger, he convinced Burger that they should give themselves up.

The two took a train to Washington, and at the Mayflower Hotel—blocks from the White House—they called the FBI. They asked to speak with J. Edgar Hoover.

While Hoover did not personally respond—it's not clear if he had been given the opportunity—FBI agents did arrive at the room at the Mayflower and Dasch and Burger were taken to FBI headquarters.

They gave their statements and turned over the U.S. currency they had brought, as well as maps of the places that they were supposed to have bombed—power plants, water supplies, train stations, factories, and more.

And they gave details of the other agents' missions.

Within two weeks, all eight agents had been arrested.

When Hoover made the announcement that the manhunt for the German agents was over, that the FBI had them in custody, the part about Dasch and Burger having surrendered and then giving up the other teams was not mentioned.

The reason for the omission, he had privately explained, was that he wanted the enemy to believe that U.S. counterintelligence had rooted out their agents.

Left unsaid: *And if anyone should happen to believe that once again the FBI Super Cops have saved the day, so be it.*

"Do you remember what those German agents told us last year?" Roosevelt said. "About Hitler sending them because he wants to bring the war to American's backyard?"

"Yes, sir."

"I would say that he's done it," Roosevelt said. "Wouldn't you?"

Hoover did not reply. He shifted in his seat, suddenly feeling the sweat in his palms.

Roosevelt looked at Donovan, who was more or less

intently studying a fixed point on the finely polished hardwood floor.

"Bill, I apologize to you and to Edgar about how this discussion has transpired. My intention was not to put anyone on the spot."

Donovan looked at him and said, "No apology necessary to me, Mr. President."

"Nor to me, sir," Hoover added. "You have every reason to be concerned."

Roosevelt shook his head. "The headlines are bad enough, but every time a light flickers in the White House, Eleanor thinks it's the end of the goddamned world!"

Hoover looked at the President, saw the toothy smile, and found himself grinning, too.

Donovan chuckled softly.

"Mr. President, it isn't that we're not pursuing the German agent angle," Hoover offered. "For example, we have agents reinterviewing Dasch and Burger." He paused. "Very simply, sir, we are checking and rechecking everything."

Roosevelt nodded solemnly. "I understand. But we have to do more. Which is why I asked you both here. Edgar, I want you to know that Bill's agents will be working on this, too."

"In my area of operations?" Hoover asked, glancing at Donovan.

Hoover saw that the look on Donovan's face could have shown that this was the first that he had heard of this plan. Or it could have shown that he was expertly hiding the fact that he had heard of this plan a day or a week ago.

Roosevelt went on: "They will be using their network of agents to see if they can uncover any intel as to who is making these attacks. Your agents will share any information that is asked of them."

Like hell they will, Hoover thought.

Hoover said, "Yes, Mr. President."

"As I said, we have to do more. This cannot continue. Especially now that it has become personal."

Donovan and Hoover looked at the President.

"In Dallas," Roosevelt explained, "they bombed the USO lounge."

"Yes, sir," Hoover said, but it was more a question than a statement.

"They have come into our country," the President explained, "and now are targeting our soldiers on our land. It is difficult enough dealing with U-boats off the coast. We cannot have every American thinking there is a German agent on every U.S. street corner."

He looked for a long moment at Donovan, then at Hoover. "Any questions?"

"No, sir," Donovan said.

"None, Mr. President," Hoover said. "And if that is all, I'd like to be excused in order to get back to the office."

"Thank you for coming, Edgar."

Hoover stood, and Donovan followed his lead.

The FBI director shook the President's hand, then the OSS director's.

"I'll let you know—both of you—as soon as I hear from the labs about the Dallas results."

"Please," Roosevelt said. "And anything else that Bill should know."

"Of course, Mr. President."

As soon as Hoover went out the door, the President looked at Donovan and said, "I think we can both use a belt right now. I'm done with the room for tonight."

"Allow me," Donovan said and went to the wooden tray with the crystal. The ice in the pitcher was about half melted.

"Should I call for more ice?" Donovan asked.

Roosevelt looked. "What's there will be fine. We'll just pretend we're students roughing it at Columbia."

"Then I'd better call for more ice," Donovan said. "As I recall, you never suffered one second in school."

"You can go to hell, Colonel," the President said, laughing. "Pour me a damned martini. A double. I think Eleanor is checking lightbulbs; we should be out of her sights for a while."

Donovan put ice in two of the crystal glasses, then poured a healthy four ounces of gin on top. He carried the glasses back to the couch and chairs and handed one of the glasses to Roosevelt.

"Victory," Donovan said, holding up his glass in a toast.

"Victory indeed," Roosevelt replied and touched his glass to Donovan's.

After they took a sip, Donovan said, "Is it just me or does anyone else suspect that Edgar does not want to believe there are German agents blowing things up in our country?"

"He's embarrassed, Bill. He knows they're out there and wants to bag them as much as anyone—probably more than anyone. But until he can, he's protecting his image like that prefect in *Casablanca*—"

He paused, mentally groping for the character's name.

"Captain Renault," Donovan supplied. "Played by Claude Rains."

Donovan and his wife, Ruth, had been among those whom the President had hosted in December in the White House theater under the east terrace for a showing of the new hit movie starring Humphrey Bogart and Ingrid Bergman.

Donovan had found the event somewhat ironic—considering that the love story was set in war-torn, present-day North Africa and that shell casings spent there in OPERATION TORCH barely a month earlier were damned near still warm—but then decided it was in fact Roosevelt relishing the irony.

"—Yes," the President picked up, enjoying himself, "*Captain Hoover* declaring, 'I'm shocked, *shocked*, to find German agents here!'"

Roosevelt made his toothy grin, then took a good sip of his martini.

"I'm damned lucky," he went on, "in the absence of this 'evidence beyond a doubt,' that he hasn't just rounded up the usual suspects and called a press conference."

Donovan chuckled.

Roosevelt, after a moment, said in a deeply serious tone, "Unfortunately, this is a humorless situation."

He looked at Donovan to make his point.

"This problem, it has to go away. As in, it never happened."

"Say that again, Frank," Donovan said softly.

Roosevelt did not make a point of reminding Donovan that he preferred to be addressed formally as "Mr. President."

"Bill, this problem on our turf must disappear. I need America's attention and energies focused on Europe and the Pacific. These German-agent headlines need to go away."

"I agree."

"And if Hoover bags these guys, he'll make sure that not only are there more headlines, but that he's pictured on every front page." He paused. "So it's up to you."

"The U.S. is not my area of operations—"

"Bill," Roosevelt interrupted. "I don't know how much clearer I can be. You do what you have to do. Do it fast. Do it quietly."

Donovan looked him in the eyes and said, "Yes, Mr. President," then took a long sip on his drink.

[**THREE**]
Newark, New Jersey
2010 6 March 1943

Kurt Bayer and Richard Koch had made good time getting to downtown Newark in the 1940 Ford sedan that
they had taken from the parking lot of the Jacksonville
Terminal Station.

In the course of the past week, they had put far more
than a thousand miles on the car. They had also put on a
succession of different license plates, stealing ones off of
cars in South Carolina and Delaware, then carefully dis-
posing of the old ones.

The car had thus blended in well with so many other
average sedans as they made their way toward New York
City. It had served them well—far better than that hor-
rendous yellow plumber's truck would have—and they
had been very fortunate indeed.

But with all of the news reports, Koch felt their luck
was in danger of running out.

Ever since they had blown up the electric transformer
station in Baltimore, every town that they had passed
through seemed to have a heavier and heavier police
presence.

The Reading Terminal in Philadelphia had been crawling with cops, as was Trenton's and even little Princeton's.

Koch thought that it could be the result of an active
imagination, but damned near every power pole along
U.S. 1 seemed to have a cop parked next to it.

And it was no different here in Newark.

It was hard not to notice the squad cars lined up outside Penn Station and, as they drove down East Park Street, the paddy wagons parked on the curb of the north side of the Public Service Bus Terminal.

Koch looked away from the cops and saw something across the street from the bus terminal that caught his interest. A restaurant sign hung from a pole on the dark brick building. Lit in bright red neon was: PALACE CHOP HOUSE.

A steak and a couple beers sounds really good right now. But not there. Too damned many cops across the street.

"After we get our room at the hotel," Koch said, "I'm going to get rid of the car. Then we can eat."

"Okay," Bayer said.

They had already discussed ditching the car at great length during the drive. They still had more missions, but now it was time to cool it, to hide out. Especially after Rolf Grossman and Rudolf Cremer's latest in Texas. The radio stations—every one since Wilmington, Delaware, that morning, till they got tired of it and turned it off after noon—had had some news about the explosions in the Dallas train station and that expensive department store.

After making it though the heavy traffic at the intersection of Market and Broad, Bayer drove a number of blocks, made a couple of turns, and finally came to Park Place.

"There," Koch said, pointing.

The Robert Treat Hotel was just down the block.

"I see it."

"Drop me here," Koch said, "then go all the way down and park around the corner. I'll get the room key, then come find you and we'll walk in. That way the car's out of sight and not linked with us."

Fifteen minutes later, Bayer and Koch carried the suitcases that contained their duffel bags through the front doors of the hotel.

Bayer saw that it was a nice hotel, not anything like the motor hotels that they had been staying in all week. The lobby featured impressive large columns, and there was marble and polished tile everywhere.

They walked to the elevators, passing two young women, a well-built blonde and a petite redhead, both about twenty, relaxing in richly upholstered chairs beside a line of lush palms.

The blonde, her tight black skirt rising up on her crossed legs, made eye contact with Bayer. She smiled. He sheepishly grinned back.

Koch and Bayer got on the elevator, and as the doors closed Bayer met the blonde's eyes again. She winked.

"Now, those," he said as the car began to rise, "were some good-looking women. Wonder who they are?"

Koch was looking up and watching the floor indicator move past 3.

"Prostitutes," he said in a matter-of-fact tone.

"Hookers?" Bayer felt as if he'd been punched. "No!"

"Yes."

"Really?"

The elevator stopped at the fourth floor and the doors opened.

"Really," Koch said, then looked at Bayer and added, "Don't do anything stupid."

Richard Koch had been gone for more than an hour. He had said it was going to take him no more than a half hour to get rid of the car.

The time was not a problem for Kurt Bayer. It was, instead, that from almost the moment that Koch had left, Bayer's stomach had started to growl.

Bayer had dug through his luggage, hoping to find a stick of the chewing gum from the pack that he had spilled in there a few days ago. There was none.

What I really want is something salty.

Some nuts or chips would be good.

He went over to the table between the two beds, and on the white notepad there, wrote:

```
R—
In the bar
KB
```

He put the whole pad in the center of the dark bedspread where Koch couldn't miss it, then went out the door.

The bar turned out to be easy to find. An open area off of the main lobby, it was noisy and smoky. There was a twenty-foot-long bar, made of nice dark wood and with a dozen tall seats, about half of which were being used. The thirty or so cocktail tables were almost all taken; some had a couple sitting and enjoying drinks at them, others two or more couples.

Bayer saw three empty seats at the far end of the bar and went and sat in the very last one, against the wall. He realized that from there he could keep an eye on the lobby and probably see when Koch came in and intercept him. Then they could go get dinner.

He looked on top of the bar and smiled—there were bowls of potato chips *and* nuts.

Bayer was reaching for a chip when the bartender walked up. He was in his midforties, tall, with thinning salt-and-pepper hair, a gray mustache, and somewhat jowly cheeks. He wore a cheap black vest, a clip-on black bow tie, and a white shirt with slightly frayed cuffs. The gold tin name tag on the vest pocket read: SEAN O'NEILL.

"'Evening," the bartender said. "What're you drinking?"

"'Evening, Sean," Bayer said. "I was thinking about a beer, but I've had a long day and think I deserve a real drink."

"You name it."

"Martini, up."

Yeah, that should either tame the rumbles in my stomach or make me ravenous.

"Vodka or gin?"

"Gin. Do you have Beefeater's?"

I'm supposed to be blending in. What good German would be drinking British booze?

"You got it, pal."

The bowl of chips was empty, and he had the nut bowl down to half full by the time the bartender brought his second martini. And still no sign of Koch.

"Thank you, Sean."

"Sure thing."

Bayer looked at the drink before taking a sip.

Better take it easy on this one, he thought. *My old man always said to stay away from gin, that it made you mean or stupid. Or maybe both.*

Now's not a good time to learn that he was once again right.

He took a sip at the same time the bartender brought bowls of fresh chips and nuts.

He put down the glass and reached for a chip from the new bowl. Right as his hand got to the bowl, there were slender, pale white fingers with long, red manicured nails reaching in ahead of him.

"Excuse me," a female's soft voice said.

Bayer turned to the voice and was met with the same sweet smile he had first seen earlier, just before getting on the elevator.

"Would you like some company?" the young blonde in the tight black skirt said, motioning at the empty chair next to him.

"Please," he tried to say but his throat caught.

He took a sip of his martini as she stepped up into the seat and put a small black clutch bag on the bar.

Well, if she's a hooker she's not getting much business on a Saturday night.

He glanced at her. She was trying to get the bartender's attention.

What the hell does Koch know? She's not one. Look at her. She's too good-looking, too young, too innocent.

She turned and caught him looking at her. She smiled, more widely this time, and for the first time he noticed that her teeth were crooked.

Bayer glanced down the bar to the far end, where the bartender was making small talk with a customer.

He raised his voice and waved his left hand. "Sean!"

The bartender turned and at first seemed to make a face. But then he grabbed a cocktail napkin and started coming toward them.

He put the napkin in front of the blonde.

Bayer said, "What would you like—"

"Mary," she said.

"A Bloody Mary?" Bayer said.

"No, silly." She giggled, and showed a bit of her crooked teeth. "My name is Mary. Mary Callahan. I'll have"—she looked at his martini—"oh, I guess I'll have one of those."

The bartender said, "A Beefeater's martini coming up," and turned away.

"Oh?" she said excitedly to Bayer. "Is that gin?"

"Is that okay?" Bayer asked.

"I guess. You like yours, right?"

He nodded. "Want to try it before you get yours?"

"Do you mind?" She smiled.

He slid the glass over in front of her and she slowly put it to her lips and took a tiny sip.

Bayer saw that when she took the glass from her lips, there was red lipstick on the glass. He wondered how he could "accidentally" get that to his lips and see what it tasted like.

"Whew!" she said. "That's strong—"

"You want to order something else?" he said and started to wave for the bartender.

"Oh, no," she said, looking intently at him. "That'll be just fine."

Her eyes twinkle!

She put the glass back on the napkin and slid it back to him.

She offered her right hand and said, "Thank you—"

Bayer took her hand and shook it.

She repeated, "Thank you—"

"Oh, Kurt. It's Kurt," he replied. "And you're very welcome, Mary."

Bayer noticed how soft and warm her hand was—and that she made no effort to immediately pull it free after they had shaken.

Sean the bartender walked up with Mary's martini and put it on the napkin before her.

She then, with a smile, removed her hand from Bayer's and picked up the martini and gestured toward him.

"To new friends," she said.

He met it with his and they clinked glasses.

"New friends," he said, grinning.

He wondered if the sudden warm feeling he had was caused by the gin or the thoughts he was having of Mary.

They both sipped their drinks.

She took a slender chrome case from the small black purse and pulled a cigarette from it.

Bayer quickly scanned the bar, found a nearby basket of matches, took a pack from it and lit her cigarette.

"Thank you," she said after delicately exhaling the smoke over her shoulder.

He smiled, then sipped at his martini, trying to fill what was beginning to feel like an awkward silence.

He tasted something different this sip, and, when he looked at the glass rim, saw that he had touched the point where Mary had sipped and left a little lipstick.

I'd like to have more of that.

But what do I say now?

"Didn't I see you earlier?" Mary asked.

Thank God!

Bayer smiled and nodded enthusiastically. "By the elevators."

"That's right. You were coming in with another man."

"Just a friend," Bayer said, not worried about revealing anything about their mission.

He and Koch, when they were on the U-boat, had come up with the simple cover story of being two friends traveling to New York, where they would be joining in the war effort.

As with the best of cover stories, it was close to the

truth. They felt somewhat like friends now. They were traveling to New York. And they would be "joining in the war effort"—though they found more than a little humor in the twist on that.

"It appeared that you had a friend, too," Bayer said.

"She's on a date."

"Oh?"

Mary smiled sweetly, but he noticed her hand holding the cigarette shook a little.

In a nervous voice, she asked, "Are you interested in a date?"

That bastard Koch was right!

"A date?" he repeated tentatively.

She picked up her martini and, as she sipped, looked over the rim at him and nodded.

Damn!

He reached for his glass and took a sip and suddenly grinned.

She took the matchbook that was in front of him, opened it, and on the inside cover wrote: "10/30."

"Till midnight," she said, her voice inviting and her left pinky first pointing to the ten-dollar fee then to the one for thirty dollars, "or for all night."

He looked at the matchbook, then looked into her eyes.

Jesus. They're still twinkling!

Well, this sure will beat hell out of hearing Koch snore all night.

He took the pen and circled "30."

Mary made her crooked smile.

[FOUR]
New York Bay
2345 6 March 1943

Francesco Nola put down the battered black binoculars, pulled back on the throttle controls, and made a hard course correction, swinging the wooden wheel so that the *Annie* headed in a due eastward direction and in line with the channel markers. The dimly lit compass face responded by rocking then spinning inside its grimy glass dome on the helm, the white number 90 finally settling in behind the black line etched in the dome glass.

Dick Canidy could tell that they were now in the Narrows, the tidal strait between Upper New York Bay and Lower New York Bay, and that on the present course, they were headed for shore.

Behind them was Staten Island, and ahead—directly ahead, as Canidy could now make out the shoreline and some docks—was the southwestern tip of the borough of Brooklyn, on Long Island.

"So after I ice up the *Annie* here and deliver her to my cousin at Montauk—he's taking her on a four-day run—I'll come right back to the city and we'll meet a little after that," Nola said.

He reduced the throttle more, causing the boat to settle in the water.

"You have my home telephone number. If I am not there, then I am at the fish market. You can get me one place or the other."

"Okay," Canidy said.

Outside the pilothouse windows, he saw the man who had thrown him the lines at the fish-market dock. The man was walking toward the bow, preparing the lines for docking.

Canidy wondered if he should offer to help, then saw on the dock a man coming out onto the pier finger. The building behind him had a faded sign reading: ISLAND ICE & SUPPLIES BRKLYN. A metal chute projected out of the top floor and reached down and out to the pier where the *Annie* was about to be moored.

Canidy watched quietly as Nola, with a mix of grace and skill, spun the boat in its own length, working the engines against themselves—starboard in forward, port in reverse—then both in concert, to back the boat in so that the ice chute could easily reach and fill the fish holds.

After a couple minutes of bumping the levers in and out of gear, the *Annie* gently nudged to a stop against the pier. Nola put the twin gear levers in the neutral position, then went out the steel door of the pilothouse to get a better view of the work on the deck.

He saw that the fore and aft lines were being tied to pilings, and nodded to his crewman.

He turned with his hand out to Canidy.

"See you soon," he said.

"Thank you," Canidy replied, shaking the offered hand.

"Just in time," Nola then said and nodded toward the dock.

Canidy looked toward the building and noticed nothing special. Then, just beyond the building, he saw a taxicab pull up to the curb.

"Mine?"

Nola nodded.

"That's some service. Especially out here at this hour."

Nola smiled and squeezed his arm.

Canidy went to the car. When he got close, he realized it wasn't just any cab.

He got in the backseat and closed the door quickly, appreciative of the warmth inside.

"Small world," Canidy said to the monster fishmonger cabbie.

The fishmonger did not reply. He put the car in gear . . . then sniffed audibly and slightly cocked his head.

Canidy heard him grunt, and watched as he quickly rolled down the driver's window and then the front passenger's window—*He'd do the back ones, too,* Canidy thought, *if he could reach them*—before driving off.

It was almost two o'clock when the cab pulled up at 2 Lexington Avenue. Other than a couple walking up the sidewalk to the Gramercy Park Hotel—a man and a woman coming in late from some formal event, judging by their attire—there was no one else around.

Nor was there anyone in the lobby as he went through, nor at the front desk.

When he got to the elevator bank, the indicators showed the cars were all stopped on upper floors.

He pushed the call button, then considered taking the steps up. About the time he decided he was just too exhausted to do that, an empty car arrived and opened its doors.

In his suite, he found his uniform lying on his bed, cleaned and pressed.

He pulled the .45 from the small of his back and put it under a pillow on the bed.

Then he peeled off his fish-slimed clothes, stuck them in a bag, and considered what to do with them.

Nobody's going to steal anything smelling this bad.

He went to the suite door, opened it, and put the bag in the hallway, looping its drawstring closure over the doorknob. Then he phoned the hotel operator and gave instructions that he needed the clothes he'd left outside his door back from the laundry service by eight o'clock, and he asked for a wake-up call.

I'll put in a call to Donovan first thing. With any luck, I can have Eric Fulmar here by tomorrow afternoon, or at least before I meet with Nola on Monday.

He then took a hot shower, pulled on fresh boxers and a T-shirt, and crawled into the soft, king-sized bed.

Ann would like this bed, he thought, yawning and rolling onto his back. *And I would like Ann in it....*

VII

"We should be going to Amarillo instead," Rolf Grossman said as he placed what looked like a very fat black cigar on the folding table of the Pullman compartment. "Strike while the iron is hot."

The "cigar" was a five-hundred-gram stick of explosive wrapped tightly in a thin skin of black paper.

"Is that a good idea?" Rudolf Cremer said, watching him compulsively put together another pouch bomb. "On a moving train?"

Grossman glared at him.

"I know what I'm doing," he said, then turned back to the table.

He put one of the acid-timed fuses—disguised to look like an ink pen—beside the explosive and its detonator, then pulled from his suitcase a small black leather pouch. He attached the fuse and detonator to the explosive, tinkered with the pen timer, then carefully slipped the assembly into the pouch.

"Now we have a half kilo with a short fuse," he said, clearly pleased with his work, "and another with a long fuse."

With his history, Cremer thought, *how the hell can he tell the difference?*

"We have no need for either until we get to Kansas City," Cremer said.

"We would in Amarillo."

The year-old Army ordnance Pantex facility, on sixteen thousand acres of Texas Panhandle seventeen miles outside of Amarillo, was producing explosive-filled projectiles—bombs and shells—round the clock.

Cremer shook his head. Grossman's appetite for blowing up things was insatiable—which of course made the *Oberschutz* more or less perfect for their mission—and taking out such an enormous target probably would make him happy only until he could explode something else.

"Why must I keep reminding you that Skorzeny's orders are that we do not go after big targets?" he said. "We are successful in what we were trained to do."

Otto Skorzeny, thirty-four, was a legendary Nazi lieutenant colonel. He had won the Iron Cross fighting with the Leibstandarte SS Adolf Hitler against the Soviets and afterward had been handpicked by the Führer to lead the German commandos. With dark hair and deep, dark eyes, he had strong good looks that were crudely accented by a scar that went from the tip of his chin, arced across his left check, and ended at his ear—a wound he received dueling with sabers as a student in Vienna.

The radio mounted in the wall of the Pullman compartment was tuned to a news broadcast—heavy on the Dallas explosions—but the station's signal was getting weak and the sound had deteriorated to mostly static.

Grossman got up and walked over to it.

"But taking out a bomb-building plant would be incredible," he said. "Imagine the secondary explosions. . . ."

Cremer could indeed imagine the incredible destruction of massive stockpiles of explosives erupting. Not to mention the setback it no doubt would cause the Americans in their war effort. But a task on that scale—if it was even possible—was best left to the Luftwaffe, not a lone pair of agents, and thus he had to constantly discourage Grossman and that had become a source of more than a little friction between them.

Cremer was convinced that taking this sleek, bright red train, with its routing from Dallas–Fort Worth to Oklahoma City to Kansas City, was the best way to put some distance between them and the blasts . . . and the crowds of cops who no doubt were swarming the area . . . and position them well for more sabotage opportunities.

During their week in Dallas, after having walked down to Union Station and collected pamphlets with each rail line's schedule, he had gone over them and determined that from Kansas City they could get anywhere they needed to be in the middle and western U.S. The Rocky Mountain Rocket, train number 107-7, ran from Kansas to Denver; train number 43, the Californian, went from Kansas City to Chicago to Los Angeles; the Mid-Continent

Special, train number 17, had sleepers to Minneapolis and Des Moines.

And so he had bought them tickets on the Red Rocket and secured for the duration of the trip a Pullman "master room" compartment.

He looked around the master room and was reminded of the railway brochure that had said it offered "the ultimate in refined comfort." So far, he could not dispute that.

This one—on the left side of the train—had a big main room, about seven by ten, with four comfortable, cloth-upholstered, chrome-frame armchairs that could be put wherever a passenger pleased. (The smaller accommodations came with fixed bench seating.) When the chairs were slid to the side, there was room to fold down the two twin-sized beds from the walls. The compartment also had a large wardrobe, plus full-length dressing mirrors. And, off the main room, an attached private bathroom with toilet, sink, and shower.

Cremer had an armchair pulled up to one of the two large windows and was looking out to the west. He noticed that the Oklahoma countryside was changing. For the last hour or so, since at least the Texas border, it had been fairly flat, barren land, with occasional clumps of trees. Now it was turning dramatically hilly, with exposed uplifts of rock—what looked like the foothills of some small mountains.

Grossman was quickly adjusting the tuning knob of the radio, anxious to hear more of the news bulletins on the Dallas explosions. After a moment, some cowboy music came in clearly. It was the tail end of a tune by Bob Wills and His Texas Playboys. Cremer had heard quite a bit of them on the radio while in Dallas and actually was beginning to like this Texas swing music.

Grossman, however, would have none of it, and after hearing a bartender in the Adolphus Hotel alternately refer to it as "Western" or "shitkicker" music had used only the latter description whenever he heard it.

Cremer was surprised that he did not call it that now but decided it was probably because the radio announcer was promising that the news was coming up next, with updates on the terror in Dallas, and Grossman would rather suffer the music than miss a report.

Grossman went back to the table and continued working with the explosives as the Red Rocket swayed and *clack-clack-clacked* its way north toward Oklahoma City.

Considering all the time and attention he gives those, Cremer thought with mild disgust, *one would think he could have properly set the goddamned fuses in Dallas.*

A half hour later, Cremer felt the train begin to slow. He looked out the window and saw that the countryside was becoming more developed. Houses dotted the land, and there were more roads that were improved—ones paved with blacktop as opposed to all the bare dirt ones he'd seen.

He wondered if they already were approaching Oklahoma City.

The train slowed even further as it came closer to town. First there were nice wooden houses in tidy neighborhoods, then the two- and three-story brick buildings of downtown proper.

Cremer strained to peer forward, and, following the tracks, could just see the train depot to the left side of the tracks. It was a small one, about half a block long, of dark red brick with a black tile roof and a narrow wooden boarding platform—all clearly too small to be that of Oklahoma City.

Then, just as he noticed the standardized signage reading NORMAN on the station's southern wall, he heard the porter passing outside the compartment door.

"Norman!" the deep, black voice announced, "Norman, Oklahoma! No stops, no disembarking! No stops, no disembarking!"

The porter's voice grew fainter as he moved up the car repeating the station information.

Cremer and Grossman exchanged glances.

"I don't like this," Grossman said and quickly put the last of the explosives back in the suitcase. The only thing remaining on the table was one of the small black leather pouches.

"Don't overreact," Cremer said. "We may just be taking on mail or something."

The train's brakes began to squeal and Cremer again looked out the window. He could see a few men standing on the platform, two in dark gray suits and black fedoras, one in the blue uniform and cap of a railway employee.

The train, with the locomotive coming even with the station, was now barely rolling along. There were no more brake squeals.

As the first of the passenger cars reached the station, the two men in dark suits began running alongside. In no time, they were outside Cremer's window—Grossman now saw them, too—and he pulled the curtains closed for a moment. The car rolled past them, and when he cracked open the curtains again and looked back he saw that the men had matched the speed of the train and were now, one at a time and with some difficulty, jumping onto the metal platform where the last two cars were connected.

Cremer's stomach knotted.

Those aren't postal clerks, he thought.

"They just jumped on the train," he said.

Grossman got to his feet, picked up the leather pouch from the table, slipped it into his suit coat pocket, and went to the door. He put his ear to the door but heard nothing unusual.

The train began to pick up speed, and when Cremer looked out the window this time he could see that they were leaving downtown.

He stood up, too, and when he instinctively reached in his pants pocket, making sure the Walther pistol was still there—it was—he noticed that his palms were starting to sweat.

Grossman opened the door a crack and looked out. Then he pulled it open more, looked toward the car behind them, then to the one ahead, and then stepped out into the hall. He glanced at Cremer before walking to the back of the car.

Cremer watched as Grossman positioned himself to

the left of the rear door's window, out of sight of anyone in the other cars, and peered back into them.

Grossman saw that the two men—one taller and clean-shaven, the other with a mustache—were going through the farthest car, systematically knocking on the door of every compartment.

Each time, the man with the mustache would stand outside the door, covering the taller man as he went in. After about a minute, the taller man would then come out and they would move to the next compartment and repeat the process.

At the fourth compartment, one of the passengers, a slender male of about thirty, came out into the hallway. He gave his wallet to the man with the mustache, who then appeared to ask a few questions as he inspected what looked like identification papers.

The man with the mustache gave back the wallet, nodded curtly, then went with his partner to the next compartment.

Grossman had seen enough. He carefully and quickly made his way back to the compartment.

Cremer closed the door once Grossman was inside. "What did you see?"

"Two men, maybe local police but probably state or FBI, clearing the train compartment by compartment. They're checking passengers' papers."

"Well, our papers are not a problem," Cremer said evenly. "My driver's license is the same as I had when I lived in New Jersey."

"Mine also." Grossman's eyes darted around the

compartment. "But I do not like how this is happening. This is no routine investigation. There probably are more police waiting in Oklahoma City."

He went to the suitcase and pulled out the other black pouch.

"What the hell do you intend to do with that?" Cremer said.

"How far from Oklahoma City are we?"

Cremer looked at him, made the mental calculations, then said, "Fifteen minutes . . . maybe less."

Grossman held up the pouch he had taken from the suitcase.

"This is the one with the ten-minute fuse. I am going to place it in the passenger car behind us. It will take them no more than ten minutes to work their way up to it. Meanwhile, we will go forward, and when it blows, and the train stops, we will get out. By that time, the train will be in the city and we can slip away in the chaos."

Cremer, thinking, stared at him.

I don't want to believe it, but he may be right.

Hell, he is right.

Why else would a couple of cops suddenly jump on a train, if they weren't looking for us? The damned radio has been nothing but nonstop reports about Dallas.

And lucky Grossman—now he gets to blow up something else.

He went to the door, opened it, and looked down the car and through the door windows. He could see the two men in gray suits and black fedoras, not in detail but clearly enough to tell that they were now about halfway through the first car. He closed the door.

"I don't like the idea . . . but, frankly, I do not have a better one."

"Okay, then," Grossman said and unzipped the pouch. "I'll start the acid fuse."

He pulled out the pen, looked at it, then quickly looked at it more closely, and whispered, *"Scheist."*

Cremer saw Grossman's face lose all color.

"What?"

"The fuse . . ."

The initial explosion of the half-kilo bomb blew out the side of the train seconds later. Grossman and Cremer had only a heartbeat to begin to comprehend what the absolutely brilliant flash and vicious concussion meant.

Within a split second, secondary explosions were triggered when the twenty or so kilograms of plastic explosive that had been packed in the suitcases—and the half kilo in Grossman's coat pocket—suddenly cooked off.

The massive blasts rocked the whole train and tore the last three Pullman passenger cars from the track, scattering the Red Rocket and its contents across the peaceful Oklahoma countryside.

[TWO]

Office of Strategic Services
The National Institutes of Health Building
Washington, D.C.
0630 7 March 1943

When President Roosevelt had informed Wild Bill Donovan in August of 1941 that he had made a few calls and found, in a town where office and living accommodations were impossibly tight, space from which Donovan could execute the duties associated with his new position as director of the Office of Coordinator of Information, Donovan at first was somewhat underwhelmed.

The National Institutes of Health? he had wondered.

In no time, however, it became clear that housing—or, more to the point, hiding—the supersecret OCOI (and then its successor, the Office of Strategic Services) in the nondescript NIH building with its innocuous name came as close to perfect as the parameters of wartime allowed.

The office of the director of the OSS was nicely furnished with a large, glistening desk, a red leather couch, and two red leather chairs. The director himself was sitting in one of the chairs, his feet up and crossed on a low glass-top table, and reading from a fat folder in his lap.

"From the looks of it, Professor Dyer has already earned his keep," Donovan said to his deputy director.

"Yes, sir," Captain Peter Stuart Douglass Sr., USN,

said. "The list of scientists he thinks will follow him is impressive."

Douglass was slender and fit, a pleasant-looking forty-four-year-old with sandy hair and a freckled face. His career in the Navy had been spent aboard deepwater vessels—most recently as the commanding officer of a destroyer squadron—and in intelligence. When FDR had given Donovan the OCOI, he said it was only just that he start his staffing, too, and—with Donovan's blessing—asked the secretary of the Navy to put Douglass on indefinite duty as Donovan's number two.

Douglass, who believed he had little hope of making admiral—and was not sure he in fact wanted such duty, especially if it meant sailing a desk in Washington—embraced the OCOI assignment because it promised to put him, as it now delivered, in the middle of some very exciting and important work.

"Question is," Donovan went on, "can we get them out before the Germans (a) find out we grabbed Dyer and that he's not simply 'missing,' and (b) decide that the loyalty of these remaining scientists is not with Hitler but soon with Leslie Groves."

Until recently—as in two weeks before—Professor Frederick Dyer, a rumpled academic in patched tweed in his fifties, had been at the University of Marburg, working under duress on the molecular structure of metals in the pursuit of turbine engine technology for the propulsion of aircraft, among other projects critical to ensuring the *Tausendjahriges Reich*—the Nazis' thousand-year empire.

The OSS—with Eric Fulmar as the mission operative and Dick Canidy as his control—had smuggled Dyer and his daughter, twenty-nine-year-old Gisella, out via an OSS pipeline. The difficult escape through German-occupied Hungary very nearly cost all of them their lives.

In the end—as in two days ago—the Dyers were escorted to the University of Chicago, where the professor joined the dozen or so scientists—including Enrico Fermi, Dyer's friend and colleague from the University of Rome—working on a highly classified project led by Brigadier General Leslie Groves, Army of the United States.

Code-named the Manhattan Project, it traced its roots to when the brilliant Fermi had fled Mussolini's fascism for the United States.

Once in the U.S., Fermi naturally had become involved with a number of other eminent scientists, many of them also Europeans who had sought freedom in America. There was the great Danish physicist Niels Bohr, the master German mathematician Albert Einstein, the Hungarians Leo Szilard, Edward Teller, Eugene Wigner, and others of remarkable scientific talent.

And among them there was talk of the very real possibility of splitting the uranium atom in a chain reaction—"fission," they called it—that would create energy on a scale bordering on the incomprehensible.

They theorized that the energy released from such a chain reaction, or continuous disintegration, of one hundred pounds of the uranium 235 isotope was the equivalent of the energy from twenty thousand tons of the high explosive TNT (trinitrotoluene).

The scale of effort to achieve this fission and then harness it in a usable manner—if, in fact, it was entirely possible, and the scientists had some disagreement over that—also bordered on the incomprehensible.

What was not disputed among these great minds was the fact that others in the world's scientific and political communities were aware of the possibilities of atomic fission and its military applications—and these others included Adolf Hitler.

Thus, the scientists in America—particularly the Hungarians Szilard, Teller, and Wigner, who vividly knew the reach of Hitler's cruel hand and the inconceivable atrocities that would follow were he to gain control of such a weapon—had to make this information known to the President of the United States.

They did so by drafting a letter, under Einstein's signature and dated August 2, 1939, that was then delivered to the White House by Alexander Sachs, an economist who enjoyed Roosevelt's close friendship.

The letter laid out everything the scientists knew about the big picture of turning uranium into an atomic bomb—what the potential uses were, where the rare usable uranium could be found, the limits of current academic funding, et cetera, et cetera. It ended by stating that it was understood that Germany had stopped the sale of uranium from Czech mines it had taken control of, and that the uranium work being done in America was being repeated at the Kaiser Wilhelm Institute in Berlin, where physicist Carl von Weizsacker—son of Nazi undersecretary of state Ernst von Weizsacker—was attached.

FDR instantly read between the lines. And he saw that this situation set up a pair of particularly difficult obstacles for the United States—not officially in the war—and the Allies:

1. They had to beat the Germans in the actual development of such an atomic bomb while not letting the enemy know that they were in fact working on one; and

2. They had to stop the Germans from accomplishing the same.

To the first problem, FDR put into play the Manhattan Project, a secret so great that only a very small circle of people—the scientists and FDR, of course, Churchill, Donovan, Hoover, the chief of Naval intelligence, an Army general named Leslie Groves—knew about it. Vice President Henry Wallace was not in that circle.

And to aid with the second problem, he established the Office of Coordinator of Information, which, as part of its agents' secret work in intelligence, counterintelligence, sabotage, and other shadowy operations, would be deeply involved both in the snatching of scientists from the Axis and in the blowing up of their assets that could be used in the development of an atomic bomb.

Donovan flipped through the Dyer file and came to a sheet that caught his interest. "'Known alloy machining, milling, and extrusion shops in and near Frankfurt'?"

"Another nice list from the professor," Douglass said. "We were aware of a couple of the major ones, but not that many, and not the scope of their production. There has to be a lot of machinery that the Germans looted and shipped back to put on line."

"Maybe Doug can take out these facilities with the drones," Donovan said with raised eyebrows.

Captain Douglass smiled warmly at the thought of his son.

While Peter Stuart "Doug" Douglass Jr. was Captain Douglass's namesake, the twenty-six-year-old West Point graduate was quite something more. Starting with the fact that he was a triple ace and a newly minted lieutenant colonel in the Army Air Forces.

He also was in England, and caught up with the OSS team involved in the Aphrodite Project, which was trying—key word *trying*, because so far they had had little luck—to convert B-17s into Torpex-filled drones that, controlled remotely, would attack and blow up German submarine pens and other targets considered highly valuable to the military, such as plants fabricating parts for tanks, attack aircraft, et cetera.

Lieutenant Colonel Douglass believed the drone to be a good idea—anything with the potential to save lives was a good idea—and he had good reason to, professionally and emotionally.

As the commanding officer of the 344th Fighter Group, Eighth United States Air Force, then-Major Douglass had lost 40 percent of his pilots to enemy fire during a bombing mission of German sub pens at St. Lazare. He vowed to do anything he could, when he could, to never allow the risking of the lives of his men in such a reckless way.

That included, one version of the story went, a furious Douglass having gone directly from his shot-up P-38F on the field at Atcham to the Eighth Air Force Headquarters building there, finding the planning and training officer who had laid out the mission—and giving the REMF a bloody nose to make his point known, not to mention remembered.

It wasn't the smartest of moves, Major Douglass had been the first to admit, but what the hell were they going to do to a graduate of Hudson High who had against all odds managed to actually take out a sub on the mission and bring back 60 percent of his force?

Worst case?

Send the poor bastard back out in his Lockheed Lightning?

The one with its nose painted with ten small Japanese flags (or "meatballs," each representing the downing of a Japanese airplane), six swastikas (signifying six German aircraft kills), and now a submarine of equal size?

Even the Army's slow-grinding bureaucratic machinery on rare occasion was capable of exhibiting some wisdom and in this case saw fit to recognize Douglass's heroism and leadership on the St. Lazare mission by promoting him to lieutenant colonel.

"I know that Doug would certainly welcome the chance to bomb them all," the deputy director of the OSS replied. "There's more than a little professional competition with our cousins in the SOE, especially after their saboteurs blew the nitrates plant in Norway last month."

Norway was a leading producer of deuterium oxide—or "heavy water," a by-product of the manufacture of fertilizer—one of only two materials (the other being graphite) that scientists found could control (essentially cool) the reactors during nuclear production. The British Special Operations Executive all-Norwegian commando raid at Rjukan had destroyed a critical half ton of heavy water earmarked for the Nazis' nuclear-development program.

Donovan nodded. "That was such an important facility, they're rapidly rebuilding it."

"Then Doug won't have to wait long for his turn at taking it out."

Donovan chuckled appreciatively.

"With any luck, he can do it safely from the controls of an Aphrodite drone," the OSS director said. "But if the Pope keeps up the pace, Doug may not get a chance."

"The Pope?"

"Fermi," Donovan explained. "Oppenheimer picked up on the nickname. Years ago, some Italian scientists gave it to the young Fermi because they said he believed himself to be infallible."

Dr. J. Robert Oppenheimer was the distinguished physicist from the University of California overseeing the scientists of the Manhattan Project.

Douglass grinned. "Oh, that one. Sorry. My mind went right to Rome. I had heard that about the nickname."

Donovan went on, "Oppenheimer says that in discussions with the Pope after they created the first atomic chain reaction at the University of Chicago in December, he, Oppenheimer, sees a completed bomb."

Douglass stared at Donovan.

"That is remarkable," Douglass said after a long moment.

"Yes, which is why the OSS is accelerating the pulling out of the scientists and the sabotaging of assets."

"Sounds like Doug is going to be busy."

"We're all going to be very busy."

[THREE]
The National Institutes of Health Building
Washington, D.C.
0655 7 March 1943

The young woman at the tall reception desk in the NIH lobby watched as the lithe, good-looking guy in his mid-twenties walked toward her. He wore a U.S. Army uniform with first lieutenant bars and had blond hair and blue eyes. He moved with enormous energy and confidence.

Seated at a small desk to the right of the receptionist station was a uniformed policeman—half-listening to a radio news bulletin about what was being described as a train derailment in Oklahoma earlier in the day—and two other cops standing guard by the elevators. They watched the soldier, too.

"My name is Fulmar," the Army lieutenant said to the receptionist. "Captain Douglass is expecting me."

She consulted a typewritten list.

"May I see some identification, please?"

Fulmar produced the identity card issued by the Adjutant General's Office, U.S. Army, that said he was "FULMAR, Eric, 1st Lt., Infantry, Army of the United States."

After she carefully studied it and studied him and smiled, she produced a cardboard VISITOR badge. Fulmar thought that that was curious; he was in the OSS, not just a regular visitor to the Washington office, and thought that the list she had checked would have somehow reflected his status.

Then he noticed there was no signage—no indication whatsoever—of the OSS and decided the standardized badge was part of the anonymity, and thus nothing more than some standard operating procedure, and attached it to his tunic using the alligator clip on the back.

One of the guards at the elevators approached the desk.

"Please show the lieutenant to Captain Douglass's office," the receptionist said to the guard.

"This way, sir," the guard said.

They took the elevator up three floors, then walked all the way down a long hallway. At the end was a doorway with a little sign labeled DIRECTOR. A police guard was posted outside. He was sitting in a folding metal chair reading the *Washington Star*.

The two policemen acknowledged one another, and Fulmar followed the first through the door and into an outer office that had a small army of female clerks. One was older and gray-haired, at a basic wooden desk with a black phone and a nameplate that read A. FISHBURNE, and was apparently in charge. Two younger women were standing at a pushcart stacked with papers and file folders and working with quiet efficiency to feed a huge bank of file cabinets. Three other young women noisily clacked away at typewriters, presumably generating more work for the women at the file cabinets.

"Good morning, Lieutenant," the gray-haired woman said with a smile. "The captain expects you."

There were two inner doors, one labeled DIRECTOR and one DEPUTY DIRECTOR.

The cop started to lead Fulmar to the latter, but the gray-haired woman said, "They're in the boss's office."

The cop looked at her and nodded. He walked to the door with DIRECTOR on it, knocked on the doorframe, and when he heard a man's voice from behind the door call out, "Come!" he opened it and announced, "Good morning, sir. Lieutenant Fulmar is here."

Fulmar heard the voice say, "Send him in, please."

The cop stepped back from the door, gestured with

his hand for Fulmar to enter the office, then went out the main door and down the corridor toward the elevator.

Fulmar stepped through the doorway and saw two officers in uniform, one a silver-haired Army colonel and one a sandy-haired Navy captain, sitting in opposing red leather chairs that were separated by a glass-top table and a red leather couch.

Fulmar came to attention and saluted stiffly.

"Reporting as ordered, sir."

The officers stood and returned the salute.

"It's a pleasure to meet you, Lieutenant," the Navy captain said, offering his hand. "I'm Captain Douglass. I think you may know my son."

Fulmar shook his hand. "An honor, sir. To meet you, and to be acquainted with Doug—with Colonel Douglass."

"That's very kind of you to say," Douglass replied, then took a step back and motioned to the Army colonel. "It's my pleasure to introduce you to Colonel Donovan." He looked at Donovan. "Colonel, may I present Lieutenant Fulmar?"

Fulmar already had his hand out, and when the Irishman took it in his mitt of a hand, Fulmar could not help but notice the very firm squeeze as they shook.

"I've heard a great deal about you, Lieutenant," Donovan said.

"Yes, sir?"

Donovan grinned. "Relax. It's very good. Otherwise we would not have asked you here."

"Yes, sir."

"Let's get on with it," Donovan said, his face somber. "It's a matter that seems to be getting more urgent by the hour."

He motioned toward the couch and chairs.

"Have a seat, please."

"Thank you," Fulmar said and moved toward the red couch.

As Donovan went to his red armchair near the fat manila folder on the glass-top table, he said, "I don't know about the lieutenant, Captain Douglass, but I would be eternally grateful for a cup of coffee."

Douglass looked at Fulmar. "How about it?"

"Please."

Douglass went to the door and opened it just enough to call out. The sound of typewriters filtered in.

"Mrs. Fishburne," he said, "coffee for three, please, and anything else you can scrounge up that we might find of interest. Thank you."

Douglass closed the door, shutting off the clacking, and returned to the red chair opposite Donovan and sat down.

Donovan, seated toward the front edge of the chair cushion, leaned forward. Elbows on his knees, he held his hands together—almost in a manner of praying—and tapped his fingertips together twice, then touched index fingers to his nose and thumbs to his chin as he considered his thoughts.

He looked directly into Fulmar's eyes.

It was a penetrating gaze, and as Fulmar looked back

into the steely gray-green eyes he felt himself automatically sit more rigidly.

"What I am about to tell you," Donovan began in a tone deeply serious, "is known by only a few people in the OSS."

"Yes, sir," Fulmar said, but it was more a question.

"The President has directed the OSS to quote quietly and quickly unquote put an end to the acts of German sabotage on American soil."

"Sir?"

"Do I need to repeat myself?" Donovan said softly.

Fulmar glanced at Douglass, who was expressionless, then back to Donovan.

"No, sir," Fulmar said. "It's just that it was my understanding that that was the FBI's territory."

"It is. Which is why what I am asking of you requires the utmost secrecy."

After a moment, Fulmar said, "Yes, sir."

"Do you have any questions?"

Fulmar nodded.

"A few, sir. The first being: 'Why me?'"

"You are the proverbial round peg for the round hole," Donovan said, sliding back in his chair to a more relaxed position and crossing his legs. "You understand the mind of a spy and the mind of a German—you speak German fluently, yes—?"

"Yes, sir."

"—And how many other languages?"

Fulmar shrugged. "Three fluently, maybe four, five passably. Living in so many places, they came to me easily. . . ."

The director nodded. "And that—and I mean your ability to blend in 'so many places,' as you put it— coupled with your actions in the rescue of the Dyers makes you our round peg."

He paused.

"You perform exceptionally under pressure . . . and we're under a great deal of pressure."

There was a long silence before Douglass broke it.

"The President—and our country—simply cannot have these agents taking the focus off of the war abroad," the deputy director said.

"Yes, sir. What would you have me do?"

"Whatever is necessary," Donovan said.

"And, sir, that would be—?"

"Whatever is necessary," Donovan repeated evenly.

The director let that sink in, and when Fulmar slowly nodded that he understood, Donovan went on:

"The FBI has been directed to share with us everything they have on all the bombings. On the surface, that sounds great. But I find at least two fundamental flaws in it, the first being that Director Hoover is not going to willingly turn over all of the information if there's a chance that he can hold something back in order for the FBI to collar these German agents and get the credit—"

"We know for a fact they're German?" Fulmar said.

Donovan showed his mild displeasure at being interrupted. "May I finish?"

"Certainly, sir. My apologies."

"To answer your question, we have reason to believe that they are agents of Germany—if not precisely German nationals—because of the pattern of evidence that they're leaving, from weapons to witnesses. There's a file—"

Douglass stood up. "I'll get it," he said and went to the big desk.

"—and in it," Donovan went on, "is everything the FBI believes we should have. It's enough to establish that in all likelihood we are dealing with German agents—soldiers trained by Skorzeny. You're familiar with Obersturmbannführer Skorzeny?"

"Yes, sir. Of course."

Fulmar's tone suggested that it was inconceivable that anyone could not be familiar with such a storied warrior, enemy or not.

Douglass brought back a folder thick with papers. He put it on the glass-top table. Fulmar glanced at it, then back at Donovan.

"And that brings me to the other flaw," Donovan went on. "The OSS at its core is military and thus plays by different rules than does the FBI. While Director Hoover has been known to stretch the rules of law enforcement to suit his needs, by and large he keeps the bureau on the straight and narrow—his intolerance of crooked cops, for example—and this rigid mind-set, having trickled down to how the rank and file fundamentally operates, limits what the bureau is capable of accomplishing. You follow me so far?"

"I believe so, sir. No risk, no reward."

"Yes. The President understands these limitations, as he does the parameters of the OSS, and thus has decided that the situation requires something more than the FBI offers. . . ."

He paused to gather his thoughts.

"These attacks," he went on, "spotlight some of our country's biggest weaknesses. The United States cannot secure its vast borders—that's a statement of fact, not a political ploy—and our infrastructure is vulnerable to subversive acts. We simply cannot protect every electrical substation, every train station, every town reservoir from attack. There are too many, and the manpower available—that is to say, everyone we are not sending to fight abroad—is far too few."

"So one clever saboteur can with little effort cause remarkable chaos," Fulmar said.

"Correction," Douglass said, "*is* causing remarkable chaos."

"And with more than one on the ground," Donovan added, "there is a force multiplier effect. Follow?"

"If the public hears of two," Fulmar offered, "they speculate that there could be two—or two dozen—others."

"It's already happening in the press reports," Douglass said. "Reckless speculation. And soon the press will draw the obvious conclusion that the Texas and Oklahoma explosions show that the size of the attacks are becoming larger by the day."

Donovan added: "Given time—and the Hoover Maxim on Criminality—the FBI would get these guys. But we don't have the luxury of time."

"'The Hoover Maxim on Criminality'?" Fulmar said. "I am not familiar with that."

Donovan's eyes twinkled as he looked at Douglass.

"You wouldn't be expected to," Douglass said with a smile. "Quoting from the *J. Edgar Book of Law Enforcement,* 'The Hoover Maxim on Criminality stipulates that all criminals—without exception—commit some stupid act before, during, or after a crime that allows for their eventual capture.'"

The director and deputy director of the OSS exchanged grins.

"Forgive us," Donovan said. "We do not mean to make light of the circumstance. It is just that the important word there as far as we're concerned is *eventual.*"

"Yes, sir," Fulmar said. "We do not have time to wait."

Donovan nodded. He liked what he just heard. Fulmar had said that he understood the urgency of the mission—and with "we" his acceptance of it.

Douglass said, "And that brings us back to doing whatever is necessary—"

There was a knock at the door.

Douglass looked to Donovan, who nodded.

"Come!" Douglass called.

The door opened and Mrs. Fishburne came through it, struggling with a tray holding three china mugs of steaming coffee and a plate piled with sticky bun pastries.

"I'm sorry that I took so long," she said, placing the tray on the glass-top table. In her hand there was a sealed envelope, with STRICTLY CONFIDENTIAL stamped in red on the front.

"This just came for you, Colonel," she said. "An FBI agent hand-carried it here. He said that his orders were to give it to you personally. It took some time for me to convince him that the director and the deputy director were not only unavailable now, but that it would be hours before either was available at all. He gave that about five seconds of thought and decided that waiting was not high on his list of priorities."

Donovan chuckled as he broke the seal of the envelope.

"You did well, Mrs. Fishburne," the director of the OSS said, scanning the message. "As you'll learn, the FBI has a very high regard of itself, and it is a noble endeavor indeed—if fruitless—to try to help keep them grounded."

"Yes, sir," she said without much conviction.

He looked up from the sheet of paper and added, "Don't be surprised, however, if you suddenly find yourself the subject of a thorough FBI investigation."

Mrs. Fishburne looked momentarily stunned.

Donovan grinned. "I'm only half kidding. If the FBI had decided you were a threat to the domestic security of the United States, Mrs. Fishburne, there'd already be an ample file on you. And they'd just be waiting for the Hoover Maxim on Criminality to work its magic."

Fulmar glanced at Douglass and could see he was trying not to grin too obviously.

"Yes, sir," Mrs. Fishburne said, clearly not at all comfortable with the explanation.

"That'll be all for now, Mrs. Fishburne," Douglass said. "Thank you."

She turned and left the room, pulling the door closed behind her.

"Well, this appears to be both good and bad news," Donovan said, leaning forward to pass the letter to Douglass, then picking up one of the steaming china mugs.

He looked at Fulmar and nodded at the coffee. "Help yourself."

Douglass sat back in his chair and his eyes fell to the message.

Federal Bureau of Investigation
WASHINGTON, D.C.

Office of the Deputy Director

*** STRICTLY CONFIDENTIAL ***

March 7, 1943

Colonel Donovan:

As an update to the previous information provided by the F.B.I. to your office on the most recent acts of sabotage, Director Hoover has asked me to inform you of the following:

---

1. That our F.B.I. agents in Texas believe with a confidence factor of 90 percent that at least two (2) German saboteurs were responsible for the Mar. 5 bombing of the Dallas department store that killed two (2) citizens and injured five (5) others;

2. That our F.B.I. agents in Texas believe with a confidence factor of 90 percent that at least one (1) German saboteur was responsible for the bombing of the Mar. 5 Dallas Union Station train depot and the U.S.O. therein, killing five (5) soldiers and injuring twenty (20) others;

3. That our F.B.I. agents in Texas and Oklahoma believe with a confidence factor of 70 percent that at least one (1) German saboteur was responsible for the bombing on Mar. 6 of the Red Rock Rail Line train en route Dallas to Kansas (casualties unknown at this time); and

4. That our agents in Oklahoma believe that in the train bombing:

(a) with a confidence factor of 50 percent at least one (1) German saboteur died in the explosion, and

(b) with a confidence factor of 100 percent two (2) F.B.I. agents in the defense

of their country lost their lives in the
explosion.

On behalf of the Director,

And with warmest personal regards,

Clyde

C. A. Tolson

Douglass's eyebrows went up.

Donovan saw that and said, "Wondering why Tolson sent that, are you?"

As deputy director of the FBI, Clyde Tolson was nearly inseparable from Hoover. Both on and off the job. Their relationship was so close in fact that rumors of homosexuality circled regularly, though Donovan dismissed the dirty tales as more of the vicious undercurrent that was Washington politics.

"A little," Douglass said as he leaned forward and passed the paper to Fulmar, and added, "Your mission's most recent intel, Lieutenant. Word to the wise: Don't take it at face value."

"Yes, sir," Fulmar said, and began reading the confidential message.

Donovan explained, "While the President told the director to keep us—the OSS—informed of any and all updates, he did not say that the director had to do so personally."

"Then using Tolson is his way of following what he considers a distasteful order," Douglass said, "without bringing himself to the level of a lowly field operative."

Douglass caught Fulmar's eyes dart at him.

"No offense, Lieutenant. No one in this room has anything but the highest regard for field ops."

Fulmar knew that that certainly was the case with Wild Bill Donovan—his reputation as a first-rate battlefield commander was above reproach, made all the more so by his Medal of Honor from the First War—and while Douglass's history was not necessarily as well known, Fulmar had to believe (a) that Donovan would not tolerate anyone but a true believer as his number two, and (b) that with Doug Douglass being one competent fearless son-ofabitch, he had had to have learned that from someone and that someone most likely was his father.

"None taken, sir," Fulmar said.

"That crack about not taking Tolson's update at face value was not entirely facetious," Douglass said.

He looked at Donovan. "I am somewhat suspicious as to why they have provided that information to us so quickly. We usually have to pry the weather report from them."

Donovan nodded. "Just take that into consideration as you review the file, Lieutenant."

"I will, sir."

"How are you fixed for a place to stay here?" Douglass asked.

"I need something, sir, but I don't anticipate for long,

maybe a night or two. I'd like to get on the trail of these guys as soon as possible."

Douglass looked at Donovan, who nodded.

"We have a place on Q Street," Douglass then said. "I'll have Chief Ellis make arrangements for that, as well as anything else you'll need."

Douglass stood, then Donovan followed.

"Good luck," the director of the OSS said, offering his hand.

Fulmar quickly got to his feet and shook the director's hand. "Thank you, sir."

"Grab that file," Douglass said, "and a sticky bun, if you like"—he nodded toward the door—"and we can be on our way."

[FOUR]
Room 909
Robert Treat Hotel
Newark, New Jersey
0115 7 March 1943

After Kurt Bayer had agreed to an all-night date with Mary by circling the "30" that she had written on the inside of the matchbook cover, Kurt had said that he had to make a couple of quick arrangements.

The first he said was that he had to go to his room and leave another note for his traveling partner.

He asked Mary about a hotel room, and when Mary replied that she did not have one—wasn't allowed to have one, she added—Bayer realized that meant he had to take care of that, see if he could get one in the Robert Treat, and, if not, then try to find one elsewhere, preferably very close by, before writing the new note.

He had considered the idea that they could have taken a chance and used the room he already had access to. But he instantly dismissed that, because they wanted the room for all night, and he told himself he'd be damned if he and Mary were going to be interrupted by Richard Koch storming into the room at whatever late hour— possibly drunk, and possibly suddenly interested in sharing Mary.

So Bayer had gone to the front desk, found that they had plenty of available rooms, put down a cash deposit to secure a nice one with a view on the ninth floor for three days to start, and then returned to the lounge with two keys.

At the bar with Mary, he had ordered them both fresh drinks—doubles, and in highball glasses, so on their way upstairs they would not risk spilling liquor from the tricky-shaped martini glasses—then paid the tab, signing it to Koch's room, and gave Mary her room key, saying that he would meet her there after he went by his room and either told Koch that he had plans for the evening or left him a note to that effect.

Bayer had found the notepad with his first note untouched on top of the bedspread and no sign that Koch had ever returned. He wondered where in hell Koch could have gone for so long—ditching a car was not that difficult—then decided he'd probably found his own fun.

He had then torn off the old note from the pad and written a new one:

```
R—
Starving. Couldn't wait any longer.
See you in the morning.
K
```

He had grinned at that.

Starving? Absolutely. But now it's a whole different hunger.

Mary had already been in the bed when Bayer finally reached room 909, though in the darkened room it had taken him a moment to notice the human form under the covers. She had all the lights turned out, the radio quietly playing some big band music, and the curtains on the big window pulled back to show the sweeping view over Newark.

As his eyes had adjusted to the dark, he noticed the tidy stack of her clothes in a chair by the window, with her shoes beneath on the floor. And he could see that she had the sheets pulled up to her nose—and that her eyes twinkled.

Aroused, Bayer had not been able to pull off his clothes fast enough.

Literally.

No sooner had he jumped naked between the sheets—at the same moment noticing Mary's wonderful warmth and sweet scent floating out—than his first attempt at coupling turned disastrous.

Bayer had been very excited—too excited, it turned out—and they had had to wait thirty minutes—despite Mary's very creative and energetic attempts to breathe life, so to speak, back into his libido—before they could again try making the beast with two backs.

They now lay on their backs in the bed, sweat-soaked and exhausted, looking at the ceiling, the music from the radio softly masking the sound of them trying to catch their breath.

After a moment, Mary inhaled deeply and let it out.

"That was worth the wait," she said, and giggled as she reached over to stroke his chest.

"Yeah, it was."

"You're very nice, you know."

He turned to her and was amazed at how much she glowed, her face soft and warm, her blonde hair bright in the night.

"Thank you," he said. "And you're amazing."

She looked back at the ceiling and giggled.

The music ended, and an announcer came on and said that that had been the melodic sounds of Glenn Miller and his orchestra and that the news was next.

Bayer instantly turned to look at the radio, then padded naked across the room and tuned in another station.

"Something wrong with the music?" Mary said, admiring Kurt's body.

"Oh, it's not the music. I'm just tired of news. And it doesn't seem right for now."

Mary giggled.

She said, "Somehow I don't think the news is going to slow you down."

Bayer crawled back in bed and kissed her on the lips. "Me, either."

"Especially if it's about those . . . explosions."

"Explosions?"

"Yeah, bombings is what they're saying in the news. They're scary, but at the same time they're kind of exciting—you know?"

What the hell? Bayer thought.

"How old are you?" he said all of a sudden.

"Twenty-two," she shot back.

He reached over, cupped her breast, and squeezed very gently as he kissed her ear.

"No, really," he whispered.

"Twenty-two."

"C'mon . . ."

"Why's it important?"

"Just curious."

"Okay. Twenty."

"Mary . . ." he whispered and squeezed again.

"Eighteen, okay? Why?"

Jesus Christ. A hooker at eighteen?

"How long have you been doing . . . this?" he said.

She sat upright. "Doing *what*?" she said defensively.

Bayer looked up at her. "What we're doing."

She looked out the window a long moment. She sniffled, and Bayer saw her eyes were now glistening.

"I think I'd better go," she said finally and threw back the sheet.

Bayer reached out and wrapped his arms around her, then pulled her back beside him on the bed.

"I'm sorry I asked."

She sniffled again and nodded.

Bayer thought, *I need to turn this back around. . . .*

"Tell me what you find so exciting about those explosions?" he said.

"Nothing, really."

"C'mon . . ."

She shrugged loose of his arms and sat up.

"Okay, I'll tell you," she said, looking down at him, her voice hard. "I see power in them."

"Power?"

"Yeah, like if I could do what they're doing I would have power."

"What would you do with the power?"

She looked out the window again, deciding if she should answer . . . and answer truthfully.

"Look," she said, her tone softened. "I like you. A lot, you know? Like I said, you're very nice."

She paused, then swallowed hard.

"Not every guy is," she went on.

"What do you mean?"

"When I was fifteen, my boyfriend—he was twenty. And he had an older buddy who ran a club over on Route 17 in Lodi, and they said I could make some really sweet money by dancing. Just warm-up stuff. No nudity, you know?"

"Uh-huh."

"And at first that's what it was. The money was great. But then I began having a drink or two while dancing, and then more, and my boyfriend said he didn't mind if I tried it topless—said he liked that customers knew I was his girlfriend and how they had to pay to see what he got for free. . . ."

She stopped and looked toward the bedside table. Her glass from the bar was there, mostly melted ice, and she took a sip.

"And then the money got better," she went on, "and the audience, you know, the rush you get from them, so I was doing more and more. And then—I guess I'd just turned seventeen—I started doing private dances and couldn't believe the money. My boyfriend said he didn't mind the private dances and I found out why—the bastard had gotten himself a new girl. . . ."

"Jesus," Bayer said softly, stroking her hair.

"So next thing I knew, with my boyfriend out of the picture, his buddy said that I owed the club so much for my drinks—which I had always paid for—and half my tips. And he said there was a way to make up the difference. . . ."

"This way."

There was a long silence. "I didn't do it till they beat me up pretty good. Lots of bruises, and I couldn't work for a couple months. So I still owed the money but couldn't pay it off. But then I healed up. . . ."

Now Bayer took a sip of his watered-down drink.

"I can see why you'd want that power," he said softly as he put the glass back on the table.

"Uh-huh."

There was a long silence, and then she said, "Let's forget about all that and you and me just have some fun."

She rolled over and draped her right thigh over his belly.

He enjoyed the weight and the warm, soft feel of it, and when she moved it and her leg brushed his groin he liked that even more.

Bayer grinned in the dark.

Do I tell her?

He said, "Can you keep a secret?"

"Sure," Mary whispered.

"You could not tell anyone else."

She snuggled up to him.

"What is it?" she whispered seductively.

"I know who's causing them."

"Causing what?"

"The explosions."

She inhaled deeply and audibly. "No!"

Ach! I shouldn't have said shit.

"Who?" she pursued.

"Well . . ."

"Do you know," she said, "or—"

She reached down with her right hand and grasped his genitals. The warmth of her hand caused him to stir.

"—are you just full of it?"

She squeezed gently.

He groaned appreciatively.

"Hey," she said, "it's like a miracle."

He was ready again and broke free of her grasp, and rolled onto her as she started to giggle.

VIII

[ONE]
Suite 601
Gramercy Park Hotel
2 Lexington Avenue
New York City, New York
0801 7 March 1943

Lit by a full moon, Ann Chambers came in and out of Dick Canidy's view as he chased her up the narrow, winding grassy drive that was lined with mature magnolia trees in full bloom. She was wearing the silk pajamas that he had bought for her at the boutique on Broadway, the pj top half unbuttoned, and every now and then Dick could hear her playful laugh float back on the cool, humid night air.

This was the Plantation, a vast tract of timberland that the Chambers family owned in southern Alabama, and the natural drive wound from a paved macadam country road past the dirt airstrip—where the Beech Staggerwing biplane was tied down—and ended a mile later, opening onto a large hilltop clearing that highlighted the property's main building, a Gone with the Wind *antebellum mansion that had been named the Lodge.*

Dick saw Ann finally dart out of the shadows of the

magnolias, glance at him over her shoulder—her long blonde hair catching the moonlight—and laugh as she went to a side entrance of the Lodge.

As Dick approached, he could see that she was pulling on the wood-frame screen door but that it would not open. The flimsy door was being held shut from the inside by a small hook-and-eye latch, and every time she pulled, the hook gave only a half inch or so—and the door then slammed back into its frame.

Dick came closer, and the bam, bam, bam *became louder with Ann repeatedly pulling at the door—and laughing hysterically. The top of her silk pj's slid off her right shoulder.*

Dick grinned mischievously, his heart beating rapidly as he closed in on her.

Ann laughed, and the door slammed bam, bam, bam. . . .

And a man's muffled voice called, "Mr. Canidy?"

Canidy shook his head, trying to shake off the fog that clouded his thought.

Bam, bam, bam.

"Room service, Mr. Canidy."

Canidy cracked open an eye and saw that he wasn't at the Plantation in Alabama but still at the Gramercy in New York.

The clock on the bedside table showed three minutes past eight.

Bam, bam, bam.

"Mr. Canidy?"

I didn't call for room service.

He slipped his right hand under his pillow, found his .45, then got out of bed and in only his boxers and T-shirt went to the door.

"I didn't request room service," he said, staying to the side of the doorframe, away from the door itself.

Using his right thumb, he pulled back the hammer on the pistol.

"It's complimentary, sir."

Canidy rubbed his eyes. He shook his head.

Complimentary?

Wait . . . that's right. Instead of a wake-up phone call, they send up coffee and tea and the morning paper at the requested time.

He took his left index finger and thumb, grasped the hammer, squeezed the trigger, and carefully uncocked the pistol.

"Just leave it at the foot of the door, please."

"Are you sure, sir?"

"That'll be fine. Your gratuity will be on the tray when you come back for it."

"Very well, sir," the voice said, and then there was the clanking of cups and saucers as the tray was placed on the floor.

Canidy walked to the bathroom, put the pistol on the top of the toilet tank, and took a long leak.

He flushed, glanced at himself in the mirror over the sink—*Smooth move, Casanova. The minute you fall for one girl, you can't even get laid in your dreams*—and washed his hands and face.

He took the white terry cloth robe from the hook on

the back of the bathroom door, put it on, slipped the pistol in the right pocket, and, somewhat sure the gun wasn't going to fall out, went back to the door.

After he unlocked it and went to open it, he found that there was some resistance. He got it open enough to peek out and saw that the resistance was because his clothes from the trip aboard the fishing boat had been cleaned and returned and were now hanging from the doorknob.

He pulled open the door completely, retrieved the clothes, and put them on the couch, then went back and picked up the tray and brought it in the room, pushing the door closed with his foot.

Candidy put the tray on the coffee table in the sitting room of his suite and looked at the *New York Times* as he poured steaming coffee into one of the two cups.

The biggest headline above the fold read: U-BOAT AT-TACKS IN ATLANTIC ON RISE AGAIN.

"Jesus H. Christ," he said disgustedly.

He sat in the armchair, unfolded the paper, and scanned the other headlines on the front page.

There was a long piece, with a large photograph showing strewn wreckage, about a train derailment in Oklahoma on Saturday. Beneath that, a report on the Luftwaffe's attack on London with twin-engine Heinkel He 111 bombers. A short piece reported that the rate of pregnancies among American teenagers had spiked. And—some really good news—the rest of the page was devoted to progress on the war fronts: the Germans withdrawing from Tunisia, the RAF bombing the hell out of Berlin, and the Australians and Americans kicking the goddamned Japs' asses in the Bismarck Sea.

He decided to start with the U-boat article and went back to it.

It reported that both of the convoys that had left the New York area in just the first week of March had been attacked, with a loss of four ships carrying matériel and one troopship.

"Shit," he said and drained his coffee cup.

He moved on to the London bombing piece and that caused him to wonder—and worry—if Ann Chambers was right now knee-deep in rubble interviewing rescuers for her profiles.

Jesus, I'm getting nowhere sitting here, he thought, frustrated. *I need to do something.*

He poured more coffee, grabbed the newspaper, and started for the head.

He glanced at the clock. Eight-twenty.

To hell with it. Close enough.

Canidy put down the paper and picked up the phone receiver. He then asked the operator to connect him to a Washington number he gave from memory.

"Switchboard oh-five," a woman's monotone voice answered.

"Major Canidy for Chief Ellis. Is he available, please?"

"Major Canidy? One moment."

Canidy took a sip of his coffee as he heard a click and another dial tone and then ringing.

"Ellis," came the familiar voice.

"How they hanging, Chief?" Canidy said.

"One lower than the other, Major. Got a heads-up for you—I overheard the boss asking if you were having any success and when you'd be headed over there. Sounded like he wanted whatever done yesterday. . . ."

Shit, Canidy thought.

He said, "Any chance you're with the boss?"

"No chance. Sorry."

"Well, if it comes up again before I speak to him, tell him I said, 'Some, and very soon.'"

"Will do. He's at home. The captain has me babysitting."

Canidy knew that Colonel Donovan's home was a town house in Georgetown, just off of Wisconsin Avenue, and that when Ellis said he was babysitting for the captain, that meant that Douglass had him keeping watch over someone at the house on Q Street.

"I was going to ask him if I could get Ex-Lax to work with me."

Ellis knew that Canidy's lower gastrointestinal tract was not the subject at hand. It was, instead, Eric Fulmar. "Ex-Lax" had been the code name that "Pharmacist"—Canidy—had assigned him on their last mission, the one in Hungary that almost killed them all.

When Fulmar learned of the code name, he did not find it at all fitting—and sure as hell not humorous—which, of course, only caused Canidy to continue referring to him by it.

Ellis didn't answer immediately.

Canidy went on: "What do you think the chances are of that?"

"Not good, Major."

"Really?"

"Yeah, why don't you ask him yourself?"

"Donovan?"

"No, Ex—" Ellis began, then caught himself. "Fulmar. He's right here."

Canidy heard the phone being passed.

Fulmar's voice came through the phone: "How about cutting out that 'Ex-Lax' shit, ol' buddy?"

"Good morning, Eric. Nice to hear your voice, too. And you don't have to thank me again for saving your ass."

The line was quiet a moment, then Fulmar said, "You know I'm grateful. But you're not going to let me forget, are you?"

"Never. That way, you'll always come running when I call."

Fulmar chuckled. "Like now? What's on your mind? Everything okay?"

"So far. But I'm in New York, up to my neck, and soon quite possibly over my head, and was hoping to maybe get a hand from you."

"Not possible. Sorry. The boss has me . . . let's just call it 'busy.'"

"Anything I know about?"

"Only if you've listened to the radio or read a newspaper lately. It's hot."

"You're the one responsible for the spike in knocked-up teens?"

"Very funny. All I can tell you is that I've been up for what seems like hours doing nothing but wading through more bullshit FBI reports. I've never read so much that said so little in my life. Except maybe your English essays at St. Paul's."

"When do you think you could break free?"

"I can't, I told you. I have to . . . Hang on a moment."

Canidy guessed that Fulmar had moved the receiver away from his head, because he could faintly hear Fulmar asking Ellis something and Ellis grunting a reply. Then he could hear Fulmar more clearly.

"Where are you?" Fulmar asked Canidy.

"New York."

"No, where are you staying?"

"Gramercy."

"Nice."

"Yeah. Plenty of room. I got a suite."

"Look, I can read these files anywhere. And I need to run down a lead there."

"Great!"

"I can be there by—what?—after noon or so."

"Room six-oh-one."

"Six-oh-one. Got it."

[TWO]
Robert Treat Hotel
Newark, New Jersey
0815 7 March 1943

Richard Koch was sitting among a small crowd in the lobby. He was reading the *Trenton Times* and smoking a cigarette when he noticed one of the two young hookers from the night before come out of one of the elevators and start across the lobby.

He smiled at the blonde as she caught a glimpse of him, but she would not make eye contact.

Still wearing the same clothes from last night, mein Liebchen? *Business must be good.*

He was admiring the sway of her hips as she went out the main doors when another elevator opened and Kurt Bayer got off.

Koch glared at him and thought, *It's about time you showed up, you bastard.*

He folded the newspaper, got to his feet, and started walking toward the main doors. He nodded for Bayer to follow.

Outside, Koch waited for Bayer to catch up.

"Good morning," Bayer said pleasantly.

"I got your note in the room," Koch snapped. "Where the hell have you been?"

Bayer looked at him before replying.

"I can ask the same: Where the hell have *you* been?"

"Getting rid of the car. Like I told you."

"You also told me that that was going to take only a half hour to do."

Koch started walking. "Come. There's a coffee shop around the corner."

As they walked, Koch added, "I had to take extra care with the car."

"Why?"

"Because of this."

He swung the newspaper, hitting him in the chest.

Bayer looked at him crossly, then took the paper, unfolded it, and scanned the headlines.

He came to the picture of a train wreck, and read the caption.

"*Ach du lieber Gott!*" he whispered.

"Yeah," Koch said.

They turned the corner and came to the door of a coffee shop.

"Read the story," Koch said. "It just gets better."

He pulled open the door and went inside. Bayer quickly followed.

The noisy small restaurant, with its open kitchen behind the counter, was quite warm, the air saturated with the smells of toast and coffee and grease. They took one of the two empty booths toward the back and, after the waitress brought them water and coffee, placed their order.

Bayer flipped the pages of the newspaper until he came to the article on the train derailment. It was a long one.

After a moment, he said, "It says they believe the derailment is connected with the explosions in Dallas."

"I know. I read it," Koch said, annoyed. "And of course they do. Who wouldn't put the two together? They happened a day and maybe three hundred kilometers apart."

He sighed heavily.

"Those bastards are out of control."

"I say it's Grossman," Bayer said, looking at him.

"It doesn't matter which one it is. Their actions require that we really have to be careful right now. There're already cops everywhere."

The waitress arrived with an armload of plates. She took two off, placing a plate of ham and fried eggs and toast in front of Koch and a plate with a tall stack of pancakes in front of Bayer.

Bayer poured syrup on his cakes, then kept reading as he ate. He shook his head.

" 'Authorities declined to speculate,' " he read aloud, talking with a full mouth, " 'if there was any connection between these explosions and the ones last week on the East Coast.' Damn!"

Mashed pancake flew out of his mouth, and he washed down what remained with a swallow of water.

"I think," Koch said evenly, "that we are okay here."

Koch had noted that no one had paid him any notice as he had waited in the hotel lobby. Now his eyes surveyed the restaurant and its customers. And, again, no one paid them any particular notice.

"We just have to not make a single mistake."

Bayer nodded.

Koch tore into his ham slice with the knife, cut off a

large piece, forked it into his mouth and chewed aggressively. He repeated the process, not saying a word until the plate was empty. Then, finished, he at once tossed the fork and knife on the plate with a loud *clank*.

He looked at Bayer.

"So, now you tell me where you were last night."

Bayer turned his attention to his plate. He casually cut more pancake and put it in his mouth and chewed slowly as he looked at Koch, then around the restaurant, then back at Koch.

"I had a date," he said, his mouth half full.

"With that hooker?" Koch said, incredulous.

Bayer frowned.

"She has a name."

"I thought I told you to be careful!"

"I was."

"No more," Koch said firmly. "It must not happen again."

"What is the harm?"

Bayer looked at him, and when Koch did not answer Bayer grinned, then leaned forward.

"I think that I can get her friend the redhead for you as a date."

Koch ignored him.

"What we are going to do," he said as a matter of fact, "is stick with our original plan but wait at least an extra three, four days to see what Cremer and Grossman do— or what gets done about them and their work."

"Fine." He shrugged and cut another piece of pancake. "I have something to fill my time."

Koch's eyes narrowed. Steam practically came out of his ears.

Koch thought, *This whole time we've worked well together as a team—but bring in one lousy piece of ass . . .*

"I'll be in the room," he said, sliding out of the booth. "We will continue this conversation there."

Bayer watched Koch's back as he went to the door and through it, then disappeared down the sidewalk in the direction of the hotel.

He made a face, then looked back at his plate and saw that he wasn't nearly finished.

What the hell. I'll take my time and eat in peace.

He held up his coffee cup for the waitress to see.

She came and refilled it, and his water, collected Koch's plate and cup, and left the check on the table.

Bayer cut another piece of pancake and went back to reading the newspaper.

He did not really understand why Koch was so concerned about the explosions in Texas and Oklahoma. The other team of agents was having significant success with blowing up things and creating general disorder. That was what they had all been sent to do. Granted, not with such big bombings, but nevertheless . . .

He shook his head and turned the page.

He came to a full-page advertisement for Bamberger's Department Store that showed new women's spring fashions. The light-haired young model wore a very flattering formfitting blouse and it took no effort whatever for Bayer to picture Mary in it. He smiled, and with that warm mental image turned the page.

Ten minutes later, he had finished with the pancake and washed it down with coffee.

He reached into the right pocket of his pants and dug around for the roll of cash that he had bound with a rubber band. All he came up with, though, was the rubber band and a fistful of coins.

Damn! All my cash went to pay for the room and Mary!

After hearing about her money woes, he had advanced her almost a week's worth of cash so that she could buy time with the club owner—and time that they could spend together.

He grabbed the check, looked at the total, then quickly counted the coins in his hand.

Just enough, but almost no tip.

As quietly as he could, he put all of the coins on top of the ticket and slipped toward the door, avoiding the waitress and anyone else.

Koch was sitting on his unmade bed in their room on the fourth floor. Bayer's bed was still the way he had left it the night before, although now there were the two duffel bags on it.

Koch had a newspaper spread out on the bed and was field-cleaning his Walther PPK 9mm semiautomatic pistol.

"Any plans for that?" Bayer said as he locked the door behind him.

"Just maintenance. When I'm finished, we can go over the plans for New York."

Bayer walked over to the duffels and starting digging in the nearest one.

Koch glanced up from his gun. "Need something?"

Bayer stopped digging and looked back at Koch.

"Cash. I literally spent my last dime paying the restaurant bill."

"What? I gave you almost three hundred dollars two days ago."

"Right. And I spent it."

"On what, for chrissake?"

"There was all that gas on the drive up," he said. "And on food. . . ."

And—damn, he won't like it—on Mary.

Koch angrily jabbed his right index finger at him. "And on that goddamned hooker!"

Bayer stared at him. "I said she has a name." He shook his head. "I paid her. So what? We have plenty more money."

Koch made a short, snide laugh.

"Not for that we don't. I control the funds, you may recall."

Bayer glared at him.

Damn him!

I need that cash.

But . . . not right away. At least I have a few days to figure this out.

He pulled his Walther from his pocket and Koch's eyes grew wide.

Huh?

Oh, now that's interesting.

So I scare you, do I?

Bayer looked down at his pistol. He pushed the thumb button at the top of the grip on the left side of the frame. That released the magazine and it dropped out of the handle. He pulled back the slide to eject the 9mm round that was in the throat, then spread out newspaper on his bed and began disassembling the weapon.

"Hand me that oil, will you?" Bayer said.

[THREE]
New York Public Library
Fifth Avenue at Forty-second Street
New York City, New York
1142 7 March 1943

Dick Canidy stood on the sidewalk in front of a huge stone lion that overlooked Fifth Avenue and held out his right arm, trying to flag down a taxicab. All the ones headed south zipped past him, and it was not until the Forty-second Street traffic light cycled to red that a cabbie heading north did a U-turn and pulled up in front of the library and Canidy.

This is all going too well, he thought as he opened the cab's back door and got in. *The other shoe is bound to drop at any moment.*

"Gramercy Park Hotel," he told the cabbie and put his heavy leather attaché case on the floor as the cab shot south toward Twenty-first Street.

What had been going well was his luck with finding research material on Sicily.

After getting off the phone with Eric Fulmar, he had moved on to taking care of the morning's three *s*'s, and in the course of covering the latter two at once—shaving in the shower—he came up with the idea of seeing what the New York Public Library had on the shelf.

And *had* was the key word, as Canidy's bag now held what little the NYPL had held on Sicily deep in its dusty stacks.

He hadn't been greedy per se—where there were duplicates of a title, he took only one—but his cache contained a dozen books, including the expected *Michelin Guide,* and—a genuine surprise—eighteenth-century British Admiralty charts ("Produced by the Royal Hydrographic Office") that showed the coastlines of Sicily and Italy and all of their islands, the details of their ports, as well as detailed information on such curious things as caves and the erosion of coastal areas.

It had taken Canidy more effort to fit all of his find into his bag than it had to sneak the loot out of the library. He had not gone out past the front desk but through the janitor's door that was ajar at the back of the building and had slipped into the stream of pedestrians coming out of Bryant Park.

Next thing he knew, he had been in front of the lion and then in the backseat of the cab that had stopped just for him.

Yeah. Something is going to go to hell at any moment. . . .

The cab arrived at the Gramercy ten minutes later and Canidy paid the fare. He went in the hotel and took the elevator to the sixth floor.

In his room, he turned on the radio and tuned in to the National Broadcasting Corporation's Blue Network, which was playing jazz. He opened his attaché case and, feeling somewhat like a mischievous underclassman in the lower school at St. Paul's in Cedar Rapids, brought out his "borrowed" library research and began laying it out.

He unfolded two of the British Admiralty charts on the couch and made a small stack of the books on the coffee table, putting them next to where he had left a pair of socks and the duck call that he'd bought at Leonwood's.

After studying the charts for a few minutes, he thought he would have a better understanding of the islands if he had Francesco Nola take him on a tour, so to speak, explaining what was what and who was where.

He then picked up the *Michelin Guide* and went to settle into the armchair. But first, he decided, he'd call room service and ask if the kitchen could put together for delivery one of those nice sliced-steak-on-a-hard-crusted-baguette sandwiches that he had had the night before at the bar and a pot of coffee.

The person answering the room service phone said that a server would have it up to room 601 within the half hour, twelve-thirty at the latest.

Canidy hung up the phone, wondering, *Okay, was*

that an undercover Navy guy or was it a member of the mob's union? And whichever one it was, how soon before my lunch order is passed up the intel line?

Three hours later, as Canidy picked up the fat slice of garlic pickle from the plate on the room service cart that had held his sandwich, there came a knock at the door. He took a bite of the pickle, tossed the remainder of it on the plate, then went to the door.

"Yeah?" he said, standing beside it.

"It's me," Fulmar's voice answered.

Canidy smiled and quickly unlocked, then opened, the door.

Fulmar, blond and lithe, stood there in a nicely cut dark gray J. Press two-piece suit, a white button-down-collar shirt, and a blue-and-silver rep tie. He held a brown suitcase in his right hand and a brown leather briefcase in his left.

"Come in!" Canidy said.

Fulmar came in and put down his bags and they embraced warmly.

Canidy took a step back and looked him over.

"Why do I suddenly feel like there's going to be a meeting with the headmaster and adults?"

Fulmar grinned.

"I don't know. We'd have to have done something significant to require one these days. The government pays us to do things we used to get in trouble for."

Canidy smiled as he grabbed the suitcase. He carried it to the far corner of the room.

"The couch folds out into a bed," he said. "Have you had lunch?"

Fulmar shook his head. "Looks like you have."

"How about a steak sandwich? The ones they make here are first-class." He gestured toward the plate on the room service cart. "That was my second one."

"Today?"

"No, I had the first one in the bar last night."

"Yeah, that'd be great. Thanks."

Canidy nodded and went to the phone and dialed room service.

"Hello? That sandwich you sent up to six-oh-one?—

"Yes, it was fine—

"No, really. I'd like another sent up, please. Yes. What?"

Canidy looked at Fulmar, pointed at the coffee cup and raised an eyebrow.

Fulmar nodded.

"Yes," Canidy said into the receiver, "and another pot of coffee. Thank you."

As he put the receiver back in its cradle, he saw that Fulmar was looking over a British Admiralty chart and the library books.

"Those," Canidy said with a smile, "are part of what brought back feelings of our dear ol' boarding school days."

Fulmar picked up the duck call and held it up to Canidy, who shrugged sheepishly.

"It was on sale. . . ."

Fulmar put it to his lips and blew. The reed vibrated a miserable *quaaack* sound.

"Sounds like that duck deserves to be shot," Canidy said, "put out of its misery."

Fulmar chuckled, then put the duck call back on the coffee table and picked up one of the dusty books and opened it.

He saw that inside the front cover there was glued a tan-colored pouch. It held a stiff card five inches tall and three wide with NEW YORK PUBLIC LIBRARY printed at the top and typewritten just below that the book's title— "Of Wine and Roses: A Lover's Tour of Sicily"—and then the author—"Sir Barry Brown"—and then a list of a dozen or so borrowers' names with chronological due dates that had been made by an adjustable rubber stamp, the most recent entry being MAR 04 38. And in long-faded red ink, stamped at least three times on the first four pages and the inside back cover: PROPERTY OF THE NEW YORK PUBLIC LIBRARY SYSTEM.

He picked up the next book in the stack, opened the front cover, and saw that it also had a similar card still in its tan pouch.

"Lose your library card, did you?"

Canidy shrugged.

"Like at St. Paul's, I intend on returning them." He paused. "Eventually, anyway."

"Well, now I don't have to guess where you're going."

Canidy raised his eyebrows. "And now I can honestly say that I didn't tell you."

"Sicily? What the hell, Dick?"

"Boss's orders."

Fulmar sighed. "Yeah, I've got mine, too."

They looked at each other a long moment.

Fulmar broke the silence.

"So, you said you needed some help?"

"I wanted to ask Donovan to let you work with me."

"I would—and maybe can—but not until I get a handle on these Abwehr bombings . . . or the FBI does."

"These bombings in the States?"

Fulmar nodded.

"Jesus. That must make Hoover happy."

Fulmar shrugged.

"All I know," he said, "is that Roosevelt told Donovan to take care of it quote quickly and quietly unquote. And here I am."

"You said you had a lead to follow?"

"In the files the FBI gave me—the ones that Donovan and Douglass told me quote not to take at face value unquote because they were nothing more than what Hoover wanted the OSS to have—"

"No surprise, with you encroaching on Hoover's territory."

"Yeah. Anyway, in there was information suggesting Fritz Kuhn and his American Nazi Party may be connected with the agents. The FBI gave them a once-over, came up with nothing. But I'm going to shake that tree, too, and see what falls out. Midnight tonight I have a date—more like a meeting—over on the Upper East Side. Remember Ingrid Müller?"

Canidy's face brightened considerably.

"Who the hell could forget her?" he said, grinning.

Ingrid Müller—tall, tanned, and white blonde—had been a sixteen-year-old sex kitten when she appeared in *Monkeying Around*, a 1933 comedy that starred Fulmar's mother, Monica Carlisle. Every red-blooded American male—and certainly the boys of St. Paul's Episcopal Preparatory School, Cedar Rapids, Iowa—went ape-shit over Ingrid. Fulmar and Canidy had tried every way they thought possible to get her to visit Iowa, including sending letter after letter to Fulmar's mother that contained everything from promises that sensible people would see as impossible to keep to outright begging.

Months passed without a single response—not at all unusual behavior for the "childless" Monica Carlisle—and the boys had given up.

Then the star's legal counsel—a young Hollywood hotshot in his twenties by the name of Stanley S. Fine, Esquire—showed up.

Fulmar and Canidy were convinced that Fulmar's mother had again sent him to put out yet another fire (if nothing else, to make them cease and desist from writing annoying letters to her) when they noticed a familiar female in his company.

It was indeed the teen starlet Miss Müller. She had been scouting locations for background on her next movie—one set at a boarding school for boys—and she said that Mr. Fine, Esq., had suggested St. Paul's ("simply as an idea, something to use as a reference without having to fly all the way to the East Coast"), and, as student escorts, he thought that one Dick Canidy, son of the headmaster, and one Eric Fulmar would serve her well.

Fine ensured, despite the best attempts of Canidy and Fulmar during her two-day visit, that neither had an opportunity to get in any trouble with Miss Ingrid Müller.

Thus, the short-term result had been that the boys were instant heroes among their classmates. And, long term, Fulmar had found himself exchanging an occasional letter with her—his being far more frequent than hers.

"I vowed never to forget her," Fulmar said.

"I remember. I also remember that you vowed to bag her. So you're batting .500."

"Maybe my luck changes tonight. She will be very pleased to know that I am seriously considering joining the American Nazi Party—"

"Of which I presume she is a member?"

Fulmar nodded.

"That's what she tells me in her letters." He paused. "And she'll be pleased I am considering joining her and the party because I believe, as a Good German, that we must win this war in any way possible. Oh, and how could I go about contributing to these German agents that the newspapers say are bombing the States?"

Canidy smiled.

"Subtle. Is this before or after you try to get in her pants?"

"Before. No, after . . . Hell, whatever it takes."

"You wouldn't consider trading missions, would you?"

Fulmar raised an eyebrow in question. "Certainly not with what I know so far about yours."

"It's pretty straightforward. You've done it before. There's another scientist to pull out before the Germans get him."

"That's it?"

"And something bigger that, according to Donovan, I'll find when I get there. I'm going to need help with that and running the underground."

"I think I'll stick with trying to bag Ingrid and shoot saboteurs."

He looked at the charts.

"But that explains your looting of the library."

Canidy nodded.

"Oh, it gets better. I'm now officially involved with the King of the Looters."

Fulmar looked at him, and shook his head.

"I don't follow."

"Charlie Lucky," Canidy offered.

Fulmar shook his head again.

"Murder, Inc., ring a bell?" Canidy asked.

Fulmar's eyes widened at the realization.

"No shit?" Fulmar said. "The mob?"

"No shit. The connection goes back to when Murray Gurfein . . ."

". . . So Luciano," Fulmar said finally, "is serving time, but, as boss of all bosses, is running the rackets from prison?"

"Exactly. And has pretty much made good on every request we—the U.S.—has made of him."

"Amazing. But, then again, there's no end to what people will do for the promise of freedom." He paused. "It's what this damned war is all about, no?"

Canidy nodded. "True. For some. Can't forget, though, that for others it is an opportunistic time . . ."

The phone rang and Canidy reached for the receiver. "Hello?"

Fulmar went back to the charts and studied them.

"Frank," Canidy said, "how are you?"

"Tonight is fine—

"Okay, got it. Six o'clock at Sammy's, at the fish market. I'll be bringing my partner, okay?"

He looked at Fulmar, who nodded his agreement.

Canidy said into the phone, "Okay, then. Thanks, Frank."

As he hung up the receiver, there was a knock at the door.

"That must be your lunch," he said, and saw that Fulmar had the duck call back in his hand.

Fulmar grinned and blew a soft *quaaack . . . quaaaaaack.*

Canidy reached the door and raised an eyebrow that asked, *What?*

Fulmar shrugged.

"You're dealing with Murder, Inc.," he said solemnly. "Just wondering when the dust settles who's going to be the real dead ducks. . . ."

[FOUR]
Fulton Fish Market
New York City, New York
1750 7 March 1943

The cab carrying Dick Canidy and Eric Fulmar, both now in casual clothes, turned south off of Beekman Street and slowly rolled up in front of the market. The long, two-story white building of concrete and brick had a series of street-level doorways that served as the entrance to the individual fish resellers. Signs were affixed above the wide doorways, each advertising the business therein: FAIR FISH CO. INC., S&R SEAFOOD, MANHATTAN FISH CO., and more than a dozen others.

Heavily clothed workers were moving about busily, carrying boxes and pushing two-wheel dollies. Trucks, both local delivery and over-the-road tractor trailers, were being steadily loaded.

"There it is," Canidy said, pointing to a doorway five businesses down. The sign above it read: SAMMY'S WHOLESALE SEAFOOD CO.

A forklift carrying a pallet with a four-foot-tall wooden bin piled high with iced-down fish was moving quickly into Sammy's. The cab dodged it and pulled up outside the doorway, its brakes squealing to a stop.

Canidy paid the fare, and they got out and started toward the doorway. Canidy carried his attaché case with the Sicily books and charts.

Fulmar sniffed and made a face. "Rather rank, huh?"

Canidy inhaled deeply—but didn't gag, which surprised Fulmar.

"This?" Canidy said. "This is nothing. You should go around back, where the boats come in. It's *really* raw there."

They walked through the large doorway and stepped around the back of the forklift that now was putting down its load beside a wooden table thirty feet long and topped with a sheet of dented, bloodstained galvanized tin.

Behind the table stood four men with long, thin-bladed filet knives. They began to methodically pull fish from the just-delivered box, and, with surgical skill—remarkable both for their spare efficient motions and for their ability to completely remove all useful flesh—began to separate tissue from bone.

The large filets were then slid down the tin tabletop, where another worker put them in a twenty-gallon scoop that hung by chain below an enormous scale suspended from a steel ceiling beam.

When the scale's long black needle rotated on the dial face to the number 20, the worker then packed the fish filets with shaved ice into smaller boxes, these made of heavy waxed cardboard and imprinted with: PERISHABLE FRESH SEAFOOD—20 LBS.—SAMMY'S WHOLESALE SEAFOOD CO. NYC.

The full boxes were then stacked on a new pallet, which, when full, the forklift would carry out to one of the delivery trucks.

All around the open-air facility, workers moved fish in

various states of processing—from full carcasses to just head and bones—by spiking them with handheld two-foot-long gaffs (cold steel hooks on short shafts). Occasionally, a couple of workers would wheel around dollies carrying forty-gallon galvanized tubs of squid and octopus.

The forklift driver—a fat, squat, rough-looking Italian with coal black eyes set deep in a weathered face—put the lift in reverse, inched it backward, and, when the forks were clear of the pallet of fish, raced the engine and manipulated a lever that very noisily brought the forks a foot off the ground. Then he very quickly backed the lift outside, where he switched off the engine and jumped free as it slowed and then came to a stop all by itself.

He walked back inside the large doors and looked at Canidy and Fulmar.

"Help you guys?" he asked agreeably.

"Looking for Frank Nola," Canidy said.

The coal black eyes studied Canidy a moment.

"The name's Canidy," he added. "Nola knows we're coming."

"Upstairs."

Canidy followed the squat Italian's eyes upward. There he saw a bare steel framework of beams supported by steel poles, painted red and rising from the concrete first floor. Above the framework was a wooden tongue-and-groove floor.

"The steps are in the back there," the squat Italian added, pointing to a far corner.

"Thanks," Canidy replied.

Fulmar followed Canidy to the back corner, then up the steps, which led to a narrow landing on the second floor and a wooden door with a small metal sign reading: OFFICE.

Canidy knocked, and then they heard footsteps approaching the other side of the door. The knob turned and the door flew open inward.

The office was dimly lit by a single bare bulb hanging from the ceiling, but Canidy and Fulmar could see well enough to tell that they were looking at the muzzle of a high-caliber long arm—and immediately put their hands up, waist high, palms out. Canidy's attaché case hung painfully on his thumb.

Behind the business end of the firearm was an Italian fishmonger, this one somewhat slender and of medium height, wearing a dark wool sweater and black rubber overalls. Canidy could not be sure in the low light of the office but he thought that this guy looked like one of Nola's men whom he had seen loading crates on the truck the previous night.

I can easily grab the end of the barrel, Canidy thought. *But even if I get the muzzle pointed away, this could get messy fast, especially if that's what I think it is and it's on full auto.*

Canidy saw some motion behind the fishmonger, and then Francesco Nola's voice called from farther inside the office. "Mario! Put that gun away!"

Another set of footsteps quickly approached the door. The door swung open completely and there stood Nola. He pushed Mario to the side, forced the direction of the muzzle to the ceiling, and then smacked him on the side of the head.

As Fulmar and Canidy put down their hands, they exchanged glances. Fulmar's said what Canidy was thinking—*We've got to deal with dangerous goons like this?*

"Nice welcoming party," Canidy said. "I'd hate to see how you host people you don't expect."

"My apologies," Nola said. "Mario, he's just a little jumpy. Come in, come in."

Canidy looked around the office once they were inside. There was a rusty filing cabinet against one wall, a grimy, threadbare couch with the stuffing poking out the cushions against another, and in the middle a big, beat-up wooden desk that had its front right leg reinforced by a two-by-four nailed to it.

"This is a very close friend of mine, Frank," he said as he gestured to Fulmar.

Nola offered his hand to Fulmar. "Francesco Nola."

Fulmar shook the hand but made no effort to offer his name.

"It's a pleasure to meet you, Mr. Nola."

"It's Frank, please."

Canidy said, "Mind if I ask where Mario got that gun?"

"Why?" Nola said.

"Can I have a look at it?" Canidy pursued.

"Mario," Nola said, "give my friend the rifle."

Mario, in a sloppy motion, swung the barrel so that the muzzle swept across Canidy and Fulmar. This time

Canidy did grab the end of the barrel and thrust it toward the ceiling.

"No offense, Mario," he said coldly, "but I've seen people killed that way."

Nola smacked the top of Mario's head again. "Idiot!"

Mario looked hurt and let loose of the stock.

Canidy held up the gun to the light from the bare bulb. He looked it over, then read the stamping on the receiver. "Yeah, just what I thought."

He looked at Fulmar, then handed him the gun. "Ever see one of these?"

"A Johnny gun, no?"

Canidy nodded. "A Johnson model 1941 light machine gun, chambered for thirty-ought-six Springfield. They're rare."

"And they're a helluva weapon. They had the semi-auto rifle version at the range in Virginia. Next to the Thompsons. I think the range master said that the LMG in full auto puts out four hundred and fifty rounds a minute. Reliably. Open bolt, no jams."

The range in Virginia was at an estate that the OSS used as its agent training facilities. They called it "The Farm." It essentially was an intense boot camp—one where all the agents in training went by their first name and only their first name—complete with instruction in all types of explosives and weaponry, domestic and foreign. The gun range had a wide range of pistols and rifles, anything the OSS could get its hands on from the field so that agents would have some familiarity in their use should they find themselves left with only, say, a German Mauser or British Sten to defend themselves.

"Johnny gun" was a word play on "Tommy gun," the nickname for the storied Thompson .45 caliber submachine gun.

"They said the LMG was in short supply," Fulmar finished, handing the gun back to Canidy.

Canidy pulled the twenty-round box magazine from its mount in the left side of the receiver, checked the action to ensure that a round wasn't chambered, then handed the gun to Mario. He inspected the magazine and then tossed that to him.

"Do us a favor, Mario. Leave it unloaded till we leave, okay?"

Mario squinted his eyes to show his disapproval.

"Do as he says," Nola added.

Mario nodded, then walked with the gun to the grimy couch on the far side of the office and took a seat, laying the weapon across his knees.

Canidy turned to Nola.

"Reason I asked where you got that," he said evenly, "is that they are in short supply, and the ones available were supposed to go to the Marines."

That's one reason. Another is: I'd like to get my hands on one for myself.

"No," Nola said, "that one came from a crate that was supposed to go to the Netherlands."

Canidy's eyes lit up.

"Really?"

He looked at Fulmar.

"Story I heard was that there was a real pissing match over the Johnny gun even being considered to take the place of the BAR," Candy explained.

The beloved Browning automatic rifle was the U.S.'s primary automatic weapon, tough as nails and reliable as hell. In many minds it had no peer, and never would, and when Boston attorney—and Marine Corps reserve officer—Melvin Maynard Johnson Jr. designed and built the first generation of the Johnny gun—a semiautomatic rifle that he felt was superior to the new M1 Garand—his battle for it to be adopted was straight uphill. In the eyes of the U.S. Army Ordnance Department, the Johnson had all the chance of being military issue that a Red Ryder BB gun or a slingshot did.

Johnson did get his M1941 LMG into the hands of some Marine Raiders. And the Marine's First Parachute Battalion came to prefer the weapon because it weighed only twelve pounds (the BAR was a hefty twenty), and because its buttstock and barrel were designed to be quickly removed and replaced, allowing for more compact packing and easier servicing in the field.

"Then," Candy went on, "some Marines praised its performance in the Solomons and 'Canal—more than one swearing it beat the BAR hands down, especially in the jungles—and the Dutch got wind of that and ordered a bunch for their colonial troops in the East Indies."

"But the Japs took the islands," Fulmar said.

"Right. And after they did, the U.S. embargoed the weapons that had come out of the Rhode Island factory and not yet shipped. So at that point no one was getting them, except now . . ."

Canidy looked at Nola.

"Would I be guessing wrong if I said that friends of Socks peddled this one?"

Nola did not have to say anything. The answer was on his face.

Canidy said, "I'm not at all happy with the idea of the mob getting them."

Nola shrugged. "What can I say? Better than the Japs."

"I heard that they had to pull a whole shipment off one of the Liberty ships."

Nola shrugged again. "If you say. I do not know. I am sorry."

Well, this is starting out as some fine partnership, Canidy thought.

He said, "Have you seen Lanza today?"

"Yes, he was here at the market."

"Was or is? I'd like to see him."

Nola walked over to the desk and picked up the phone and asked for a number.

"This is Frank Nola," he said after a moment. "Is Mr. Lanza still there?" There was a pause. "At his office? Thank you."

He broke off the connection by pushing the receiver hook down with his index finger, then asked for another number.

"Mr. Lanza? Frank Nola—

"Yes, sir, those fish were processed, packed, and loaded—

"Probably three days. The *Annie* should be out right now—

"Yes, sir, I will. Mr. Lanza, I have Mr. Canidy here. He wants to see you—

"I will. Good-bye."

He put the receiver in its hook and looked at Canidy.

"He said to come by his office. He has something for you. He's going to get something to eat, then he'll be back there till midnight."

"In Meyer's Hotel?"

"Room two-oh-one."

"Okay," Canidy said, carrying his attaché case to the desk. "In the meantime, I hope I can find something that you do know about. I brought some charts of Sicily and the islands. Think we can start with a tour?"

Nola nodded. "Yes. And I may have other things that would be of help."

Canidy unfolded the chart that covered the southern coast of Sicily.

"We run boats from here at Porto Empedocle," Nola began, pointing to a midpoint on the southern coast of the island, "across the Strait of Sicily down to the Black Pearl, then over to Tunisia." He paused. "Do you have a chart that shows Africa?"

"Hang on," Canidy said and pulled the *Michelin Guide* from his attaché.

Nola took it and flipped to a regional map that included a sliver of the northern African coast just under Sicily, then continued, "To here at Nabeul, then up and around Cape Bon and into Tunis itself."

Canidy pointed at the Sicilian island in the strait that was closer to Tunisia than to Sicily. "The Black Pearl?"

Nola nodded.

"Pantelleria," he explained. "It is volcanic rock—black rock—about fourteen by eight or nine kilometers. It's known for its capers, figs, lentils, grapes. I have cousins there. Rizzo is the family name. Many Rizzos there. They are *tonnarotti*."

Canidy shook his head.

"Tuna fisherman," Fulmar translated.

Nola smiled and nodded. "Bluefin tuna. You would like it. They take a number of boats and work the nets, surrounding the big fish like cowboys herd cattle. The nets close in and the great tuna struggle to escape, and the water, as you can imagine, becomes a brutal swirl of fish and blood."

Fulmar said, "Those fish can be four hundred pounds."

Nola smiled again.

"Yes. Some as big as some cattle. And when you catch the entire school—twenty, thirty fish or more—it is called a *mattanza*." He paused. "That is a word that also has come to mean 'massacre.'"

Canidy studied Nola, who clearly was happy with this tale of his family heritage, then glanced at Mario on the couch.

Maybe there is some fight to these people after all, Canidy thought. *Not blooded in human battle, but unafraid of being around blood and violence.*

"So how far from here to here to here—Porto Empedocle to the Black Pearl to Tunis?"

"About one hundred and fifty kilometers," Nola said. "One way."

"And how often does your family run the route?"

"Every day. There are boats traveling in both directions. They usually take two, three days—when there are no patrols or other problems, such as mechanical breaks—fishing as they go."

"What if they did not fish?"

"Straight across? Less than a day, considering the seas."

Fulmar said, "Tell us about the patrols."

"Germans mostly. Sometimes Italians. They usually do not stop us. But sometimes they board the boats, make sure we are doing what we say we're doing. Sometimes they take our fish. Confiscate it?"

Fulmar nodded. "Harassment."

"Yes. They say it is a price of doing business." He paused. "One captain from another family refused to give up his catch—he had been stopped twice that month—and the Germans shot his boat full of holes. So he lost the catch and the boat . . . and was lucky to live."

Canidy said, "How many boats do you have and what size?"

"There are—or at least there were when I was last there—nineteen boats. Eight of them are deepwater boats that average twelve meters in length. The others are smaller—maybe six meters—and completely open."

"And the crew for the big boats?"

"Two to six. Depends on the time of year—more in May and June, when the big tuna move through—and who is available."

Canidy pointed to the chart, at the southern shore of Sicily.

"Let's say I was coming into port on one of your boats. What would I see? Who would I see?"

Nola's eyes brightened and his narrow face spread with a broad grin.

"Oh, you would see the most beautiful port in your life. And the most wonderful people."

Canidy said, "I need details, please. Specifics."

Nola nodded agreeably.

"Not a problem."

He went to a box across the room and took from it a heavy leather-bound volume some two feet square and at least three inches thick.

He brought it back to the desk and said proudly, "My family photographs."

He opened the cover and pointed to a somewhat faded black-and-white photo that dominated the first page. It showed a score of heavyset middle-aged and older men, ten of them, sitting in straight-backed wooden chairs and the other half standing behind them, all in dark suits and shoes and white shirts.

"These are the padrones," Nola said. "The leaders of Porto Empedocle."

Canidy thought, *Jesus Christ, that is one tough unattractive crowd.*

"This was taken about five years ago. Some are still there."

He pointed to two of the men standing. They were a bit taller and far more slender than most of the others. They resembled Nola.

"This one is my father," he said. "And next to him, his brother, my uncle Ignazio, who was on the town council."

He pointed at a very fat, very gray-headed man seated in the middle chair. "This was the mayor, Carlo Paglia. A very wise man."

And looking mean as hell, Canidy thought.

"The Nazis took Mayor Paglia and Uncle Ignazio off to prison. Some of the others fled to Tunis, but most stayed."

He sighed and turned the page.

Nola went through the album, describing each photograph, where it was taken, and pointing out that location on an admiralty chart—or, if in Tunis, on the 1935 tourist map of Tunisia that he had produced—then writing down names of who was who. He set aside duplicate loose photos for Canidy to keep.

The majority of the images showed Sicily. It clearly was a more robust and happier time. The towns built along the hills were busy. The people looked full of life. They ran their businesses and raised their families. They swam the clear turquoise waters and played on the beaches of pebble and sand, strolled the crowded palazzos and shopped the open-air markets that offered plentiful meats and vegetables and fruit.

That likely was not the case now, not with everyone forced to work for the war effort. The Germans also took the majority of their food production and shipped it to feed others elsewhere. Rationing was widespread—not to mention discontent with Mussolini and fascism.

After two hours, Canidy and Fulmar felt that they knew the extended family of Francisco Nola and the families of the padrones damned near intimately. Both those in Porto Empedocle and Tunis.

Nola folded the sheets of paper, then handed them and the photographs to Canidy.

"Thank you," Canidy said.

He put them in his attaché case.

"Frank, how soon do you think you will be able to leave?"

Nola looked back at him blankly.

"Leave?"

"Yes. Leave. You *are* going with me, right?"

"That was not the plan," Nola said.

"Well, then it is now."

"No, it is not possible for me to go with you."

Canidy exchanged glances with Fulmar, then looked back at Nola.

"Why the hell not?"

"I cannot say." He glanced at the folded papers. "Once you locate my family, the letter of introduction will do the rest. You will have many people."

Canidy started stuffing the books and charts back in his attaché case.

Dammit! I knew this was going too smoothly.

"What the hell happened to the guy who wanted to blow up all of the Germans himself?" Canidy said furiously. "Where the hell is he now? Jesus H. Christ, Frank!"

"He still stands before you," Nola said stiffly, his voice wavering with emotion.

Canidy shook his head, then looked him in the eyes.

"Frank, I'm going to need more than family snapshots. I need hard intel. How many troops and exactly where? Who is in charge of harbor security, of town security? The locations of minefields on the beaches and offshore, and what's been booby-trapped. I need documents on enemy ops. And more. . . ."

"And you will have that," Nola replied evenly.

Canidy stared at him for a long time. Then he looked as his watch, then at Fulmar. "Let's go see Lanza. Ready?"

Fulmar nodded.

"I'll be in touch, Frank," Canidy said sharply.

He grabbed his attaché case and they went out the door.

Canidy and Fulmar crossed South Street and started walking the block north toward Meyer's Hotel.

"Sonofabitch!" Canidy said. "I don't know if I'm

madder at Nola for saying he's not going or at myself for assuming he was going."

"I would not worry about that too much," Fulmar said. "You have what appears to be good information to get going now. Each bit—"

"I know, I know. Each bit of info leads to more info. But I needed a lot yesterday."

Canidy stopped walking.

When Fulmar stopped and looked back at him, Canidy said, "There's just something about this that doesn't feel right."

Fulmar laughed. He checked the immediate area around them, then said, "Are you fucking kidding me? *Everything* about this doesn't feel right!"

Canidy shook his head.

"Thanks, pal. Thanks for making me feel better."

The door to room 201 could have used a fresh coat of paint. It actually could have used a complete refinishing since it had, judging by the fat flakes of paint that were peeling off, already been painted four or more times, layer upon layer. But then if renovation started with the door, there would be no end to it. The whole damned hotel needed work.

Canidy, still fuming at Nola's announcement that he was not going to Sicily, knocked on the door harder than he realized and chips of paint came flying off.

"Easy, Dick," Fulmar said.

The door swung open quickly and noisily and Joe "Socks" Lanza stood there.

"What the hell?" he said.

He looked at Fulmar.

"Who's this?"

"A good friend," Canidy said.

Lanza looked past them, down the hall, then said, "Let's not talk in the hall."

He turned and walked back into the room. Canidy and Fulmar followed.

The room was bare and ratty but brightly lit. It had a desk that was a mess of magazines and newspapers, and four mismatched chairs, one behind the desk. There was a single window that overlooked South Street, and the stained bedsheet that served as a curtain was pulled closed.

"I just got the news that Frank Nola is not going to go with me," Canidy said.

Lanza sat down behind the desk. Canidy and Fulmar took seats across the desk from him.

"Yeah—and?" Lanza said.

"And I thought that that was what you were going to get for me—someone to get me into Sicily and to the locals there."

"He didn't give you any names?"

Canidy grunted.

"I've got more names than the fucking Palermo phone book."

"Then what is the problem? You use that list, you will

get what you want. That is a promise. Those names—"
Lanza reached into his coat pocket, pulled out an envelope, and handed it across the desk "—those names and
this are all you need."

Canidy took the envelope, opened it, and unfolded
the letter.

It was written in English and in what appeared to be
Sicilian. Canidy's eyes fell to the former:

```
March 1943

    The bearer of this letter is Mr. Richard
Canidy.
    With this letter, the bearer brings to
you my many good wishes.
    It is requested of you in turn that the
bearer be given the same respect and con-
siderations that would be given if I were
to personally appear before you.
    Your friendship is appreciated and it
will not be forgotten.

Charles Luciano

(Salvatore Lucania)
```

It was clear that the date and the first line, slightly mis-
aligned with the other lines, were newly typed.

"You keep a stack of these around?" Canidy asked, his
tone sarcastic. "Just type in a date and a name and
you're—what?—instantly made?"

"It is necessary with Charlie being away," Lanza said, clearly not pleased with being mocked. "He signed that letter. It will be honored."

Canidy raised his eyebrows dubiously.

"We'll see. But this is one reason why I wanted Nola."

"Look, Charlie Lucky said to give you whatever the hell you wanted and we will. But it is not possible for Nola to go with you."

Canidy's eyebrows went up again.

"Anything?" he repeated.

Lanza sighed.

"Anything but Nola—"

"For starters," Canidy interrupted, "I want one of the Johnson LMGs, like the one that you gave Nola."

Lanza looked into Canidy's eyes and frowned slightly.

Bingo, Canidy thought. *It was Lanza. Why am I not surprised?*

Canidy glanced at Fulmar and added, "Make that two. We will each need one, with a full ammo box."

Lanza considered the request for a long quiet moment, then said, "What else?"

"How many do you have?" Canidy asked.

Lanza did not respond, verbally or physically.

"You want to tell me where the hell you got them?" Canidy pursued.

Lanza didn't answer.

"They were supposed to go to the Marines," Canidy said pointedly. "I can bring a lot of goddamned heat down on you for grabbing them."

Lanza's eyes narrowed. He studied both Canidy and

Fulmar, then, after a long moment, picked up the telephone receiver and dialed.

"Yeah, it's Joe. Put two of those new sticks in a box and put them in the trunk of the car—

"Yeah, those sticks. Don't ask questions. Just do it. Make sure they're complete. . . . What? Yeah, complete. You know what I mean."

He hung up the receiver and stared at Canidy.

"Bringing in 'heat,' as you say, would not be wise. The fact is—and you can check this out—it was the military that ordered those guns pulled off of a Liberty ship"—he outstretched his left arm and pointed with his index finger at the window covered with a bedsheet—"right over there across the river. So it was your guys that did that. And here we're doing as you ask. So easy on the threats, huh?"

"Those pulled from the ship were ones for the Dutch?"

Lanza made a thin smile.

"There. You already know."

"That doesn't explain why you have them."

Lanza shrugged.

"A small part of a total shipment got lost between the ship and the warehouse," he said simply. "Some guys found it."

"And didn't turn it over?"

Lanza made the thin smile again, then said dryly, "That's not the way it works."

Canidy shook his head.

"What the fuck does it matter?" Lanza said casually.

"So instead of, say, a hundred boxes locked down and collecting dust, now there's only ninety-nine. Or ninety-eight. Whatever."

He paused to make his point.

"And now you're going to get yours. Ones you wouldn't even know about—let alone get—if they'd been turned in to be locked up for who the hell knows how long."

Jesus Christ, Canidy thought, *he's beginning to make sense.*

Canidy looked to the desk, at the newspaper there, then at Fulmar—and he had a wild idea.

What the hell? What's to lose? This whole damned dance with the devil is wild.

Canidy reached forward and took from the desk a copy of the *New York World-Telegram.*

One of the headlines read: MORE BOMBINGS LEAD TO MORE QUESTIONS.

"Let me ask you about something else," he said, holding up the newspaper. "What do you know about these bombings?"

"Not much. Less than you, I'd guess."

Canidy locked eyes with him.

Lanza said, "It's not our guys, if that's what you're asking."

"Can you ask around?" Fulmar said.

Lanza shrugged.

"I'll keep my ears open," he said after a moment. "Anything else?"

"Not right now," Canidy said.

Lanza stood up.

"Then I'll show you the way out."

They left the office, went down the hallway to the back of the hotel, then down a flight of wooden steps that led to the alley.

It was almost completely dark there, but the yellow of the taxicab made itself known. As did, Canidy noticed, the hulking silhouette of the monster fishmonger.

"You get the sticks?" Lanza asked the driver.

"In the trunk."

"Good. They now belong to these guys. Take them wherever they want."

The driver wordlessly got in behind the wheel and slammed the door closed.

Canidy turned to thank Lanza but he had already gone back in the hotel.

Fulmar and Canidy got in the backseat.

"Gramercy," Canidy said to the driver. "I think you know the way."

IX

The monster fishmonger opened the trunk of the cab, and inside there were three parcels, each wrapped in the same heavy brown paper used for packing seafood. The two smaller packages were cubes about eight by ten inches; the one larger parcel was flat and rectangular, some two feet long, a foot wide, and eighteen inches high.

Fulmar reached in for one of the smaller parcels, expecting it to be lighter than the big one.

"Jesus," he said. "That's heavy as hell."

"That's because that's a can of thirty-ought-six," Canidy said, standing there holding his attaché case.

Fulmar picked up the bigger box.

"Much better."

"About twenty-five pounds?" Canidy said.

"Yeah."

"That'd be the 'sticks.' I have only one free hand. I'll carry them while you get the cans."

Fulmar raised an eyebrow.

"Gee, thanks, pal."

In the suite, Canidy put the large parcel on the coffee table in the sitting room. Fulmar entered a moment later, somewhat struggling with the weight of the two metal cans of .30-06 caliber ammunition, one awkwardly cradled under each arm.

He pushed the door closed with his right heel, then put the cans on the floor with a solid *thump, thump*. He tore off the brown paper wrapping.

"I'm going to hit the head," Canidy said and started in that direction.

The ammo boxes, dark green with a stencil of yellow lettering on the side indicating the contents, each had a metal handle that folded flat against the lid. Fulmar pulled up a handle as he worked the lid latch.

"It would have been far easier to carry these using the handles."

Canidy chuckled.

"Yeah, and far easier for anyone to have recognized them as ammo cans," he answered from the bathroom, then swung the door shut.

When he came back into the room a few minutes later, Fulmar had the brown paper off of the sturdy cardboard containers holding the Johnny guns and was opening the lid to the one on top.

He looked inside and said, "Oh, shit. Original packing."

Canidy pulled back the lid to get a better look.

"Oh, shit, indeed. I *hate* Cosmoline."

The rust preventative that coated the entire gun—metal and wood—was a petroleum jelly much like Vaseline—but stiffer and stinkier and harder than hell to remove completely. It had a nasty tendency, particularly in hot weather, to ooze out of every pore of the weapon, notably from the stock, and onto the shooter's face, which was the last place anyone wanted greasy oil when they were hot and sweaty.

"How're we going to get it off?"

"How else? Same as usual. Make a mess. And hope we get most of it off. . . ."

Some forty minutes later, the floor was a pile of petroleum-fouled hotel towels. But the Johnny guns practically gleamed.

"I knew it!" Fulmar said disgustedly, holding out his hands.

"What?"

"Look at me. There's fucking Cosmoline all over me. And I need to take a quick shower before I see Ingrid."

Canidy began laughing.

"A shower? Good luck. You're going to bead water better than a goose's ass!"

Fulmar made a face.

"I'm sorry," Canidy said, not at all convincingly and visibly trying to suppress more laughter. "Really. Look, maybe I'd better go for you. I'd probably have a better chance of bagging her, anyway."

"I'll go like this before I let that happen."

Canidy, smiling and shaking his head, got up and went to the door.

"Be right back," he said and left.

Fulmar walked into the bathroom, turned on the sink faucets, blending the water till the temperature was as hot as he could stand it. He began soaping and scrubbing the petroleum jelly from his hands and forearms.

After ten minutes, there was a knock at the door.

"Shit."

With no clean towels, he shook his hands to try to dry them as he went to answer the door.

"Yeah?" he called.

"Housekeeping," Canidy answered in a falsetto voice.

Fulmar turned the knob—getting on his hand the Cosmoline that Canidy had smeared there when he had gone out—and opened the door.

There stood Canidy with a Cheshire cat grin and holding a stack of five fat bath towels.

"Midnight requisition," Canidy said in his normal voice.

He entered and tossed the stack on one of the armchairs.

Fulmar carefully pulled one from the middle, where Canidy's oily hands had not touched.

"Ingrid thanks you," Fulmar said.

"I can think of plenty of ways she can do that personally."

"I'm sure you can."

Fulmar took the towel back into the bathroom and started running the shower water.

Canidy walked over to the cans of ammunition, unlatched the lid of one, and popped it open. It was packed with shiny brass cartridges. He reached in, took a handful, then started feeding them round by round into one of the six magazines that came in each Johnny gun cardboard container.

When Fulmar came out of the bathroom, he was wearing his suit pants and was buttoning the top button of a clean white dress shirt and snugging up the knot of his blue-and-silver rep necktie.

He saw that Canidy was taking another towel—one of the clean ones he had just procured—to a Johnny gun and methodically rubbing off more Cosmoline. The magazines were all now full of ammunition, lined up neatly next to the ammo cans.

"This gun's about as good as it's going to get," Canidy said. "That is, without sitting for a couple hours under a summer sun to melt out the remainder."

"It looks nice."

"Any need to take it with you tonight?"

Fulmar considered that a moment.

"Thanks, but that's not practical. And not necessary. I have my .45"—he patted his lower back—"and"—he patted his left forearm—"my baby Fairbairn."

Under the shirtsleeve, in a leather scabbard, was a

stiletto-shaped knife that Fulmar used as the situation demanded—he pulled it out first if absolute silence was required or used it as a backup if making noise was not a factor.

Fulmar subscribed to Canidy's hand-to-hand combat school of thought: If you were close enough to stick a blade in someone's brain, you damned sure were close enough to put a bullet in it instead.

The Fairbairn had been invented by an Englishman named William Ewart Fairbairn, who ran the Shanghai police force. He developed the black, double-edged blade for close combat with street thugs. Lately, he could be found at The Farm in Virginia, teaching OSS agents how to silently kill using his knife, or a silenced .22 caliber pistol, or a number of other highly effective tools and methods—including a newspaper rolled into a cone.

The "regular" version of the Fairbairn was issued to all British commandos, its scabbard customarily sewn to the boot or trouser leg.

Fulmar's smaller model, which he had bought from an English sergeant at SOE's Station X, looked a lot like the big one but instead featured a six-inch-long, double-edged blade and a short handle just long enough for fingers to be wrapped around it. It was carried, hilt downward, in the scabbard hidden between the bottom of his left wrist and the inside bend of his elbow.

Canidy knew that Fulmar, as he had fled Germany with Professor Dyer and Dyer's daughter, Gisella, had used the baby Fairbairn quite effectively to scramble the brains of a string of German SS officers who had had the misfortune of getting between them and safety.

"Right," Canidy said. "That should be enough to protect you as you attempt to secure the fair maiden's affections."

"One can only hope."

Fulmar pulled on his suit coat.

"Changing the subject," Canidy said, "I was doing more than cleaning your weapon while you primped in there."

"Yeah?"

"This has nothing to do with your qualities as a roommate but I decided that I may not be here when you get back." He paused. "Probably won't be."

"Why is that?"

"Well, I have, as you say, enough information to get started . . . and the clock is ticking. I'll take my new friend Johnny here and get to work. Unless you think there is anything that I can do to help you."

Fulmar looked off in the distance in deep thought.

"Not for me, Dick," he said finally. "But I do wish I could go with you."

"Get done what you have to and maybe you can."

Fulmar nodded.

"I'll take care of the room. Just tell them when you're leaving it for good."

"Thanks, Dick."

They stared at each other a long moment, then embraced.

When they finally released one another, Canidy was

not sure of his voice and simply nodded good-bye as Fulmar quietly picked up his overcoat and went out the door.

[TWO]
New York City, New York
0015 8 March 1943

The traffic at midnight had been nearly nonexistent and the cab had flown up First Avenue. Too fast for Fulmar, who did not want to arrive too early. He wanted a little time to clear his head—walking in crisp, cold air always seemed to work—and to get a good look at Yorkville before meeting Ingrid Müller.

He had the cabdriver drop him at the northeast corner of Second Avenue and Eightieth Street, which was just inside the southern edge of Yorkville.

This section of Manhattan's East Side—known for its heavy concentration of German residents and their shops and restaurants that recalled dear ol' *Deutschland*—covered an area that went from about Seventy-ninth Street up to Ninety-sixth or so, and from the East River on over to Third Avenue.

Ingrid Müller had told Fulmar to meet her at Wagner's Restaurant and Market, Eighty-fifth at Second, and as the cab drove off he started walking slowly in that direction.

He was surprised—though he wasn't sure why—that there were still quite a few people out and about in the cold at this late hour.

As he passed a dimly lit bakery and coffee shop—the sign read: KONDITOREI KAFFEEHAUS—he looked inside and saw that it was about a quarter full of patrons.

That impressed him, but not quite as much as the reason why it took a bit of effort to see the people inside: From the top of the shop's window, next to a chalkboard menu, hung a huge American flag. It filled half of the big window, and he guessed that if they could have put a bigger one there, they would have.

As he approached the next block, Fulmar saw that someone had pasted on the side of a redbrick apartment building a series of U.S. Navy recruitment posters so that they covered—mostly, anyway—the pro-Nazi graffiti beneath.

Block after block, he passed more nicely kept shops and apartment buildings.

By all appearances, Yorkville seemed just another normal New York neighborhood.

If you didn't look too deeply, it'd be hard to believe it's a boiling pot of subversion. . . .

Ahead, Fulmar saw the brick and glass façade to Wagner's Restaurant and Market.

The establishment's name was painted in large gold lettering on the main picture window, above a round, red neon sign—RHEINGOLD EXTRA DRY—advertising beer. Its street number was painted in the same gold lettering, but much smaller, on the glass panes above the dark wooden door.

Fulmar glanced inside the window, past the blinking neon sign, but did not immediately see Ingrid Müller.

He grabbed the big brass handle of the door, pulled hard, and went inside.

The first thing that he noticed was the blast of heat that greeted him.

He pulled off his overcoat and draped it on his left arm, over the sleeve concealing his baby Fairbairn.

He saw that Wagner's was more of a bar and grill than a real grocery, such as Schaller & Weber's, which he had noticed on Second Avenue just up the block.

The interior of Wagner's had dark-stained paneled walls. The ceiling was of pressed tin in a burnished gold color. The bar, also of dark wood, ran the length of the right side of the room—where a series of four U.S. flags hung from staffs in a row above the mirrors. There were wooden tables and chairs in the middle of the room and a line of booths down the left side.

At the back of the restaurant was the "market"—two open refrigerated cases, the kind found in full-service grocery stores, these containing packages of kielbasa, bratwurst, potato salad, and such, all menu items that had been prepared in the kitchen on the premises for carryout.

About half of the bar's twenty or so stools were taken—including by a half-dozen sailors in uniform—and three of the tables were each occupied by couples enjoying their cocktails.

Fulmar noticed motion on the left side of the room, and when he looked he saw in a booth a blonde woman in a dark outfit waving to get his attention.

She was sitting alone, smoking a cigarette, and had on the table in front of her a cup of what he guessed was probably coffee.

My God! She's gotten even more gorgeous.

He smiled and made a direct line for her table.

As he walked up, she smiled.

"I knew that had to be you," she said. "You haven't changed . . . but, then, you have."

She remained seated but held out her right hand. When he reached to take it, she leaned forward and turned her head to offer her cheek. Fulmar took her hand, bent over, touched his right cheek to hers, and made the sound of a kiss. She turned the other way and he touched his left cheek to hers, and again made the kissing sound.

Damn, she has soft skin.

Fulmar looked at her. She wore no makeup that he could tell.

And she doesn't need it.

Her fair skin was flawless. She had a soft, narrow face with high cheekbones, a thin nose, delicate lips, high eyebrows, and deep, ice blue eyes. Her hair was rich and thick, heavy with big waves. And her dark outfit tried but failed to hide the fact that she was fantastically built.

"It's great to see you again, Ingrid. You look sensational."

She smiled appreciatively.

"That's very kind of you to say."

She gestured to the seat across the table from her.

"Please, have a seat."

Fulmar tossed his overcoat onto the seat and slid in the booth after it.

The cushioning or the springs—or both—in the seat were soft or old—or both—and he instantly found himself sitting in a sort of self-formed bowl.

The back of this bowl pressed at his lower backside, which, in turn, pushed at the nose of the .45 tucked in the small of his back. He discreetly reached back and repositioned the pistol so that it would not fall out of his waistband.

Ingrid said, "I'm so glad that we could get together again. It's been—what?—five, six years?"

"Ten," Fulmar said.

"*Really?* No! That long?"

"And some ten thousand letters," he added with a smile.

She blushed.

She looked down momentarily as she absently ran the long, thin fingers of her left hand through her thick, wavy golden hair.

When she looked back up, she took a puff of the cigarette she held between the tips of her right-hand index and middle fingers, then exhaled as she leaned forward. She rested on her right elbow, her wrist cocked, her thumb angling the cigarette upward.

"If you're trying to make me feel guilty," she grinned, "you're being successful."

"I apologize."

"Please don't. They were very sweet letters, and I should be ashamed for not responding to them."

"Well, I imagine you get quite a bit of fan mail. You

can't answer every one. And lately you *have* been writing me back. . . ."

She smiled a smile that said, *Thank you for letting me off the hook.*

After a moment, she said, "Would you like something to eat or drink?"

He nodded. "Is that coffee?"

"Tea."

"Actually, I have a weakness for the power of persuasion."

She cocked her head quizzically.

"How so?"

"That neon sign in the window?"

She looked at it, then back at him.

"What about it?"

"I'm convinced it's there for me," he said with a straight face, "and for me alone."

She laughed. It was a deep and husky laugh—one that had become, in addition to her stunning looks, her signature on screen.

Fulmar waved to get the bartender's attention.

"A Rheingold, please," he called.

The bartender nodded.

Fulmar looked at Ingrid, who was pushing aside her cup.

"Make it two," she said with a smile. "Suddenly, this tea tastes like acid."

Fulmar turned back toward the bartender, who was drawing Fulmar's beer from the tap.

"Make it two."

"Two Rheingolds it is," the bartender replied.

Fulmar turned back to Ingrid.

"So," she said, "how is your mother?"

Fulmar did not immediately reply.

"You would probably know better than I," he said finally, without emotion.

She raised an eyebrow.

"I thought you knew," he explained.

She shook her head.

"My mother and I don't talk. I don't exist to her, at least to her as Monica Sinclair, Star of the Silver Screen."

Ingrid reached out with her right hand and gently squeezed Fulmar's left wrist. He liked the warm feel of her hand, and its strength.

"That's so sad," she said softly.

Jesus Christ, Fulmar thought, looking into her eyes. *They're even more sensual in person than on screen. Can she turn that on and off as needed—or is it sincere?*

He shrugged.

"You get used to it," he said.

She looked off into the distance.

"And all this time," she added, "I thought that it was just me that brought out the bitch in Monica."

"Well, welcome to the club."

Ingrid shook her head sadly.

She caressed his wrist, then looked more closely at it.

"You have unusually dry hands," she said suddenly.

It was more a question than a statement.

Fucking Cosmoline, Fulmar thought.

He said, "That's a long story. Had trouble washing some gunk off of my hands."

She stared at him with a look of amazement.

"You seem to deal with things so well. Nothing seems to bother you—"

She paused as the bartender arrived with the two glasses of beer.

He placed one in front of Ingrid, then one in front of Fulmar.

"Danke," Fulmar said.

"No problem," the bartender said.

The bartender showed no reaction, one way or the other, to Fulmar thanking him in German and walked away.

Fulmar smiled at Ingrid.

"Let's change the subject, huh?"

"Okay," she said.

She let go of his wrist and put her hands in her lap.

Shit! he thought. *Maybe we should get back to discussing Sweet Ol' Mom. . . .*

Fulmar picked up his beer.

"To reunions," he said, holding it toward her.

She grinned.

"Why not?" she said, picking up her beer. "To reunions."

They touched glasses and took sips.

Fulmar put his glass on the table and leaned forward.

"Tell me about yourself."

"What do you mean?"

"What are you up to these days?"

"I read the terrible scripts that my agent in Hollywood sends me, then scream at my agent for sending me terrible scripts."

"What's wrong with them?"

She let out her trademark laugh loud enough that, Fulmar saw in his peripheral vision, two of the sailors at the bar turned and looked and smiled along before going back to their conversation.

"What's *not* wrong with them!" she said. "Forgive me, but these are roles even your mother would not take."

She looked wistful.

"It's hard in these days of war," she went on, "particularly with a name like mine, to get good parts. I'm looking at changing agents. There's a very young guy named Ovitz who I like a lot. Funny guy, and sharp as razor."

"Stan Fine mentioned him once," Fulmar said. "Had nothing but nice things to say, and that I understand is unheard of in Hollywood."

He took a sip of beer.

"So you've got some time on your hands between scripts?"

She narrowed her eyes.

"What do you mean by that?"

Fulmar glanced around the room before replying.

"What we sometimes talked about in our letters."

She raised one of her thin eyebrows, then looked at her cigarette and took a long pull on it.

Fulmar said, "You know who my father is, yes?"

She nodded as she exhaled the cigarette smoke toward the ceiling.

The memory of when she learned that was very clear in her mind.

Years earlier, in one of Monica Sinclair's weaker moments—she'd been stone-drunk after a long day of being extremely difficult on the set—Ingrid had been told about "that sonofabitch" with whom Monica had had a fling.

And by whom she had had an unwanted son.

Monica Sinclair had vividly described the Baron von Fulmar as not only "a miserable fucking prick of the highest order" but as one highly placed in the Nazi Party and as the general director of the very important Fulmar Elektrische G.m.b.H.

So, Ingrid knew, not only was Fulmar arguably as German as anyone in Yorkville, but he was unquestionably better connected than probably everyone there. Including Fritz Kuhn, whom Hitler tolerated but did not necessarily like.

She looked him in the eyes.

"And," he went on, "you have alluded to the fact that you are friendly with Fritz Kuhn."

Ingrid quickly looked away.

"I'd prefer we not talk about that here."

She picked up her beer and took a healthy swallow.

Fulmar did the same, then put down his glass. He leaned forward.

"I want to help," he whispered.

"Help what?"

"The Bund."

Fulmar noticed that the mention of the German-American Bund—the federation of American Nazis—seemed to pique her interest.

"Especially," he went on, "if there's any connection to the bombing of the American cities."

Ingrid looked at him a very long moment—he thought he saw sadness or maybe even some disappointment—but she did not say a word.

She looked away, lit a fresh cigarette, took a puff and exhaled.

She looked back at Fulmar, her ice blue eyes calculating, then drained her beer and stubbed out her barely burned cigarette.

"Let's discuss this in my apartment," she said with a smile.

Fulmar smiled back.

Yes, let's discuss this in your apartment.

This . . . and maybe how I get in your pants.

He turned to the bartender and pointed to their table. "Check, please!"

[THREE]
Room 909
Robert Treat Hotel
Newark, New Jersey
1829 7 March 1943

Mary was late.

Kurt Bayer stood looking out the big window of the hotel room, trying to see if he could get a glimpse of her coming down the sidewalk to the hotel. It was no use. At this distance, from the ninth floor, it was impossible to distinguish many details of the people beyond the kind of clothes they wore—suit or skirt—and the coloring—dark or light—of that clothing.

He checked his watch again.

She was now almost exactly an hour and a half late.

When she had been only a half hour late, he had gone from being excited about her arrival to the early stages of being annoyed. And at an hour, he had started getting mad.

But now, after nearly ninety minutes, he had begun to worry about her.

And I have no idea how to check on her, he thought, frustrated. *I can't very well go down to that topless dance bar—if I could find the fucking thing—and ask around about her.*

Bayer knew, too, that he wasn't about to go ask Richard Koch for any help, either. They had spent all day together going over again—for what in Bayer's mind had to be the fiftieth time—their plans for putting a bomb on a New York City transit bus.

At one point, after Bayer had asked Koch for just a few dollars—which Koch reluctantly gave him—Koch had gone after him about Mary, had gone on and on and on about how the relationship had to end. Period.

Koch had even tried to make Bayer admit that not only was the relationship stupid but it was dangerous, too, and he wanted him to promise to think only of the mission.

To which Bayer had promptly stood, glared at Koch,

said that he wasn't about to walk away from a woman he thought he might be falling in love with, and then stormed out of the room and went to his own.

Where, now some two hours later, he waited and worried.

I'm going crazy in here, he thought as he turned away from the window. *Maybe going downstairs and meeting her there will help.*

If nothing else, I'll get to see her sooner. . . .

He picked up his Walther PPK pistol from the bedside table, slipped it into the right pocket of his woolen winter coat, and went out the door.

As he approached the bank of elevators, he saw that the floor indicator above the right pair of doors showed that that elevator was stopped at the eleventh floor. He looked above the left set of doors and saw that the needle of its indicator was moving; the car was coming up, now passing the seventh floor.

Maybe she's on it. . . .

The needle of the indicator moved past 7, then 8, and then 9. He heard the car itself actually pass his floor. The needle then showed that it had stopped on 10.

Damn!

He pushed the DOWN button, illuminating it.

The indicator of the right elevator began moving. The needle moved past 10, approached 9—then passed 9 and kept going all the way to 1.

What the hell?

He looked at the DOWN button. It was still illuminated. He stabbed it twice with his right index finger anyway.

He next heard the sounds of the left car coming down from the tenth floor, then the clunking of the mechanism that opened its pair of doors on his floor.

The car was empty.

Bayer quickly entered it, but as the doors started to close he had a sudden desperate thought.

What if she comes up while I'm going down?

He stepped one foot out of the car, into the path of the closing doors, and they tried to close completely. With considerable effort, he fought the mechanism and, after a moment, forced them back open.

He stood there, leaning against the door, trying to decide what to do.

This is driving me nuts. What is it with this girl that's making me act this way? Ach!

He shook his head, stepped back inside the car, pushed the button labeled L on the wall and sighed as the door mechanism clunked the doors closed.

Bayer spent a frantic twenty minutes checking the lobby of the hotel, then the sidewalk outside—going all the way to the street corner in both directions—then the lobby again, before taking a seat in the same upholstered chair in the lobby that Richard Koch had waited that morning before breakfast.

With his clear view of both the elevator bank and the

front door, he watched a steady stream of guests going to and from the elevators. He even noticed that at least once the elevators had carried a guest or guests plural to the ninth floor.

But no Mary.

After about ten minutes, he had had enough.

He got up, walked to the elevators, and rode the left one back up to the ninth floor.

When Bayer stepped off of the elevator, he noticed movement to his right and looked toward it.

Standing in front of the door to the room at the very end of the hall was a heavyset man of about thirty, medium height, wearing a tight-fitting dark suit and a hat. He was also very hairy—he had almost fur overflowing his shirt collar and cuffs.

Bayer recalled seeing him get on the elevator in the lobby when he had first gone downstairs. Now the man apparently was having some difficulty getting his key to unlock the door to his room. When they exchanged glances, the man shrugged his shoulders. He looked embarrassed or anxious—or both.

Bayer turned in the other direction and walked to his room.

He unlocked the door of 909, turned the knob, and began to push open the door. As he did so, the first thing he noticed was the sound of soft sobbing coming from inside.

Mary!

He threw open the door.

There on the bed, he saw her curled in the fetal position, her back turned toward him.

She had kicked off her heels but still wore her winter coat. She had on a navy blue, knee-length skirt, white blouse, and, over her blond hair, a flower-patterned navy scarf.

"Mary!" he said, slamming the door harder than he meant.

She responded by sobbing more deeply, her body trembling with the effort.

Bayer quickly went to her and reached out tentatively to touch her. His right hand gently grasped her left shoulder. She recoiled at first, pulling free of his hand.

He softly sat on the bed and touched her shoulder again. This time, she did not pull away, and when he tugged gently she slowly—and with what was obvious pain—rolled toward him, stopping as she lay on her back. She had the scarf completely covering her face.

He reached down to pull back the scarf and give her a kiss. She held the fabric tightly, and he had to tug a couple of times before she let it slide back.

Bayer was shocked at the sight.

So horrible was her bruising and swelling that he automatically exclaimed in German, *"Ach du lieber Gott!"*

One of Mary's eyes was swollen completely shut. The other had broken blood vessels. Her ears were bruised, as though she'd been repeatedly slapped. Her nose was bloody—he wondered if it was in fact broken—and she had a busted upper lip.

He was not sure but it looked like she might have lost one of the teeth that helped form her goofy little gap.

He looked away from her face and cautiously down along her body. It was then that he saw that her neck was also bruised—four horizontal stripes of blue-black on the left side of her throat, three on the right, that strongly suggested someone had taken both hands and tried to strangle her. And farther down, beneath the white blouse, dark shapes on her breasts that indicated the beating had been widespread.

He could not comprehend an act so vicious against a girl so beautiful.

His head spun.

He inhaled deeply.

He began to cry.

"What happened, Mary? Who did this?"

She did not reply. She pulled the scarf back over her face, rolled back over into the fetal position, and continued to sob.

Bayer attempted to softly stroke her back to console her, but when he did she made a strong reflex and he guessed that she had been beaten on her back, too.

He stood up and anxiously paced the room.

"I've got to get you to a hospital."

Mary shook her head twice and grunted, "Uh-uh."

Bayer thought, *Christ, she's right. I can't take her. If they started asking me questions, they might think that I did this.*

And even if they don't, they will ask who I am, and that's a question I can't afford to answer. . . .

He checked her over cautiously.

After he had determined to the best of his ability that she did not seem to have any life-threatening injuries—he was relieved, too, to see that she hadn't lost any teeth—he went in the bathroom, ran cold water in the sink, and soaked a hand towel in it. He wrung out the excess water and went back to the bed.

"Here. Let me try to clean up some of this."

She didn't move at first, but after a moment she slowly rolled onto her back.

He pulled back the scarf, then removed it from her head entirely, tossing it to the side of the bed. He began to softly dab at the dried blood on her lip, taking care not to reopen the wound.

When that blood was cleared, he refolded the towel to make a clean area, then moved to her nostrils and worked to clear them of the caked blood.

When the hand towel had turned completely red, he went back into the bathroom, rinsed it out, wet a second one, then took both of them to Mary.

He folded the fresh towel lengthwise and draped it across her forehead. Then he took the towel that he had rinsed and went back to softening the dried blood and dabbing it off.

A half hour later, Bayer carefully began undressing Mary.

He removed her coat, then unbuttoned her blouse and pulled it back.

The bruises across her belly and back almost made him nauseated.

He helped her into the bathroom and into the shower, then gently dried her with a towel and put her in bed.

Then he pulled up a chair, turned on some soft music, and gently stroked her hair until she fell into a deep sleep.

When Bayer awoke the next morning, Mary was curled under the covers with only her head visible. She was looking at him with her one good eye.

She tried to smile but the effort clearly hurt her.

"Good morning," Bayer asked softly. "How do you feel?"

She shook her head twice slowly.

"Can I get you anything?"

She shook her head again.

"Are you going to be all right?"

She nodded.

Bayer stood. He walked into the bathroom, filled one of the glasses with water, drank it all, then refilled the glass and brought it to Mary.

"Here," he said, holding out the glass. "Try some of this. You need to drink."

She closed her eye but did not move.

Bayer stared at her, wondering what to do next. Then he saw that she was moving her feet, ever so slightly, then her legs. He realized that she was attempting to reposition herself—and that it was taking great effort.

She has got to be in terrible pain.

"Can I help?" he said softly.

She shook her head, then rolled onto her back and used her elbows to inch herself up, pulling the sheet with her as she went.

Bayer quickly put the glass of water on the bedside table and started adjusting the pillows to better support her.

When she was sitting up and as comfortable as could be expected, she reached over and picked up the glass. She sipped the water tentatively, drinking only about a quarter of the water in the glass.

She sat there, her good eye closed, and slowly breathed in and out. After a moment, she brought the glass back up to her lips, took a deeper sip than before, then opened her eye and watched as she put the glass back on the table.

She looked at Bayer and mouthed, *Thank you*.

He said very slowly and softly but with some force, "Who did this, sweetheart?"

Mary closed her eye, shook her head, then slid down on the bed, back beneath the sheets.

She pulled the cover over her head and went back to sleep.

[FOUR]
OSS London Station
London, England
0915 10 March 1943

As a professional aviator, Major Richard M. Canidy, United States Army Air Forces, knew that to get from New York City to Algiers the faster, more efficient routing—the term "faster" being somewhat academic, as there really was no way in hell to quickly cover such a vast distance—was to go south, then east, then northeast.

That little adventure—about five days in transit if you were lucky, longer if you weren't—meant taking a Boeing C-75—one of the massive tail-dragger transcontinental Clippers with four 900-horsepower Wright Cyclone engines that the USAAF had taken over from Pan Am—to South America via Cuba, British Guiana, and Brazil, then getting aboard a converted B-24 bomber for the transatlantic leg to Dakar, French West Africa.

With a fuel stop in the ocean on a speck of rock called Ascension Island.

If good fortune allowed you to find the refueling stop, and to make Dakar, then came the long flight over the Sahara Desert, then another over the Atlas Mountains to Marrakech, then a four-hour hop to Algiers.

To the weary traveler at that point, the ragged little Maison Blanche Airport looked more lovely than Washington National Airport during cherry blossom season.

Conversely, Canidy knew, the northern routing, while arguably not as "fast" or efficient to the Mediterranean

Theater of Operations as its southern counterpart, had at least two things going for it:

One—which appealed immensely to Canidy the Aeronautical Engineer, who had a profound sense of self-preservation—it *did not* require, in an aircraft potentially flying on fumes, the terrifying task of trying to find a speck of solid surface on which to put down in one of earth's largest bodies of water.

And two—which appealed to Canidy the Love-Struck—it *did* mean he could stop and see Ann Chambers en route.

If pressed, Canidy was not sure which was the stronger sales point, but together they created a deal that simply could not be passed up.

And so he had gone from the Gramercy Park Hotel in New York City to Elizabeth, New Jersey, and there caught an Air Transport Command C-54 aircraft that ferried him and twoscore of his fellow comrades in arms to Gander Field, Newfoundland, then on to Prestwick, Scotland.

Canidy found himself in London in almost no time.

Hauling a suitcase in each hand—one containing his Johnny gun and the six magazines full of .30-06—Dick Canidy entered the Berkeley Square building of OSS London Station, cleared through security, and made his way upstairs to the office of Captain Helene Dancy, WAC.

Canidy looked through the doorway into her office, which was outside the doorway to that of her boss, David Bruce, the chief of station.

She was standing in front of a filing cabinet, impatiently flipping through folders. Canidy noticed that despite exuding her usual attractiveness, she did not presently have a look of overwhelming joy.

"My, don't we appear happy," Canidy said.

When she turned and looked at who had had the nerve to interrupt her with some sort of sarcasm, the flames in her eyes could have bored holes in cold steel.

But then she saw just who it was and her eyes softened, and a big smile showed her brilliant white teeth.

"Dick!" she said, slamming the cabinet shut.

"Bad morning?"

"The usual FUBARs. I'm just not in the mood to deal with them today."

"Fouled up beyond all recognition? Or the other, worse F-word?"

"The other," she said, absently wadding up a sheet of paper. "What brings you back?"

She looked at the suitcases.

"Are you moving in?"

"I take it that you really don't know?"

She shook her head.

He bent his head toward Bruce's office behind her.

"How about him?"

"Not that I'm aware of."

"Is he in?"

She shook her head.

"He's not in the office?" Canidy pressed. "Or the country?"

"Both."

"Great! I didn't particularly want to see him, anyway."

She shook her head and smiled. "You're impossible."

"How about Colonel Stevens? I was told to see him when I got in."

"I can call, if you like."

"Thanks, but I'll just go down to his office. I wanted to stop here first—a courtesy to Colonel Bruce."

"Something tells me there's more to it than that."

She said it with a knowing smile.

Candy made a face of shock and put his hands up to his chest, palms out.

"What!" he said with mock indignation. "I cannot believe you would suggest that my intentions are anything less than completely honorable!"

"Take it on down the hall, Major," Captain Darcy said, laughing. "Would you like me to bring you two something to drink?"

"I always said you were the best, Captain. Coffee would be great."

She playfully threw the wadded-up sheet of paper at him as he turned to leave.

Lieutenant Colonel Ed Stevens was seated behind the desk in his office, leaning back in his chair with his feet up. In his hands was a thick stack of papers, about half of which rested on his lap and the other half, which he'd already read, on his chest.

When Candy knocked on the doorframe, he saw that the graying forty-four-year-old was deep in thought.

"Still trying to solve the world's problems, Colonel?" Canidy said.

Stevens's stonelike face looked up and smiled when he saw Canidy in the doorway.

He put the papers on his desk, then stood up.

"I've been expecting you," he said. "Drop your bags in the corner."

As Canidy did so, Stevens came out from behind the desk.

They shook hands.

"Great to see you back so soon."

Canidy shrugged.

"What can I say? When I left, it didn't look like I'd ever be back. But I found that if one prostrates oneself before the boss, the boss will send one back out to draw enemy fire." He paused. "Lucky me, huh?"

Stevens shook his head.

"You're damned good at what you do, Dick. Don't you forget that."

They looked each other in the eye a long moment, then Canidy broke the silence.

"Any word from Stan Fine?"

"Only that he's in Algiers and setting up shop in what he describes as 'loosely controlled chaos.'"

Canidy grinned.

"Can you get me the details on how to find him there?"

Stevens nodded.

"Done."

"And give him a heads-up I'm en route?"

"Done."

There was a knock at the door and Captain Darcy brought in a tray with two china mugs of steaming coffee, a third mug half filled with milk, and a small bowl of sugar. She placed it on the desk.

"Thank you, Helene," Stevens said.

"Thanks," Canidy added, picking up one of the mugs.

"You're welcome, gentlemen," she said. "Let me know if you need anything else."

She smiled and turned and left.

Stevens walked over to the desk and picked up a mug of coffee and a folder.

"I got an Eyes Only from Colonel Donovan via Chief Ellis that said you were coming, and that Donovan wanted me to pull any intel the SI Italy desk here had on your Professor Rossi."

Stevens handed over the brown folder that had come up from the Secret Intelligence branch in the building's basement.

Canidy flipped it open and saw that it held only a few sheets of paper.

"Not much there," Stevens said, "but what we do have is fresh. Rossi, for example, was seen just last week at the University of Palermo."

Palermo? Canidy thought. *That's the north side of Sicily. Francisco Nola's people are in Porto Empedocle, on the south side. Not that you couldn't get between the two by boat. But that might be like saying you can get from New York to London by boat—complete with the damned Germans trying to sink you. . . .*

"Does Bruce know about this?" Canidy asked.

Stevens shook his head.

"The boss made it clear only you—and I—had the need to know."

Canidy raised his eyebrows.

"That wasn't my idea, Ed."

"I know, Dick. You shouldn't sweat it. It's not the first op that's been kept supersecret—and I suspect that it won't be the last."

Canidy nodded.

Not telling Bruce about the mission to nab Professor Dyer immediately comes to mind, he thought.

He looked at the folder and said, "Eisenhower will throw a fit if he finds out."

General Dwight David Eisenhower was Supreme Commander Allied Expeditionary Force, who had just enjoyed enormous success leading the Allies' amphibious landing in North Africa—OPERATION TORCH—and looked to repeat that with the taking of Sicily and Italy—OPERATION HUSKY.

Stevens nodded. "Uh-huh."

"Well, so be it. The boss has his reasons. Ike can play the game, too."

"Which reminds me," Stevens said. "A word to the wise, my friend. Steer clear of Lieutenant Colonel Owen."

"Who the hell is that?"

"Warren J. Owen. He's one of Ike's gatekeepers at AFHQ in Algiers. On the fast track. Ivy League fellow—*Hahv*ard '36—who smokes cigars for the pretense, not because he likes them. And drinks—or at least talks about drinking—expensive wines, ones you've never heard of. You know the type."

Candily made a sour face and nodded.

"Worse," Stevens went on, "he has a remarkable knack of bullshitting out both sides of his mouth. Trouble is, I think he really believes what he says."

Candily chuckled.

He said, "Reminds me of Turkish officers. When one solemnly tells you, 'It is no problem,' what he means is it's not a problem for him."

Now Stevens chuckled.

After a moment, Stevens added, "And if all that wasn't bad enough, this Owen is a ticket puncher."

Candily shook his head.

"I won't mention any names," Stevens went on, "but someone said the other night at the Savoy bar that if Owen could get an I Wuz There ribbon for using the women's restroom—and there was absolutely no risk of a shot being fired in anger in his direction—he'd be front of the line."

Candily let out a belly laugh.

"Yeah," Stevens smiled, "that's what everyone at the bar did, too. Laugh. Apparently, it's not a secret. And, at least in my opinion, it's not a good way for people to think of an officer who ranks so high—especially one sitting at the right hand of Ike."

"I agree. Does this Colonel Owen have any other stellar qualities?"

"Well, he does go by the book. Strictly. Which is why

I think that Ike likes him. But his going by the book really means that he doesn't like making waves, specifically doesn't like anyone else making waves."

Stevens stared at Canidy.

"Which means—"

"I know, I know," Canidy said, holding his hands up chest high, palms out. "I get it. Which means he won't like me. Especially if he gets wind of this." He waved the folder. "Ike has made it clear (a) that he doesn't think much of the OSS, and (b) that he damned sure doesn't want us going in ahead of the rest."

Stevens raised his eyebrows.

"Exactly," he said.

"So, I'll deal with it," Canidy said.

Canidy looked at his wristwatch, then changed the subject.

"I've got one stop to make to deliver some girly things"—he nodded at his suitcases—"then I'm going to hop out to the airfield at Scampton and hitch a ride there on one of the B-17s that the Royal Air Force is ferrying to Algiers."

Stevens looked to the suitcases, then back to Canidy and smiled warmly.

"Good for you. But watch yourself, my friend. When I said that you should not forget that you are good at what you do, I meant at being a spook. A woman in love is a far more dangerous proposition."

Canidy grinned.

"Duly noted, Colonel."

———

When Lieutenant Colonel Ed Stevens had called down for one of London Station's motorcars to be made available to Major Richard Canidy, the Brit in charge of the vehicle pool had told him that he was terribly sorry but all of the standard-issue vehicles in service—a small fleet of nondescript English-made sedans—were in use. The garage, unfortunately for the moment, was stark empty.

But when the Brit had heard the disappointment in Stevens's voice, he quickly offered one option: If it was to be a local errand, his brother—who had just pulled up to bring him his sack lunch of a sardine sandwich—could do so in his personal vehicle.

Stevens had immediately accepted the kind offer.

Canidy stepped from the building with a suitcase in each hand. Two British male civilians in their early twenties—they looked almost like twins—approached him.

"Mr. Canidy, sir?" the one on the left, who wore a tie and jacket, said.

Canidy nodded. "Yes."

"I'm Robert, sir. And this is my brother, Harry."

Canidy nodded.

"Thank you two again for your kind offer."

Canidy saw that Harry was looking at the suitcases with what appeared to be mild shock.

"Any problem?" Canidy said.

"Those are to go with you, sir?" Harry said.

"Sure. Why?"

Harry looked at Robert with a raised eyebrow. Then the brothers at once turned to look toward the street, the gap between them opening and giving Canidy a clear view of what he instantly surmised to be Harry's personal motorcar.

It was a candy apple red 1937 Austin Seven 65—nicknamed "Nippy"—a tiny, two-seat convertible barely bigger than the passenger's compartment itself. It looked to be six, maybe seven feet long, not quite three feet wide, and the top of the chrome-plated frame of the windshield looked as if it reached about as high as Canidy's hip.

It might be best, Canidy thought, *if right now I don't say a word.*

Robert turned back to Canidy.

With classic English understatement, Robert said, quite unnecessarily, "It'll be a bit tight of a fit."

Robert then smiled and revealed thin gray teeth that could have used the attention of an orthodontist.

He added cheerfully, "But my brother Harry works miracles."

He looked at his brother.

"Isn't that right, Harry?"

Harry looked back at Robert wordlessly—and, Canidy thought, more than a little dubiously.

"Right!" Robert answered for him.

Robert grabbed one of Canidy's suitcases and said, "So off you go!"

After a moment, Harry grabbed the other suitcase and

made himself busy with taking rope from the trunk of the Austin, positioning the suitcases on the lid of the trunk, then repositioning them, then tying them down.

After a few minutes, despite the car visibly squatting under the additional weight, it looked as if Harry had been indeed successful.

Even he appeared surprised that he had pulled off the miracle.

Robert went to the left door and opened it.

"Here you are, Mr. Canidy."

Canidy squeezed into the passenger's seat as Harry hopped behind the steering wheel.

Inside, it was so tight that they touched shoulders.

To make some room, Canidy stuck his left arm out of his "window" opening—there were no actual glass side windows, nor side curtains, just an opening—and rested it on the top of the doorframe.

This car is so low that if I'm not careful and my arm slips off this door, I'll drag my damned knuckles across the cobblestones.

Canidy turned to Harry.

"We're going to Woburn Square," he said.

Harry made a face that suggested some ambivalence.

"Do you know where it is?" Canidy said.

"Quite," Harry said. "It's just that . . ."

"What?"

Harry hesitated, visibly thinking.

"Nothing. I could be wrong."

He grabbed the knob of the stick shift with his left hand and moved it into first, grinding gears as he pushed.

When the sounds of metal being tortured ended, indicating that the gears had finally properly meshed, he revved the 747-cubic-centimeter engine to a high whine, let out on the clutch pedal, and the tiny motorcar lurched into traffic.

The car, clearly far overloaded, rode like a brick. At almost every bump, it bottomed out, and the jarring repeatedly shot up Canidy's spine to his jaw. He began to wonder if walking and dragging his suitcases would have been better than this torturous ride.

Harry seemed oblivious.

He ran up through the gears, the little engine roaring mightily. He wove through the heavy Wednesday traffic, then headed down Brook Street. At Hanover Square, he suddenly downshifted, wrestled the wheel to the left, and shot toward the traffic circle.

Canidy worried that if his luggage didn't go flying off the trunk lid, then its weight being suddenly shifted was going to cause the Nippy to go up on its two right tires—maybe even flip.

It didn't, and Harry accelerated heavily out of the circle, then shifted into high gear.

He picked up Mortimer Street and headed east.

As they went, Canidy could see the clear evidence of the recent bombings by the Luftwaffe that he had read about in the New York papers.

Some shops had their windows blown out while other shops were gone completely, their buildings demolished.

There were lines of women and children outside markets and laundries and more.

In the next block, two London bobbies sat sipping tea at a table on the sidewalk, taking a break from walking their beat. All that remained of the tea shop was part of the brick wall that held the store's wooden signage; the rest of the building beyond that was gone.

As Harry got on Gower Street, Canidy realized that the destruction was looking much worse.

And Woburn Square was only blocks away.

He turned to speak to Harry but found that he was so close that he almost put his nose in Harry's ear.

He looked forward again, out the windshield, and said, "How bad were the bombings in this area?"

"Spotty. Some parts the bombs did some serious damage. But other parts went untouched."

Canidy thought about that a moment.

"And Woburn Mansions?"

In his peripheral vision, he saw Harry shaking his head.

"Not great," Harry replied.

They made the next block with only the sound of the Austin whining.

As they turned onto Woburn Mansions, Canidy felt a real fear take hold.

It took him a moment to get his bearings because so much had changed.

He saw the park, then recognized the point in the park where 16 Woburn Mansions would have been in relation to it.

He looked hard and had trouble believing his eyes.

The building with Ann Chambers's flat—the very one

that had once survived other bombings with only its limestone façade scorched black from the fires—was now rubble.

Sixteen Woburn Mansions—and everything to its right and left—was gone.

Bombed to nothing but rubble.

And what about Ann?

Oh, shit!

X

Kurt Bayer passed through the front doors of the hotel carrying a brown paper sack that was imprinted in black with: TRENTON PHARMACY/WE DELIVER CITY-WIDE/PHONE HILL 4-3466.

In the bag, he had a fifty-tablet bottle of double-strength aspirin, a roll of two-inch-wide sterilized gauze, a roll of white fabric adhesive tape, a pair of blunt-tip scissors, a pint bottle of the topical antiseptic Mercurochrome, and a fifteen-piece box of Whitman's Sampler chocolates.

He scanned the lobby for any sign of Richard Koch. He did not see him, even in the cushioned chair where the agent usually sat to read the newspaper and smoke cigarettes.

On one hand, he was glad, because if Koch learned that he had used the cash he'd given him for Mary again, Koch would no doubt launch back into his speech about the relationship having to end.

On the other hand, however, he did grudgingly admit

that he admired his partner and knew that he could use some wise counsel right now to help Mary.

When Bayer got to the ninth floor, he noticed motion at the end of the hallway to the right. When he glanced that way, he expected to see the hairy, heavyset man in the tight suit. He instead saw a tall, dark-skinned man in casual slacks, shirt, and leather jacket. He had black hair that was nicely trimmed and a neat, thin black mustache.

And he was, as the heavyset man had been, having apparent difficulty getting his room key to work in his door.

Guess the fat guy didn't report it, Bayer thought as he approached room 909, *and if you don't report it, it won't get fixed.*

Bayer put his key in his door, unlocked it, and opened it just enough to slip inside quickly and quietly so as not to awaken Mary.

That, he immediately saw with the light of the bedside lamp, hadn't been necessary.

Mary was awake. And sitting up, albeit clearly with some discomfort.

"Hi, sweetheart," he said.

She made her gap-tooth smile.

"Hi."

He held up the paper bag for her to see.

"I went to the pharmacy, got you some stuff."

"Thank you."

Bayer took off his winter coat, put it—with the Walther pistol in the pocket—on the upholstered chair by the coffee table, then walked over to the curtain.

"Okay if I open this? It's a beautiful morning. Might make you feel better."

"I guess."

He slowly pulled back the curtain with his left hand and soft morning light from the western exposure began to fill the room.

When it was all the way open, Bayer turned—and almost dropped the bag.

The morning light emphasized Mary's injuries. Her bruising had turned deeper during the night, so much so that, for example, places on her face that had been separate spots the night before had melded into one big blue-black bruise.

I swear on my mother's grave that I will get the bastards who did this. . . .

Bayer walked to Mary, removing the box of chocolates from the bag as he went.

He sat beside her on the bed and held out the box.

"For you."

She grinned.

"That's sweet. Thank you."

She opened the box and put it on the bedside table, beside the telephone.

They stared at each other a long time, then Bayer broke the silence.

"Please, Mary, you have to tell me what happened."

She closed her eye but said nothing.

"Were you robbed?"

She shook her head.

"Did someone take the money that I gave you?"

She started softly crying.

"I'm sorry, sweetheart. I don't want to make you cry more." He paused. "But I *have* to know."

She opened her eye.

"You won't get mad?"

"Mad? Why would I get mad? Just tell me who did it."

She was silent a moment.

"Okay . . ." she began, then inhaled deeply. "Donnie."

"Donnie? Donnie who?"

"Paselli."

"Who the hell is Donnie Paselli?"

Mary started crying and sniffling.

Bayer got up and went to the bathroom for a tissue. He pulled one from the box, then grabbed the box and brought it back and put it on the bedside table. He pulled out another two tissues and handed them all to her.

She gently blew her nose—the effort itself proved painful—and coated the tissues with a soupy, blood-laced mucus.

When she paused, Bayer took the tissues, threw them in the tin trash can that was under the bedside table, and gave her two new ones to hold to her nostrils.

She looked at him, then looked away, then said, "They call him Donnie the Ape—Donnie 'the Ape' Paselli."

"Okay. But why—"

"He's the guy who I told you beat me before. You know? The guy I'm supposed to give half of my money I make?"

Bayer was silent.

You didn't give him the fucking money I gave you? Jesus!

"You didn't give him the money . . . ?"

Mary shook her head.

"I had late bills, rent . . ."

She sniffled.

"Please don't hit me," she whispered.

Hit you? I want to hug you—but I'm afraid that that might hurt you even more.

"Shhhh," he said.

His head spun.

I need to talk to Koch. This has gotten way out of hand.

Bayer leaned forward, toward the bedside table, and picked up the receiver of the phone. He dialed o, then sat upright again.

"Operator, please give me room four-ten."

There was a long pause as the call was put through.

"Yeah," Bayer then said into the phone. "It's me—

"Where? I'm in the hotel—

"That can wait. Look, I've got a serious problem—which means *we've* got a serious problem—one that you're not going to like—

"No, I can't tell you here—

"Stop shouting! I really need you to get off of that right now, and meet me in room nine-oh-nine—

"Right. Nine-oh-nine."

Bayer put the phone back in its cradle. He looked at Mary.

She was watching him, and he could see stark terror in her one good eye.

———

Not five minutes later, there was a knock at the door.

Damn, that was fast, Bayer thought. *He must be furious.*

Bayer went to the door, turned the knob—and suddenly felt the door being violently forced open.

In the next moment, he was conscious of three things happening simultaneously: There was a hand squeezing his throat. He was being pushed against the wall to the right of the bed. And he was looking down the muzzle of a pistol.

Holding the small-caliber semiautomatic—he did not recognize the make, but right now he did not exactly have a very good view of anything except where the bullet would exit immediately before it blew out his brains—was the tall, dark-skinned man who had been at the end of the hallway when Bayer had stepped off the elevator.

"Not a fucking word," the man said evenly, almost calmly.

Bayer, pinned to the wall, tried to nod his understanding.

Mary let out a pathetic whimper.

Both Bayer and the man looked toward her.

"Get out of the fucking bed, Mary!" the man said. "I want to see your hands."

Bayer's eyebrows went up when he heard the man say her name.

How does he know?

Then the man, as if reading Bayer's mind, looked at him and said, "I'm here to collect the money the bitch owes Donnie."

He turned back to look at the bed.

"Move it, Mary!"

"Okay, okay, Christopher," she said.

Mary struggled to get out of the bed but finally did so and stood there naked and bruised and bent, modestly trying but failing to cover her breasts and crotch with her marked arms and hands.

That, you sonofabitch, is a new low, Bayer thought, staring at the man.

The man appeared unmoved.

He motioned with the pistol at Mary and said, "You! Go close the door!"

Bayer watched as she shuffled feebly from the bed, passed where he was pinned against the wall, then crossed the room to the door. She pushed it but was so weak that when the door swung on its hinges it closed but did not click completely shut.

Bayer, his voice sounding strange due to his vocal cords being constricted, asked the man, "How much?"

"Three hundred bucks, plus another hundred as a penalty."

Beating her almost to death wasn't penalty enough? Bayer thought.

Bayer nodded his understanding.

He tried to swallow.

The man said, "And I want it fucking now."

Bayer nodded again.

"I have to get it from my wallet"—he nodded toward the upholstered chair—"in my coat."

The man looked at the coat in the chair.

"Mary," he said, "bring me that coat!"

Mary shuffled from the door to the chair. With some difficulty, she pulled the coat off the chair and started dragging it across the room.

"Hurry, goddammit!" the man said.

[**TWO**]

Richard Koch, who had hung up the phone after Bayer had called and immediately gone to the elevator and taken it up, walked down the corridor of the ninth floor.

He looked at the room numbers on the doors on the right side as he went and saw that he was getting closer to 909. He came to 903, then 905. When he got to 907, he looked ahead and saw what had to be the door to 909.

It was open a crack.

He took another step—then heard from the inside of 909 a strange man's voice say, "Hurry, goddammit!"

It made Koch's skin crawl.

He instantly got low to the floor, then reached in his pocket, pulled out the Walther PPK semiautomatic pistol, and worked the slide to chamber one of the 9mm rounds.

He started moving toward the door, pistol up and ready.

He came to the doorframe of 909—the side where the door had its hinges—and stopped just shy of it.

He leaned forward, in the direction of the knob, and tried to get a look through the crack.

All he could see, though, was some furniture and a window with its curtain wide open.

He listened and heard a woman weeping, then the strange man asking, "Which pocket is it in?"

Pocket? Koch thought.

Then he heard another man's voice grunt something. It was mostly unintelligible, but clearly it was Bayer's— and he sounded under duress.

I have no idea how many people are in there . . .

He pushed on the door gently. It moved, opening another two inches.

He waited to see if there was any reaction to that from the inside.

There wasn't, and so he took another look through the now-larger crack between the door and its frame.

What he saw horrified him.

It was Bayer's hooker, standing naked—and brutally bruised from head to toe.

She held Bayer's coat.

What the hell did Kurt do to her? And why?

And is that her pimp here to settle the score?

Bayer said he had a problem . . . said that we had a problem.

Stupid son of a whore!

I told him something like this could happen.

Koch took a deep breath, stayed low, and started pushing open the door very slowly.

[THREE]

Christopher "the Enforcer" Salerno took great pride in his street name, and in the fact that he had earned it by being good at what he did—"debt collection," he called it.

The thirty-one-year-old had been settling scores for almost ten years, not counting his teenage years, when he had dropped out of high school in Hoboken and hustled on the streets for whoever would hire him to do whatever.

Having worked nearly a decade exclusively for Donnie "the Ape" Paselli, he considered himself not only a professional—but *the* professional. He trained to keep his skills sharp. He worked out daily to stay in top shape. And he never took anything for granted, particularly in the middle of a collection.

Right now, his adrenaline was rushing. He knew that he had to keep it under control while at the same time using it to get the job done quickly and efficiently.

So far, everything had gone pretty much as planned.

After Mary had not paid Paselli his cut and Salerno had had to have her beaten—during which she had babbled some nonsense that her trick, "Kurt," claimed to be a German agent responsible for all the bombings that were in the news—they had tailed the stupid hooker right back to the hotel, right back to her stupid trick.

Then Paselli had waited down the hall to get an idea of what they were up against to get his money. Then he had sent Salerno to complete the transaction.

Salerno had his Colt Model 1908 .25 caliber semi-automatic pistol pointed at Bayer's forehead. It was a small, cold-blue-steel vest-pocket model barely as big as his left hand that held it—but it got the job done. He had his right hand firmly squeezing Bayer's throat.

A head taller and some thirty pounds heavier, Salerno had no trouble keeping control of the guy.

But that damned Mary is taking too long getting me that coat with the money.

"Hurry, goddammit!" Salerno said.

When Salerno looked over his shoulder at her, he saw that her one good eye had quickly looked to the door, then back at him.

Salerno looked at the door, too.

It was moving slowly open.

With his hand still squeezing Bayer's throat, Salerno quickly pulled him from the wall and spun him so that he stood between him and the door. He put the muzzle of the pistol against Bayer's skull, right behind his left earlobe.

"One sound," Salerno said calmly, "and you're—"

The door suddenly swung wide open and a man entered in a crouched position, his pistol sweeping the room.

Shit! Salerno thought.

Salerno squeezed the trigger of the tiny Colt. There was a *crack,* and then the slide of the pistol cycled rapidly, ejecting the spent casing—it landed on the bed—and feeding a fresh round into the breech.

Bayer started to crumple to the floor.

Mary screamed something unintelligible.

Salerno ignored it.

Using Bayer's body as a shield, he shoved him toward the man who now was moving toward them, then dropped to the floor and rolled left.

The man fired one shot at him, then another.

Neither found their target.

Salerno quickly squeezed off four shots.

Two of them went wild, missing the man completely.

The third .25 caliber bullet hit him in the groin area—stopping him not at all.

The fourth found his right knee, however, and caused him to fall forward, over Bayer's body and toward Salerno.

When the man hit the carpet, Salerno quickly put the muzzle of the tiny Colt to the base of the man's skull and fired the last of the six rounds.

He then quickly reached into the front pocket of his trousers and brought out a full magazine of .25 caliber ACP ammo.

Salerno swapped the fresh magazine for the spent one, racked the slide, and aimed the muzzle right back at the man's head.

The man did not move.

Salerno looked at Bayer. A steady trickle of blood ran from his left ear.

He was dead, too.

Neither had an exit wound; the small-caliber bullets clearly had bounced around inside their skulls, scrambling brains and bringing quick death.

As Salerno picked up the man's pistol—*Huh! A Walther. How about that?*—and stuck it in his coat pocket, the man passed his last gas.

Salerno heard Mary sobbing uncontrollably.

He walked across the room looking for her, following the sobs.

He found her curled up on her left side on the tile floor of the bathroom. She had her arms wrapped over her head, her ears covered.

Salerno stepped closer and saw that there was blood coming from her neck.

One of my shots must have got her.

He shook his head.

What a waste. If only she'd done what she was supposed to . . .

He leaned over and put a round behind her right ear.

The crack echoed in the tiled room.

Her body quivered, then went limp.

Salerno went back into the main room.

He picked up the coat that Mary had tried to carry across the room, dug through its pockets, and found a pistol in the right one.

What the fuck? Another Walther, identical to the other.

He put the second pistol in the other outside pocket of his coat.

He dug in the coat some more but found no money.

"You lying sack of shit," he said.

He went through Bayer's pants pockets and found no money there, either.

He kicked the body.

Then he went to the second guy and picked through his pockets.

Bingo.

Salerno came out of the right pocket of the pants with a roll of cash. He pulled off the rubber band, flattened the bills, and counted the money. Five hundred and thirty-one dollars. He rolled it back up and wrapped the roll with the rubber band.

In the left pocket, he found a key to room 410.

Maybe there's more where this came from . . .

Salerno went to the telephone, asked the operator to connect him to a number he provided, and after a moment said into the receiver, "I got the cash. But it got ugly. Need to get rid of three—huh?—yeah, three. Had a surprise guest. Take care of it, okay?"

A moment later, he put the receiver back in its cradle.

When he did, he noticed the open Whitman's Sampler box of chocolates next to the telephone.

He raised an eyebrow, then picked through the selection. He took out a chocolate-covered cherry and popped it in his mouth. He swallowed it after just two chews.

He licked his lips, looked again at the selection—then grabbed a fistful of the chocolates from the box, stuck them in his coat pocket, and went out the door.

[FOUR]
Algiers, Algeria
1625 12 March 1943

Major Richard M. Canidy, USAAF, awoke abruptly when he felt himself being bounced—bodily lifted a couple of inches, then dropped—and it took him a moment to get his bearings and figure out what the hell just happened.

Snug and warm in a lambskin flight suit, he quickly recalled that he had gone to sleep—a deep sleep, it turned out—while lying on the floor next to the bulkhead of the cockpit of the B-17.

He could have tried to sleep in one of the fabric sling seats that the aircraft had lining one side of the fuselage. But he knew that that would have been terribly uncomfortable, despite the fact that he could have strapped himself into the seat for security.

The alternative—lying on the floor, against the bulkhead—was somewhat riskier. If the plane, as it had just now done, dropped suddenly—the pressure in Canidy's ears and sounds from the airstream told him they were rapidly descending—he would get bounced in the air.

The bouncing was a calculated risk, but it was a hell of a lot more comfortable than sleeping in the slings.

Canidy was in the last of a flight of four B-17s. Each was a mammoth marvel of aeronautical engineering. The B-17 had four twelve-hundred-horsepower Wright Cyclone engines. Its cruising speed of 182 miles per hour gave it a range of two thousand miles while carrying a bomb payload of three tons. (It could carry as much as three times that but with a reduced range.) And it was armed with thirteen .50 caliber machine guns mounted all around the aircraft.

The routing of the Flying Fortresses had taken them from England south over the Atlantic Ocean, down the western coast of Spain, then on an almost due east vector over Morocco and into Algeria.

Thankfully, the trip had been uneventful.

But Canidy knew that wasn't always the case with the B-17.

Word had gotten around the USAAC that when General Eisenhower had flown pretty much the same routing a month ago to the Casablanca Conference to meet with President Roosevelt, Prime Minister Churchill, and all of the other top generals, he had been in a Flying Fortress—and the aircraft had lost two of its engines.

On the growing chance that the B-17 would not make its destination and that they would have to ditch, Ike had wound up spending most of the trip wearing a parachute harness.

Canidy felt his big bird turn on final for the Maison Blanche Airport.

He got up, and went to one of the fabric seats and strapped himself in.

He sighed.

All signs suggested that they were going to get on the deck at Algiers just fine.

But that did not mean that he did not have much to worry about.

He was still sick to his stomach at the thought of Ann Chambers gone missing . . . and maybe gone forever.

I spent every possible second chasing down anyone who might know anything about her.

Small wonder I just now slept so hard. . . .

As soon as Canidy had contacted Ed Stevens, Stevens had said he would immediately have people continue looking for Ann. He would message Canidy the minute he heard anything.

And when Canidy had spoken with Ann's bureau chief at the London office of Chambers News Service, the editor—who also had not heard a word from her since the bombing—promised to honor Canidy's request that he pass along any news to Lieutenant Colonel Stevens.

People disappear all the time in war . . . and then reappear.

Please, Lord, I never ask for anything, especially for me. But I pray You let Ann reappear. . . .

The scene outside of Base Operations, in the airport parking lot, bordered on comical. A crowd of some fifty or so natives swarmed in all directions. There appeared to be no logic as to where they went and why.

Canidy stood there for a moment with his suitcases and watched in amazement. He thought that it resembled what happened when you took your shoe and tapped the top of an ant mound—the ants suddenly appeared and swarmed every which way.

He felt a hand touch his right hand and then his suit-case being picked up.

"Hey!" he said, turning to see who it was.

There was a tall, thin, dark-skinned man in a well-worn, tan-colored suit and a collarless white shirt. He had a narrow, clean-shaven face with intense almond eyes.

"Taxi! Taxi!" he said in broken English with a faint French accent.

He nodded toward the parking lot.

Why the hell not? Canidy thought.

The man made a path through the crowd and Canidy followed, carrying the suitcase that contained some cloth-ing and the Johnny gun.

The parking lot looked more like a junkyard. Not one of the vehicles appeared to be in sound operating condi-tion. And when Canidy saw the man stop at a 1936 Peu-geot 402, it made him long for the tiny Austin "Nippy."

The black paint on the guy's taxi was severely faded and much of it had been overtaken by rust. The sedan had no trunk lid, no front fenders, the rear bumper was crushed into the bodywork and the back window was broken out completely.

The man put the suitcase in the lidless trunk, then motioned for Canidy to give him the other case to put with it.

Like hell!

And have someone come along and steal them while we're in traffic?

Canidy shook his head and pointed to the backseat.

The man looked, understood what Canidy meant, and moved the case out of the trunk and into the car. The second case went next to it. Then Canidy got in beside them.

"Villa de Vue de Mer," Canidy said.

"Villa de Vue de Mer?" the driver repeated with some surprise.

What the hell is wrong with that?

Stevens said that's where Fine was based, at the Sea View Villa.

"La Villa de Vue de Mer," Canidy said again with conviction.

"La Villa de Vue de Mer," the driver said, nodding repeatedly, "La Villa de Vue de Mer."

It was a twenty-minute drive from the airport into downtown Algiers.

It wasn't that long of a distance—twelve, maybe fifteen kilometers—but the narrow roads were in bad shape and they were packed with more of the craziness that was at the airport. It was a third-world mix of traffic that included not only cars and trucks but people on foot and horses pulling wagons.

Canidy, on a positive note, did notice that the weather was absolutely beautiful, the temperature mild, the late-afternoon sky cloudless and bright blue.

As the car crested a hill, the city and the naturally circular harbor—with the Mediterranean Sea just beyond—came into view.

At the port docks was a colorful fleet of wooden fishing boats. And anchored in the harbor were a half dozen or so United States Navy vessels and twice that many Liberty ships. Silver barrage balloons—beginning to reflect the early golden hues of the sunset—floated above the ships, their steel-cable tethers discouraging attacks on the ships by enemy aircraft.

The driver, tapping the horn occasionally, wound the taxi down the city's narrow lanes.

The car made a right turn and drove past the luxurious Hotel St. George. It sat on the lush hillside overlooking the port.

Canidy knew from his research that the hotel had been built in 1889. It was of a French Colonial style—with a brilliant white masonry exterior—and it was surrounded by beautiful, well-kept gardens and rows of towering palm trees. The interior was said to be impeccable, with grand, gilded ceilings and walls adorned by thousands of multicolored, hand-painted tiles.

Canidy also knew that the supreme commander had made the St. George his Allied Forces Headquarters. And with Eisenhower's AFHQ came all the brass, and all their aides.

Probably a good idea to keep clear of the place.

They drove on and came to an open market.

The cabbie slowed and rolled past, slow enough for Canidy to be able to get a good look at the tables of produce and dried fish for sale.

He studied the people waiting in lines and the ones at the front, haggling. A tall, olive-skinned man, with thick black hair cut close to the scalp, a rather large nose, and a black mustache, walked past his window—and Canidy did a double take.

They made eye contact, but then the man quickly looked away.

Damn! If that's not Francisco Nola, it's his genetic twin.

Canidy looked again, hard, but the guy had started walking away and then disappeared into the crowd.

Incredible . . . but then I guess maybe half of the people here could be part of Nola's genetic pool.

The crowd cleared out from in front of the car and the driver picked up speed.

He turned on a narrow street that went uphill, drove another three blocks, and pulled to a stop in front of a large, French Colonial–style villa. It resembled the Hotel St. George, except that it was maybe half as large, and its masonry exterior was a faint pink color.

There was no signage to indicate the place was anything more than a private residence.

"La Villa de Vue de Mer," the driver said with some finality.

He stepped out of the car.

Canidy got out of the backseat dragging one of the suitcases, then reached in and pulled out the other. He had no idea how much to pay the driver, who stood watching him.

He motioned to the driver with both hands, palms out and fingers spread, to wait right there.

The driver looked at him suspiciously, then nodded.

Canidy went to the large wooden door of the villa, looked at it, and noticed that it had a heavy brass knocker and, next to it at eye level, a smaller door about four inches square.

He knocked and after a moment the small door opened.

A very unfriendly looking face, belonging to what looked like a local male who was about age fifty, appeared in the opening.

He said nothing but raised his right eyebrow as if to ask, *Yes?*

Canidy glanced over his shoulder at the driver, who was watching with what appeared to be a mixture of curiosity and annoyance.

Canidy looked back at the door and said, "Pharmacist for Pharmacist Two."

Lieutenant Colonel Stevens had told Canidy that he would use the code names from the last mission in his heads-up message to Fine.

The unfriendly face contorted as if it had encountered a foul smell.

What the hell? Is this the right place?

"*Pharmacien pour Pharmacien Deux,*" Canidy repeated in French.

The unfriendly face left the opening and the little door closed and locked.

Canidy stood there, wondering what to do next.

He looked at the cabdriver, then smiled, nodded, and held up one finger to say, *It'll be just another minute, buddy. Everything's okay.*

After a couple of minutes, Canidy could hear what sounded like something large and heavy sliding on the inside of the big, heavy door.

Then the door swung open.

There stood the fit and trim Captain Stanley S. Fine in the uniform of the USAAF.

Behind him was the fifty-year-old man with the unfriendly face.

Fine looked past Canidy.

"Nice wheels," he said with a smile.

Canidy shrugged.

Fine motioned for the man to get Canidy's bags.

"Good to see you again," Canidy said, offering his hand.

He looked back out the door.

"How much should I give the cabdriver?" he added.

Fine said something in French to the man with Canidy's bags.

The man put Canidy's bags inside the door, then went back out to the driver. Canidy heard the man and the driver begin to noisily negotiate the fare.

"Let's get a drink," Fine said. "You're in time to watch the sunset."

Fine closed the door, and Canidy then saw what had caused the sliding sound on the big door: a long, wooden four-by-four beam that, when in place across the door, was held by a U-shaped steel cradle bolted to either side of the doorframe.

Fine saw Canidy looking at it.

"Keeps out the riffraff," Fine said. "Well, most of it."

He put his arm around Canidy as they walked.

"You got past it."

Fine poured two glasses of single malt scotch, neat, and brought them out onto the tiled balcony where Canidy leaned against the masonry wall.

The view from the villa was incredible. The city spread out below on a gentle slope that went all the way down to the port, maybe ten kilometers' distance.

The sun, now a red ball melting into the horizon, set the sky ablaze with deep reds and oranges. It cast remarkable lights on the ships and barrage balloons in the harbor, and on the houses and buildings of the city.

"Very, very nice," Canidy said softly, taking one of the glasses. "Must be hard to get used to."

Fine laughed and touched his glass to Canidy's.

"Unfortunately," he said, "I don't think I could ever get used to something as spectacular as that."

They both took sips of scotch.

They watched the sky for a moment, then Fine added solemnly, "That said, I hate to spoil the moment but I've always believed that news that's not good always should be dealt with at the soonest opportunity."

Fine took from the inside pocket of his tunic a folded sheet of paper and held it out to Canidy.

"This is not bad, per se," he said. "It's just not what you want to hear."

Canidy quickly unfolded the sheet.

"'Nothing new at this time,'" he read aloud.

"I'm very sorry about Ann. Wish I could be the one to deliver good news."

Canidy took a big sip of scotch, then looked at Fine.

"I wish that you could, too."

He looked out at the view. The sky was quickly darkening and the lights of the city began to twinkle on.

Damn, Ann would love this. . . .

"Let me tell you what we've got going here," Fine said after he had poured them each a fresh drink, "and then we can get into what you need."

Canidy stood, leaning against the balcony wall.

"Great. Start with this villa. How'd you get it?"

"It belongs to Pamela Dutton, widow of one of Donovan's law school buddies who made a mint in shoes, if you can believe it. Women's shoes. She has—maybe it's *had*—family here and split her summers between here and Italy, where they had the shoes made. She let us take this place over for ten dollars a year on the condition we'd protect it from the unwashed. And so now it's our main OSS installation."

"How does AFHQ feel about that?"

"Well, they aren't exactly thrilled. We've been put under the direction of AFHQ—"

"Which is based at the St. George, right?"

"Yeah. The brass is, anyway. And unless they specifically ask us for any intel—which we're supposed to supply, and gladly will, but more than a few there don't like us—we avoid the place."

Canidy nodded.

"Same old story."

"Unfortunately. But we don't have time to dwell on that. We're in the very early stages of using the Corsica model of assembling teams. These we'll insert in France to supply and build the resistance. The usual setup: The leader is an intel officer, and there's a liaison and the two radio operators who report to him." He paused. "We're not where I'd like us to be timewise, but I just got here."

Canidy nodded.

"I remember."

"The SOE," Fine went on, "has its finishing school down at Club des Pins. It's a swank, resort-type place on the beach that they've taken over. They're training their people—and mine—in telegraphy and cryptography and such. They even have a jump school. And . . . that's about the sum of it."

"Nice."

They silently sipped at their drinks.

Fine broke the silence. "So . . . you're going in yourself."

It was more a question than a statement.

Canidy nodded.

"It's necessary, Stan. We need this guy out now. And I need to get a handle on whatever it is the boss is after there."

And, should I not make it back, what the hell.

Ann didn't, either.

"The trick," Canidy went on, "is getting into Palermo."

Fine was quiet a moment.

"How about PT boats out of Bizerta?"

The wooden-hulled patrol torpedo boats were faster than hell and armed to the teeth. The eighty-foot-long Elco model, powered by triple twelve-cylinder, fifteen-hundred-horsepower Packard engines, could make more than forty knots. They could be armed with .50 caliber machine guns, torpedo tubes, depth charges, even a 40 mm Bofors medium antiaircraft gun.

"That's tempting. I had considered PTs, but then decided they were too open and it was too far. Plus, it's really helpful to have good seas and a moonless night with them."

Fine nodded.

"How about a sub?"

"That would work. Happen to have an extra sitting around?"

Fine chuckled.

"Not quite," he said. "But there is going to be a re-supply of Sandman in Corsica that leaves out of here in three days."

"The Corsicans who were recruited through the French Deuxième Bureau," Canidy said.

"Right. They'll take the *Casabianca* and go ashore on Corsica by rubber boat."

Canidy looked at him.

"Try to pay attention, Stan," he said, and with his hand that held his drink he pointed toward one o'clock. "Corsica is a chunk of rock in the water out in that direction."

He pointed to three o'clock.

"Sicily," he went on, "is another chunk of rock in the water more or less out thataway."

Fine chuckled again.

Fine said, "Any reason they couldn't drop you there after dropping the team on Corsica?"

Canidy thought about that a long moment.

Fine went on: "And wait for you offshore on the bottom till you come out?"

Canidy looked at him, then his eyes brightened.

"Wait," he said. "What about dropping me off on the way and picking me up on the way back? We plan for the pickup in the same place they drop me—just like how the teams do it—with a backup site."

Fine nodded thoughtfully.

"That could make sense," he said. "But . . . what if there are problems in Corsica before they get back to you . . ."

"Beggars can't be choosers," Canidy said, and shrugged. "I've been stranded before."

Fine considered that.

"If that's what you want, Dick, I don't see why not." He paused. "But then, I'm learning there's a lot that I think is okay and someone is always more than happy to tell me otherwise."

"One Colonel Owen?"

He nodded.

"And others . . . but they can be handled," Fine said finally. "What about you—anything you need?"

"No, but thanks. I brought what I thought I'd need, including a nice new Johnson LMG."

Fine's eyebrows went up.

"Nice," he said. "Where'd you get that?"

Canidy told him about how he and Fulmar each got one from Joe "Socks" Lanza.

"Amazing," Fine said when he had finished. "But then again, I guess not. Not after you've seen all the shady characters running around this town."

"That reminds me," Canidy said. "I thought I saw a guy I knew in the market this afternoon—but he's not supposed to be here."

"This place is white-hot with the anticipation of the Husky Op," Fine said, his tone matter-of-fact. "There're spies here from every Allied power. Then we've got the Communists, the Fascists—and of course the Nazi spies, who no doubt are putting two and two together. It would surprise me not one bit if the pope himself came walking through town. . . ."

Canidy, deep in thought, gazed out across the water.

"So they just might be expecting someone like me slipping into Sicily. . . ."

Fine nodded solemnly.

"Yes, unfortunately the odds are good that they would."

"The boss must understand that."

They were silent a moment.

"Wait," Canidy said again. "I do need something else from you. When I get ashore, I'd like to set some things to blow in case I need a diversion or two. So, some Composition C-2?"

"Not a problem."

"Okay, then. That's it."

"Good. Let me make a call, then we'll get some dinner."

[FIVE]
1010 East Eighty-third Street
New York City, New York
0135 8 March 1943

Eric Fulmar followed Ingrid Müller out the door of Wagner's Restaurant and Market. As they walked west, there was an awkward silence, which Fulmar desperately wanted to break while consciously avoiding the mentioning in public of anything about the German-American Bund.

"So," he said finally, "have you seen any good movies lately?"

"Not really. You?"

"*Heaven Can Wait* was pretty funny."

"*Heaven Can Wait* simply made me sick."

Fulmar looked at her.

"Why?" he said, incredulous. "I thought it was hilarious. And very romantic."

She looked at him.

"I auditioned for the lead role."

"Oh. Sorry I mentioned it."

They did not speak again till after they were across Park Avenue.

"Don't get me wrong," Ingrid said, switching her clutch between hands. "Gene Tierney did a marvelous job as Martha Strable. She's a doll. I do love her." She paused. "But I really wanted that part—*needed* that part."

"What happened?"

"It's what I told you earlier—it's what *didn't* happen."

Fulmar gave that some thought.

"I don't follow."

"Ernst said the studio wouldn't go for me."

"Ernst?"

"Lubitsch. The director."

"Oh, yeah."

"Maybe I should just change my goddamned name and start over. Or become a director; clearly, it's okay for someone behind the camera to be from Berlin. But not an actress. . . ."

She let that thought drop as she stopped in front of the grand entrance to a high-rise apartment building.

The three-foot-square cast-bronze signage on the brick wall to the right of the door richly announced: ROY-ALTON TOWERS.

"Here we are," she said simply.

Behind the pair of thick glass doors was a doorman—about thirty-five, every bit of six-four and two-twenty, wearing a dark blue uniform with gold piping—and he pushed open the left door with no apparent effort.

"Good evening, Miss Müller," he said formally.

She answered with her husky laugh as she entered and passed him.

"Harold, don't be silly," she called over her shoulder. "It's 'Good morning.'"

The doorman smiled.

"Yes, madam. Of course it is. Good *morning*."

Harold looked suspiciously at Fulmar.

"Good morning to you, sir," he said stiffly.

Fulmar nodded and pressed past, catching up to Ingrid at the bank of elevators.

He looked around the expensively appointed lobby. There was polished marble almost everywhere, and, looming above, a grand chandelier that looked impossibly big and bright.

Whatever roles she's getting, Eric thought, *the money must be pretty good. This place didn't come cheap.*

The elevator on the far left was waiting with its doors open and Ingrid motioned that they should get on it.

"Shall we?" she said.

Inside, Eric saw her push the 10 button. It lit up, the doors closed, and the car began to ascend. They rode up in silence.

And, interestingly, her home is not in Yorkville . . . nor particularly near it.

Third Avenue may as well be the proverbial train tracks separating her town's good and bad sides.

He glanced at her and smiled.

She smiled back.

So it would appear that my sweet Ingrid does not wish to live among her fellow Germans in Yorkville.

What does that tell me?

The elevator reached the tenth floor and the doors opened.

Fulmar saw that the floor there was a smaller version of the main, first-floor lobby—a wide application of the same beautiful polished marble and a looming, though smaller, chandelier.

There also was a picture window that faced south. Fulmar went to it and saw that it allowed for a grand view of the city in that direction, as well as decent ones to the east and to the west.

He found that, with a little work, he could see just past the apartment building to the west—it was on Fifth Avenue—and catch part of the Metropolitan Museum of Art that was behind it, and beyond that the vast dark area that was Central Park.

"Nice," Fulmar said.

"This way," Ingrid said with a smile.

She started down the hallway, pulling a fob that held a couple keys from her clutch.

Halfway down the hall, she stopped in front of a door. It was painted a cream color and, at eye level, had a four-inch-square frame with 1011 in it. There also was a black doorbell button.

She tried to put one of the keys into the lock but was having some difficulty.

She's nervous. You'd think I was her first gentleman visitor. . . .

Fulmar stepped closer.

"Can I help?"

She worked more quickly with the key and it found its home.

Without looking at him, she said, "There, got it," then turned the knob and pushed open the door.

She motioned with her right hand and said, "After you."

Fulmar nodded and started to go through the doorway and into the dark apartment.

"The switch is here on the left," she offered, reaching her hand in to hit the light.

There was the sound of something moving inside, behind the door—and the hair on the back of Fulmar's neck stood straight on end.

With his left hand, he quickly swatted her hand away from the switch before she could turn it on. At the same time, he threw back the tail of his jacket with his right hand and pulled out his .45, thumbing back the hammer as he brought the gun up. Then he threw his full weight into the door and followed it to the wall.

But it didn't hit the wall.

It stopped about eight inches shy of the wall, and when it did there came a heavy, soft thud from behind it and the sound of a man's grunt. Then there was a dense, metallic *clunk* near Fulmar's feet—

Was that a pist—?

—and then the *crack* of a small-caliber round going off.

It was a fucking pistol hitting the floor!

"Get out!" Fulmar called to Ingrid.

"Be careful!" Ingrid said.

He pulled back on the door and slammed his weight into it again, causing another thud and grunt. He reached around and grabbed at the person behind the door, found what felt like an arm, yanked hard, and threw the person to the floor facedown.

In the ambient light, Fulmar could make out that it was indeed a man.

Fulmar put his left knee on the man's neck, forcing his face to the right, then stuck the muzzle of the .45 to the man's right ear.

"Make a fucking move and your brains—"

"Eric, don't!" Ingrid said. "He's FBI!"

She flipped on the lights, and it took a second for Fulmar's pupils to contract as they adjusted to the brightness.

Fulmar now got a good look at the man.

He was smaller than Fulmar, about five-five, one-thirty, and in his midthirties. He wore a rumpled dark suit, dark blue shirt, dark patterned tie, and scuffed black leather shoes. His face and neck were bright red, thanks to the way Fulmar had him pinned to the slate floor. And he had a bloody nose.

Guess the door got him good.

Some three feet away, at the foot of a tall curtain, was the pistol that the man had dropped. Fulmar recognized it as a small-frame Smith & Wesson .38 caliber revolver, a five-shot model with a two-inch barrel made for the military and police.

Apparently, the man had had a round under the hammer

and when the gun had struck the slate floor the impact had caused the hammer to move and fire off a round.

I have no idea where the damned bullet went, Fulmar thought. *Just lucky it didn't hit anyone.*

Ingrid quickly closed the door, then knelt beside Fulmar.

"Eric, please—"

He looked at her.

"You know this guy?"

She nodded.

"Who is he?"

"F-B-I," the man grunted angrily.

Fulmar looked down at him and saw the man's angry right eye staring back.

What Fulmar did next took Ingrid—not to mention the man—completely by surprise.

Fulmar started laughing, slowly at first, then more deeply.

Of all the people I could run into, I run into one who's on our side. . . .

The man's angry eye darted about in its socket.

"Get off me!" the man grunted.

Fulmar looked at Ingrid.

"Is he really FBI?"

She stared wide-eyed back at him and nodded slowly.

"What's so funny?" she said.

"I can't say," Fulmar replied as he reached down with his left hand, dug into the man's inside coat pocket, and brought out a small leather wallet.

He flipped it open and saw a badge and an ID card.

Well, shit. So much for wild sex with Ingrid tonight. . . .

Fulmar stood and tossed the wallet on the floor beside the man's face.

Ingrid Müller came into the living room from the kitchen carrying a small, light blue bag made of a thin, soft rubber material in one hand and a small, stainless steel pot in the other. She had just filled the rubber bag with crushed ice and a small amount of cold tap water, then sealed its screw-top opening. The pot was about a quarter full of tap water.

Eric Fulmar and the FBI guy—"Agent Joseph Hall," it had said on his ID—were seated opposite one another on leather furniture.

Not just any furniture, Fulmar thought, looking around the now brightly lit apartment. *This is the good stuff—designer stuff found in museums.*

Ingrid's taste in furnishings ran toward the modern school—less is more. That included her artwork, oil paintings that were hardly more than huge floor-to-ceiling canvases painted in thick textures of a single hue only slightly darker than the walls.

Thus, there did not appear to be much in the large apartment, but what there was was very nice and fashionable.

The main living area, with its light gray-green slate floor, had as its focal point what Fulmer believed to be pieces—*Probably knockoffs of the real thing,* he thought, *but still outrageously expensive*—by the very serious designer Le Corbusier.

There was a chrome-and-black-leather couch and two chrome-and-black-leather chairs (the ones he and Hall were sitting in) positioned around a four-foot square glass-top table with a chrome-framed base that mimicked that of the chairs and couch.

It was all situated on a kind of finely woven rope mat—*"Sisal," I think it's called*—in a cream color.

The styling of the furniture was boxy, square, and though visually stunning—*like its owner*—it was unbelievably uncomfortable.

Fulmar, taking care not to spill on the leather the scotch on the rocks that Ingrid had made for him, shifted in his seat.

It's like sitting in, well, a damned box.

A well-upholstered box, but a backbreaking box nonetheless.

"Here you are, Joe," Ingrid said, handing the ice bag to Hall.

The FBI agent pressed the ice bag to his neck and glared at Fulmar.

Ingrid put the pot on the glass top, then stepped around the table and sat on the black leather couch.

"What's with the pot?" Fulmar asked.

"If Harold comes up and says someone reported they heard a shot, I act like the silly blonde I am and say my heavy pot got too hot and I dropped it on the table."

Fulmar raised his eyebrows. "Might work."

"You've clearly never seen me act."

She smiled, then went on:

"As I was saying, I've made my connections in the German community here available to the FBI. I'm an American citizen and this is my way of helping in this awful war."

"And you were willing to sell me out."

Her face turned very serious.

"If your intention," she said, her voice hard, "was to aid and abet the enemy, then you bet your ass I'd do anything that helps stop Hitler even a minute sooner. And that includes bringing people to speak with a 'member of the Bund'"—she nodded at Hall—"someone about whom I can easily act, if challenged, that I had no idea he's really with the FBI."

Fulmar smiled.

"I admire your loyalty," he said after a moment. "It's why I approached you."

"To get to those German agents?"

Fulmar saw Agent Hall's eyes brighten.

"Maybe," Fulmar said. "Maybe not."

"Which is it?" Hall said harshly.

"It's none of your business," Fulmar said.

"I am a law enforcement officer of the United States government," Hall snapped. "You *will* answer my questions. Or you will go to jail."

Fulmar chuckled.

"I don't think so."

He paused.

"Tell me, Agent Hall, what do you know about any connection between the Bund and these German saboteurs?"

"I'm afraid that I'm not at liberty to discuss such information."

"Because you won't—or because you can't, because you don't know?"

Hall stared at him.

"I'm the FBI," Hall said. "I ask the questions."

Fulmar chuckled again.

"You were almost with the fucking New York City coroner's office."

Hall tried to ignore that.

Fulmar looked at Ingrid.

"Please excuse my language."

Hall said, "Tell me again, in what capacity are you here asking such questions?"

"You're the smart one." Fulmar grinned. "You figure it out."

"Look, I've about had enough of your attitude—"

"No," Fulmar said evenly, "it doesn't work that way. How about you get the hell out of here and go try to figure things out. I've got work to do."

As it turns out, Fulmar thought, *your work.*

No doubt the FBI is still hoping and waiting those German agents just turn themselves in.

Fulmar stood.

Hall just looked up at him.

"I wasn't kidding," Fulmar said. "Get up and get the hell out."

Hall turned to Ingrid.

"Joe," she said, "you should do as he says."

Hall made a face, then stood up. He held out his left hand, palm up.

"What do you want," Fulmar said, "subway fare?"

"My revolver."

"Considering recent events, I don't think I feel too comfortable with you having it right now." He paused. "I know where you work. I'll see it gets back to your office. Meantime, maybe you won't have to explain what happened to it."

"You can't—"

"I can," Fulmar interrupted. "And I am."

He pointed toward the door.

"Out. Now."

Hall turned for the door.

"This won't go unchallenged, Fulmar."

He slammed the door as he left.

After a moment, Ingrid said, "Do you think he'll cause trouble?"

"No, of course not. He's not stupid. He knows who I am and now thinks he knows what I came to you for. He does not want anyone to know what happened here; it's in his best interest to pretend tonight never happened."

He paused, then chuckled.

"Hell, when he calms down in the next hour or so he'll probably become terrified about whether he should file an official report for the discharge of a bureau firearm. They probably track his rounds."

Fulmar smiled. He drained his drink and put it on the glass-top table.

"I'd better go," he said. "Thank you—it's been an interesting evening."

Ingrid slid up beside him and put her head on his shoulder.

Fulmar felt her thick hair softly flowing from his face to his shoulder. He smelled the sweet lilac of her perfume.

"I feel like I should somehow apologize," she said, and added softly, "How about, um, we make it an interesting *morning*?"

Then he felt her hand on his left buttock.

Fulmar looked at her and grinned.

She made her husky laugh.

She added, "It's what I said before: you know how to handle things. And . . . I like the way you handled that guy."

She squeezed his cheek.

Fulmar thought, *And I like the way you handle a guy, too.*

XI

[ONE]
39 degrees 10 minutes 2 seconds North Latitude
13 degrees 22 minutes 3 seconds East Longitude
Aboard the *Casabianca*
Off Palermo, Sicily
2010 19 March 1943

Over the course of the previous four days, since leaving Algiers, Dick Canidy had come to admire Commander Jean L'Herminier, the submarine's chief officer.

Canidy found that L'Herminier was truly an officer and a gentleman, as well as a first-class submariner. Though the commander had a compact frame—five-seven, maybe one-forty—the way he carried himself made him seem much larger. He spoke softly, but there was strength in his voice, a confidence that he knew exactly what he was doing.

And the thirty-five-year-old had real balls. This wasn't the first time he had pushed his ship hard and fast.

The Agosta-class *Casabianca*, ninety-two meters long and diesel powered, had been launched February 2, 1935, at St. Nazaire, France. She had been armed with antiaircraft guns and eleven torpedo tubes and carried a complement of some fifty men and four officers.

L'Herminier had pushed the sub to make the nearly five-hundred-nautical-mile trip from Algiers to just north of the northwestern tip of Sicily in four days. During nighttime hours, he ran her as much as he felt comfortable on the surface, which allowed approximately twice the speed than when she ran submerged during the daylight hours.

He had used a somewhat similar tactic four months earlier, when on November 27, 1942, he and his entire crew escaped from Toulon, the Mediterranean port in southern France. Most of the vessels of the French Navy had just been scuttled there to keep them out of the hands of the Nazis, who had invaded in retaliation of the Allies' OPERATION TORCH.

L'Herminier had set a hard course of 180 degrees and sailed the *Casabianca* as fast as she would go to Algiers, and there joined the Allies.

And now he was about to send Canidy to the shore of Sicily.

"Ready, Major?" Commander L'Herminier asked.

"At your pleasure, Commander," Canidy replied.

Stanley Fine had told Canidy that it had been L'Herminier who had come up with the efficient method of putting agents ashore.

The process involved first making a daylight reconnaissance of the shoreline by periscope to locate an appropriate landing spot on shore for the team. ("You don't want to drop them off at a tall rocky cliff, for example," Fine had explained.) The next step was to submerge there and lie on the seafloor till dark. Then, in the safety of darkness, the sub would surface and the agents would disembark to infiltrate ashore either by swimming or by inflatable raft.

The process had worked flawlessly on Corsica, Fine had said, and was quickly being adopted as the standard.

Canidy was dressed in nice slacks, a dark-colored sweater, and a navy blue Greek fisherman's cap that he had pulled from the wardrobe room the OSS maintained at La Villa de Vue de Mer. These clothes were in fact from Sicily—possibly even once belonging to the shoe magnate Dutton himself—and while they did not fit Canidy perfectly, they were close enough.

He had one other set of clothing from the OSS wardrobe in a black rubberized duffel that also contained his Johnson LMG, the six magazines of .30-06 ammunition for it, four full magazines of .45 ACP for his Colt pistol, ten pounds of Composition C-2 explosive, two packages of cheese crackers, a one-pound salami, and a canteen of water.

In a waterproof canister were the fuses for the Composition C-2, his coded notes of Nola's family contact information—*If for some reason I should find myself in Porto Empedocle*—the copy of what he considered his "Charlie Lucky's You're an Instant Mobster!" form, and his OSS credentials.

In his pocket, kept close at hand, was a tin pillbox with ten or so aspirin—and two glass ampoules of cyanide acid. When he had put them in there, he had thought, *Well, if the aspirin doesn't cure a headache, an ampoule sure will.*

Commander L'Herminier looked one final time in the periscope, and when he was satisfied with what he saw—or, more important, didn't see—he turned to his executive officer.

"Take her up please," the captain of the boat ordered in French.

The deck of the submarine was still much awash with seawater as Canidy and a pair of sailors wordlessly came down the conning tower ladder. Canidy carried his duffel. One of the sailors carried a partially inflated rubber boat, a paddle that folded, and a bellows. The other sailor carried a rope ladder.

Out on the deck, just forward of the conning tower, the sailor with the rope ladder began tying it off to hard points while the sailor with the rubber boat fully inflated it.

When both were finished, Canidy was less than enthused.

As far as he was concerned, the rubber boat that had been provided for him to transition from sea to shore left quite a bit to be desired.

"Boat" is a rather fanciful description, he thought, eyeing the rubber doughnut.

It was not much better than a large truck-tire inner tube, and he began to strongly suspect that that was exactly what it was. Or at least a modified version of one, with a circle of rubber material vulcanized to its bottom to serve as a sort of floor.

Its chief—if not sole—positive attribute was that being so small it would not be hard to hide once he reached shore.

He was grateful that he had had some practice getting in it back in Algiers. But now that he stood on a wet sub deck out in the open sea, that training seemed rather far removed from the real world.

He shook his head.

"Now or never, I suppose," he said, not necessarily to the sailors.

"Yes, sir," they said almost in unison.

The paddle was tied to the boat and then the raft tied with two lines—the second being backup in the event the first came loose—to the foot of the rope ladder. The sailors slowly slid the boat down the side of the sub.

The sailors came to attention and saluted Canidy.

"Good luck, sir," the one who attached the ladder said.

"Thanks," he said, returning the salutes. "I think I'm going to need it."

He adjusted the straps of the duffel that he had slung over his right shoulder, then got to his knees beside the ladder and, with great effort, began working his way down its difficult rungs.

As he descended, he heard the sound of water lapping against the hull. With the lapping getting louder, he knew he was close to the surface of the water.

He found the rubber boat bobbing in the sea.

Carefully, and slowly, he reached out with his left foot and tried first to locate the damned thing and then, if successful, step into it.

After a moment, he felt the familiar sensation of his shoe touching rubber.

But the boat bobbed away.

When he tried again and reached farther with his foot—his right foot slipped on the rope ladder.

He clung to the ladder with his hands with all his energy.

He hung by his hands a moment—*Now, that was close to disaster*—then one at a time put both feet back on the ladder, and when he was sure of his footing he slowly reached again for the boat.

He got it.

He then carefully managed to get his right foot in the ring of rubber. He knelt—his knees getting soaked from water that had collected inside the boat—and slowly worked his hands down the rope ladder.

He was completely inside now and floating just fine.

Here's where I suddenly flip.

Or the sub starts to submerge with me still attached.

Moving as quickly as he dared, he untied the paddle, then the lines attaching the boat to the ladder.

He tugged twice on the ladder to signal he was free of it, then with his hand pushed off of the sub hull.

The fucking massive sub hull, from this perspective, he thought, looking up and watching the ladder being recovered.

He took the paddle, unfolded it, dipped the blade in the water to his right and stroked.

The boat made almost a complete revolution.

Shit!

Forgot about that . . .

He carefully reached the paddle out in front of him, toward shore, dipped the blade again, and brought the blade straight back toward him.

The rubber boat moved forward.

He pulled this way for about five minutes when he suddenly felt the boat moving far more quickly than he could possibly paddle it.

What the hell?

Then he remembered.

Backwash from the sub's screws.

Thanks, guys!

He looked back, but the big boat was gone in the dark or the depths . . . or both.

And he suddenly felt very alone.

He rode the rush from the backwash. Then, when it had died out, he began paddling again.

Ten minutes later, he felt the rubber boat's bottom hit sand.

[TWO]
Gramercy Park Hotel
2 Lexington Avenue
New York City, New York
1315 8 March 1943

When the taxicab pulled up outside the hotel, the driver saw that he was going to have to wake up the passenger in the backseat. The guy had fallen asleep almost as soon as he had gotten in at the corner of Fifth Avenue and Eighty-third Street.

"Hey, buddy!" the cabbie said, looking in his rearview mirror. "This is it."

Eric Fulmar rubbed his eyes, opened them, and yawned.

"Great," he said, and looked out the window. "Thanks."

He paid the fare and got out and went through the revolving door of the hotel.

Heading for the elevator, he passed the front desk, then stopped and went back.

"Good morning," he said to the desk clerk. "Any messages for suite six-oh-one?"

The clerk turned and checked one of the cubbyholes in the wooden honeycomb behind him and retrieved two yellow sheets.

He looked at them, then turned and held them out to Fulmar as he made an unpleasant face.

"A couple for you, Mr. Canidy," he said curtly.

Fulmar nodded.

He didn't think it was important to correct him.

And he was too tired to give a damn about whatever bug was up this guy's ass.

"Thanks," Fulmar said.

Fulmar read the messages as he took the elevator up.

One was from housekeeping, saying that they were sorry but that they were going to have to place an extra charge against the room for the cleaning of the "oily" towels.

That probably explains why the guy made a face.

But what do I care?

He grinned.

I'm "Mister Canidy."

The other message had only a date and a time—it was from noon, just an hour ago—and a telephone number: WOrth 2-7625.

Fulmar opened the door to the suite.

He saw that it had been neatly made up. His luggage had been moved from the corner of the sitting room back into the bedroom. And there was a set of fresh clean towels hanging in the bathroom.

There was absolutely no sign that Major Richard Canidy, United States Army Air Forces, had been there.

I wonder what Dick did with my Johnny gun? Or did he take them both?

Fulmar looked around the suite for the Johnson LMG, first in the sitting room—under and behind and inside

the Hide-A-Bed couch—and next in the bedroom—
under the bed and between the mattress and box springs.

Then he went to the clothes closet. It wasn't on the
floor in there. But at the top of the closet was a deep,
dark shelf that held extra comforters and pillows and he
reached up and felt under the blankets.

Bingo.

Fulmar looked and saw that Canidy had rewrapped
the boxes, both the heavy, cardboard one with the
Johnny gun broken down inside and the other, metal
one with the thirty-ought-six ammo, and hidden them
well.

Thanks, pal. I may need this. . . .

He covered the boxes back with the heavy blankets
and pillows, then went to the phone and called the number that was written on the message.

When the call was answered, he recognized the voice
of Joe "Socks" Lanza.

"Fulmar," Fulmar said. "I got a message to call this
number."

"Yeah," Lanza replied. "I asked around, like you
wanted."

"And?"

"You're not going to find out anything where you
were last night."

What the hell?

"How do you know where I was last night?"

"How do you think? You were in a bar, no? Talking
German to the bartender."

When ONI—Naval intelligence—in New York City

had been trying to think of ways of casting a wide net to spy on the German-American Bund in Yorkville, it had been Lanza's idea to use William "Tough Willie" Mc-Cabe's union guys who serviced the bar vending machines.

Lanza told them that the forty-seven-year-old Mc-Cabe had a small army of low-paid thugs from Harlem who ran numbers in the bars, then collected the money.

They were in every Yorkville bar every day—and they knew every bartender.

And what they learned, Lanza learned.

Fulmar thought, *If you consider saying one word—Danke—talking German, then okay, Joe Socks, you got me.*

But he's on the money about it being a dead end.

Jesus! Does he know about Ingrid, too? And Hall, the FBI guy?

"Okay," Fulmar said. "So if not there, where?"

"Take the cab out to Lodi."

"Jersey?"

"Yeah. There's a place on Route 17 called Lucky's Pink Palace. Ask for Christopher. He's expecting you."

"When?"

"Now."

"Now?"

"Thought you were in a hurry. If you want to wait . . ."

What I want—thanks to Ingrid . . . oh boy, that Ingrid—is to fall on the bed here and take a long nap.

But that's just not an option right now.

"Okay. When will the cab be here?"

"It's there now."

"It's here now," he repeated, incredulous.

He yawned.

"Okay. Thanks."

Fulmar heard the connection go dead.

Fulmar went out the revolving door of the Gramercy and saw what he thought was Lanza's taxicab waiting at the corner.

He started walking toward it. The cab's engine started and then the car began rolling toward him.

For a moment, Fulmar thought that he might be mistaken—the monster fishmonger was not behind the wheel—but then the car stopped when its back door was even with him.

He opened the door and asked the driver, "This Joe Socks's?"

"Yeah," the driver said.

Fulmar saw that the driver was a tiny guy, maybe five-two, one-ten—*probably has to jump around in the shower just to get wet*—and about age thirty. He had a two-day growth of black, stubby beard and wore a dark work shirt, corduroy pants, and a black leather Great Gatsby driving cap.

Fulmar got in the backseat.

"Where's the big guy?"

"What big guy?"

Fulmar shook his head.

He looked out the window and yawned.

"Never mind," he said and settled in for a nap.

A jarring sensation abruptly awoke Fulmar from his deep sleep.

At first it felt like the taxi had hit a wall or something. But when he looked out the window and back to where they'd just been—down what he guessed was Route 17—he saw that the cabbie had just jumped a curb to reach a parking lot.

This part of Route 17 was a hellish-looking thoroughfare through a rough part of town. It had two lanes in each direction—with vehicles bumper-to-bumper—and traffic lights as far as the eye could see. It was lined with cheap used-car lots, greasy burger and fried chicken joints . . . and strip clubs.

Fulmar looked out the front windshield.

In front of the car was a two-story building almost the size of a high school gymnasium. It was built of cinder blocks and had been painted completely hot pink. It had a flat roof and no windows. The front wall had two steel doors at street level, one labeled ENTRANCE and one labeled EXIT.

Painted on at least three sides, as well as illuminated on the pink neon sign atop the twenty-foot-tall steel pole near the curb, was LUCKY'S PINK PALACE.

The very top edge of the walls, just below the lip of the rooftop, had GIRLS! GIRLS! GIRLS! repeated over and over in lettering three feet tall.

Fulmar noted that the parking lot was packed and that the crowd had a disproportionate number of work trucks.

"Looks like the place," he said.

The driver grunted, then drove around to the back side of the building.

There were two steel doors in the back wall, one at ground level and one on the second floor, at the top of a set of rusty steps that served as a fire escape. The lower door read: NO DELIVERIES 11A.M.–2P.M. The upper door: NO ADMITTANCE! FIRE EXIT! KEEP CLEAR!

When the cabbie nosed the car into a parking place, the car's bumper tapped the bumper of the one parked in front of it.

He shut off the engine.

"I'll wait here for you." He pointed to the top door. "Just knock on the office door up there."

As the cabbie tuned the dash radio and adjusted the volume, Fulmar opened the back door, got out, and walked toward the steel steps. He could hear loud music coming from the inside of the building.

At the top of the stairs, he looked at the steel door. It had three industrial locks and one peephole.

They don't want anyone getting in this way. . . .

He knocked. There was no reply for a moment, then he heard one of the locks open, then a second, then the third.

The door opened a crack and a thick Italian accent said, "Yeah?"

"I'm looking for Christopher," Fulmar said. "Joe Socks says he's expecting me."

After a moment, the door opened just enough for Fulmar to squeeze through.

Once inside, he saw the guy who had opened it—a really fat guy, easily two-forty, probably two-sixty, in baggy slacks and a dark shirt, its tail untucked—slam the door shut, then start throwing the dead bolt locks.

There was nothing at all exceptional about the office. It had two standard gray steel desks with wooden swivel chairs on casters, half a dozen regular wooden chairs scattered around the room, a couple of pictures of the Jersey shore on one wall, a large four-by-four calendar for the year 1943, with the days to date crossed out, on another. There was a dartboard hung on a wooden interior door. And one tall tin trash can, overflowing with old discolored newspapers.

A big, hairy guy sat behind one of the desks and a thin, dark-skinned guy with a thin mustache was behind the other.

The fat guy stared at him.

The thin guy got up and came out from behind his desk.

"You Fulmar?" he said.

"Yeah."

"Christopher," he said, his tone of voice flat.

He offered his right hand.

Fulmar shook it and was impressed by the strong grip.

"Why don't you give us ten minutes?" Christopher said to the really fat guy.

"Whatever you say, Christopher," the obese guy said and started opening the dead bolts again.

When the obese guy was gone, and Christopher had locked the door, the hairy guy behind the desk said, "Joe Socks says you're looking for something?"

"Some*one*," Fulmar said. "I'm sorry, but you are—?"

"In charge."

He smirked.

Fulmar looked at him.

Okay, have it your way . . .

"Okay. Short version. Lanza has agreed to help me find the German agents who are setting off bombs in the U.S."

Neither responded to that.

Fulmar looked at Christopher, then back at the hairy guy.

"And," Fulmar went on, "Lanza said you guys knew something that would help."

After a moment, the hairy guy nodded.

"Keep this in mind: I'm only doing this because Joe Socks said to."

Fulmar nodded. "I understand."

The hairy guy opened the top drawer of his desk, removed a pistol, and held it out.

Fulmar took it, checked to see if it was loaded—it was—then said, "It's a Walther."

"It's what we took off the guy who didn't pay his bills."

"Okay . . ." Fulmar said.

He made a motion with his right hand that said, *Give me more.*

"Story we got was that he'd been boasting that he'd been doing the bombings."

"Was he?"

The hairy guy shrugged.

"Where is he?" Fulmar quickly said.

"Gone."

"Where?"

"Gone."

"Look," Fulmar said. "I've got to have more to go on than that. 'Some nameless guy at a Jersey strip club says the bomber is quote gone unquote.' I'd deserve to have my head handed to me if I reported back with just that."

The hairy guy stared back at him.

"Okay," he said after a moment, "that horny Kraut told my hooker that he and his partner had been doing the bombing on the East Coast and that there was another team in Arizona—"

"Texas?" Fulmar said.

"Yeah, Texas. Whatever. I was damned if I was gonna give the guy up to the fucking FBI, dead or alive. He owed me for my hooker. So we went to squeeze him—nobody cheats me, *ever*—and his Kraut buddy starts a fucking shoot-out."

He paused, then went on:

"They lost. And now the sonsofbitches are fish food."

He made a thin smile.

"That enough 'to go on'?"

Fulmar thought for a moment.

"Is this pistol all you found? No wallets? No IDs?"

The fat guy glanced at Christopher and jerked his head to say, *Give it to him.*

Fulmar turned and saw Christopher holding out what looked like a pen.

"Found this in a duffel in their room. Maybe you can make something of it."

Fulmar took it and looked at it closely.

It's an acid fuse disguised as an ink pen.

And where there's smoke, there's fire.

Or maybe explosives . . .

"There wasn't anything else in the bag?"

The hairy guy looked at him with a blank face.

"Nope."

My ass. Of course there was.

But . . . okay . . . I'm not going to get anywhere with this.

You keep whatever you got.

"I need to use your phone," Fulmar said.

"Help yourself," the hairy guy said, motioning to the black one on his desk.

Fulmar gave a number to the operator.

"Switchboard oh-five," a woman's monotone voice answered.

"Fulmar for Chief Ellis."

"Hold one."

There was a clicking sound, then a familiar voice.

"Ellis."

"Got a pencil handy?"

"Huh?" Ellis said, then recognized Fulmar's voice. "Uh, yeah . . . okay, go."

"Message for the boss: 'Fire out. No trace.'"

"'Fire out. No trace.' Got it. Congratulations. And interesting timing."

"How's that?"

"The other guys report the other fire is out. It's on the news."

"Really?"

"Yeah. You coming home now?"

"See you soon," Fulmar said and hung up the phone.

All the way back to Manhattan, with the Walther and acid-fuse pen in his pockets, Fulmar tried to find holes in what just happened.

There really isn't any way to absolutely know if all the fires are out.

Maybe all the agents aren't dead.

Maybe others are laying low.

Then again, maybe there aren't any others.

The only way to find out for sure is to wait and see if there are any more bombings, while keeping the intel lines open.

Which I can do from Washington while working on something else.

Like going to work with Canidy.

He sighed.

But all that can wait till after I see Ingrid again.

The cabbie tuned the radio in the dash to a new station. The programming was going to a commercial break.

The announcer said, "The news is next after this message from one of our sponsors."

An obnoxious advertisement, sponsored by the Tri-State Ford Dealers, came and went, and then the announcer's voice came back on again.

"And now for today's breaking news," he said. "In a press conference in Washington, D.C., a half hour ago, FBI Director J. Edgar Hoover—"

Fulmar said, "Turn that up, will you?"

The driver did, and they both listened as Hoover said, "I repeat, we have found no evidence to suggest that this train wreck in Oklahoma was anything more than a very tragic event involving a gas leak. . . ."

Say it often enough, Fulmar thought, *it becomes the truth.*

Fulmar said to the driver, "That's all I needed to hear. You can turn it down or change the station."

He looked out the window and wondered what Ingrid was doing right now.

[THREE]
Palermo, Sicily
2240 19 March 1943

First impressions were important, Major Richard M. Canidy, USAAF, knew, and the thing that most impressed him about Sicily was how it appeared utterly unaffected by the fact that there was a war going on.

Although he had taken great care to evade any German or Italian coast watchers when he had landed just up the beach from Mondello, and when he had deflated the rubber boat and buried it, and then when he had passed through the tiny seaside town, his efforts seemed misspent.

He had not seen a single soul.

There had of course been a dog, and a slew of damned feral cats—but not a single human being.

Mondello may as well have had its sidewalks rolled up.

It was only now, as Canidy continued to walk the ten-plus kilometers to Palermo, paralleling a two-lane macadam road but staying far off it, that he finally saw someone.

It was a man, and he was inside a small stone house off in the distance.

Canidy saw him through the window and watched as he walked across the room—and blew out the candles for the night.

Amazing, Canidy thought, shaking his head and looking up at the twinking stars in the dark sky. *Is the whole island on snooze?*

He started walking again.

I don't know.

But I do know that the last thing I'm going to do is let my guard down.

I plan on being back at that beach when the sub returns in six days. . . .

———

Canidy came closer to the capital city and its glow of lights began pushing back the pitch-black night.

Now, as he entered the outskirts of town with its brightly painted modern buildings constructed of masonry, he finally saw some people. He passed a man, then another, then saw a couple holding hands as they walked across a piazza.

Not many, but at least it was some life.

He walked until he came to what he recognized from photographs was the Quattro Canti district. It was the city center, the medieval "four corners" area, and its ancient Norman-built stone buildings loomed in the night shadows.

He looked around, then walked on, heading in what he thought—*hoped*—was the direction of the University of Palermo.

I may as well check it out now, in the dark, with no one around.

Who knows? Maybe I'll get lucky and bump into the professor.

He chuckled.

Yeah, right.

Fifteen minutes later, after covering five blocks and backtracking two, he found affixed to a street-corner wall a metal sign with an arrow and the word UNIVERSITÀ.

Voilà! Canidy thought.

Or is it "Eureka!"?

He reached the university after three blocks.

The school itself was a disappointment. There was

no campus. And with no campus there were no fields for playing sports, no complex for housing students— nothing that gave a genuine sense of a school.

There was, instead, only more of the same masonry-style buildings he had seen in the modern parts of the city. Across the top of the main building's façade was basic signage, the black block lettering on a white background proclaiming: PALERMO UNIVERSITÀ.

Canidy walked up and got a closer look in the big window of the main building.

There was a security guard inside, sitting on a wooden folding chair with a billy club resting across his knees— and sound asleep.

The funny thing to do would be to bang loudly on the window and watch this guy go flying.

It'd also be the stupid thing to do.

Canidy looked around some more and found that the lights were out all around the university's building, the doors locked tight.

At a corner, he came to a coffee shop. Its door was open, and he could hear the sound of voices floating out.

He walked to the door and looked inside. There were eight students at the small round table and they had books with them. But judging by the fact that a couple of the girls were sitting in the laps of the boys, it appeared that the last thing they were there for was the study of academics.

One of the girls—a beautiful twentysomething with dark, inviting eyes, jet-black hair, and large breasts barely restrained by her sleeveless blouse—noticed Canidy at the door and smiled at him.

He grinned back, then walked on.

Love conquers all.

He turned onto a street named for Leonardo da Vinci—earlier, he'd passed one named for Michelangelo—and followed it downhill. He could see the port in the distance.

When he reached the bottom of the hill, he saw that there were a number of boats moored in the port. They were tied either to the long pier or to buoys in the harbor.

He also saw that there was absolutely no one around.

He surveyed the area.

At the pier was one large cargo ship, eighty, ninety feet long, with a flat deck that had large hatches and tall booms. It was the biggest vessel in sight. The rest were all fishing boats of various brightly painted wooden designs, six of them about forty feet in length, but the bulk of them were about twenty feet long and, interestingly, pointed at both ends. There were a half dozen more of these twenty-footers pulled up on the shore of pebbles, lying on their side, apparently in for repair of some sort.

Overlooking the port were apartments and homes built almost to the water's edge. They were dark and quiet.

Dockside was a series of shops, including what looked to be a fish market, their doors and windows closed and locked. Lining the outside wall of the fish market were wooden tables painted in bright greens and yellows and reds. He had seen similar ones at the Fulton Fish Market.

They were built at a thirty-degree angle, with deep sides to hold ice, for the display of fresh-caught fish.

Something on the dock moved and Canidy crouched behind a corner of an apartment.

He looked again, and saw a cat standing next to where one of the twenty-footers was tied. The boat was covered almost completely by a tarp, and as Canidy watched the cat leapt from the pier and landed in the middle of it.

Almost immediately, the cat came flying back onto the pier—and not by choice, Canidy saw.

The tarp was pulled back and an angry male stuck his head up. He slurred something in Sicilian at the cat, then threw a bottle for good measure.

Canidy chuckled softly.

Sounds like someone had a bit to drink tonight and had to sleep on the boat.

Or maybe that's where he always sleeps.

I've had worse. . . .

Canidy caught himself in a yawn.

I'd like to settle into one right now myself.

But no matter which one I pick, that'll be the one where the owner is casting off lines at oh-dark-hundred—and finding me aboard, snoring, will not be the highlight of his day.

Or mine.

Canidy then looked back at the beached twenty-foot boats.

But no one's going fishing in those anytime soon.

He walked down to the second-farthest one. It was

turned on its starboard side, its hull facing the fish market and shops. He pulled back on its tarp and saw that the interior had been gutted. There was a very long, smooth area where he could crawl in and pull the tarp back for concealment.

He looked at his watch and saw that it was now almost one o'clock.

May as well get rest while I can.

He took a long leak on the pebble beach, then settled inside the boat, put his .45 under his duffel, rested his head on top of it, and yawned.

And the Gramercy Park has the nerve to call itself a luxury hotel. . . .

The sound of small diesel engines came loudly across the water and almost echoed inside the boat hull where Canidy lay rubbing his eyes.

Judging by the light coming in the edges of the tarp, he figured it was just turning dawn and a glance at his wristwatch confirmed it. Both hands were on the six.

Men's voices filled the air, and there was the sound of foot traffic on the wooden pier.

Canidy peeked out of the tarp, saw there was nothing but another boat hull looking back at him, and crawled out of the boat.

He peered around the boat. The piers were bustling with fishermen loading their boats for the day; some boats had already cast off lines and were headed out of the harbor.

Some of the shops were now open. Canidy noticed

the smell of coffee on the salt air, and that someone had put ice in the display tables outside of the fish market. Customers were already coming and going.

Canidy turned around and relieved himself in what he thought was probably the same spot he had five hours earlier. He started to grab his duffel and throw it on his back but stopped. He made a close examination of the boat and the work done on it thus far and decided that the boat had not been touched in months.

No one's coming in the next hour or so.

He slipped the .45 into the small of his back, adjusted his Greek cap, then headed for the shops, hoping he might get lucky sneaking a cup of coffee.

As he walked across the beach, he studied the steady traffic going on and off the pier. All of the men looked approximately the same—same dark pants and sweaters, same olive complexions, and pretty much the same head of hair (though this varied greatly; some had beards or mustaches while others were clean-shaven).

Canidy stepped up on the pier and joined the line headed to the shops. He followed two men into one and saw that it wasn't a shop so much as a bare-bones communal room. There were two wooden tables. On one were baskets of fruit and breads. On the other, in the corner, were two big coffeepots. One was being refilled by a tiny, wrinkled woman who Canidy guessed had to be eighty, eighty-five.

Hell, she could be a hundred and eighty-five, for all I know.

The fishermen were freely helping themselves, no one paying for anything.

The woman looked at Canidy and she moved her thin wrinkled lips into something of a smile. She poured coffee into a chipped and stained white porcelain cup and held it out to him.

Jackpot.

He smiled and nodded his thanks, then turned to leave, grabbing a fig from a basket on the way out.

Outside, standing beside one of the iced-down display tables, he took his first sip of coffee and looked out across the piers.

The boat with the drunk who'd thrown the cat off early that morning still had the tarp across it.

Sleeping in . . . must've been some bender he was on.

Canidy looked past that boat, to the end of the pier, where it made a *T,* and saw a good-sized fishing boat, about fifty feet, just arriving. Painted on its bow, just below the rusty anchor mounted there, was: STEFANIA.

Two more of the same-looking men—olive-skinned, dark clothes, dark hair, et cetera, et cetera—jumped off the *Stefania* and secured her lines to cleats on the pier.

Canidy took another sip of coffee—and almost blew it out when he saw a third man get off the boat.

It just can't be . . .

He had to get a better look and quickly joined the line of fishermen walking out on the pier.

As he approached the *Stefania,* it became clear that he was not seeing things.

Although the guy had his back to him, there was no doubt whatever that this guy was *not* average. He was big and burly—easily six-two, two-fifty—and towered over everyone else.

And then Canidy saw who was onboard handing the big guy a wooden crate.

I knew it!

Canidy stepped closer and said quietly, "I don't suppose there's fish in that box, huh, Frank?"

Francisco Nola turned to look but did not appear to be particularly surprised to see Dick Canidy standing on a pier in Palermo.

The monster fishmonger, however, almost dropped the wooden crate into the sea.

Nola looked around the pier, then jerked his head toward the cabin of his boat.

"C'mon aboard," he said softly in English to Canidy.

Nola said something in Sicilian to the monster fishmonger, then turned to go into the cabin.

Canidy hopped aboard and followed.

"So you couldn't come with me," Canidy said, "but here the hell you are."

Nola was standing next to the helm of the *Stefania*, his arms crossed. He stared at Canidy but did not speak.

"What the hell is that all about?" Canidy said, his voice rising.

Nola glanced out the window before replying.

"This trip was planned before you were sent to me," he said.

Canidy shook his head in disbelief.

A member of the crew came up from down below carrying another crate. He went out of the cabin without saying a word.

"What's in the boxes?" Canidy said.

Nola did not immediately reply.

"Chocolates," he said finally.

"Bullshit!"

"And medicine."

Canidy stared at him.

"That I believe. What else?"

Nola shrugged.

"Does it matter?"

Canidy ignored that.

"Maybe weapons?" he went on.

Nola looked out the window, then back at Canidy.

"You know whose side I'm on."

"How did you get this stuff into Algiers?"

"If you know who loads the Liberty ships in New York, you can figure out who unloads them here."

Canidy nodded, and thought, *And a crate here and a crate there that goes missing, or isn't listed on a manifest . . . doesn't exist. Nice.*

"How do you get to come in and out of here? They let you?"

"Not everyone. We have to wait till a German named Müller is away or otherwise distracted." He paused. "We have always run an import-export business. Olive oil, tomatoes, and more out. Merchandise in. It is overlooked now because you can always find someone willing to look the other way if it is to his advantage."

He held up his right hand and rubbed his thumb and index finger together.

"Why didn't you tell me you did this—that you ran boats here?"

Nola grinned.

"You didn't ask."

Canidy made a sour face.

"I don't think it's funny."

"Look," Nola said reasonably, "I would have. But you were interested in Porto Empedocle."

Canidy stared at him.

Dammit. He's right. That's when I thought we were going to bring the professor out that way.

"I thought that that was where we'd bring out Professor Rossi."

"Rossi?"

"Yeah. Know him?"

Nola shook his head.

Canidy said, "He's at the university here—"

"Yes," Nola said. "His sister is my cousin's neighbor. They used to sometimes have dinners, then play cards. Dr. Napoli and Dr. Modica, too, but no longer. I hear both are dead."

"I thought you said you didn't know Rossi?"

"I don't. I said his sister—"

"Jesus Christ!" Canidy exploded.

What is it with this guy?

He should be a lawyer!

Or maybe I should ask better questions . . .

I'd better start again.

"Sorry, Frank," Canidy said, and took a deep breath.

"Can you get me to Rossi?"

[FOUR]
Port of Palermo
Palermo, Sicily
1805 25 March 1943

The *Stefania*, her diesel engine idling, was moored next to the huge cargo ship when Dick Canidy helped Professor Arturo Rossi aboard.

Rossi, carrying a suitcase packed with his papers from his office at the university, tried to move too quickly and nearly fell into the dark water.

Canidy took the suitcase and Rossi awkwardly rushed again to get aboard.

He made it, and Canidy then handed the suitcase over and hopped aboard with his duffel.

As he helped the professor into the cabin, Canidy thought, *He's been in high gear since the very second he understood that I could get him the hell out of here.*

Keeping him under wraps the last few days has been tough.

And no wonder.

He loses two dear colleagues—one to a heinous disease, the other shot in front of him by that Müller from the SS— then is tapped to take their place in that hellhole of a villa.

It was the same as a death sentence.

Canidy helped Rossi get comfortable on a bunk down below.

At least the villa is history . . . or will be in two hours, when Nola's men fire the fuses to the C-2 I set for them.

Canidy looked out the porthole at the harbor.

But I still don't know what the hell Donovan meant about something bigger.

Maybe it was the viruses . . .

"Thank you," Rossi said.

"You're welcome, Professor."

Rossi looked at him oddly.

"Something bothering you, Professor?"

He shook his head.

"Just what are you going to do about the Tabun?" Rossi said.

Tabun? Canidy thought.

He said, "Tabun, as in gas?"

"Yes. That's also why you're here, no?"

Canidy did not answer.

"Why Tabun?" he said.

"You've seen how few Germans there are here," the professor explained.

Next to none.

"Yeah."

"Well, in anticipation of an Allied landing on an island it can barely hold because they're stretched so thin, the Germans have very quietly brought in their first shipment of the nerve agent."

Jesus! That stuff is worse than yellow fever. It targets

organs, and it makes muscles twitch till the victim collapses from exhaustion—and dies.

"Where is it?"

Rossi pointed out the porthole, to the darkened cargo ship moored nearby.

Canidy dug into his duffel and came out with the last two pounds of Composition C-2, then went topside.

Nola stood at the helm.

"You ready?" Nola said.

"You have any men on the dock?" Canidy replied.

Nola shook his head.

"They are all aboard. There's no one out there."

"Give me ten minutes," Canidy said, and reached to set his watch.

Nola touched his watch to adjust it.

Canidy said, "Mark."

Canidy then went out of the cabin, jumped on the pier, and ran toward the cargo ship.

Nola looked at his watch. Nine minutes had passed since Canidy left.

He stuck his head out the door of the cabin.

"Cast off the lines," he called to his men.

The men untied the bow and stern lines from the cleats on the pier, then leaped back aboard, coiling the lines as they went.

Nola checked his watch.

The second hand swept the face.

Ten minutes.

He looked back to the pier, saw no one, and frowned.

His right hand reached up and bumped forward the lever that controlled the transmission.

As the *Stefania* slowly moved ahead, Nola turned the wooden spoke wheel to port and her bow began to angle out toward the open sea.

Just as the transom cleared the end of the pier, Nola heard a heavy *thump, thump* aft of him.

He did not turn around to look.

It was the unmistakable sound of feet hitting the deck.

The *Stefania* was dead in the water—her engine off and all lights out—just north of Mondello, which was just below the Villa del Archimedes at Partanna.

It had been an hour since she had left the dock at Palermo, and Dick Canidy, sitting on the transom and peering toward shore through a pair of battered binoculars, was beginning to question his skills.

He let the binocs hang from the strap around his neck, looked again at his watch, then back toward land— and then there came a small explosion followed by a second one, and then by a much louder one.

It lit the night.

"That third one," he said to no one in particular, "must have been the fuel cell cooking off. Or . . . maybe there was something more onboard that ship."

"Whatever it was," the professor replied, "judging by the fire plume, it totally consumed everything aboard."

There was a loud rush of water about one hundred

yards north of their position. Everyone turned to see the great black bulk of a submarine. It was lit by the glow in the sky.

Canidy turned to the professor.

"There's our ride," he said. "Too bad we can't stick around to see the villa go up. That's going to be one of my masterpieces."

Turn the page for a special preview of
the next book in the Men at War series

THE DOUBLE AGENTS

Available in June 2007
from G. P. Putnam's Sons.

"You very well would be shot for saying such a thing," SS Standartenführer Julius Schrader said.

SS Obersturmbannführer Oskar Kappler—an athletic thirty-two-year-old, tall and trim, with a strong chin, intelligent blue eyes, and a full head of closely cropped light brown hair—did not trust his voice to reply. The lieutenant colonel stood stiffly, and simply stared at the colonel, a pale-skinned, portly thirty-five-year-old of medium height who kept his balding head cleanly shaven.

"Of all people, my friend, this you should understand," Schrader added.

Taking care not to spill coffee from the fine porcelain cup that he carried on its saucer, the Standartenführer rose slowly from his high-back leather chair then moved out from behind the polished marble-top wooden desk that dominated the large office.

Kappler's eyes followed Schrader as he walked across the floor, also of highly polished stone, past oversized portraits of Adolf Hitler and Joseph Goebbels—the images of the Nazi Germany leader and his propaganda minister striking Kappler as more oafish than inspiring—and over to one of the half-dozen floor-to-ceiling windows with heavy burgundy-colored drapes pulled back to either side.

Sipping from the cup, Schrader looked out at the busy Port of Messina and, five kilometers distant across the Strait of Messina, to the toe of the boot that was mainland Italy. The morning sun painted the coast and rising hills in golden hues and turned the surface of the emerald green sea to a shimmering silver.

Schrader sighed, then added pointedly but softly: "Or, perhaps worse, you would be sent to suffer a slow death in a concentration camp."

Both men—Nazi officers in the *Sicherheitsdienst*, the SD, the intelligence arm of the SS—knew far more about that than they wished. Punishment for anything less than total commitment to *der Führer* and the success of his Third Reich was swift and brutal. And they both personally had witnessed incidents in which those merely suspected of being suspicious—civilians and soldiers alike—had been summarily shot or shipped off to spend their final days toiling in the death camps.

For those so sentenced, a bullet served as the far better option, even if self-administered . . . as it sometimes was.

Obersturmbannführer Kappler wanted to speak but found it hard to control his voice so that it did not waver.

Schrader surveyed the port. Cargo vessels flying the flags of Germany and Italy were moored at the long docks, loading and unloading, the cranes and ships creating long, defined shadows in the low angle of the sun.

At anchor inside the sickle-shaped harbor were warships—two aging destroyers and a heavy cruiser, the latter easily twenty years old—from the Third Division of the Italian navy, the *Regina Marina*.

Schrader thought, *The ships look beautiful in the morning light, but the fact is the merchant vessels have been weeks late getting here. Supply to all of our ports in Sicily—especially those in the south and far west—has been getting slower. Food, munitions, everything.*

And the Regina Marina *treats us like some kind of stepchild, providing only weak, aging vessels for our protection.*

It is hard not to agree with my old friend . . . though I dare not say so.

Schrader, still looking out the window, stated in a matter-of-fact tone, "We go back very far, Oskar. I have always supported you. I must strongly counsel you not to continue with such talk, and will, even at great risk to myself for not reporting it, ignore that you ever said anything of the kind."

He turned to glance at Kappler. He saw him looking off into the distance, slowly shaking his head in frustration, if not defiance.

Kappler cleared his throat, swallowed—and found his voice.

"Juli," he began softly but with determination, "I of course have always appreciated everything that you have done for me. And I certainly value your counsel. But . . ."

Schrader held up his hand, palm outward, in a gesture that said *stop*.

"But nothing," he said. "You will serve here as ordered, as will I, and we will honor the *Führer* and the Fatherland. Period."

Kappler looked at his friend, who for the last year also had been his superior in the SS office in Messina. Their friendship dated back a dozen years, to when they had been teammates on the university polo team in Berlin. Schrader, then in far better shape, had held the key position of number four player, while Kappler was the number three player.

Then, as now, Kappler knew Schrader expected him to follow his lead.

"But, Juli, I have heard from certain sources in Berlin that Hitler will not be able to adequately defend Sicily. With his focus on fronts of higher strategic value—France, Russia, others—he cannot afford to send the forces necessary to do so. And when that is realized by the Italian military—who some say would just as well fight against us, which is to say not fight any invasion—we'll be left to defend this pathetic island alone. We'll be overrun."

He walked over to the window and stood beside Schrader.

"Take a closer look out there, Juli," Kappler said, making a dramatic sweep with his arm. "What do you see? A tired old city—no, not even that—a tired old town that has been neglected by its own. And what has Mussolini done for Messina? Same that he's done for all of Sicily: Nothing but make promise after promise, all of them empty. Yet here the Sicilians sit, so close that they can almost reach out and touch the shore of Italy—and its riches."

He paused, then pointed to the northwest, where the low masonry buildings at the edge of the city gave way to much lesser structures—fashioned of really no more than rusted corrugated tin and other salvaged metal and wooden scraps—near the foothills.

"And there," Kappler went on, his tone of voice becoming stronger. "Those shanties. Do you think that any one of the tens of thousands in those miserable conditions have any reason to fight for Mussolini? No. Of course not. Nor does the average Sicilian feel loyalty to him. And certainly not the real leaders, the members of the Mafia—many of whom you will recall you and I helped Il Duce imprison. They feel exactly the opposite. They despise Mussolini." He paused. "They despise *us*."

Schrader made a *humph* sound, and shrugged.

"What do you expect?" he said. "This is war—"

"But," Kappler interrupted, "you would think that we're an occupying force. We're not. These people do not know—or choose not to acknowledge—that we're fighting on the same side, Juli."

He let that statement set in, then added: "If you do not agree, then answer this: How do we go about ensuring their allegiance?"

He looked at his friend. When finally there was no answer, only silence, he answered the question himself: "We do it with threats, Juli, with coercion and fear. Just as you and I fear being found not to be in complete and total lockstep with—" he made a disgusted wave of his hand toward the portraits on the wall— "the high party and its ideals."

Schrader looked at Kappler, then at his coffee cup, and drained it.

"This is complete nonsense," Schrader said. "I have been given no intelligence that says—"

"Do you really believe that they would *tell* you that? From what I hear, no one tells the *Führer* anything that the *Führer* does not want to hear. His temper is legendary."

Schrader snorted. "So it is said. I would not wish to have been the unfortunate one who had to report the news last month of von Paulus's defeat."

Kappler nodded solemnly.

The *Wehrmacht* had been dealt a devastating blow by the Russian Red Army. Field Marshal Friedrich von Paulus and his Sixth German Army—strung out too far while battling a wicked Stalingrad winter—had been damn near obliterated.

It was a loss that even now Hitler had not come to completely comprehend—quite possibly *could* not, considering that people were prone to report that which would keep them alive . . . not necessarily that which the *Führer* needed to hear.

"Precisely," Kappler said. "And apparently that temper is worsening with his misfortunes of war. First, he basically loses North Africa and—worse—refuses to concede it. Now, mere months later, this travesty in Stalingrad. What makes you think he is even thinking of Sicily? Maybe he's more concerned about Corsica and Sardinia. They're closer to the mainland. If I were him, I would pull back and protect against mainland invasions closer to home—particularly ones from the east and west—battles that I can win." He exhaled audibly. "Not save some island."

He looked at Schrader, who returned the look but said nothing.

Kappler then quietly offered: "You know there have been attempts on Hitler's life."

"Rumors," Schrader snapped.

Kappler nodded, and said, "Possibly. But credible ones. He's weakening."

Schrader stared at Kappler, looking in his eyes for something that he feared Kappler might be holding back from saying.

Schrader knew the Kapplers were an old family that was well connected in Dortmund—and thus well-connected at high levels in Berlin thanks to Oskar's industrialist grandfather's steel mill in *Ruhrpott*, the Ruhr Valley, supplying critical materials to the war effort—and Kappler could very well have access to quiet information that Schrader never would.

"Only a fool would try to assassinate him," Schrader finally said, reasonably.

"Only a fool would try *and fail*."

Schrader stiffened and with a raised voice said, "You're not suggesting—?"

"I'm not suggesting anything, Juli," he said evenly. "I am, however, saying that there appear to be real cracks in Hitler's grand plan. And that wise men make their own plans for different courses of action."

Schrader walked wordlessly over to the desk, took a deep breath and exhaled it, then picked up the carafe from the sterling silver coffee service at the front edge of the desk. He gestured with it, offering Kappler a cup.

"Sure you won't have some?" he asked, his voice now casual, and after Kappler shook his head, Schrader shrugged, and poured himself a fresh cup.

"'Different courses of action,'" Schrader said, conversationally. "What does this mean?"

"Just look at what Hitler has sent us to prepare for a possible invasion. Not men, not matériel. No, he has left us Il Duce's tired army to fight with our own thin forces."

As Schrader absently stirred three spoonfuls of sugar into his coffee, he said, "There is no reason we could not get additional reinforcements."

Kappler made a sour face.

"Come now, Juli. The German forces have only so many men, and we're losing what we have at a growing rate. If Hitler were planning to reinforce Sicily, why would he have us overseeing Sturmbannführer Müller's work? And let me remind you what that professor from the university in Palermo said: That such weapons do not discriminate. That they are as likely to kill us as they are any enemy."

Schrader made eye contact, pursed his lips, and nodded. He returned to his leather chair, sat, and sipped slowly and thoughtfully at his coffee.

He knew that Kappler was of course privy to all of the secret SS operations on Sicily, and that these included Müller and the plans for chemical and biological weapons.

For one, Kappler was the supervising officer of the SS major—Hans Müller, a twenty-eight-year-old with a violent temper matching, if not surpassing, that of Hitler—who was in charge of the Palermo SS field office and its operations.

Near Palermo, in an ancient seaside villa, the SS was advancing the Nazi experimentation—begun in the Dachau concentration camp—of injecting Sicilian prisoners with extract from mosquito mucous glands to keep alive a strain of yellow fever. That was to say, until the sickened hosts died of malaria. Then new hosts—often members of the Mafia brought in from the penal colonies that had been established on tiny outer islands just north of Sicily—were infected with the disease that the SS had imported.

For another, Kappler was aware—although Müller as yet was not—that shipments had begun of crates labeled SONDERKART.6LE.F.H.18T83 that contained 10.5-cm howitzer shells. These were not the usual *ack-ack* anti-aircraft munitions for firing from the Nazi's light field howitzers. These rounds contained the chemical agent code-named T-83 that attacked the human central nervous system.

Commonly called Tabun, the German-developed chemical was one of the easiest to produce on a massive scale and was efficient to a horrific level. Mostly odorless and colorless, it quickly caused its victims to have convulsions, restricted breathing, triggered loss of bowel control—and ultimately loss of heartbeat.

Death by Tabun was relatively swift . . . but intensely painful and gruesome.

Kappler knew that Müller was not aware of the Tabun munitions, nor that a first shipment was already in the Port of Palermo, aboard a cargo ship, mixed in with other military goods and listed, more or less innocuously, on the manifest by its code name.

Müller did not know because Kappler had decided not to tell him until he thought it was necessary to do so.

In short, Kappler had told Schrader that he did not trust the hothead with knowledge—let alone control—of such a powerful weapon, and Schrader had quietly concurred.

After a moment, Kappler asked, "What do you have to say about that, Juli?"

Schrader leaned back in the leather chair, staring at the coffee cup, and with an index finger slowly rotated the cup on the saucer as he considered it all.

How do I agree, Schrader thought, *without encouraging Oskar to take one step too far, to act on a "different course" perhaps too soon?*

He sighed.

"I will allow that what you say is conceivable—" he began.

"*Ach du lieber Gott!*" Kappler flared. Dramatically, he raised his hands heavenward, palms up, and looked upward, as if seeking divine input. "Of course it is, Juli! And that is why I speak of this with you, my friend, so that wise men can make plans, not just be left twisting in the wind . . . a deadly contaminated wind."

Standartenführer Julius Schrader looked exasperated.

"Yes, yes, Oskar. So you have said. Yet you have not shared with me what these different courses of action might be."

Kappler approached the desk, then went to the coffee service and poured himself a cup. He started to pick up the coffee cup, then for some reason decided otherwise.

He buried his face in the palms of his hands, his fingertips massaging his temples. After a moment, he removed his hands, looked at Schrader, and quietly said, "I have also heard—from trusted sources other than those I have mentioned—that there are certain members of the SS who are setting up routes to safety should we not win this war. Routes for them, for their loved ones. And then there are other routes that set aside their funds."

Schrader stared into Kappler's eyes. After a long moment, his eyebrows went up.

"Yes," Schrader said. "I have heard of that, too."

Schrader leaned forward, and placed his cup and saucer on the desktop. The fine *clink* that the porcelain made as it touched the polished marble seemed to echo in the silence of the large room.

"I have also heard," Schrader said, his tone quiet, his words measured, "that those caught making such plans—or even suspected of such—are being charged with treason . . . and so are being dealt with in a vicious fashion. And if you and I have heard of this 'planning,' then no doubt it is known to—"

There was a faint rap at the door, and both men turned quickly—and more than a little nervously— toward it.

The massive dark wooden form slowly swung open just enough for a boyish-looking young man—easily a teenager—in the uniform of an Italian naval ensign to step though. He stood at an awkward attention, and saluted stiffly.

Kappler noticed that the ensign's uniform was mussed, that he had a crudely shorn haircut, and that his eyes appeared to be without thought.

He doesn't look old enough to shave, Kappler thought as he and Schrader absently returned the salute. *He looks, in fact, like a very simple boy, one plunked off a farm . . . or maybe out of the shanties . . . and stuck in the first sailor suit they could find, nevermind the fit or lack thereof.*

"Herr Standartenführer?" the young ensign said tentatively.

"I am Standartenführer Schrader," Schrader said with what Kappler thought was a touch too much authority. "Where is Tentente de Benedetto?"

Italian navy lieutenant Antonio de Benedetto—a fifty-five-year-old Sicilian, five-foot-two and one-eighty, with a sun-baked complexion as coarse as that of the volcanic rock of nearby Mount Etna—had two months earlier been recalled to the *Regina Marina* and there assigned to serve as the chief naval aide/liaison—and, it was strongly suspected, chief spy—to the Messina SS provisional headquarters.

He of course had been neither requested nor needed, but the Italians insisted that they be allowed to properly serve their SS guests and comrades in arms. And so the squat Sicilian had become a fixture around the office.

The young ensign looked uneasy, and avoided eye contact with Standartenführer Julius Schrader by looking five feet over his head, to a point on the high wall near the portrait of Hitler. He still held his salute, though now it was not quite so stiff.

"He is ill, Herr Standartenführer. I am Guardiamarina Mentesana. I was asked to take his desk today, as no one else was available."

Christ! Kappler thought. *They send us children and old men to fight a war!*

"Guardiamarina Mentesana," Standartenführer Julius Schrader said stiffly. "Did anyone, perhaps even Tentente de Benedetto, inform you that you are to wait to be admitted after you knock at the door? That you do not simply knock and then enter?"

Guardiamarina Mentesana's eyes, still fixed on a point on the wall five feet above Standartenführer Schrader's head, suddenly grew wider.

"No, Herr Standartenführer. I was not so informed."

As if suddenly remembering he was still saluting, he quickly brought down his hand, then held out a folded sheet of paper as he walked to the desk.

"This message just came in, Herr Standartenführer. It is marked 'urgent' for you."

"Danke," Standartenführer Schrader said, taking the paper. "That will be all."

"Yes, Herr Standartenführer."

Guardiamarina Mentesana saluted, turned on his heels, and marched back to the door, then went through it.

When the door was pulled closed, Kappler said what he was thinking: "That's what we can expect to repel the enemy? Children? It is bad enough that the Italian men are ill-equipped and poorly trained. What can we possibly expect of their children?"

Schrader was unfolding the sheet of paper as he replied, "Never underestimate the effectiveness of youth, my friend. I seem to recall a young man in university who time and again bravely rode polo ponies into battles that others greatly feared."

Kappler snorted.

"Battles?" he began. "I seem to recall that the teams were reasonably evenly matched and that we shot wooden balls, not bullets." When he saw Schrader's expression change dramatically, he said, "What? What is that about?"

"It's from Müller."

"Müller? Why is he not messaging me?"

"He reports explosions of unknown causes," Schrader said as he refolded the sheet and held it out to Kappler, "and felt that I directly should be made aware of them. According to this, protocol would appear to be the least of our worries . . . ."

As Kappler took the sheet, he muttered, "The bastard."

He scanned the message.

"Scheist!"

He looked at Schrader, then said more softly, "The Tabun?"

Schrader nodded just perceptibly.

"Berlin won't be pleased that we allowed this to happen," Schrader said.

Kappler didn't reply for a moment. Then he said: "Worse, if word gets out that we have a nerve agent, and thus there are plans to use it, Churchill may make good on his threat to retaliate in kind . . . ."

"I believe it was the American President Roosevelt who said that," Schrader offered.

"Churchill, Roosevelt—does it matter?"

Kappler saw in Schrader's eyes that he clearly understood the ramifications of that.

"No. Of course not. You should leave for Palermo at once, Oskar. Take whatever and whomever you think necessary. Report back as soon as you can."

W.E.B. Griffin is the author of six bestselling series: The Corps, Brotherhood of War, Badge of Honor, Men at War, Honor Bound, and Presidential Agent. He has been invested into the orders of St. George of the U.S. Armor Association, and St. Andrew of the U.S. Army Aviation Association, and is a life member of the U.S. Special Operations Association; Gaston-Lee Post 5660, Veterans of Foreign Wars; China Post #1 in Exile of the American Legion; and the Police Chiefs Association of Southeast Pennsylvania, South New Jersey, and Delaware. He is an honorary member of the U.S. Army Otter & Caribou Association, the U.S. Army Special Forces Association, the U.S. Marine Corps Raider Association, and the USMC Combat Correspondents Association. Visit his website at www.webgriffin.com.

William E. Butterworth IV has been a writer and editor for major newspapers and magazines for twenty-five years, and has worked closley with his father for several years on the editing of the Griffin books. He lives in Texas.